SKYBORN

Books by Eric R. Asher

Shop ebooks, audiobooks, and paperbacks at ericrasherstore.com

The Theme Park at the End of the World

The Steamborn Series

Steamborn

Steamforged

Steamsworn

Skyborn

Skyforged

Skysworn

Stormborn

Stormforged

Stormsworn

The Vesik Series
(Recommended for Ages 17+)

Days Gone Bad

Wolves and the River of Stone

Winter's Demon

This Broken World

Destroyer Rising

Rattle the Bones

Witch Queen's War

Forgotten Ghosts

The Book of the Ghost

The Book of the Claw

The Book of the Sea

The Book of the Staff

The Book of the Rune

The Book of the Sails
The Book of the Wing
The Book of the Blade
The Book of the Fang
The Book of the Reaper
Dreams of the Forgotten Dead
Garden Gnome Graves

The Vesik Series Box Sets

Box Set One (Books 1-3)
Box Set Two (Books 4-6)
Box Set Three (Books 7-8)
Box Set Four: The Books of the Dead Part 1
Box Set Five: The Books of the Dead Part 2

Mason Dixon: Monster Hunter

Episode One
Episode Two
Episode Three
Episode Four

Want to receive an email when one of Eric's books releases?
Visit ericrasher.com to get started.

SKYBORN

THE STEAMBORN SERIES, BOOK FOUR

By

ERIC R. ASHER

The past is not always the truth.

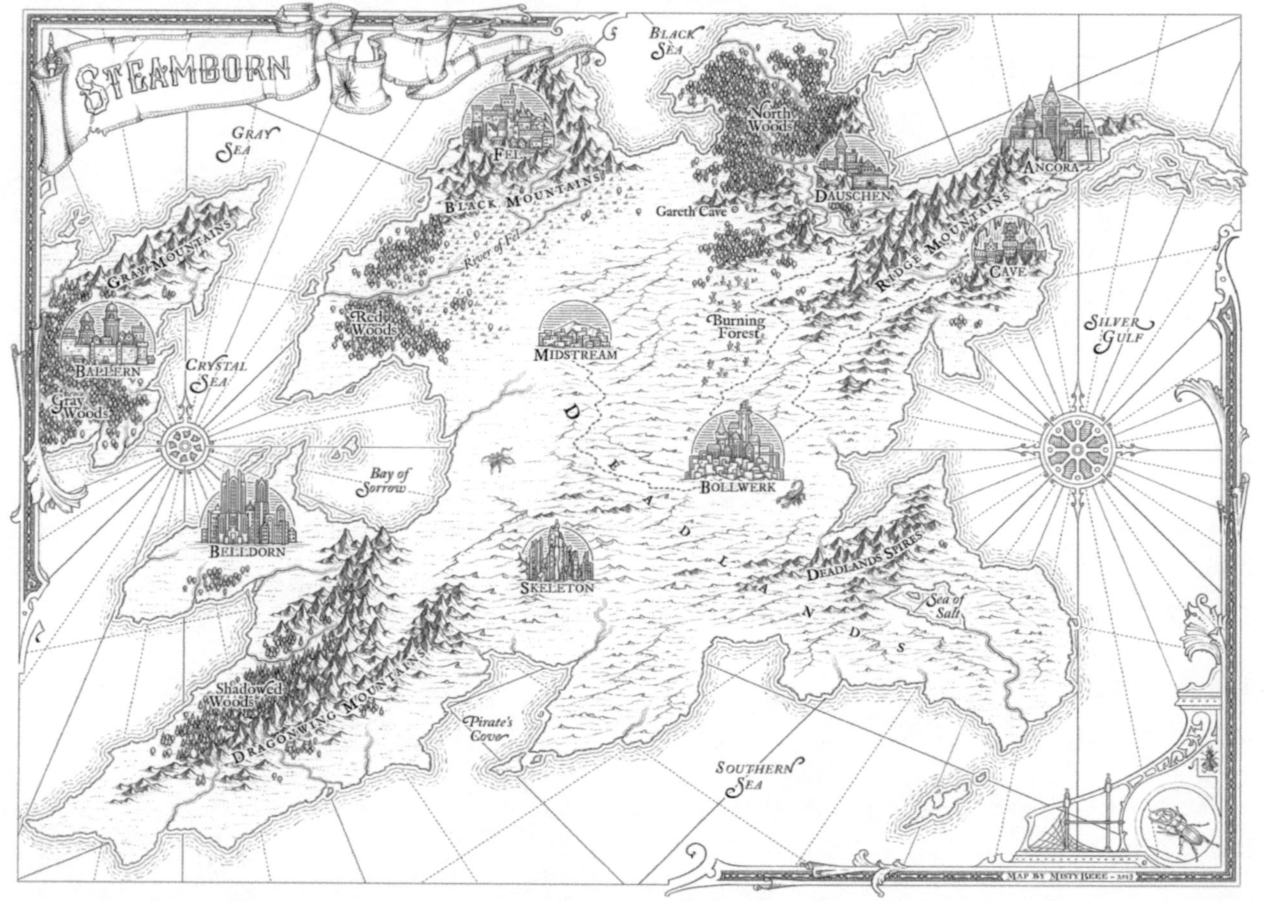

STEAMBORN
GRAY SEA
BLACK SEA
North Woods
FEL
BLACK MOUNTAINS
Gareth Cave
DAUSCHEN
ANCORA
RIDGE MOUNTAINS
CAVE
River of Fel
Red Woods
Burning Forest
SILVER GULF
GRAY MOUNTAINS
MIDSTREAM
BALLERN
CRYSTAL SEA
Gray Woods
D E A D L A N D S
BOLLWERK
Bay of Sorrow
BELLDORN
SKELETON
Deadlands Spires
Sea of Salt
Shadowed Woods
DRAGONWING MOUNTAINS
Pirate's Cove
SOUTHERN SEA
MAP BY MISTY BEEE - 2013

CHAPTER ONE

URI WEAVED THROUGH the sea of people. Countless citizens milled about below banners hung above an endless wall of vendors. It never sat right with her, this kind of celebration whenever Ballern went to war. She was proud to be on the crew of the Nightingale, one of the most storied airships of the entire fleet, but another battle wasn't something to celebrate. At least, not until they'd won.

Annoyed as Furi might be at the bright smiles and merriment around her, it didn't stop her from picking up a handful of skewers from a favorite chef. She eyed the braised meat with some suspicion as vendors, even her favorite vendors, were known to substitute less savory things.

"The finest Pill-Bug you'll find this side of the seas, child," he said from behind a mustache as wide as his head.

She was almost seventeen now, and old enough not to be called a child. Furi narrowed her eyes as she nibbled on a corner of the topmost cube of meat. A little chewy, but a burst of rich broth and salt backed up everything the man had said. She jammed the skewers between her fingers while digging in the leather pouch at her side.

"Thanks, Chef. Good as always."

"That's lovely praise from a Skyborn connoisseur as yourself."

Furi grinned at the man despite herself. Most of the people who lived in the city used "Skyborn" like a curse, as if those who dwelled on the docks were somehow *less* than the rest of them. But not Chef Jakon. The man might have spent his days cooking for royalty in the palaces, but it was his cuisine on the streets Furi wanted.

Chef Jakon wiped his hands on a stained towel before taking the two square coins from Furi. The bulbous golden spires of Ballern's towers had been worn down on the coin's faces, but it would spend just as well.

"Keep the extra. I … won't be needing it for a while."

Jakon frowned at Furi, and she met his gaze despite every instinct to fidget. "Your tunic." The chef's frown deepened. "You go to war."

"It's the right thing to do."

The chef shook his head. "No, my friend. War is rarely the right thing to do." Jakon looked at the citizens around them before leaning closer to Furi. "You will not be dissuaded?"

Furi hesitated. "No."

"You're still looking for your friend who left for the same war, yes?"

Rin. He meant Rin. A dear friend whom she could not remember a time without. Well, at least not a time before he'd deployed to fight the "godless heathens of Belldorn," as he liked to call them. Furi had never understood that. Never understood how Rin, one of the smartest people she knew, couldn't see it was their own leaders crushing the Skyborn beneath their heels. It saddened her he could be as blind to the corruption of Ballern as so many were.

"Furi?" Chef Jakon asked.

She shook herself out of those thoughts and offered him a smile. "I don't think I'll ever see him again, but I'd like to find out what happened to his ship."

The chef flipped a coin back to Furi, and it smacked against her palm. "You'll need this more than I. Be safe." He leaned over the booth, whispering into her ear. "Do not give your life for those who would not do the same. War is not what you think it is, and you will not forget the horrors you see."

A frisson of fear crawled down Furi's spine. She nodded to the chef and hurried away, snacking on the grilled Pill-Bugs. But despite the deliciousness of the skewers, they tasted like ash on her tongue. She knew war was terrible. She knew there were awful things waiting across the sea. But Furi didn't believe all the people of Belldorn were evil, just as she didn't believe all the people of Ballern were good.

She still had the golden coin in her hand when another vendor flagged her down. A woman with a radiant smile stood inside a booth filled with exquisite hair ties and two gowns that looked fit for a princess.

"That is quite a long braid you have there." After a hesitation and a glance at Furi's coin, she added, "My lady."

"Thank you. I could use a new tie."

Furi didn't need to know any more about the vendor. She could already tell the woman had no patience for those who were less than royalty or didn't at least work in the palaces. The vendor likely would have thrown Furi out if she realized she was Skyborn and lived on the airship docks. Furi hadn't missed the fact the woman had chased off two Skyborn who weren't in uniform.

The vendor pursed her lips, eyed the straight lines and leather satchel at Furi's waist, and then held up a finger. "I have just the thing for you." The woman turned away, showing a surprising level of trust that Furi wouldn't pocket her wares and run. Crystals caught the light in the woman's own braid, casting a rainbow of color through the graying brown bun atop her head.

When the vendor faced her again, she held up a rich green hair tie. It wasn't gaudy or pompous, unlike a great many things in her tent. "Now, I see you wear the Nightingale's colors. This should match exactly. It's woven from the leftover fabric we used to make the ship's flag."

Furi took it and pulled on the edges, smiling at the dense weave, which had the feel of an elastic band. It was certainly nicer than anything she planned to bring onto the ship, but she had another concern. "I don't think I can afford this."

"For you, one who defends our fair city? A mere two silvers, and it's yours."

Furi didn't question the vendor further, as that would approach the realm of haggling, which would be a dead giveaway she was Skyborn. To most vendors, the Skyborn were only known for their lack of wealth and penchant for stealing. Furi pulled two silvers from her pouch and dropped the gold coin and the hair tie inside.

"Oh nonsense, give me that tie. I'll fix your hair for you."

Furi handed it over and turned around, almost losing her balance when the woman yanked the old tie out of her hair. She grunted, thinking her dark hair would be quite a bit thinner after the vendor was done ripping it all out.

"There. Now have a look at that."

Furi looked to the side, glimpsing the mirror the vendor held out. The streak of emerald in her dark braid matched the hem of her tunic. It looked right, it felt right. She didn't hide the smile that lifted her thin lips and crinkled the skin around her small eyes.

"Be brave out there, and serve your city well." With that, the vendor set the mirror down and turned to greet another shopper.

Furi patted her braid, double-checked to make sure both clasps on her satchel were secured, and continued down the street toward the city wall. It was built of the same beige and faded red brick as much of the buildings within. There were no vendors set up in the tunnel that led outside the walls, and Furi let her fingers run across the rough stone as she walked into shadow and back out into the sunlight.

The Crystal Sea was at high tide, which meant the historic docks on the shore were nearly underwater. But that was the perfect time for the fisherfolk to haul up both fish and the water beetles much of Ballern subsisted on. Two men wrestled with a long fishing pole, casting the bait out as far as they could before collapsing to the dock in exhaustion.

Furi smiled at the sight and then turned to the vendors lining Ballern's outer walls, more than she could hope to visit in a single day. Every space between the small stone guard shacks was crowded with craftsmen and shoppers alike. The scent of the sea filled the air, complementing the nearby grilled fish.

She stopped at a tinker's stall, marveling at the useless gadgets strewn across the tabletop. She supposed some of them might provide some benefit, but most were toys for kids. And that was something she would have no use for on the Nightingale.

Furi whiled away a few hours watching the churning mass of Ballern citizens. She didn't miss the fact that the upper class, clad in finely cut fabrics and jewelry, stayed inside the walls while she found far more people like herself closer to the shore. She wasn't sure if she'd ever feel like she fit in with upper-class people, despite the relative kindness of vendors like the woman who had sold her the hair tie.

Furi was near one of the stone docks that stretched out into the Crystal Sea when she heard the scream. It echoed around her, bouncing off the old steel warship permanently docked as a reminder of what had once been. She couldn't make out what people were saying as she scanned the area, trying to find the source of the commotion.

But two small words sent a bolt of fear down her spine. "Red Death!"

More of the shoppers screamed and started to scatter, but Furi frowned at the palm-sized beetle buzzing toward her chest. She'd seen Red Death, and they were like an armored crawler in both size and tenacity, but this little beetle was not that. She supposed if she were wrong, she wouldn't have to worry about it for long.

One of the fisherfolk charged the bug, lashing out with his pole. Furi snatched the bug out of the air on pure instinct, hugging the rather annoyed beetle to her chest. It buzzed and pushed against her with its bright red wings before finally giving up and settling in to chew at her tunic.

"Don't you even think about that," Furi muttered, holding the bug out farther from her chest.

"Thank the gods you caught him! My dad was ready to kill me." A small girl, not much more than ten, beamed up at Furi.

"It is the Great Machines you should thank, little one," a cloaked man said, extending his hand and a heavily tattooed forearm.

Furi stepped in front of the man, shielding the girl from him. The disciples of the Children of the Dark Fire were easy enough to recognize. If their black cloaks didn't stand out enough in the searing heat of the day, the flame tattoo formed of steel plates and rivets could not be more obvious. Not to mention their constant prattling about the Great Machines.

Furi yelped when the beetle managed to catch her forearm in its mandibles, but it quickly let go. She took the moment of distraction to turn her back on the cloaked man, who grumbled and walked away.

"Oh yeah, he'll give you a nip if he isn't happy," the girl said.

Furi glanced back to watch the cloaked figure blend into the shadows near the edge of the dock.

"Not him," the girl said, exasperated. "The beetle. Here, give him to me."

Furi handed the bug over, raising an eyebrow when the girl pulled it to her chest like a stuffed toy.

"My dad will pay you, you know. It's hard to catch a breeding pair, and this slippery guy almost got away."

"No need," Furi said. "I'm … just glad you have your pet back."

"Pet? Oh no, I'd never keep a Crimson Beetle as a pet. They'd eat every bug on the farm if I did that. We sell them to the flower peddlers. Keeps the worse bugs out of the gardens, you know?"

Furi glanced back toward the wall where one of the flower peddlers had set up a sweeping booth, crowned by a violently bright bundle of purple blooms. A man waved, and the girl gave an exaggerated nod.

"That's my dad. Thank you again!" She grinned before sprinting away, leaving Furi somewhat baffled at the exchange, but also amused at the looks of horror the girl got when someone screamed, "She's carrying a Red Death!"

It was easy to forget how sheltered some of the people of Ballern really were. Furi hoped it would stay that way, and that the wars they fought would never reach their own shores. Three rapid cannon shots echoed out from the city as the royal airship signaled the start of the day's second block of celebrations. That meant she didn't have much longer to spend in the markets. She'd need to get back to the Nightingale soon.

She brushed at her tunic where the beetle had snapped a handful of threads. Her commanding officer was not going to be amused.

✧　✧　✧

FURI MADE HER way back through the crowds, passing the celebration's main stage where a cadre of masked performers put on a show. All of them wore brilliant colors as they performed the play of the founding of Ballern.

She didn't stay to watch, instead circling around the small space near the back of the courtyard that led to an alley just wide enough for two people to pass each other. No vendors were allowed to set up in the narrow alleys, and Furi only passed two other people in the shadow of the city courts. The place made her skin crawl. It was in that same building her father had been sentenced to a prison camp for speaking out against the expulsion of Gray Woods refugees.

A conflict in the nearby forest had ravaged the small villages, leaving thousands homeless. Some turned to Ballern for aid, but for whatever reason, the leaders of Ballern would not intervene against the warlords.

They accepted refugees into the city for a time … before the executions began.

Furi shivered and hurried away from the shadows.

The street stood vacant, as none of the celebration was scheduled to take place on Breckenridge. It was an odd thing to see one of the main thoroughfares so empty. Two of the restaurants had opened but were mostly empty as the city joined in the festivities.

Curved roofs towered above Furi, flanked by taller buildings that were squared off, which, in turn, were dwarfed by the spires for which Ballern was known. As Furi passed beneath the oldest of those old towers, a stone construction with slanted sides that took up almost an entire city block, the distant airship docks came into view.

While most of Ballern had preserved its history, keeping ancient buildings repaired and updated, even in the slums, the docks were another beast entirely. Steel scaffolding soared into the skies, linked together by platforms and cabling in the northwestern corner of Ballern. The only access to the docks—other than flying into one—was the cable elevators for the common folk, and the gondolas for royalty.

Furi waited at the base of one of those steel towers, two groups preceding her before she finally managed to catch a lift. Even in times of celebration, the lifts weren't enough to meet the demand for them.

"What in the three hells happened to your tunic?"

Furi stiffened and looked around at her fellow passengers. At first she thought the voice belonged to her commanding officer, but a knot of dread untied itself when she saw Beck's hooded eyes filled with mischief.

"Dammit, Beck. Almost gave me a heart attack."

The lift lurched into motion, causing most of the occupants to stumble. But not Furi or Beck. Growing up on the docks taught you something about balance that earthers didn't have.

"Did you see the flags?" Beck asked. "Looks like they called for us to come aboard early."

"What?" Furi asked, squinting as if that would help her see through the fast-moving mesh on the lift.

"Are you telling me you just happened to wander back here when they were calling for us to return to ship?"

Furi pursed her lips. "Maybe."

Beck shook his head. "The first call was almost half an hour ago. You really are the luckiest soldier in the company. Let me see that tunic."

Furi didn't argue when Beck slid his hand just inside her collar to better inspect the bite from the beetle. She trusted him, having grown up near the second gas chamber atop the airship docks. He'd been a friend and a regular sight before that.

Beck opened the pouch at his waist, flipped through two pockets, and pulled out a needle and thread.

"Are you serious?" Furi muttered.

"This is for my sake too. You think I want to run laps around the Nightingale with our squad? You think *the squad* wants to run laps?"

Furi rolled her eyes. "Fine, fine."

Beck worked on the pull, deftly adding stitches in just the right places so when he pulled it tight, Furi could scarcely tell where he'd patched it. He bit his lips as he often did when he was thinking, folding the collar of her tunic out and slicing the thread on the edge of his ring.

Furi adjusted her tunic when he leaned away, nodding at his work. "There. Now I won't have to run laps."

"You two are adorable," said an older woman beside them.

Whatever Furi had been about to say fled in a moment of horror, embarrassment, and maybe a little disgust. Beck was like a brother. An *annoying* brother.

So when he said, "Yeah, next week is our fifth anniversary," and the woman just said, "Aww," Furi wanted to leap out of the lift to whatever fate awaited someone who fell from those great heights. Thankfully, the lift stopped, and she didn't need to do anything quite so dramatic.

CHAPTER TWO

RELIEF FLOODED FURI'S chest when her tunic passed inspection. She didn't have time to empty her satchel in the barracks, so she headed for the briefing hall instead. After boarding, not even an hour went by before they weighed anchor and the Nightingale took to the sky. She'd have to thank Beck later.

Walking along the outer rail, past the upper bank of massive fore-cannons, Furi watched an entire squadron of destroyers pull away from the docks, skirting the huge gas chambers that supported the structure's edges. Sailors hurried in and out of the armory below the towering smokestacks, prepping the cannons before they'd so much as cleared the docks. Furi's suspicions that this was no routine mission sharpened.

She reached the armored door near the center of the ship, flanked by enormous fuel cells, gas chambers in their own right, but armored to withstand most any attack. Inside, the auditorium was already filled. She looked for Beck, but their company was spread out in no conceivable order. That was unusual.

Sailors were still filing in when one of the ship's commanders stepped to the podium.

"I am sure many of you are wondering why our deployment has been rushed. We have received word that the holy terror, the one named Charles von Atlier, was struck down in Dauschen by our alliance with Fel. With Bollwerk's most powerful ally removed, it is time for us to bring the armored city to its end.

"The fleet makes for Bollwerk, and the glory of Ballern. Once Bollwerk is secured and reinforced, Belldorn will be surrounded, and we will remove the stain of their legacy from this world."

Sailors erupted into applause and shouts, but something didn't sit well with Furi. Bollwerk and Belldorn were different, to be sure, but they were still home to people, families, and children. That was not the kind of target she ever wanted in her sights. Give her the soldier, the faceless few who had signed up for war.

But never the children.

"Once the bombing of Bollwerk is complete, our priority is to secure the airship docks. You have your orders, and the cannons are already prepped. Say your prayers, to the gods or the Great Machines, and make your peace with whatever may come. This is your moment of victory, and the long-awaited triumph of Ballern!"

After the group was dismissed and started filing out of the auditorium, someone elbowed Furi. She turned to find Mei, one of the Nightingale's gunners and someone she'd come to think of as a friend.

"You look like someone just ate your favorite pet."

Furi grimaced. "I just, you know, there are kids in those cities."

"Kids who will grow up to be holy terrors, you mean. Easiest way to deal with that is to remove the threat before it becomes a threat."

Furi cringed at those words. "That's terrible, Mei."

Mei smirked. "No, Furi, that's war. You'll understand when you're older."

"You're nineteen. That's literally one year older than me."

"And all the wisdom that comes with it!" Mei laughed and hurried on ahead when another gunner motioned for her. "Bye, Furi!"

She waved, but Mei's words grated on her mind. How could anyone think like that? Mei had a little brother. How would she feel if someone killed him just to keep him from growing up? It was a stupid question, she knew, but was it any more so than what they had just been asked to do?

Furi ground her teeth and made her way to the bow of the ship. The Nightingale's flag flew beside her, the massive green cloth snapping in the wind. She wondered if it was the same flag the vendor had used to make her hair tie. She remembered the little girl with the beetle and shivered at the thought someone might murder a child to save a future that might never be.

✧   ✧   ✧

THEY HAD BEEN hours in the skies. Half the crew thought Bollwerk would never see an attack coming until it was far too late. Furi doubted that very much. No city survived without spies and scouts. And Bollwerk had survived for several decades.

The destroyers formed a magnificent V, made up of the finest ships Ballern had ever produced. It was an imposing sight, and one Furi had never seen outside of the festivals and parades around her own city. What would it look like to an enemy?

She smiled at the thought before she remembered where they were heading and how many innocents might die. There was no turning back now. She could only help bring a quick and decisive victory. Keep the casualties to a minimum, and perhaps when this tour ended, she could find a new job. Get a place to live off the docks, or maybe teach music to some of the Skyborn again. She wasn't bad on an ocarina, and music could soothe her on the worst days.

A glint near the horizon to the south interrupted Furi's thoughts. She frowned and leaned down to one of the many telescopes mounted along the bow.

Nothing. There was nothing there but clouds.

But then the clouds thinned enough for the flash to come again. She shifted the telescope, latching onto a sight she didn't fully understand: a small airship, its gas chambers sleek and contained by a wide metal band until it almost formed a puffy number eight. The cabin sat at the bow instead of below the chambers, and something like wings extended from the sides.

Shadows appeared at the edge of the small craft—three faces she couldn't fully make out. Two vanished.

"We have an airship above us," Furi said, pointing with the full length of her arm.

A nearby commander took the scope from Furi. "Tourists," he muttered. "That ship is far too small to be a military vessel. Not much larger than a clipper."

He handed the scope back to Furi a second before the first explosion rocked the Nightingale. Screams rose around them as two sailors dashed onto the deck near the bow, covered in flames.

Furi stared, horror warring with the need to do something. It was only a moment before she grabbed one of the fire blankets from a brass compartment at her feet and dove toward the screaming sailors. She didn't even have the first one extinguished when another explosion tore the far side of the deck out from under the commander. He fell into nothing, chased by a burning man.

Nothing felt real. The world slowed as Furi's heart hammered in her chest.

A secondary explosion deafened the world around her, and one of the giant fore-cannon mounts spiraled off the Nightingale in streamers of black smoke and brilliant flame.

"Mei!" Furi cried, her voice cracking. Mei was stationed at those cannons.

"Raise the flags!" a surviving commander screamed. "Attack!"

The brilliant green of the Nightingale's colors was quickly replaced by red flags along the sides of the warship. Through the smoke and flame,

Furi could see the other destroyers mimicking the signal flags.

The deck of the ship shuddered and dipped, sending the crew stumbling about as they tried to adjust the remaining cannons. But the destroyer's cannons were huge, slow, and took time to aim. They weren't meant to lock onto a ship so small and so fast.

It wasn't long before the Nightingale leveled out and started rising again as other destroyers fired on their attacker. More than once, it looked like the tiny ship would be blown to pieces before it lurched to the side.

Furi tried to spot the attackers again, following the aim of a surviving cannon. She was surprised to find the ship nearby, just inside a cloud bank, before another explosion rocked the deck and brought the cannon to a grinding halt.

A rapid staccato came to life, the sailors grabbing small handheld cannons to fire back at the ship. But a moment later, the pattering of those shots was drowned out by more explosions tearing through men and armor alike as Furi dove to the deck, too close to the hole so many had already fallen through.

Even as she thought it, a bloodied sailor tumbled and fell. There was no scream, no flailing, just a red-stained rag doll hurtling toward the earth. Furi took one more glimpse at the ship as she braced herself against the bow.

Two faces, younger than she was, stared out from the ship. A young girl, pale with brilliant red hair, and a boy with dark hair—an Ancoran, she was almost sure.

Another destroyer fired as the small ship shot into the clouds, faster than any airship Furi had ever seen. There was only so much training could prepare them for. And this had gone far beyond that.

The ship broke down into panic and fear and chaos. Furi threw two extinguisher grenades into the worst of the flames, but they did almost nothing. Once those were spent, she hurried toward the opposite side of the deck, horrified to see both sides of the ship were now on fire.

It was a scene repeated time and again, as her burning shipmates flung themselves off the sides or through the damaged floors. She made her way up to a storage well where the cannons held their ammunition. She immediately wished she hadn't. Nothing could have survived in that scorched and blackened ruin. Mei was gone.

Furi took a few rapid breaths and hurried down a ladder. She was nearly to the deck when they collided with another airship, the screams of metal joining the screams of her shipmates. She lost her grip and slammed onto the deck, losing every last bit of air in her lungs. Tears rolled down her cheeks as she gasped for breath. A handful of sailors had reached the racked emergency gliders, and they leaped from the destroyer wherever they could.

The Nightingale was in a death spiral now, a terrible dance between two flailing destroyers. If the last of the gas chambers were compromised, it would be a much quicker end.

Streaks of light cut through the sky, and one of the distant destroyers exploded as if its entire structure had been forged from cannon powder.

Two of Ballern's destroyers returned fire. Thunder drowned out the screams and cries all around her.

Furi caught a glimpse of their target, an impossible hulk covered in more cannons than she thought might exist in the entirety of Ballern's fleet. And there were *two* of the insane ships. She'd heard the stories. She knew what they were.

Porcupines.

One of the hulks flashed with light as multiple cannons fired at once, and another of Ballern's destroyers took a pounding. It did not crash. Its red flags switched to white, and the other surviving destroyers followed suit, rising higher and making a slow turn in retreat.

The Nightingale's flag broke away, burning the air above Furi, even as the blood of her friends and allies pooled across the deck around her. Flames burst from the sides of the destroyer, turning the escaping gliders into screaming balls of fire and ash.

Her only hope was to hang on until they were close enough to slide down the landing lines. But even then … even then the ship might crumble down on top of them all.

Furi wept.

✧   ✧   ✧

"Furi?" a voice called out. "Furi!"

Her eyes flashed open, shocked to find Beck standing above her.

"We have to go! Come on." He pulled her up, leaning against the railing as the ship spiraled closer to the earth.

"Give me the glider or you're dead."

Beck turned slowly, pausing when he found a sailor with a handheld cannon leveled at him. "You shoot me with that, this glider isn't going to do you much good."

"Give it to him," Furi hissed. "I have another way."

Beck frowned and glanced at Furi before sliding out of the glider. The sailor took it and backed away, keeping the cannon locked on the pair until he reached the far side of the deck.

Furi grabbed the nearest landing line and tossed it over the edge.

"*That's* your other idea?"

"Put your gloves on. We have to time this right. Slide to the bottom and wait until we can drop into a sand dune or something."

"Or something," Beck muttered, but he still slid his iron-palmed gloves on.

Furi glanced over the edge. They didn't have too long now. She hopped up, took a deep breath, and slid down the steel line. Her gloves sparked when they hit frayed bits of the landing line, and she had no illusions that the sting on her legs from hitting them was going to need time to heal.

She was almost at the bottom when Beck joined her.

The ship's spiral was slow now, but the descent was accelerating. They needed to drop soon, or they might as well have been on the destroyer that exploded.

"Furi, we're still five stories in the air."

"Look. Aim for the tall dune when we circle around." It was almost clear but for one bulbous cactus the size of a Pill-Bug.

Beck followed her gaze and grimaced. "I'm going to hit the cactus."

Even as the ailing ship turned, swinging them out in a blistering breeze, Furi loosened her grip and fell.

One thing she learned immediately was that sand dunes were not as soft as the snow in the north. Her teeth rattled together, sprays of rock and sand flying into the air as she rolled over in a violent spiral. She came to a stop a third of the way down the hill, and despite her pain, laughed when she saw Beck.

"I hit the damn cactus!"

He was bloody and his arm had half a dozen stickers impaling it, but they were alive. And that was something.

✧   ✧   ✧

THEY HADN'T MADE it far from the dune and the cactus when the first of Bollwerk's defenders arrived. Only, they didn't wear the colors of the city of rust. They wore the colors of Belldorn.

"Don't move," a woman said, raising her visor. "Surrender and we'll get your wounds treated. Despite whatever you may have heard of our city, you'll find sanctuary with us."

Furi and Beck exchanged a glance. She gave him a small nod and the tension in Beck's posture loosened.

"I'm Furi," she said, dropping her armored gloves into the sand.

"Beck."

The woman nodded. "Call me Eva. Let's get you some water."

CHAPTER THREE

"SURE YOU DON'T want to come with us?" Jacob asked. He rubbed at his arm without thinking, pulling on a bandage and wincing.

Samuel gave him a small smile from the doorway to Bat's house. "No, kid. I have to get things in order here. And they're going to need some help reorganizing the guard. I'll head to Cave in a few days."

Alice hesitated, then threw her arms around the Spider Knight, crushing him in a quick hug. "You better." Her brilliant red hair stood out like a fire next to Samuel's dark strands.

"I'll keep the workshop ready for you." Samuel traded grips with Jacob. "Once Smith and Mary get back to help with the reconstruction, I figure you'll both want to use it."

Drakkar offered a shallow bow and inclined his head. "Cave will welcome you, my friend. We welcome all who stand against tyrants, and all who flee from them."

George the Walker reared up, flexing dozens of legs in a rolling, mesmerizing pattern. Drakkar patted the Walker's head before loading their last pack of canteens. It had been a surprise to see Drakkar returning from the stables with none other than their trusty George. Jacob hadn't been sure if the Walker had survived, and he was happy to hear Bessie was still in the stables as well.

"We'll be back," Jacob said. "I want to help with the reconstruction too. I think some of Charles's old friends will help. Try Baddawick. Then maybe we can go back to Cave together."

Samuel waved as the group hopped onto the back of the Walker and surged forward, weaving through the people walking down the streets of Ancora, until they reached the front gates. The damage in the Highlands wasn't insignificant. Some of it had been patched over by the people who lived there, and by the innkeepers, but broken weathervanes and blood still stained the streets. As they passed through the gateway to the Lowlands, Jacob's chest tightened.

While there were remnants of the Butcher's handiwork in the Highlands, the Lowlands were still a ruin that stretched as far as the eye could see. A few patrols were out, clearing any unwanted invaders like the Red Death and Carrion Worms, but it would take weeks to construct a new temporary city wall. And likely years to repair the stone in full.

Jacob and Alice clung to the saddle while Drakkar steered them through the ruins. They'd only rested behind the city walls of the Highlands for a day, which didn't feel nearly long enough to Jacob. The trip into the remains of the Lowlands was made in silence.

None of them mentioned the ruined buildings and the many bodies that would need to be tended to. That was for another time, once the reconstruction began in earnest. Alice watched the landscape roll by, tucking an occasional strand of windblown hair back into her braid.

Drakkar guided them toward a steep drop that made Jacob's back stiffen.

Once, there had been a lift on the cliffside. One Jacob could slide down with the right gloves, but the drop he remembered was far too steep for a Walker. Except now it wasn't. Now what should have been a huge fall was cluttered with shattered stone and fallen houses.

Dust rose around the Walker's legs, churned up by the rapid movement and weight of the beast.

Alice glanced back at Jacob, tears in her eyes. She knew where they were, too—not far from where they'd once lived. She squeezed his hand

and turned back to the carnage surrounding them.

As fast as they'd plunged into the destruction, George carried them onto the outer path, over the remnants of the city wall.

Jacob felt like he could breathe again as the destruction faded behind them. He wanted to rebuild now. Start salvaging what he could. But there was more to be done before they could focus on the reconstruction.

He closed his eyes for a time, feeling the rise and fall of the Walker beneath him as Drakkar's deft hand steered them out of the mountains and back onto the plains. He remembered walking that distance with Alice and Charles and Samuel. It had taken hours upon hours. But now, with the speed of a well-trained Walker, they were already in the grasslands, the Bull's Horn of the Ridge Mountains looming in the distance.

✧   ✧   ✧

IT WASN'T LONG before they stood once more at the entrance of Cave. The first time Jacob had come to the underground city, he wouldn't have believed there was anything hidden behind what appeared to be a solid stone mountainside.

But now the grounds leading away from the entrance were worn down, the grasses trampled by countless people fleeing Ancora and taking shelter in Cave. Jacob suspected it would be a long time before many of the citizens of Ancora returned.

He reached out to the Devil's Hammer, a skeletal brass hand clutching a steel orb. He raised it on its hinge and let it fall against the gong hidden behind it. The familiar click and whirl inside the wall echoed up around them, and then there was only silence.

Jacob frowned as the walls started to move. He'd expected one of the Guardians to interrogate them, much the same way they had the first time they'd visited with Charles. Now, there was only a shadow near the entrance, who simply said, "Welcome to Cave."

"Thank you, brother," Drakkar said with a nod to the Guardian.

Jacob turned to Drakkar. "Is that why they didn't question us? Because you're here?"

"No, Jacob, even the Guardians can be questioned. It is not unknown for citizens of Cave to turn traitor against their own city. But in rare times, when Cave is a refuge for more than the people who live here, we are generous with granting passage. Perhaps it is because of our past."

"What about your past?" Alice asked after a long yawn.

Drakkar grinned, showing brilliant white teeth against his dark skin. "I think you already know the answer to that. Cave was long a stronghold of pirates and thieves."

Alice perked up. "What kind of pirates? That's what I can never find in the history books. Did they steal precious metals? Or rare spices?"

Drakkar laughed quietly. "Some, yes. But many more stole people."

"What?" Jacob asked.

"Perhaps I should explain better. Not all the cities of the world are as benevolent as Ancora. You had disparity between the Highlands and the Lowlands, but others, like Ballern, forced their poor into labor and jobs no one else would want. The poor are sent to the front lines of every battle, while the rich trade peacefully with the nations at war."

"What does that have to do with stealing people?" Jacob asked.

Alice sighed and rolled her eyes. "You can be awfully dense some days. They didn't steal people, they freed them. Took refugees across the sea."

"That anyone had to do that is appalling."

Drakkar nodded and steered George the Walker toward the stables, passing through another layer of stone. Here, beyond the gates, the supports for the city's structure grew noticeable. Thick steel propped up much of the passage they started down.

"What was it Charles said last time we were here?" Jacob asked.

"Something about a Scorpion's Trial?"

"He survived it," Alice said. "What is it, Drakkar?"

The Cave Guardian didn't answer as he guided George into his stable. The Walker immediately stuck his face into a trough full of Sweet-Flies. Only when they'd all disembarked did Drakkar respond.

"The Scorpion's Trial is a way to show how much of a stubborn fool you are."

"What?" Jacob asked as a stable hand chuckled.

"A scorpion is not unlike a Tail Sword, only diminutive. Fools still follow an old pirate code, letting themselves be stung by a scorpion."

Jacob glanced away. "And then what happens?"

"They live, or they die."

"Idiots," Alice muttered. "Who would ever do something like that?"

"Pirates who wished to prove themselves loyal to a guild. What most folk who visited did not realize was that the scorpions were almost always harmless. But if you happened to be someone the pirate captains disliked, well, let us say they would not be so harmless."

"You're talking about murder," Alice said, following Drakkar down an adjacent hall, off to the opposite side of the stables.

"You will find a great deal of talk is about murder when it comes to pirates."

Alice and Drakkar continued their back and forth as they made their way into a roughly hewn hallway. Jacob saw the golden glow at the end of the path and his heart rate spiked. As they drew closer to the end, Cave's noise and general buzz grew louder than he remembered.

When they turned the corner, he understood why.

The towering streetlamps with their wide copper reflectors still lit the town, but the cobblestone streets were choked with people. Where Cave had once been bustling, it was now the equivalent of the square during Festival in Ancora.

"Well," Drakkar said. "I must admit this is a sight I have never seen."

He led them down the hill, from the stables where small cottages and three-story inns sat side by side, various architecture crammed into too limited a space like a book meant to document every style of building from across the world.

The last time they'd been in Cave, Jacob remembered buskers on many of the street corners. But now, with the mass of people, he couldn't see them at first, only hear them, until they moved farther into the city. Musicians were set up close to the buildings, taking whatever coin the passersby would throw. With such limited space, the more extravagant shows were still nowhere to be seen.

"Where are we going?" Jacob asked, raising his voice to make sure Drakkar could hear him over the din.

"We make for the only place in Cave you go when you need information. The Rock Inn." Drakkar led them past a towering building, a strange thing with a high platform that seemed to hold another house above it. It wasn't until they reached the next street that Jacob realized where they were.

Beside them was the old church with sweeping Gothic doors, but more important to him at the moment were the dark stairs that led to a wooden entrance. Across the doors, spelled out in smooth river stones, was "The Rock Inn."

Inside was nothing like Jacob remembered. It was still a small bar, surrounded by booths, but now there were enough people that he wasn't sure he'd be able to cross the room. Drakkar had no such hesitation, weaving between patrons and practically dragging Jacob and Alice with him.

"Watch your pockets," Drakkar said. "This is ideal for a pickpocket."

Jacob didn't need that warning. He'd been one of the best pickpockets in Ancora before the Fall. He recognized some faces, people from the

Lowlands, though many whose names he didn't know. All the same, it was a relief to see survivors from his old life.

Drakkar pulled his hood down and sidled up to the bar. He gestured to the barkeep, who looked annoyed for a moment until recognition softened his expression. He hurried over to greet them, much to the annoyance of some of the waiting customers.

"Drakkar," he said. "Rumor was you were dead. Sacrificed yourself for the Ancorans."

"I plan to avoid that for a time. Preferably until I die of old age."

The barkeep reached out and wrapped his hand around Drakkar's forearm, and Drakkar returned the gesture. "What brings you back now?"

"The Butcher is dead, and what remains of Ancora is safe for now."

"Doesn't matter too much to me either way. As long as a man has coin, he's welcome in my shop."

Alice leaned forward, but before she could say anything, Drakkar held up a finger and gave a tiny shake of his head. She frowned at the Cave Guardian and crossed her arms, but let whatever she was about to say slide.

"We're looking for two refugee families from Ancora. You know where we could find them?"

The barkeep cursed under his breath. "Everywhere. Can you give me more information than that?"

"One woman has hair like mine," Alice said. "Another we're looking for has a bad lung from being in the mines. He'd be on medicine."

The barkeep nodded. "The sick are currently staying in the Temple of the Cave Guardians. If he needs medicine, you'll likely find him there. As for the woman you described, I've seen her around. Look to the east, closer to the sea caves."

"Thank you," Drakkar said.

"I have a couple rooms set aside should you need a place to stay to-night. Rooms are hard to come by, so the price will not be cheap."

Drakkar ushered Jacob and Alice toward the front door. Jacob had almost forgotten that the barkeep was the owner of The Rock Inn. And while that may have been the name of the bar, a large portion of the building served as a proper inn.

Drakkar adjusted his cloak at the bottom of the stairs, fidgeting with the dark metal clasp on his chest.

"What's wrong?" Alice asked.

Drakkar's fingers froze, and he offered a small smile. "You are too astute at times, Alice. For many years I called the Temple of the Cave Guardians my home. You may think of it as a monastery with, well, fewer rules."

He led the way back up the street, angling to avoid the worst of the crowds along the cobblestones. "It is the home of all who would become Cave Guardians. Even the Nameless. Perhaps, especially the Nameless."

"Isn't your brother one of the Nameless?" Alice asked.

"Yes," Drakkar said, weaving past a vibrantly dressed cluster of musicians who gathered between two stone staircases. "But you must understand. I reclaimed my name, Alice. I left many of the teachings behind. It was a dishonor done to my brother. Though he has always denied it, I fear it wounded him deeply."

Jacob glanced back at the group whose music followed them down the next street. He was fairly certain two of them were from the orchestra that had performed on the day Ancora fell.

Drakkar didn't say any more as he led the way up the stairs to the Temple of the Cave Guardians. It didn't look much like a temple to Jacob. It was tall, three stories at least, and four if you counted the strange house perched atop it on stilts. The roof had been carved from rectangu-lar sections of stone, giving it the appearance of the lid to a jar Charles once had on his workbench.

Jacob kept looking up until Drakkar pushed through the dark wood of the front door. The door itself was some ten feet high, nearly reaching the second story, but the cacophony of laughter and talking that greeted them didn't fit Jacob's expectations for a makeshift hospital or a monastery, for that matter.

Everything inside that place was sharp angles. The columns stretching from the first floor up through wide holes in the second were each square, each inlaid with an impossible mosaic so fine and detailed at first Jacob thought they were paintings.

What wasn't stone, or part of the mosaics, looked like aged bronze and brass more fitting for the halls of Bollwerk than tucked away in a hidden city. Jacob suspected there was a great deal more to the history of Cave than pirates and honor.

"Welcome to the Temple of the Cave Guardians," a cloaked figure said as he stepped forward in greeting. "You are welcome to explore. The gates are open to all who do not mean harm." He focused on Drakkar. "Even those who have taken names once more."

"You have my thanks," Drakkar said with a small bow. "Where will we find the sick from Ancora?"

"Most shelter on the second floor. I would start your search there." The cloaked figure took his leave, circling behind a thick column and vanishing into shadow.

"You know him?" Jacob asked.

"Yes. But when I stayed here, he was much younger. And much angrier. Time changes a great many things, Jacob. A great many."

As they made their way through the wide expanse of the first floor, Jacob noticed discolorations on the tiles beneath their feet. Areas where the old stone was more vibrant gave away the fact more structures once filled the room.

Even as the thought crossed Jacob's mind, Alice asked, "What used to be here? You can see signs of a lot more set up across the floors besides the cots and benches."

"The Cloister Halls," Drakkar said. "They were once graced with carved arches of flowers and trees, but age and traffic ruined them. Once a place to be at peace and ponder what good you could do in the world, they provided splinters more than anything else in the end. I think the only thing I miss about those walls is how they stopped the echoing in these larger rooms."

He led them around the back of the rearmost column. It was smaller than the others, and Jacob was somewhat surprised to find a lift installed.

Drakkar smiled at the confusion on Jacob's face. "We do not shun technology here. Come, let's find your parents."

It wasn't the fastest lift Jacob had ever been on. One story took almost as long to climb as ten had in Bollwerk. But it felt stable, the gears were quiet, and as his eyes adjusted to the dim candlelight inside the lift, he was surprised to find braided cables strung over basic pulleys. It was striking in its simplicity, but obviously effective.

"I'd love to see the engine they're using to drive this."

"It's an old steam engine." Drakkar hesitated. "One of Charles's designs."

"What?"

Drakkar nodded. "A secondary engine for the Titan Mechs he designed during the Deadlands War. Archibald may be able to tell you more. I'm not sure how many of Charles's notes survived from those times."

Jacob looked up at the pulleys and cables and smiled, imagining Charles would be quite happy one of his wartime designs ended up being repurposed into something useful. Even good, he might say.

The lift came to a smooth stop and Drakkar pushed the latticework to the side, ushering Jacob and Alice out.

"Mom?" Alice said almost immediately.

And then Jacob saw her as the crowds passed and thinned. The same fiery hair as Alice, just over by the railing that surrounded the gap in the floor around the nearest column. She'd lost weight since they'd last seen her, as many had when the supply chains were broken in the conflict with the Butcher. But as Alice's mom turned, looking for a familiar voice, Jacob gasped at the sight behind her.

CHAPTER FOUR

ALICE WAS ALREADY running to her mother, but Jacob couldn't take his eyes off the woman she'd been talking to. A woman who now held both hands over her mouth and sobbed when she saw Jacob.

Drakkar glanced between the two and raised an eyebrow. "I take it that is your mother?"

Jacob nodded.

"Perhaps you should go say hello?" Drakkar laughed and clasped him on the shoulder. "It does seem likely she would like to greet you."

Jacob blinked and slowly met Drakkar's gaze. "We've been a bad influence on you. Mary would be proud." Jacob flashed Drakkar a grin and sprinted toward his mother.

"Jacob," she whispered as she wrapped her arms around him, nearly breaking his ribs. "We weren't sure … we didn't know if …" She didn't say anything more, just crushed him, a tremor running through her while her curly hair tickled his nose. He could have sworn her hair looked grayer in the short time since he'd seen her last.

"I'm alive, mostly," he said, knocking on his leg.

His mother pushed him back and glanced down. "We'd heard rumors about Charles leading the resistance. Rumors about a one-legged apprentice who helped bring down the Butcher." She smiled at him, her eyes red.

"One and a half legged, really."

His mother let out a small laugh.

"I guess it *was* him that crazy drunk was rambling about in The Rock Inn."

Jacob turned toward the new voice, then paused, trying to understand what he was seeing. It was his dad, yes, but the man's lips weren't so pale and his skin was more vibrant. He was slow to stand up, but he looked stable, almost like his old self. Jacob tried to say something, but choked up as he hugged them both.

After all he'd seen. After all he'd done. He hadn't been sure he'd ever see his parents again. Wasn't entirely sure they'd survived the horrors inflicted on Ancora by the Butcher. But now they were both here, alive, and his dad looked better than he had in months.

"Are you staying?" his dad asked as they broke away.

Jacob hesitated. "Not for long. We have to get back to Ancora and help with the reconstruction."

"I'm proud of you."

Jacob didn't know how to respond to that. It felt good to hear the words, but he'd done things no one should be proud of.

"Who's your friend?"

Jacob glanced back. "Oh, right, rude of me. Mom, Dad, this is Drakkar. He's saved us more than once. And saved Samuel even more. Drakkar, this is Mags, and Leo."

"Don't let the Spider Knight hear that," Drakkar said with a smile. He bowed to both of Jacob's parents. "It is an honor to meet you both."

Jacob caught a bit of Alice's conversation when she said, "They told us you'd be down by the caves, wherever that is."

"Oh, that would have been a good place to find me," her mom said. "They have quite a wonderful Pilly stock here. I've been helping them in the stables where I can."

Alice noticed Jacob looking at her and then glanced at Drakkar. She briefly introduced them before turning to Jacob's parents. "How did you all end up here together?"

"After you two *vanished*," Alice's mom said, "we kept each other company at Bat's home. Until … until things got worse. We fled to Cave with help from Baddawick and the tunnels beneath Bat's house."

Alice nodded and turned to Jacob's dad. "You seem to be doing a lot better here."

"All thanks to the Cave Guardians. They treated me with a vile concoction of moss and lichen, but I must admit it helped far more than the medicine in Ancora."

Jacob had a hard time reconciling the memory of his frail father with the recovering man in front of him. Where other citizens of Ancora had lost weight due to some level of starvation, his father looked healthier than he had in recent memory.

There was almost guilt, knowing Jacob and his companions had not dealt with that kind of struggle. They'd had their own issues, no doubt, but food had not been one of them.

"Now tell me," Jacob's dad said. "What do you hope to do to help the reconstruction of Ancora? That kind of devastation isn't the sort of thing one person can fix."

Jacob bristled at his father's words. That wasn't how he'd been raised; that wasn't the ethic his father had instilled in him. "Charles was the greatest tinker in Ancora. The least I can do is help where he would have. And I'll help as much as I can."

His father sat down on the cot and took a deep breath. "There was a time when I would've been with you. Out there with the masons who will help rebuild the walls. I might be better, Jacob, but I'm afraid those years are long past me now."

There was some understanding Jacob gleaned from those words. His father might have improved, but the illness had taken its toll.

"Rest while you can," Jacob said. "Dauschen and Ancora are both compromised. Cave might be the safest place you could be for now."

Jacob's father gave him an awkward smile. "Safe from what? The Butcher is dead. You saw to that."

Jacob wasn't sure how much he should say. If they'd learned one thing, there were ears everywhere. And in a city once known for its spies and pirates, Jacob felt caution was a wise course of action.

Alice saved him from having to answer the question. "I'm going back with Jacob. At least for a while. You can't imagine the things we've seen. I don't want you to have to imagine the things we've seen. Like he said, rest here while you can. It seems like a good home."

"It is the best kind of home." Drakkar lowered his voice. "Should you have need, send a letter addressed to Samuel in Ancora. We have come to an agreement with Baddawick. He will pass on any message received in Samuel's name."

Alice's mom frowned at that. "What better is that than sending a letter directly to you?"

The smirk on Alice's face gave her mom pause.

Barely above a whisper, Alice said, "It won't be the letter itself that gets to us, only what it says. Trust me on this."

"Very well. You've managed to keep yourself alive this long. I guess I've done okay raising you."

Alice grinned at her mom.

Jacob's parents exchanged a glance, and his father shrugged. They didn't pry any further into Drakkar's suggestion. Jacob was thankful for that, as he didn't want to explain to them how the various radios of Archibald's spy network operated. And while it was true they wouldn't have access to a transmitter at all times, someone from their party would likely be near one. It wouldn't take too long for a message to reach them.

"Will any of you be returning to Ancora?" Drakkar asked.

Jacob's mom squeezed her hands together and held them close to her chest. "Not now. I can't look at our home like that. I can't see what's left of the Lowlands again."

The conversation trailed off on that note, until Drakkar broke the silence. "Have you already eaten?"

Everyone shook their heads.

Drakkar smiled. "If you don't mind a small walk, I would be happy to introduce you to the best fishmonger in Cave."

DRAKKAR LED THEM deeper into Cave than Jacob had ever been. He'd always thought the main cavern with The Rock Inn and the Temple of the Cave Guardians contained most of the city. They slowed at times, waiting for his father to rest on his cane. But it gave Jacob more time to take in just how large Cave really was.

The first passage Drakkar took them through looked identical to the main entrance to the city. It bent to the left, and then the right, and then they were standing inside a new cavern at least half the size of the first.

"How big is the city?" Alice asked.

"Perhaps a bit smaller than the Highlands of Ancora," Drakkar said. "The prime cave, which welcomes all to the city, is the largest. But there are three more chambers like this, and farther out a network of hovels, home to only a few families."

"It's quite wonderful, isn't it?" Alice's mom said. "We aren't far from the stables here. They have quite a large glowworm farm. But it's really the Pill-Bugs you should see."

Jacob noted the architecture was different in the second chamber. More stone, and crude brick, and less of the fine woodwork he saw in what Drakkar called the prime cave. It was a long walk at their leisurely pace, and Jacob hoped they'd be able to sit down soon for his father's sake.

As if reading his thoughts, Drakkar said, "One more hall and we'll be there."

The last corridor was the longest Jacob had seen in Cave. It curved gently before sloping down. The lower they got, the better the lighting was, but he did not see torches in the walls, only a handful of glow worms grazing on lichen. But no glowworm could emit a light so intense.

It wasn't until they stepped out of the corridor that Jacob understood. The world opened in front of them. A tall arcing cavern encompassed the entire area, but the front of it was broken, fallen away into the endless sea known as the Silver Gulf.

Storefronts and small dwellings rose all around stone docks. A cluster of wooden ships bobbed on the waters, rolling up and down with the waves. The broken cavern provided shade and cover against the blinding sun glistening on brilliant clear waters.

Dozens of fisherfolk lined the piers, casting lines and hauling up traps near the shore. It was a surreal sight, and one Jacob could have stayed and watched for hours.

"Come," Drakkar said. "Lakkan's restaurant is not far."

He led them closer to the far south wall of the cavern. It was a strange thing, seeing the Silver Gulf so clearly. Jacob knew it was the same waters not so far from Ancora, but the way the mountain city had been built among the peaks and hidden behind the city walls, the sea was a rare sight indeed.

Drakkar turned back to the group, a wide smile across his face as he gestured to a humble structure built of dark wood. Inside was a single chef, a row of barstools, and a single bar top.

"We aren't open for business yet," the chef said.

"Not even for a very old friend?"

The chef didn't pause his rapid knife work, only glanced up and cast a small smile toward Drakkar. "Perhaps I can make an exception."

"Lakkan, it is good to see you." Drakkar turned to the others, holding a canvas flap out of the way and ushering them inside. "Take a stool. I hope you're ready to have fish ruined for life."

The chef didn't acknowledge Drakkar's compliments. Instead, he paused and met the Cave Guardian's gaze. "Is your warmongering done so soon?"

"No more than your fish mongering."

Lakkan blinked at that retort. "I never thought of you as one for humor."

Drakkar flashed a brilliant smile. "Perhaps my companions have been somewhat of a bad influence."

"Good." Lakkan harrumphed. "In that case, they are most welcome."

Jacob studied the interior. While most was raw wood, the kitchen and stove itself looked like something the finest Highlander would envy. Lakkan twisted a knob and flames burst to life.

"How did you do that?" Jacob asked. "I don't see a fuel source."

Lakkan narrowed his eyes. "You brought a tinker."

Jacob blinked at that, but Drakkar laughed.

"The rest of you aren't tinkers, are you?" Lakkan sighed. "They can be exhausting."

Alice elbowed Jacob, who felt his cheeks turning red.

The chef opened a compartment in the floor, hauling up a strange metal box. The door swung open, and inside were dozens of small containers. "We use the colder water to keep things fresh." He popped the lid off two containers and dumped the contents into a frying pan. The entire room filled with an earthy, sweet scent, and Jacob found his embarrassment fading.

"As to your other question, tinker," Lakkan said. "There are veins of gas that run through the walls. We simply plug them, and harvest the power within. A natural gift, much the same as what gave birth to the Burning Forest, we suspect."

"That's amazing," Jacob said. "How long do your gaskets last? At least I assume that's how you're blocking the gas."

At that, Lakkan offered a small smile. "We replace them every few months. There is a corrosive element here in the caves. And it is better to be safe than dead."

"Have you had explosions?" Alice asked.

"Don't you pester the chef, too," Alice's mother said.

Lakkan gestured out toward the Silver Gulf. "We did not always have such a striking view of the sea. If you walk out to the edge of the piers, you will find some jagged remnants of Cave's old wall below the waters."

Alice raised her eyebrows.

Lakkan harrumphed. "Yes, so now we change the gaskets."

He added the contents of another container to the pan, the room filling with steam and an intense hissing.

"What is that smell?" Alice's mom asked. "Is that a batch of Sea Claws?"

Lakkan grunted in confirmation. "We have excellent fish in the shallows, but the crevices formed when the wall collapsed are an ideal habitat for the Sea Claws." He didn't turn around as he dropped a handful of green ribbons into the pan, tossing it about before finally removing it from the heat.

Drakkar grabbed a stack of shallow rimmed plates from the end of the counter, laying one at each table setting. Lakkan poured a bit of his concoction across each plate, making sure everyone had a piece of the shelled claw, and several small fish.

"It is always chef's choice here," Drakkar said. "But I have yet to see a bad choice."

"Do we need a spoon?" Jacob asked, almost whispering to Drakkar.

Lakkan laughed at that. "Not here. Use your hands and drink from your plate. Tinkers."

Jacob's dad smiled at him and took a sip from his own plate. "How did it get tender so fast?"

"The closest thing to a Sea Claw on land is likely a Pill-Bug. Similar in flavor, perhaps, but an entirely different flesh. I assure you, you would not enjoy an overcooked Sea Claw. It would be more like chewing on a gasket."

"This is so good," Alice said, leaning forward over the bar.

Jacob's mom smiled before her expression fell a little. "Can we afford this?"

"Afford?" Lakkan asked. "You have returned my friend to me. And a friend of a friend does not pay in this place."

"Ever?" Alice asked.

Lakkan let out a low laugh. "Today."

Jacob nibbled at the Sea Claw. There was a hint of that rubber texture he was used to from Pill-Bugs. But there was more, almost a sweetness to it. And the sauce Lakkan had added made for a wonderful experience, bringing brine and char together into a single bite.

"I've never had anything like it," Jacob said. "Thank you. I think George needs to learn how to make this for The Fish Head."

Lakkan hesitated at that. "You know the proprietors of The Fish Head in Bollwerk?"

Drakkar leaned back on his stool and smiled. "Part of Lakkan's family is from Midstream."

"Oh!" Alice set her plate down. "Do you know Gladys and George? They're friends of ours. Gladys is going to be the best princess."

Lakkan didn't respond for a moment, and Drakkar laughed.

"Not bad for a tinker's apprentice and one overly fond of books, eh Lakkan?"

Lakkan ignored Drakkar's barb. "I only met Gladys once, but George has been good company on more than one night. A taste for sake that one, and a fine taste at that."

Jacob remembered not feeling so fine after his last encounter with that drink, but he nodded along with Lakkan's story.

"It has been a long while since I saw them, though. Before the darkest times came. Before the warlords wrapped all the Deadlands in an iron grip. Gladys was newly crowned. An infant. If not for George, I do not know what would have happened to the royal line."

Jacob was pretty sure he knew. That would have been the end of it. The end of their legacy, and the last gasp of Midstream, itself.

"Archibald is helping defend Midstream," Jacob said.

Lakkan scoffed. "The Bollwerk king?"

"I don't think he's a king, exactly."

"In all but title. And he is the man who abandoned Midstream to its fate. To what end? The end of all, I suppose."

"He did offer shelter to George and Gladys and what remained of the guard," Drakkar said.

Lakkan grimaced. "He should have put Rana down the first instant that warlord took power in the wastes near the Burning Forest."

"Rana?" Alice asked.

Not entirely thinking things through, Jacob blurted out, "Oh, Alice killed Rana to rescue Gladys."

Lakkan stared, slack-jawed before composing himself. "I am glad to hear of his demise."

"You did *what!*" Alice's mom barked out.

Jacob froze mid-bite and gave an awkward smile to a now-glaring Alice.

"And I suppose *you* are the tinker who executed the Butcher," Lakkan muttered.

"What?" Jacob's mom hissed.

"Ha!" Alice said, the focus now off of her.

"He may be," Drakkar said, "but that is something which should remain quiet. We do not know how deeply Fel's network penetrated Ancora's allies."

"I would hardly call Cave an ally of Ancora."

"You have taken in countless refugees. It is enough for an empire of ill intent to take notice."

"Well done," Jacob's dad said, patting his knee.

"Well *done*?" Jacob's mom said, unable to keep the exasperation from her voice. "He … and you just … how could you say that?"

"I didn't have a choice, Mom. It was us or him. He chased us to Bollwerk and sent Ballern's warships after us because of what we knew." It was a slight exaggeration, Jacob knew. No one had specifically sent warships after *them*, but it sounded like a better excuse.

Jacob's mom cursed under her breath. "Anything stronger to drink than water, Lakkan?"

The chef grinned. "I can fix you up."

✧ ✧ ✧

THEY SPENT ANOTHER hour with Lakkan as he regaled them with evermore ridiculous stories of the madness that sometimes happened on the sea. Jacob hoped one day he'd be able to go out on those ships and see how they could stay afloat in the storms like Lakkan described.

When the time came for Lakkan to open to his regulars, the group said their goodbyes and headed back into the heart of Cave. Jacob and Alice agreed to an evening of rest over at The Rock Inn. But in the morning, they'd return to Ancora.

Now they knew their families were safe. It was time to help the city rebuild.

CHAPTER FIVE

Gregory Mordair sat on the jagged stone throne of Fel. He kept enough loyalists close to him that the day to day running of the empire was usually not so taxing. But the takeover of Ancora had not gone as smoothly as he planned. His idiot brother, concealed for decades among the Parliament, failed in a proper coup.

Dauschen's destruction weighed on Mordair's mind far more than the failures in Ancora. All he needed in Ancora was chaos, and there was plenty of that to go around. He had not suspected Charles to be such a problem in his old age. A small smile lifted the edges of Mordair's mouth, though no one could see it behind his metal mask. He doubted Charles had expected *him* to be such a problem either.

Sometimes the destruction of one's enemy decades after the fact was just as sweet.

The King of Fel focused on the man in chains before him. There was little that bothered Mordair as much as disloyalty. The disturbing trend among the population to question royalty had the potential to become a problem. There was a time not so long ago that a handful of executions would quell the masses. But much to Mordair's annoyance, more of the population were willing to risk death.

He adjusted the spiked breathing mask on his face, long the symbol of his family line in war. Though it had not often been worn outside of battle, things had changed.

"Now, traitor, tell me of these pamphlets." Mordair had already read them. Their pages were filled with conspiracies that the king had lost his mind, was simply warmongering for his own personal gain, and cared nothing of the population at large. The irony, of course, was that a great many of those conspiracies were true.

The man slowly raised his eyes to the king. Hair matted by blood covered one eye, and a magnificent bruise stretched from ear to chin. "I have nothing to say that wasn't said already. Do with me as you will."

Mordair leaned back in his throne. "I believe we have had a misunderstanding. It is not so much you I am interested in. It is who gave you the stories."

"So they're true," the man whispered.

"Truth is a fickle beast. The fact there are fragments of it in your stories—and that is all they are—is dangerous."

"You murdered families in Ancora. Families no different from mine. You want us to believe they deserved to die because they put a kink in your trade route."

Mordair laughed. "Defiant. I can respect that. Let us see if your wife feels the same." Mordair gestured to a guard at the back of the room.

The man on the floor did not respond.

They escorted a petite woman in heavy robes across the room. Unlike her husband, she was free to walk on her own, or flee to her death, if she chose. It took time to convince a populace they were powerless. But the easiest way was to offer them small freedoms before crushing the dissenters.

The King of Fel had grown used to loyalty. He had expected some resistance as the nature of his campaigns came to light. There were always fractures, even in the most loyal populations, and witnessing the destruction of the city would make many question their leadership.

But the ringleaders of these so-called spies could not be allowed to continue. The pamphlets had been found in more than one dissenter's home. Some abandoned, the owners fleeing to some far-off city. But Mordair needed the population. They were a convenient shield against any possible invaders.

The nearest guard tried to force the woman to her knees, but her hand slid inside the heavy robes. Mordair watched, somewhat detached, as her hidden blade found a joint in the guard's armor. Blood sprayed from his neck as she turned on the king himself. Two more guards pounced, impaling her with their pikes as she collapsed to the ground.

Mordair stood and took two steps down toward the dying woman. What he didn't understand was the impassive look on her husband's face.

The prisoner leaned over to kiss his wife goodbye. But when he straightened, and smiled at Mordair, a small metal orb gleamed between his teeth.

"Down!" one of the guards screamed, diving for Mordair.

Almost in slow motion, their captive bit down, setting off the small explosive. Shrapnel tore through the guards. The prisoner and his wife died in an instant. The nearest guard, the one who had dove for Mordair and taken the brunt of the shrapnel, gurgled and reached out to his king. Mordair shoved him away with his boot and stepped down to the corpses of their prisoners.

The king exhaled and leaned down beside another dead guard by the chained prisoner. He picked up the small metal box, now dented from the impact of shrapnel. Inside, he found the latest pamphlet they had meant to print.

It spoke of new evidence that Mordair had funded the warlords of the Deadlands. That he was responsible for the fall of Midstream, the razing of the villages around Gareth Cave, and the new aggression emanating from Bollwerk.

Mordair crumpled up the paper and walked over to a small torchère at the base of the throne, tossing the paper in.

He turned to the Red Hand. "I don't know who was feeding them information, but I want every informant found."

"Of course," the Red Hand said. "Should we cancel the march, sir?"

Mordair slowly shook his head. "No. Pull a detail off to clean up this mess. But the march goes on as planned. We need to remind these people who feeds and protects them, and where their loyalties should lie."

"It shall be done." The guard gave a short bow to Mordair and turned to exit through a decorative steel door.

Mordair made for his chambers to the rear of the throne. The leather apron he wore would need to be changed. Too many questions would arise if he showed up with blood splattered across his chest. It was only then he noticed the burn on his left biceps. A small bit of shrapnel had found him, and that was the closest an enemy had come to him in a very long time.

There was an excitement in that. An escalation that had not happened in the city in recent memory. The conflict to come would be memorable indeed.

✧   ✧   ✧

THE OLD FLAG of Fel had been a symbol of weakness and ruin when Mordair took power. It was a pale and colorless thing. Now he stood on the balcony of the king's courts and watched the procession below. Vibrant red flags emblazoned with an abstract black Tail Sword hung from the dark gray stone buildings and the airships floating silently overhead.

For all the kingdom knew, this was simply a show of respect for Mordair's fallen brother, the most honorable Newton Victor Burns. And perhaps some small part of it still held that meaning. But Mordair had a different reason for these marches. He made it a point to deploy their military forces inside the city at minimum four times per year. It was a stark reminder of how much power those who spoke up against Fel could bring down on their family's heads.

Some were too soft to see it, or too caught up in blindly supporting their king. But Mordair knew even his staunchest supporter could waver and abandon the city if they learned the truth of things. So, instead, there were reminders and rallies and, occasionally, disappearances.

Like those two fools earlier that day. Their home would be found abandoned. Others would assume they'd fled the city. Only four guards and Mordair himself knew the truth.

The great orator and warrior of Fel, known only as the Red Hand, stepped to the foremost armored crawler as it slowed, lifting a polished brass transmitter to her mouth, one that reached the amplifiers mounted across every crawler.

"Only with the great sacrifice of Newton Victor Burns have we obtained a great victory. Our rivals in Dauschen are no more, thrown down from their mountain fortress by a decisive blow from our king. Only he had the foresight to bring down their base and collapse their mountainside docks.

"Now, with Ancora brought to heel, only Bollwerk remains as a blockade to our domination of the Deadlands. Rejoice, citizens. For you will soon be a part of the greatest empire this world has witnessed in its long history."

Few knew what had happened in Dauschen. And the handful who wouldn't keep silent were themselves silenced. There was no room for dissenters under the rule of Mordair. But it would not always be that way. He only needed the shield until it was time to join his allies in Ballern.

The Red Hand continued, detailing the king's plans he'd not yet spoken in public. "Soon we will take once more the city known as Midstream." The longer she spoke, the more fervent her words became until, at the end, she was nearly shouting. "From there, beneath the absolute power of Fel, we will launch a strike on Bollwerk that will change the landscape of the Deadlands for all time!"

Mordair shivered at the cheers and screams that responded to those words. Like loyal pets trained to attack, these fools would die for an empire that cared little for the blood that fueled it.

With Belldorn's allies weakened, Ballern would have their opportunity, and Mordair would move through the ranks of their ruling class like a malignant parasite. He grinned beneath his mask as the citizens of Fel took up the booming chant of the citizen's oath.

One thing Newton had never fully understood was patience. Patience was not infinite. Patience was the means to wait for an opportunity. And then strike.

CHAPTER SIX

"I T FEELS STRANGE to be leaving them here in Cave," Alice said.

Jacob secured the ties on one of his packs and glanced up at her. "Our parents?"

"Yes."

"We can stay longer if you wish," Drakkar said.

Jacob shook his head. "I know they're safe here. Ancora needs us."

Alice nodded, as if trying to convince herself that she agreed with everything Jacob was saying. "You're right. We need to get back and help where we can. One day we'll have the Lowlands rebuilt. Then we can bring our parents home."

In some ways, Jacob hoped Ancora would be different, not so separated between the Highlands and Lowlands. But he'd seen enough over his life to know that a change like that would take a great deal of time. For now, they could help with the reconstruction, and maybe in the future they could help heal the divide inside Ancora.

Alice started to fold the blanket on the cot where she'd slept. The Rock Inn hadn't had many rooms left, but the innkeeper had a couple extra cots for Alice and Jacob.

"You can leave that," Drakkar said. "The innkeeper will straighten things. And my back thanks you for leaving the bed to me. Now, if you have all of your things, let us head for the stables."

The trio waved to the innkeeper as they exited. It was good Drakkar knew him, and well enough that he could acquire a room, but Jacob wondered about the rest of the overcrowded city. How many people slept on floors and alleys while they enjoyed a cot. He supposed it was better than those worst off in Ancora. At least here in Cave every citizen had a roof over their head.

Drakkar led them away from the inn, winding up through the more familiar streets of Cave. Jacob had only seen a small part of the city before. It was an odd thought now, knowing just how deep Cave went. One day, when they had more time, Jacob wanted to return and explore that cavern on the Silver Gulf.

A stable hand greeted them when they returned for George. He fetched the Walker's saddlebags without question, and without Drakkar asking for them.

Alice walked over to one of the other pens, peering inside at a large Jumper. "She looks like Bessie."

Jacob stepped closer. "She's not all gray, though."

"Not from Ancora," Alice said. "Their hair grows in different patterns and colors, depending on their environment. I wouldn't be surprised if this Jumper wasn't from the Deadlands at all."

Jacob frowned. "Her armor sure looks like a Spider Knight's."

The stable hand overheard their conversation. "She doesn't belong to a Spider Knight of Ancora. Some of the soldiers around the Sea of Salt also ride Jumpers. If you look there on the wall, you'll see more leg armor than anyone in Ancora uses. Especially on a Jumper."

"Wouldn't that be too heavy a load?" Alice asked.

The stable hand nodded. "Some people who ride Jumpers don't want them jumping."

Jacob could understand that. He'd had more than one rough ride on Bessie's back.

"This should be all of your saddlebags. There's an extra package of dried Sweet-Flies in there. Good for your Walker, or you."

Drakkar exchanged grips with the stable hand. "I appreciate your care. Be safe and travel well."

"I won't be traveling anywhere for a while. I've heard what happened in Ancora. Sounds like staying underground is the place to be."

Drakkar inclined his head. "Alice, Jacob, it is time."

✧ ✧ ✧

THE TRIP BACK through the mountain paths didn't take as long with George well rested and fed by caretakers who specialized in Walkers. George sped across uneven terrain, his legs pumping and churning through the dirt without hesitation.

Jacob was about to shout a warning that there was a Red Death ahead of them, but George simply charged over it, impaling the black carapace briefly with his pinchers, and then trampling the beetle into a ruin.

Drakkar glanced back with a smile. "I do not think we need to concern ourselves with a lone Red Death."

"Apparently not," Alice said.

The Walker was a bit rambunctious after that. George surged up onto some boulders flanking the path, giving his riders a wild time trying to hold on.

"Can you stop him from doing that?" Alice asked. "Jacob nearly lost his pack."

Jacob frowned at Alice. "You didn't have to tell him that." Jacob tightened the straps and resecured it to his back. It obviously hadn't been a good idea to let the pack ride free in front of him.

Drakkar leaned forward and dropped a dried Sweet-Fly onto the Walker's face. The food vanished in an instant, and Drakkar continued feeding George, who suddenly became much less interested in the boulders along the path. He kept to the center, and Jacob dozed off with the rhythmic roll of the Walker's stride.

It was Alice's words that shocked him fully awake. "One of Bollwerk's warships is still over Ancora."

"I see it," Drakkar said. "Hold tight. We're going to take George up the wall by the old lift."

"By the old lift?" Alice asked. "Drakkar, that's nearly a sheer cliff."

"Yes? Make sure the saddlebags are tight, closed, and your packs are secure."

Alice stared at the Cave Guardian somewhat in disbelief. But after a moment's hesitation, she started checking the buckles and tightened her own pack against the gray sweater she wore.

Jacob did the same, watching the road vanish beneath the Walker's stride. The path and cliffs that led to Ancora looked far off, but after he'd finished checking his own pack and saddlebags, they were already at the wall.

The thing Jacob noticed first as they neared the lift was the fact the remaining bodies around it had been cleared away. Part of him wondered what had been done. Had they all received burials? Or had it been like the old wars Charles talked about, where one massive funeral pyre sent the dead on their way? Another part of war Jacob never wanted to know.

"Hold on," Drakkar said.

George slowed for only a moment before Drakkar gave him two quick pats on the head between his antennae. With that silent signal, the Walker climbed onto the wall. Bits of rock pattered down while Jacob locked his legs across the segment he was seated on.

He and Alice both kept their hands bound to the straps of the saddlebags. It was both annoying and inspiring to see Drakkar casually riding on a near-vertical Walker. He made it look effortless, and in that moment, Jacob felt it was anything but.

As fatigue leached the strength from Jacob's fingers, George mercifully crested the cliff and surged into the ruins of the Lowlands.

Jacob hadn't spent much time near that old lift. Before the city fell, it had always been guarded by city knights. When Jacob was a more active pickpocket, knights were the kind of people he tended to avoid.

But as they cleared the ruin of the old city wall and slithered onto the street where their school had once stood, Jacob's chest tightened. There were only a few buildings left standing in the Lowlands. And perhaps that in itself was an exaggeration. There were only a few ruins he could recognize.

But beyond those clusters of fallen stone and wood loomed the unmistakable outline of Charles's old lab.

As if she'd seen it at the same time, Alice leaned back and squeezed Jacob's hand.

"I want to go back," Jacob said. "Charles had more hiding spots than what we raided. I want to see if there's anything else he left behind."

"It is unlikely," Drakkar said. "The Butcher raided that same lab. Do you really think they missed that much?"

Jacob shrugged, even though Drakkar couldn't see it. "Maybe they did. I just … I have good memories of the place."

"I miss him too," Alice said.

"Perhaps tomorrow," Drakkar said. "For now, we need to find Baddawick."

"Are you sure we shouldn't talk to Archibald?" Jacob asked.

"Archibald has already departed. Look closer at the airship above you. That is not Archibald's."

Jacob squinted at the massive warship. It's not that it wasn't one of Archibald's, but Drakkar was right. It was not the warship that had landed after the battle with the Butcher.

"I trust Baddawick more, anyway," Alice said. "If anyone is going to know who is left from the construction crews and who is helping rebuild the city walls, it's going to be Baddawick."

It made sense to Jacob, though he figured some of the Spider Knights might also be aware of happenings around the city. But the idea of returning to the Wild Horse Inn was not unwelcome.

Deeper into the Lowlands, Jacob could see more of the progress that had been made in the short time they'd been away. There wasn't much more in the area that had been done to the remnants of the city wall, but the remains of invaders and buildings alike had been pushed aside to make a narrow path.

George followed the path on instinct alone. Drakkar didn't guide the Walker as they sped past debris.

Alice's hands tightened on the saddlebags' straps, and her posture stiffened as they reached the wreckage of the square. It was hard to reconcile the fact that this place, still stained with blood, had hosted Festival so recently.

Jacob could make out the fractured stage and the splinters of more than one vendor cart. Beyond the ghost of the square, they skirted a crater in the road. Jacob had little doubt what had made that. One of the compound bombs, possibly one that he'd dropped while he fled from the horde with Charles.

"Look," Drakkar said, pointing toward the east mountains.

At first, Jacob wasn't sure what Drakkar was pointing at, but then he saw it. Along the side of the plateau where the Lowlands sat, more of the wooden city wall had been erected, the temporary structure stretching all the way back to the towering stone walls of the Highlands. It still left them open to attacks from invaders, but provided a modicum of protection.

Alice glanced back. "Do you think it's Ambrose working on the walls? It always did seem to be one of his priorities."

Jacob nodded. "It could be. We'll have to ask Baddawick. Or we can ask Ambrose, if we run into him."

Drakkar adjusted the reins and guided George to the west, where a central street had been better cleared than the one they were on. Jacob's grip tightened as they crossed rubble pushed to the edge of the road, and then they were on the relatively clean cobblestones closer to the High-lands.

The gates stood open, flanked by a handful of guards. Drakkar raised a hand in greeting, and two of the men motioned them in.

Jacob could see minor progress in the cleanup of the Highlands, but it was clear most of the efforts had gone into rebuilding the wall. Drakkar steered the Walker toward the stables just inside and to the left of the city gates.

"Is that Samuel?" Jacob asked, watching a Spider Knight take off down one of the streets.

"No way," Alice said. "That wasn't a Jumper, and I don't think Samu-el would be riding around without a helmet."

George made a straight line for the same stable they'd left a couple days before. The Walker was almost as much a creature of habit as his keepers. They disembarked, checking the saddlebags with a stable hand as Drakkar explained that the dried Sweet-Flies should only be used as a treat.

While Drakkar was engaged, Alice started walking down the row of stalls. Jacob followed, peering in on the various mounts currently staying in the city. Several of the stables were empty, but others held Jumpers and their slower-moving cousins, giant black and tan Stalkers, spiders that dwarfed the Jumpers.

Jacob paused by a stall with a mantis. They were a favored mount of the wealthier families in the Highlands. This one was a brilliant emerald green and its eyes shifted, staring at Jacob with an unnerving gaze.

Alice's squeak caught Jacob's attention. She threw open one of the solid gates and hurried inside. Jacob jogged over and found her nestled against a furry gray Jumper. The spider chittered and bounced on its legs, smacking Alice repeatedly with its pedipalps.

"Bessie!" Jacob followed Alice into the stall to scratch the spider between its many eyes. "It's good to see you."

The Jumper still had a few bald spots on her legs where her injuries from the previous week's battle were healing. Other spots were still bandaged, salve soaking them through.

Alice grinned at the spider. "Have you seen Samuel? I bet you miss him, don't you?"

"There you are," Drakkar said. "Come, let us make for the Wildhorse. Then we can rest at Samuel's."

Alice and Jacob gave the spider one more scratching and then made their way out of the stables.

"She looks good," Alice said.

Jacob nodded in agreement as he followed her back into the streets of Ancora.

The Wild Horse Inn was crowded, but not nearly so raucous as it had been before the attacks on Ancora. Now tables were packed with a mixture of people from the Highlands and Lowlands, and Jacob was somewhat surprised to hear Baddawick wouldn't let anyone pay for their meals.

"Not to worry," Drakkar said. "I am sure he will still profit from the drink and the spectacle."

"Incoming!" a bartender shouted. One of the tables launched its tray across the room, where it was neatly caught by a server and added back to a stack.

It still brought a smile to Jacob, but the room was far more somber without the jangling crescendos of a piano. The only sounds were clinking glasses and shouted orders, and tables kept mostly to their own hushed conversations.

Two armored forms flanked the bar, and Jacob had a sudden flashback to running away from city guards not so long ago. Now they only nodded in greeting as he joined Drakkar and Alice on a trio of barstools.

"Baddawick!" Drakkar shouted, startling the nearest guard. "I can see your hair from here. Come, speak with us."

A wild tangle of white hair appeared at the kitchen window, barely restrained by a pair of goggles with more lenses attached to them than Jacob could count. Baddawick grinned and disappeared for a moment before throwing open a door beside the closest guard.

"Drakkar! Jacob, Alice, it's good to see you all. A Dragon's Bane for the Cave Guardian."

A bartender nodded and started fixing a drink.

"Sweetwing Tea?"

Alice nodded. Jacob shrugged, but gave in after Alice glared at him.

"Just because it has wings does *not* mean it's nasty."

Drakkar looked like he too was about to protest the drink when the bartender delivered it, but Baddawick raised an eyebrow and waited for the Cave Guardian to take the first sip.

"The drink is excellent, Baddawick. You have my thanks."

Baddawick dried his hands on a towel. "What do you need today?"

"Can you tell us who is directing the construction of the temporary walls?"

Baddawick stroked his beard. "Can't say I remember the chap's name. But Ambrose would know. He's already starting a new stone wall in the northwest corner of the Lowlands."

"Stone?" Alice asked, taking the two Sweetwing Teas from the bartender and handing one to Jacob.

"Yes, indeed. Says he's tired of the Lowlands not being just as safe as the Highlands. Has a good size crew of volunteers hauling stone from some of the ruined houses." Baddawick paused. "I reckon it'll cause some supply issues when we start rebuilding those homes, but the old lift should be repaired by then. Bring some new stone into the city that way."

"Maybe Archibald would help. If he's leaving one of the warships stationed here, they can haul more than anything Ancora has."

"Archibald has enough problems to deal with," Baddawick said. "If we get desperate, we can reach out to Bollwerk. But Ancorans are a hearty bunch. We look out for each other."

Drakkar looked up from his drink. "Do not flaunt your independence to the point of folly."

"Ack," Baddawick said with a grin. "Using my own words against me? I thought better of you, Drakkar."

Drakkar matched Baddawick's grin. "I do appreciate the drink."

"On the house, and I'll hear no more about it. You mean to help Ambrose with the wall?"

"I do now," Jacob said, drawing Baddawick's eye.

"The last apprentice of Atlier. The smiths around this city will expect much of you, Jacob. Except the city smith. Reckon he got a bit more than he expected."

Jacob felt a small embarrassment flushing his cheeks at that. He sipped at the Sweetwing Tea. It was a concoction he'd never been fond of with the strange pearls at the bottom that popped in his mouth. But this was the best he'd had; sweet, yes, but a hint of herbs balanced out the musty flavor of the flies.

Drakkar threw back the last of his drink. "Thank you for the drinks, Baddawick. We will be staying with Samuel for a time should you need to contact us."

Baddawick turned his collar down, showing the bright copper of a transmitter. "Reckon I can reach you anytime."

Drakkar inclined his head. They said their goodbyes to Baddawick while Jacob and Alice finished their teas. It would be good to rest. Jacob expected tomorrow to be exhausting.

CHAPTER SEVEN

T HEY STOPPED INTERMITTENTLY on the walk to Samuel's house. An older woman wanted to speak with Drakkar, telling him how a Cave Guardian once saved her husband on the road to the Ridge Mountains. Jacob ducked into the candy shop as they passed the old hospital. Both buildings had been damaged in the attack on Ancora, but were already under repair.

Cocoa Crunch in hand, they made their way up the street until Samuel's towering home came into view. It was hard not to think of it as Bat's home, but Jacob knew it wasn't anymore. Bat had sacrificed himself in the battle of Ancora against the Butcher.

They entered Samuel's house through the open workshop, and Jacob ran his fingers along the workbench. He remembered working on the nail gloves and bolt gloves there with Charles. Jacob also remembered when the city guard had come for him, and Charles stopped them dead.

He followed Alice into the house, rubbing his fingers together to brush off the dust. The old couch and chairs where he'd once stayed with his parents were still in the entry room. A low chatter whispered through the halls, at least a dozen people in that room alone, and Drakkar nodded to those who paid attention to them.

"Is Samuel home?" Drakkar asked.

The older man he questioned only responded with a blank stare.

"You won't get answers out of that one," a familiar voice said.

Even as Jacob turned around, he heard Alice say, "Samuel! Trying to give us a heart attack?"

The Spider Knight grinned. He wasn't much older than Jacob and Alice, only recently crossing twenty years of age. Jacob had never seen him look so old in all the time he'd known him. The conflict with Fel had taken a toll, and it was one Jacob saw in himself in the mirror.

Drakkar traded grips with the Spider Knight.

Samuel gestured to the spiral stairs in the corner. "I kept your rooms empty upstairs, though you'll find the house is a bit more crowded than last time you were here. There's food in the kitchen if you need it. My home is yours."

"We saw Bessie at the stables," Alice said. "Is she healing well?"

Samuel nodded. "They're taking good care of her. I think she'll make a full recovery."

"That's great to hear," Jacob said.

Samuel held up a finger. "I went by Charles's old place yesterday. I found something for you."

Jacob exchanged a glance with Alice as the Spider Knight disappeared down the hallway. Samuel returned shortly after, a brown and tan booklet in his hand. Not a booklet, Jacob realized with a start. But a journal.

"I think it's one of Charles's old workbooks. Quite a few sketches in there, and I thought you'd like to have it."

Jacob started thumbing through the pages as soon as Samuel handed it over. Not only was it filled with illustrations Jacob had never seen before, but Charles's handwriting revealed gear ratios and tensioner settings for half a dozen different designs.

Alice elbowed him in the stomach. "And what do we say?"

Jacob smiled and closed the book. "Thank you. I've been wanting to go back to Charles's lab. Where did you find this?"

"We were looking for more bolts for Ambrose. We moved a barrel, and that was underneath it. Well, it was actually underneath a cracked floor tile. Strange hiding place for a journal."

Jacob nodded. "That's why I want to go. There's no way we got everything out of that lab. And I know the Butcher raided it, but his soldiers might not have found everything."

"Do you know where we can locate Ambrose?" Drakkar asked.

"Of course. He's always working on the northwest wall. Well, the southwest wall of the Highlands, which is …" He stopped and shook his head. "You know what I mean. Tell you what, meet me at Charles's old lab in the morning. We can search the place, and then I'll take you straight to Ambrose. Why don't you get some food and rest tonight?"

"That sounds great to me," Jacob said through a yawn. It was ridiculous to be tired already. But he found that lately it was hard to get enough rest, and they needed to take it when they could.

They hauled their bags up the spiral stairs to the topmost floor. Jacob wasn't sure if Samuel's house was three or four stories, considering part of it was underground, but it was a lot of stairs either way.

Drakkar continued to the end of the hall while Jacob and Alice ducked into their shared room. Alice dropped her pack on the corner cedar chest with a thud. Jacob was a bit slower, carefully sliding Charles's journal into the back pocket.

Alice flopped onto the edge of the bed. "I could go to sleep right now."

"Me too." Jacob checked underneath the bed, where he'd once stashed some glowworms. The portable cot was gone, likely being used by one of the families downstairs. "Cot's gone. I'll take the floor."

Alice dismissed the thought with a wave. "The bed's big enough for two. It's fine. Besides, I'll feel bad if you die because you got a kink in your back. Just no knives under the pillow this time, yes?"

Jacob blinked at Alice. "That's not fair. I just … I didn't mean …"

Alice grinned at Jacob, her laughter ringing through the room. "Come on, let's get a snack. Then we can get some sleep."

✦   ✦   ✦

Jacob found a bottle of mineral oil in Charles's old workshop after they ate. He took it back to the small room that he shared with Alice, needing to address an annoying squeak in one of the plates on his leg.

"And you're sure you're not going to poison yourself with that?" Alice asked.

"No, no. It's safe for food. Charles told me Baddawick used it on all of his cutting boards, not to mention any of the machines that process the restaurant's food."

It still felt strange having the leg of a Biomech. He wondered how much maintenance Smith had to do with the many pistons and gears embedded in his chest. Jacob pushed some of the tubing aside that flowed with his blood, finding a joint closer to his ankle that was the source of the squeak.

He put only a drop of oil on it and worked it in with his thumb. When it was silent, he closed the oil and wiped off the excess with a rag.

Jacob paused when he saw Alice studying the complex inner workings of his leg.

"It's quite a marvel, really. How the retractable anchors in your foot fit inside that thing. Not to mention the tubing."

Jacob smiled and snapped his leg closed. "I have to admit it's not all bad."

Alice yawned and crawled under the covers.

As tired as Jacob was, he couldn't resist thumbing through Charles's journal. The fact Samuel had found it, so intact, gave him a small hope they'd find more of the old tinker's writings.

"Going to read a little?" Alice asked.

Jacob nodded and glanced back at her, a wide smile lifting his lips when he saw *The Dead Scourge* propped up in front of her. Archibald's book had given them insights into the Deadlands War. And, in turn, Jacob felt that had given him some insight into the things Charles had experienced. The things that had shaped the man he knew.

But the journal was different. It showed Jacob the meanderings of a tinker. He followed the designs on the first few pages, each one marked with a small X in the top center of the page. Page after page was lettered the same way until he came to something that looked like a rudimentary air cannon. Those illustrations had a checkmark on top.

Jacob read deeper into the journal, which showed the evolution of the weapon Charles had invented. He could see it from the earliest incarnation, when he used a Burner with an attached boiler, to a hybrid with both the Burner and a pump, and six pages later, the design he knew so well. The angles of the barrel were exact, the slide for the pump, details of the ammunition, everything.

The schematics were comprehensive enough Jacob was sure he could build another air cannon. But those thoughts trailed off as he reached the second half of the journal. The aged paper had schematics for what appeared to be a mechanical hand. At first, Jacob thought that was what it was, but the measurements made little sense. What would the point be of a six-foot-wide hand?

But as the following pages detailed enormous joints, and how to attach the hand to a similarly oversized arm, Jacob's heart skipped a beat. The journal ended with the details of a lever system to control both the grip and angle, and Jacob realized he was looking at the schematics for part of a Titan Mech.

Daylight vanished from the window as Jacob read. The more he studied the schematics, the more an idea took shape in his head.

"Alice, I think I could use these designs to replace the pulley system they use on the walls." Even as he said it, he thought about how efficient the construction crews were at raising the walls. But this could help with the stone. He would have to consider it further. Maybe in the morning Ambrose could give them a better idea of what Jacob would be getting himself into.

"Alice?"

Alice was deep into sleep, *The Dead Scourge* tucked under one arm, and a blanket wrapped around the other. Jacob knew from experience he wouldn't be getting much of the blanket that night.

He smiled and set the journal down, climbing into bed next to Alice as his imagination cycled through Charles's writings. The last page kept rising to the surface of his thoughts. It was clear a few pages had been torn out of the journal, but not the pages between the Titan Mech schematics and the final drawings. A simple child's toy, not so unlike the one Alice had gotten Jacob at Festival: an automaton that performed a simple task when a coin was placed on top of it.

Even as Charles had designed tools of war, his mind had been elsewhere. Jacob wished the old man was still around so he could ask him about that. But for now, the journal would have to be enough. Maybe this was something else Jacob could help repurpose to be beneficial.

Sleep did not come quickly, but exhaustion won out in time.

✧　✧　✧

THE NEXT MORNING, Jacob felt better rested than any time since the battle of Ancora had ended. Samuel's house bustled with activity, and he and Alice were two of a dozen people passing through the kitchen for breakfast.

Jacob eyed Samuel with some suspicion. He was used to the Spider Knight complaining about most everything, but now he looked happy cooking on the old stove for his many guests.

"You're up," Samuel said when he caught Jacob's eye. "Marjorie, take over for me, would you?"

An older woman took the spatula from Samuel as he untied his apron. Beneath, he was already wearing the armor of the Spider Knights.

"Where are we going first?" Alice asked.

"Ambrose." Samuel glanced at a clock on the wall. "His crew should already be outside the gates. You two slept a bit longer than I expected, so we should be able to find him now."

"Have you seen Drakkar yet?" Jacob asked.

Samuel grimaced. "Yet? He dragged me out of bed before the sun had risen this morning. Only fifteen minutes early, I guess, but *still.* Do you know how important an extra fifteen minutes of sleep can be?"

Jacob exchanged a grin with Alice.

"He's waiting out in the workshop. Grab your packs and let's be on our way."

Alice shoveled the rest of her eggs into her mouth in two impressive gulps before placing the dishes by the sink. After a quick trip upstairs to retrieve their packs, they headed to the workshop. Hunched over the bench was the cloaked Cave Guardian. He thumbed through a book before glancing up at Samuel and the others.

Drakkar eyed Samuel. "I thought you might have perished from your lack of sleep."

Samuel opened his mouth as if to respond, but then fell silent for a moment. "You know what? Let's just go find Ambrose."

They were halfway down the street that led past the candy shop when something boomed outside the walls. Jacob glanced up, confused as to why a cannon on Bollwerk's warship was smoking.

"Trouble with some Red Death," Samuel said, answering the unspoken question. "They're keeping the worst of the hordes away from the construction crews."

"The *worst* of the hordes?" Alice asked.

"Yes. The Spider Knights are taking care of the rest. And whatever

Carrion Worms slip through."

"Are you going to bring Bessie today?" Jacob asked, somewhat hoping to have the giant Jumper at their side.

Samuel shook his head. "She heals fast, but I don't want to risk injuring her further. We can walk today." He paused and opened the long pack thrown over his shoulder. "But you'll likely want to have this."

Jacob caught the air cannon midflight, the cold metal smacking against his palm. He nodded and fastened the holster across his shoulder, so it sat flush against his back. Alice opened her own pack, sliding one hand into a bolt glove, and locking a wrist launcher on either arm.

"I suppose you'll just use your big stick," Samuel said, eyeing Drakkar's staff.

"It is a rather pointy stick, so yes."

"It should be enough while we're being escorted by a noble Spider Knight," Alice chimed in.

Samuel took a deep breath and turned to the gates. "Right then. Let's find Ambrose."

CHAPTER EIGHT

A SMALL ROW of storefronts had survived the Fall. Jacob looked into the windows at undisturbed tea settings and then through the rounded bay windows of a clockmaker's shop. It was jarring, seeing something so unscathed in the ruin that surrounded them.

And it wasn't merely the wreckage of the buildings themselves.

"The smell," Alice mumbled, covering her mouth. "It's worse than yesterday."

"It will fade soon," Drakkar said. "The worst of the rot has set in. Be on the lookout for Carrion Worms."

"There have been a few," Samuel said. "One of the old cabins near the far west wall collapsed on a family and …" He trailed off, glancing back at Jacob and Alice.

"I don't think you need to worry about giving us nightmares," Alice said. "We've seen enough."

Jacob wasn't sure he agreed. It was one thing to be in a fight, but it was another thing entirely when he'd been fleeing the hordes with Charles. When he saw the mass drag Bradley Piers to the ground to be consumed …

He shivered and turned back to the cleared street ahead of them.

Most of the invaders had been removed, or at least pushed far enough off the streets to not be an obstacle. A few more shops were still standing closer to the city walls, but as they crossed into the residential areas, following the wide stairs that led downhill, the full scope of the devastation crashed into Jacob once more. They weren't speeding by the wreckage on the back of a Walker this time.

He tried to focus on the cobblestones and the distant shouts of what he now realized were the construction workers on the walls. But it was hard not to stare at what had been. And what had been done to the Lowlands.

Alice rubbed at her eyes, but said nothing while Drakkar kept a solemn watch over the debris. Jacob realized that was probably the smartest thing any of them were doing. Carrion Worms could be tricky and explode from the earth in the most unlikely of places.

"Hold!" A loud voice boomed as they rounded the corner at the bottom of the stairs and the rebuilt sections of the wall came into view. Jacob recognized the speaker giving hand signals to the men operating a pulley system to hoist large stones and set them onto the base.

The pale gray block, some three feet in length, cracked down on the stone below it with a thunderclap.

"Not so hard!" Ambrose shouted. "You don't want to pick up the pieces if one of those shatters."

As the crew straightened one behemoth stone, masons chiseled away at the foundations of what used to be homes. They were harvesting the largest of them to become part of the city wall. It was smart, but Baddawick was right. They'd run out of stone before they'd finish.

"Ambrose!" Samuel said.

Ambrose dusted his gloves off and turned when his name was called. He paused and held a hand above his eyes to dim the sun. He had grown a rough beard since Jacob had seen him last, but the smile was familiar. He remembered that smile when Charles had shown him the nail glove.

"Samuel," Ambrose said, trading grips with the Spider Knight. "Jacob, Alice. It's good to see you again. And I've heard tales of the Cave Guardian."

"*A* Cave Guardian," Drakkar said. "Though I am not of the order of the Nameless."

"An honor, regardless." He turned to his crew. "Mount the steel first, then grind the stone. Can you handle that?"

A somewhat grumpy and begrudging affirmation came back.

Ambrose grinned at Samuel. "They're a good crew, but you need to keep them in line sometimes."

"Where are the Spider Knights?" Samuel asked.

"Other side of the wall. Cleaning up whatever the warship missed in that last barrage."

Jacob eyed the structure of the wall. A series of bolts ran along the base, connecting through brackets mounted to the stone. But the bolts looked small, too small to keep things in place long term.

"Are you bracing those bolts with anything?" he asked before he could think more about it.

"Only the brackets at the base."

Jacob thought back to the crush of invaders hitting the walls during the fall of Ancora. While these walls were stone, they still weren't as thick as the Highlands, and he wasn't sure how much they could withstand.

"Have you thought about putting an angled bracer on? Forty-five degrees, bolted to the center of the wall?"

Ambrose's eyebrow rose a hair. "I've thought about it, yes, but the few bolt gloves we have can't handle that kind of force. We need to drill the stone out and anchor it more traditionally. That would take time."

Jacob nodded. "That makes sense. Maybe when the wall is done, they can be added." He rubbed at his cheek. "I do have some ideas, though. Let me try some things to see if I can speed up the process."

Ambrose gestured toward the wall. "I won't say no if you can save us some time. Rebuilding this wall is a race. I don't think we'd be able to do it if Bollwerk hadn't left one of their warships here."

The chittering screech of a Jumper pierced the air around them. Conversation froze as they turned toward the sound. Scuttling around the far end of the wall, scattering the workers, came a trio of Red Death. Brilliant black carapaces adorned with a red skull flashed in the sunlight.

The first of the Red Death spread its wings, only a blur as the beetle reared up to strike down one of the workers. But even as Jacob drew his air cannon, the Spider Knight on the Jumper pounced. He leaped from his mount, halberd extended as he slammed down onto the back of the Red Death. The wings softened his landing, as the blade cut through the beetle's head and sparked against the cobblestones.

Jacob paced forward, raising his air cannon and taking aim as the second Red Death charged toward them. The boom of the cannon preceded an eruption of gore. The beetle collapsed and slid through the debris near the base of the wall.

Though Drakkar and Samuel were ready for the third, they didn't need to be. The knight's abandoned mount streaked over the wall and pounced, fangs extended as it slammed into the Red Death and tore the beetle apart.

It was unusually aggressive behavior for a Jumper, and even Samuel took a step back from the chittering mount.

The Spider Knight rolled off the dead beetle and slid a silver whistle out of his pocket. Two notes played in a rapid crescendo caught the spider's attention. It dropped its prey and hurried back to the knight.

With a nod to the nearest construction crew, the Spider Knight remounted and returned to the opposite side of the wall.

Ambrose took a deep breath and turned to Jacob. "I can tell you one thing. It's certainly not boring in the Lowlands these days."

✦   ✦   ✦

THEY SAID GOODBYE to Ambrose for the time being. Jacob's mind churned over a dozen different ideas as Samuel led them deeper into the

Lowlands. The cleared trails through the debris narrowed. More and more, they had to step around homes fallen into the streets and the broken remains of invaders.

It was the piles of those remains that shifted that were the most un-nerving. Occasionally, a small buzz or click rose from the ruins, putting the entire group on edge.

At the lowest point in the road, they no longer had a path. Instead, they climbed the rubble, making their way past burned-out storefronts and the collapsed façades of family homes that had stood for decades.

Jacob's focus returned to keeping his footing. It was trickier now on rough terrain. Smith had told him it would take time for his balance to be more instinctual as it once was. He didn't notice it much on level ground, but walking over stone and wood and broken furniture made it far more obvious.

The hill grew steep, and slowly they made their way out of the worst of the debris field.

He heard Alice sniff. When he glanced back, she was rubbing her eyes. Jacob frowned and looked around the area. It was only then that he realized they were back in their old neighborhood. Somewhere in that collapsed ruin was her home, and his.

The thought tightened his chest, and he slowed, reaching out to squeeze Alice's arm. She offered him a weak smile. They continued on, trailed by Drakkar.

The old observatory Charles used to use as a workshop was in a less densely populated part of the Lowlands. That also meant there was less debris in the streets, and the risk of breaking their ankles grew infinitely less severe as they started up that steep hill. It also helped that the row of homes nearest to it had survived. One of the roofs had collapsed into the street, but the stone slabs were easily skirted.

Samuel led them south, cutting through a relatively clear area before starting back up the hill Jacob had once fled down with Charles.

The strange cone shape of the observatory drew Jacob's eye. It looked different in the sunlight as they came closer to it. Now he could see the gouges and scrapes along the sides where invaders had torn through the area. The fact the observatory had not burned down, or been toppled by the invaders, might have been more than luck.

"Look at the claw marks on the side," Jacob said.

Samuel stopped and studied the exterior of the observatory. "They only go a few feet up. I would've expected the invaders to climb to the top, considering it's one of the highest structures."

"They slid off it," Alice said.

Jacob nodded. That was his assessment too. And it explained the long drag marks across the metal plating.

Samuel tried the front door, but the heavy handle just clicked, and nothing moved. "Good. Still locked."

"I'd hoped it would stay locked," Jacob said. "Do you think … I don't want anyone else messing around with Charles's things."

"I only brought Ambrose and a couple of his workers to help me with the barrels. Doubt many people have been here since the Fall."

"The workshop of Charles von Atlier," Drakkar said. "To think I learned to call him a friend."

"Cave Guardians didn't appreciate Charles much, did they?" Samuel asked.

"No," Drakkar said. "We have a long memory. And what was done in the Deadlands War was unforgivable. Though the more I learn of that history, the more I understand why it was done. But the best intentions do not always excuse the worst offenses."

Jacob made his way to the loose paneling hidden along the outer wall he'd so often used to sneak into Charles's workshop. It resisted for a moment, and then gave way with a small squeak.

Shadows and quiet waited inside the observatory. It was not as dark as when he'd visited with Alice once in the middle of the night. Now there was enough sunlight to make out most of the shapes in the workshop, even if darkness still hid in the corners.

Something thunked down on Samuel's shoulder and he screeched, dancing in a circle, trying to see what was attacking him.

Alice grabbed him by the arm. "Stop!" She raised her hand, and a furry gray Jumper leaped into her palm. "See? It's just a little Jumper."

Samuel's eyebrows scrunched together. "Of course it is. Of course I'm fine."

Drakkar's grip on his spear relaxed as the Spider Knight's panic slowly resolved.

"Where did you find the journal?" Jacob asked, picking up a long bolt he thought might be useful to Ambrose. He'd have to test it back in the workshop.

Samuel shook himself, suppressing a shiver. He glanced at the workbench off to the right and then focused on the shelving to their left. Samuel walked to the far end.

"Here, under this broken stone."

"I'm surprised Charles left a broken stone," Alice said. "That seems like the kind of thing he would've fixed."

Jacob agreed. He crouched down and lifted half the broken stone out of its resting place. There didn't appear to be much underneath it other than more stone. He glanced up at the sunlight coming through the cracks in the observatory roof.

"I need a lantern."

Alice shuffled through the remnants on the workbench and pulled up a lantern with a small reflector. Her hand slid into one of the pouches at her side and retrieved a Burner, clicking the igniter and dropping it into the lantern.

"Thanks," Jacob said as he took the lantern. He squinted in the flickering light, running his fingers around the edges of the unbroken stones. It *wasn't* like Charles to leave something broken like that. Other than the panel on the side of the observatory, Jacob supposed.

Three sides of the stone were simply that: finely cut rock pulled from the earth and formed into tiles. But his fingers caught on something on the fourth side. He sat the lantern down and lay his head flush with the floor. He didn't stop the smile that crawled its way across his lips.

"What is it?" Alice asked.

"I think it's the edge of the puzzle lock."

"A what?" Drakkar asked.

"It's like a safe," Alice said. "Some of the old homes in Ancora have them. But why wouldn't he have just put the journal in there too? Why leave it under a stone where anyone could find it?"

"I don't know," Jacob said, shaking his head. "But I'd like to find out."

He pushed on the indentations at the edge of the stone, tried prying them out with his fingernails, and even twisted them, but nothing would budge. "I wonder if it's rusted out?"

"We can break it out with a hammer," Samuel said. "Take it back to the workshop?"

"No. It's too heavy for that." Jacob frowned and sat up, looking around the room. "I need a chisel or something thin. Something we can use as a lever."

Alice started opening some of the remaining barrels and crates and looking inside. She moved from one to the next, eventually making her way over to the workbench again.

"Try underneath," Jacob said.

Alice crouched down, looking up into the darkness underneath the workbench. Jacob knew there were pockets and ledges Charles had never filled in where the old tinker liked to randomly leave tools. One by one, Alice dragged out an old hammer from the ledges, two woven baskets, and a blackened bar that looked like a broken lever.

"I think this will work." Alice made her way across the observatory and dropped the edge of the broken lever into the gap between two of the stone tiles.

At first, she tried prying up the stone that held the puzzle lock. But it didn't so much as shudder.

"Try the other one, the stone next to it."

Alice did, and the edge of it popped up with little effort.

"Yes!" Jacob said, studying this new side of the puzzle lock.

Alice let the stone drop to the floor with a thud. "Heavier than they look."

"Are you sure about this?" Samuel asked. "Charles always liked those stories about booby-trapped treasures. Maybe we should be a bit more careful with this."

"As hidden as this is?" Jacob asked. "I think we'll be okay."

He slid the catch on the side, a motion quickly followed by three clicks and a tremor in the top of the tile. Jacob worked his fingertips under the stone and lifted. The resistance was gone now, other than the weight of the rock itself, and when Drakkar saw it move, he hopped in to help lever it off what waited beneath.

"What is that?" Samuel asked.

"There's another layer to the lock," Alice said.

Jacob frowned at the large dial, shaped like a carriage wheel but infinitely more complicated.

"Steamsworn?" Drakkar whispered.

Jacob looked up at the Cave Guardian. "What do you mean? Do you recognize these symbols?"

"They are letters. From an old language the villages near Bollwerk once used. And one I have not seen much of outside of Bollwerk." Drakkar trailed off, running his fingers along the outer circle. "But this, this reads Steamsworn."

"What else does it say?" Alice asked, leaning closer.

"Nonsense mostly. Words without order. Grave. Find. Flames. I do not understand. Me in?" Drakkar frowned.

"It's the oath!" Alice said, her voice rising with excitement. "The oath of the Steamsworn. Find me in that Steamsworn grave."

Jacob twisted the bronze spokes, raising an eyebrow when the copper letters rose and turned, revealing another ring of words under them. The language beneath the upper ring, Jacob recognized. The words were in the more familiar script common in Ancora.

"Flames," he said, tracing the lower ring. "Hell, steam."

"The lower ring is the first verse," Alice said.

Jacob pulled on a spoke deeper inside the mechanism. The lower plates spiraled around each other in a mad dance like the workings of a clock. They came to rest with more words from the oath, but now in a different order.

"If it's supposed to spell out the oath, it's never going to match up. The ratios are wrong."

"Look closer," Alice said, picking up the lever once more.

Jacob frowned as she dug the metal into the gap on another side and lifted. But he did look closer. He'd almost missed it in the shadows, another layer to the mechanism, but one that didn't appear to have a knob or lever or anything to manipulate it. He pushed on it gently with a finger.

"It's thoroughly stuck."

Samuel held his hand out and took the lever from Alice, pulling up the last stone flanking the puzzle lock. "Something here." He let the lever clatter onto the stones, then pulled a switch on the side.

Nothing happened.

But when Jacob turned the knob again, the words no longer moved at the same rate. Still, there was no possible way to line them up.

"Anything on your side, Alice?"

"A button, I think?" She pressed it in and something clicked. Now with the turn of the knob, a copper plate etched with "Through the" slid in behind the plate with "black we."

"That's it! Alice, your side shifts the tracks, like tumblers in a lock. Samuel's lets me rotate the options, and there has to be another."

"There is," Drakkar said, sliding out a slender lever on the fourth side.

Another turn, and now only the topmost layer moved. Jacob's brow furrowed, trying to piece together in his mind which options needed to be switched to get the remaining spiral of words in order.

"Drakkar, you'll have to help me with the top. I can only read the bottom layer."

"Tell me what it needs to say."

"I think it's the oath. The entire oath."

They spent nearly an hour crouched over the puzzle box embedded in the floor, reciting the lines of the oath and Drakkar translating the old script as they went. One mistake would send the entire order into chaos and they'd have to reset the puzzle, which in itself took time.

Finally, after much cursing and more tries than Jacob expected it to take, the bottom layer was complete.

Through the black we ride once more

Within the flames our fortune's told

The gates of Hell lie broken wide

Within the steam, no hold abides

Drakkar directed him, getting the last of the top layer in order.

Though he couldn't read the words in that odd script, he knew the meaning of them all. Under his breath, he recited the last lines with two final twists of the knob.

Feared and cast upon the stones
We fight to save the sacred lives
When all is done and all are safe
Find me in that Steamsworn grave

A quiet click followed by two loud thunks was the only indication something had changed.

Samuel wrapped his fingers under the edge of the puzzle lock and lifted. Hidden hinges squeaked, and Jacob half expected the room to explode in some kind of mad trap. Thankfully, no such surprise waited below—only empty darkness.

Until Alice held the lantern over the hole.

CHAPTER NINE

"W HAT *IS* THIS?" Jacob asked, looking down into the slender chamber underneath the observatory. He slid over the edge and dropped down before Samuel could so much as shout a warning not to.

A small ladder led back up to the lip of the hole. But behind that ladder sat an aged set of armor. Crumbling leather propped up a bronze helmet and the Steamsworn Fist on the pauldrons.

"There's a ladder," Jacob said. "Feel it out with your feet. It's hidden just below the lip. I don't think we'll all fit down here, though."

"I'm coming down." A moment later, Alice's boots clicked on the ladder rungs.

"What is it?" Samuel asked.

"Old armor," Jacob said.

"Jacob," Alice said. "Look behind you."

He turned and froze. Carved into the wall was a shelf not more than three feet across. And on that shelf sat a haphazard pile of books. One Jacob recognized immediately. Another copy of *The Dead Scourge*, but as he thumbed through the pages, he found notes in Charles's tight scrawl.

Alice looked at another title and shook her head. "What is this?"

Jacob glanced at the odd design. A building like a pyramid with the top cut away. Huge pipes flowed into it from either side with some kind of formula written above it. It was math Jacob didn't know. And it was either more complicated than anything he'd learned, or it was from another language.

Alice took her pack off and started sliding books into it. "Come on. We can read them in better light at Samuel's."

"Charles left them locked up here for a reason, Alice."

"Maybe so the wrong kind of people wouldn't realize he was Steamsworn?" she said. "I don't think that's a worry at this point, considering you're a Biomech."

Jacob held a finger up to protest, then thought better of it. She had a point. He slid his own pack off and took a few of the books.

It was beneath the last that they found the torn pages. Pages that matched the journal Jacob had been reading.

"Oh, wow."

Alice leaned closer. "More Mech designs?"

"It's the rest of the Titan Mech specifications. Alice, we could *build* one using these. I mean, it would take years, but it could be done."

Alice pursed her lips. "Jacob, Charles stopped building things like that for a reason. I don't think he'd want you going down the same path."

Jacob rifled through the other pages. There were more than Titan Mech designs in those lost journals—the final air cannon specification, half a dozen Burner variations to create firestorms and scour buildings, and something not unlike the chainguns Smith added to the airships.

The last page was a design for a hidden blade, built for assassins, and mounted on a spring strong enough that it would both strike and retract faster than most people would notice. There was no use for something like that outside of killing, and the thought sent a chill down Jacob's spine.

He nodded to Alice and slid the last of the pages into his pack. "Just for research."

Alice rolled her eyes and started up the ladder before she paused. "That's not a wall."

"What?" Jacob asked.

She hopped off the ladder and reached over to the wall by the armor. It fluttered when she touched it and the curtains slid away when she pulled.

"Okay, now I can see why Charles kept *that* hidden."

"Kept what hidden?" Samuel asked from above.

"Weapons. Lots of weapons. Looks like a chaingun, something like the air cannon, and cartridges for long-range bolt guns."

"Leave them. No one needs to know that's here."

Jacob reached down and took the bronze Steamsworn Fist off the collar of the old armor before sliding it into his pocket.

Alice grabbed a device that looked much like the wrist launchers she wore before holding a finger to her lips. She slid it into her backpack along with several of the curved clips filled with bolts.

Jacob eyed Charles's stash before grabbing a small version of the air cannon. It was no bigger than his forearm and likely couldn't hold enough air to do any serious damage. But any chance to explore Charles's inventions was a chance for him to learn. A chance for him to get better.

Samuel sighed with relief when they finally exited the hideaway. They set the puzzle lock back in place and scrambled the knobs, sealing Charles's small armory back into the shadows.

"Why wouldn't he have used that stuff against the Butcher?" Samuel asked.

"If it's all as old as the armor," Alice said, "I doubt any of it still works."

Drakkar dropped the stones back into place, and once more, it looked like no one had been there.

✧   ✧   ✧

OTHER THAN SIGHTING a Carrion Worm from a distance, the trip back to the Highlands was mercifully boring.

Alice grimaced and readjusted her backpack as they crossed into the city. "Sometimes I forget how heavy books can be."

"Only when we drag half a library with us," Jacob muttered, sweat pouring from his brow.

"We did offer to help," Samuel said, raising a hand in the air and taking a stilted, far too formal tone. "But no! What noble mission is this? When dragging a crazy inventor's notebooks around, help would be dishonorable. Who could accept help such as that?"

Drakkar chuckled when Jacob and Alice nearly set Samuel on fire with their glares.

Alice frowned and raised a hand to shield her eyes. "Is that Baddawick?"

Jacob squinted at the group of a dozen or so people gathered along the far side of the street inside the city walls. "Unless my mom's old duster came to life, I'm pretty sure that's him."

"That's not very nice, Jacob," Alice said.

Jacob thought about the semi-soft wiry brush she used to dust their old home, and it seemed like a perfect description of Baddawick's hair. "Well, I didn't say it to be mean."

"Just don't say it to *him*."

Jacob blew out a breath. "Fine, fine."

Their steps slowed as they grew closer to the group around Baddawick. Jacob could make out the words now, and they both hurt his heart and made him want to help rebuild the Lowlands as fast as they could.

Baddawick pulled a family of three to the side. "Now, you three can share a room at the hospital. You don't have to be separated, but you, sir, need to get that leg checked out. Tell them I sent you. And tell them I'll pay for any medicine you need."

He didn't wait for the teary-eyed family to thank him before he turned to the next group, dragging only two small, worn pieces of luggage with them. "You two. I have a small closet with a bed above the bar at the Wild Horse. Come, stay with me. Whatever food and drink you need is yours."

"Baddawick!" Samuel shouted, drawing the old tinker's eye.

"My boy! What are you doing here? I thought you all were off with Ambrose?"

Samuel gestured to Jacob and Alice. "The kids needed to bring some supplies back to Bat's … back to my house. Who are these people?"

"Refugees from Dauschen." Bat lowered his voice, but Jacob doubted the words were missed by anyone nearby. "Situation is bad over there. Not enough food to go around, I'm afraid. And the last airship they'd been using to transport people crashed into Bollwerk's docks. It's still floating, but it will be a week or more before it's airworthy. Which means it's not leaving Bollwerk until then."

"Can't Archibald send another ship?" Jacob asked.

Baddawick smiled. "I'm sure he would if he could spare it. Alas …" He gestured to the shadow of the massive warship above them. "They only send supply ships back and forth, and they aren't large enough to meet the demands. Perhaps you should visit Bollwerk and see what can be done. I'm sorry to be rude, but the rest of these folks have traveled on foot from Dauschen. Along the old tracks where they could, but not all the tracks have survived. Maybe you could build some of your storied gliders for them? It could help them move around the collapsed city and perhaps through the mountains themselves."

Jacob was well aware of the damage done to the tracks. They'd been bombed out to keep Fel's army at bay. It hadn't exactly all gone to plan. He listened closely to Baddawick's words as they walked past the sweets shop and back toward Samuel's.

"The rest of you are with me," Baddawick said to the refugees. "We'll give you one room per family where we can, but some will need to pair up. I'm afraid the Lowlands here in Ancora fared even worse than much of Dauschen."

Jacob wasn't so sure of that. They'd dropped the entire base there off a cliff, sending the main airship docks into ruin. With a start, and a gut-wrenching realization, Jacob contemplated the fact *he* had made Dauschen's situation worse. He glanced back at the trail of people heading toward the Wild Horse. That was something he'd have to set right.

Perhaps when they were done helping Ambrose, he could help Dauschen as well.

So much to do, and only one lifetime to get it done.

✧   ✧   ✧

Jacob and Alice dropped their bags in the workshop before crashing onto the barstools.

"I'm done," Alice muttered. "Bury me now, or build a funeral pyre from this mountain of books."

"You don't mean that," Jacob said with a laugh. "About the books anyway."

Alice narrowed her eyes.

"I don't know," Samuel said as he and Drakkar made their way through the workshop. "I'd like to host more people here. If Baddawick is doing it, I feel like I should do more."

"Help guard the wall," Drakkar said. "Or at least those who are re-building it."

"If they could get it done sooner, I'd feel better about opening my doors to more people. I don't want anyone already sheltering here to go hungry." Samuel frowned and then raised his eyebrows. "Drakkar, don't you have masons in Cave? Artisans who could help with the reconstruc-tion?"

"Theoretically, but many in Cave are not particularly *fond* of Ancorans."

Samuel dismissed the thought with a wave. "Even now? After they've been sheltering with them for weeks?"

Drakkar crossed his arms and nodded slowly. "It is … possible."

Samuel stepped closer to the Cave Guardian. "That's what I need to do, Drakkar. Come with me, back to Cave. We can recruit masons and anyone willing to help." He lowered his voice. "Bat didn't just leave me his house. There's a small fortune hidden inside the walls. We can hire them."

Drakkar relaxed and a slow smile spread across his face. "Now you speak the language of pirates. Language that all the people of Cave will listen to."

"Then you'll come with me?"

Drakkar nodded. "I would have been returning there in a matter of days, regardless. As much as there is a burden on Ancora from the damage of the Fall, a different burden has been levied against Cave. You may not have noticed the strain on the temple while we were there, but I fear it is dire. They need more hands, and more supplies."

"I can give them some money if it will help."

"Of course it will help."

"Good. Then it's settled. We make for Cave."

"I have to help Ambrose," Jacob said. "I can't go back with you. Not now. And what Baddawick said about returning to Bollwerk? Maybe working on the gliders? I think it could help too."

"Do what you need to," Samuel said. "You're welcome to stay here as long as you need."

✧   ✧   ✧

As much as Jacob wanted to explore Charles's old journals, he wanted to help more with the reconstruction. Alice sat beside him at the workbench, hunched over an old book on climate theory. Jacob didn't understand the attraction. If it was wet, it was raining, and if it was sandy, you were probably in the desert. Predictions and forecasting didn't seem all that necessary, and he said as much out loud.

Alice tapped the top of the book and sat up straighter. "You say that now. But over a century ago, they used to have huge sandstorms in the Deadlands, and far more flooding around the coasts. So much I wouldn't be surprised if that's part of the reason Ancora was built in the mountains."

Jacob grunted and leaned all his weight into the tensioner he'd mounted to the workbench. A heavy spring slowly gave in to his coaxing as he worked the lever in a full one-hundred-and-eighty-degree arc. When the spring snapped into place on its designated post, he turned back to Alice.

"We have sandstorms in the Deadlands now. It doesn't sound so different."

"These lasted for *days*. They were entirely different, Jacob." Alice eyed the length of spring mounted to the tensioner and slid down to the far end of the workbench. "That's massive."

Jacob plucked the spring, and it sang like an out of tune piano wire. "It'll save Ambrose loads of time if it works."

"And if it doesn't work?"

Jacob pursed his lips. "Best not to think about that, really." He settled a long U-shaped piece over the spring until the threaded holes lined up with the base. Satisfied, he stuck a bolt through either end. One side—by the square plates that would drive an anchor into stone—had the bolt cut short to allow more clearance.

"Do you remember the bombs Charles talked about?" Alice asked.

"How could I forget?" Jacob asked. "Practically the last thing I heard before a Tree Killer ate my leg."

"Well, this book talks about a wasteland in the far west."

"Like the Skeleton?"

"No, Jacob. The other side of the sea. Past Ballern in the deep forests."

Jacob whistled. "Okay, but if it's in a forest, how is that a wasteland?"

Alice blew out a breath. "It's not a wasteland *now*. But centuries ago, it was. Scorched to nothing like the ruined city of the Skeleton."

"And why is that in a book on climates?" Jacob asked, tightening the last nut.

"Because they tried to fix the climate."

Jacob blew out a laugh. "Fix the climate? With what?"

Alice turned the book around and held it up. On the page was a squat-looking building with pipeworks surrounding it.

"How big is that?"

Alice frowned. "It uses a unit of measure I'm not familiar with, but it says it took hours to walk the perimeter. I'd guess it's nearly the size of the Lowlands."

Jacob cursed. "That's madness." He raised the arm of the tensioner to release some of the pressure and then lifted the new mechanism off it. It worked on the same principle as the bolt glove, but it was sized much larger.

"That's practically a cannon," Alice said.

"I like that. A bolt cannon." He tried to pull the lever back on the side of the cannon, but the spring fought him every inch of the way. "That's going to need some work. I could make it a two-handed draw ... mount a bar to the back of the plates ..." Jacob gritted his teeth, shaking with the effort of cocking the bolt cannon, but it finally clicked into place.

"Ok, I'm going to stand outside the door for this," Alice said, sliding off the stool.

"I think I'd like to stand outside with you," Jacob said with a laugh.

"Maybe we can get Samuel to push the button …" He slid the long bolt into the chamber, pleased when the small magnet held it in place. With a good deal of caution, Jacob lined up the end of the bolt gun with a stack of broken stone they'd gathered from the street. He sat a steel plate on top.

"It's not flat against the stone," Alice said. "Do you think that will matter?"

Jacob bit his lips. He wasn't sure. "One way to find out." He clicked the release on the end, and the bolt cannon almost leaped out of his hands. The explosive crack as the bolt hit steel and stone startled him, far louder than he'd expected. The room fell silent and only dust drifted through the air.

"That's not terrifying at all," Alice muttered.

Jacob moved the bolt cannon. The plate had bent slightly, but the bolt had been driven in to its head. "Wow. That worked. Usually, things break before they work."

A moment later, the back of the bolt cannon fell off, and the spring launched itself out the back end, impaling itself into the ceiling. Jacob looked up at the dangling spring and then grinned at Alice. "That's better."

Alice tried to move the metal plate beneath the bolt. "That's solid. It didn't shatter." Then she tried to move the stones. "Uh, Jacob. I think you bolted this to Samuel's floor."

When he didn't answer, Alice looked up. He was nodding to himself. "Jacob?"

"I have an idea to help restore the railway between Dauschen and Ancora. What if we mounted the arm of a Titan Mech to a flatbed? It could haul building materials and place them with minimum effort for the construction crews."

"That would be brilliant, but how do you expect to build something like that here? And … the stone is still bolted to the floor?"

Jacob glanced at the stack of immovable rock. "That's … we can fix that. But as to building the arm, it wouldn't be here." He smiled. "Bollwerk. We can improve the gliders and get the materials I need for a Titan Mech. *And* we can get help building bolt cannons."

Alice sighed and looked at the pile of books they'd gotten from the observatory. "Now I'm going to have to choose."

CHAPTER TEN

J ACOB AND ALICE stood in a cleared area of the Lowlands, not far from
the city gates. They could have traveled with Drakkar and Samuel,
back to Cave, and then reached out to Bollwerk from there, but Jacob was
eager to get back into Smith's workshop. One idea after another came to
him, inspired by some of Charles's sketches in the journals, and he didn't
have the tools for many of those ideas at Samuel's.

Instead, he'd contacted Archibald about finding a ship traveling
between the two cities.

Alice was seated on the remnants of a stone bench in what used to be
a garden filled with flowers. It had all been buried in rubble, only to be
shoveled away in the cleanup efforts. Jacob crouched to see which of the
books had held her attention for the past hour.

"*Eastern Conflicts of the Modern Age*, again?"

Alice nodded. "Which is a bit ironic now, considering it's older than
the Deadlands War. I still don't understand some of the expressions they
use, and some of the words are a mystery, but the context helps."

"Where are they?" Jacob asked, squinting at the sky. "Archibald said
the supply ship should be here by now. A 'quick' stop in Dauschen, and
then a delivery here."

"What I find fascinating," Alice said, continuing like Jacob hadn't
spoken, "is that this book ends after what we learned was the inciting
event of the Deadlands War. The founding of Fel and the alliance with
the warlords, right? But *this* text calls that the end of the wars. This book

was published by a Ballern house. It's as though they've completely ignored the fact Ballern financed Fel and supported their war efforts in the destruction of Midstream and the Deadlands villages."

Jacob sat down on the bench beside Alice. "It's easier to control a people who don't know their own history."

"Exactly, Jacob. But …" She trailed off and closed the book. "It has things about Bollwerk in here too. I don't know if they're propaganda or rooted in truth, but it says the Speaker who preceded Archibald was assassinated."

"Not so unusual in wartime."

"No, but this says it was a militant group *led* by Archibald."

Jacob frowned. "A hostile takeover? In Bollwerk?"

"Maybe? It was a different time. Think about it. They were riddled with Mechs back then. Soldiers who had literally gone mad from the metals in their bodies. It's possible he seized an opportunity."

Jacob glanced up when a shadow crossed their path. A small airship circled above. And as it crossed the path of the sun and revealed itself in full, Jacob smiled up at the Skysworn.

"Are those pirate flags?" Alice asked, her attention entirely refocused. "What in the world are they doing?"

The Skysworn dropped in a lazy spiral until the ship was no more than thirty feet above their heads.

"Heard you needed a ride," a voice boomed as a shadow leaned over the railing.

It hadn't even been a week since they'd seen Smith, but Jacob grinned at the sight of him. A rope slammed onto the stone ten feet to their left.

"Do you honestly expect us to climb that?" Alice shouted up at Smith.

The rope jerked a few times, and two gray streaks slid down it. Jacob laughed as he caught the wheels. They already had a Burner inside the belay mechanism, and it wasn't one of Charles's designs. The holes alternated in size, and Jacob studied it further until Alice snatched it out of his hands.

"We can look at them onboard." She glanced out at the ruins of the Lowlands and shivered. "I've seen enough of this place for a while." Alice wrapped a leather strap around her palm and latched the wheels onto the rope. A click of the ignitor, and a burst of heat sent her into the air.

"Right then." Jacob pulled the spring back on his own pair of wheels so the gap between the upper and lower wheels opened before locking on the rope again. The igniter was more resistant than what he was used to, but it eventually sparked, and flames flickered around the edges of the Burner before the wheels jerked him into the air.

It was hard not to smile, soaring through the sky like that, the wind whipping through his hair. But the aerial view of the Lowlands was sobering, at best. He knew it was good to take small pleasures where he could, but it was a stark reminder there was work to be done.

✧   ✧   ✧

THEY FOLLOWED SMITH to the cockpit after stashing the wheels in one of the slanted holds near the cabin. The Skysworn rose higher into the air with every passing moment.

"I will let Mary tell you why we are flying the pirate colors," Smith said in answer to Alice's question. "It is not my place to say."

Mary's head snapped around at those words as she scowled at Smith. "Like we're keeping secrets from these two. Come on now, Smith. Jacob, Alice, it's good to see you. Pull up a jump seat. I don't have all day to get to Bollwerk."

Jacob reached down and pried the edge of a jump seat up from the floor. It slid out quietly, folding down into a fairly uncomfortable wooden torture device, complete with restraints.

"Oh, this is nice," Alice said, patting the padding on her jump seat.

"A cushion!" Jacob said. "Why don't they all have cushions, Smith?"

"Because I only had time to do one since we saved the city. Is that so terrible?"

Alice and Mary exchanged a laugh as Smith dropped into a seat closer to Mary.

"Take us to your pirate treasure," Alice whispered.

"Ugh," Mary said, throwing her head back. "I almost missed you two, but I'm getting over that feeling. Ready to jump, Smith?"

"Everything was ready back in Dauschen. Before you agreed to make this extra trip to Ancora."

Mary pulled a lever on the controls, and Jacob caught the edge of the flags retracting onto the deck. "To answer your question." She threw two switches and checked the spherical compass rotating by the windshield. "We had to make good with a deal we struck before the Fall. But we ran into a little trouble along the way. With Dauschen all but destroyed, and Ancora's military compromised, pirates are getting bold again."

"What do you mean?" Alice asked.

"Word travels fast. Speakers and kings aren't the only ones with spies in the cities, Alice. Pirate activity in Cave has spiked, and rumors are circulating that Pirate's Cove is organizing under its own banner. A raiding party already attacked a supply ship bound for Midstream, and more than one clipper has been sighted around Bollwerk."

Jacob knew clippers were small, fast airships that had only one real advantage. They could run down, or escape, just about anything else in the skies. But they weren't durable, and some of the engines weren't reliable, which was likely why it was usually pirates who ran them. If your entire life was a risk, what was one more gamble?

"So, we fly the black flags to ward off other pirates."

"I do not think it was necessary," Smith said. "It is not as if the stories of the Skysworn have paled in time."

Alice perked up at that. "Tell us more. You keep teasing us about your dark and daring history, and then you don't tell us anything."

"We've told you enough," Mary said.

"Bah," Alice muttered, flopping back into her jump seat.

The Skysworn tilted forward as Mary adjusted their bearing. It gave them a terrible view of the Lowlands around them. But Jacob frowned when he noticed the cleared area off to the west. It was too far inside the city to be part of the wall.

"What is that?" Alice asked, pointing to the same area Jacob was studying.

Mary shifted a lever, and the Skysworn leveled out, taking the wide vacant area out of view. "They're building a proper airship dock."

"In the middle of the Lowlands?" Jacob asked.

"That is what Archibald said." Smith rubbed his hands together and took a deep breath.

Alice exchanged a glance with Jacob. "What about all the homes there? That's a rather large area."

Smith nodded. "It is, but the city will not need as many homes now. Entire families were lost in the Fall, and many who survived will never return. That is a kind of trauma some folks will spend their entire lives avoiding."

The Skysworn accelerated, pushing Jacob back against his seat as Mary slowly pushed the lever for the thrusters forward.

Jacob was torn at the idea. The thought of Ancora having its own airship dock that could cater to the largest trading vessels was an exciting one. But that it came at such a steep cost was terrible.

Apparently, Alice had the same thought. "Even if those homes were destroyed, the family still owns the property. They can't just take it."

"Don't kid yourself," Mary said. "Speakers and parliaments and governments have a long history of taking whatever they please. There may be benevolent aspects to the Parliament in Ancora, but money speaks louder than lives."

Alice's eyebrows rose. "That's kind of dark."

"I've seen worse. And some of it from people I called my friends."

"Baddawick served in Parliament for years," Alice said.

"And?"

"He's taking in refugees from Dauschen. Giving them room and board and food at no cost. He doesn't have to do that."

Mary cast a glance over her shoulder and smiled at Alice. "Baddawick's one of the good ones."

"It is the men and women full of nothing but ambition you must be cautious of," Smith said. "Some understand their people far too well."

"Isn't that a good thing?" Jacob asked.

"Not if they've learned how to manipulate you and are willing to do it," Smith said. "If they know your ambitions, they can convince you to do almost anything. They understand drive and desire better than most."

Smith looked to Mary, whose knuckles whitened as she strangled a lever.

Jacob met Alice's gaze. She shrugged, and they let the conversation trail off into less consequential things.

✧   ✧   ✧

THEY WERE ONLY a couple hours into the trip before Alice pulled out a book again.

Jacob did the same.

Smith leaned over to examine the old journal. "What is that from?"

"It's one of Charles's old journals. From the Deadlands War."

Smith whistled and studied the page a bit closer. "I am sure Archibald would be interested in that."

Jacob had thought the same thing, but he worried all Archibald would want the journal for was warmongering. Jacob liked the idea of repurposing Charles's inventions, even if he knew there were more battles to come.

"I'm thinking about building one of these arms, from the Titan Mech?"

Smith's eyebrows furrowed. "What do you hope to do with that?"

"I think we could mount it on a railcar and use it as a portable crane. The tracks between Dauschen and Ancora could be rebuilt much more quickly. If we could mount it on a base, something like a puffing demon, I think Ambrose could use it to rebuild the city walls too."

Smith nodded along with the idea. "There are a handful of smiths in Bollwerk who could help. If you can prove the concept, I am certain Archibald would allow them to travel to Dauschen."

Jacob picked his bag up from the floor and slid the long bolt cannon out of the main pouch. "This is the other thing I'm working on for Ambrose. It's a bit difficult to load the mechanism right now because of the spring, but it'll fire a bolt through a steel plate and anchor it into stone."

Smith took the long square cylinder and squinted at the locking mechanism. He primed it with ease using one hand, but Smith's biomechanics gave him more physical strength than any wall workers would have.

"I was thinking about adding a footplate you could stand on, and then a handle mounted between the spring and the launching plate."

Smith tapped the end of his nose. "That would work, but if you can fit the mechanism for a ratcheting lever inside of it, anyone could use it."

It was a simple solution, and one Jacob was annoyed he hadn't thought of himself. In the space he'd planned to mount the handle he might be able to mount the cog for the ratchet. He just needed two wide plates—one for the crank itself, and another to anchor it through the other side.

"I don't think he heard you," Alice said.

Jacob looked up and blinked. "Sorry, what?"

Smith smiled at him. "Go back to thinking. You will find the supplies you need in my workshop. I am sure Archibald will welcome you."

"I want to find a library in Belldorn," Alice said.

Mary turned away from the controls and the blue expanse spread out before them. "Belldorn has a great many libraries. You'd love the Crown Library."

Alice closed her book and looked up. "You aren't exactly talking me out of the idea."

Mary laughed. "Why would I? I love Belldorn."

"You love Eva," Smith whispered.

Jacob caught Mary's glare and laughed.

"Don't you start too," Mary said. "Don't forget you're on a pirate ship. It's not unheard of for pirates to throw their captives overboard." She ruined the threat with a wink.

"Come with us," Smith said.

"To Belldorn?" Alice asked.

Smith nodded. "We'll stay the night in Bollwerk, but Belldorn is our next stop."

Jacob didn't like the idea of Alice going on to Belldorn without him. Being around her was the only time he felt like himself after all that had happened since the Fall. But if he was going to be cooped up in Smith's workshop, it wasn't like he'd exactly be entertaining to be around.

"You should go," Jacob said. "A library you've never been in? How can you say no?"

"I might be able to find something there," Alice said, hugging the old book to her chest. "Maybe I can fill in the gaps between what happened between the old wars and the Deadlands Wars and whatever Belldorn's rivalry with Ballern really is."

Mary frowned and looked down at Alice's book. "What the hell did you find in there?"

So Alice told them the story of what they'd found inside the old book from Ballern. About the wild shifts in the climate and environment that happened after the old wars. But they were still missing pieces, still didn't fully understand what had turned the conflict with Ballern into a centuries-long skirmish.

The cabin grew silent for a time, until Jacob remembered another question he had. "Is my glider still in your lab?" Smith had taken it after the conflict in Ancora. He wanted to examine the layout of the spring mechanisms Charles had designed.

"Yes, I did manage to straighten out some of the more damaged parts, but I am afraid you still have some work to do."

"That's okay. I'm going to try improving the design, make it easier to steer. Alice and I were thinking we could send some of them to Dausch-en. People are making the trip to Ancora on foot, but it would be safer with gliders."

"It would be safer on a ship," Mary said, exasperation plain in her voice. "We could carry people back and forth. Not a great many at a time, but we could still help."

"Archibald didn't say anything to you?" Jacob asked.

Mary didn't answer, and that told him all he needed to know. Maybe he could talk Archibald into using some of the supply ships to move people too.

"Archibald must choose his priorities," Smith said. "And those priorities will not always agree with your goals."

Jacob knew that, but he also knew Archibald wanted weapons. Though Jacob didn't favor the idea, if it would save lives of those traveling between the cities, he could be persuaded. Or perhaps, more accurately, he thought he could persuade Archibald. But another idea stirred in the back of his mind. The Titan Mech arm might have more than one use. If they mounted it on something that could climb the frame of an airship dock, the construction in both Dauschen and Ancora could be accelerated.

Jacob pondered those thoughts as Bollwerk appeared on the horizon, the great rusted walls shielding the towering metropolis of bronze and stone and copper from the worst the Deadlands had to offer.

CHAPTER ELEVEN

F URI LISTENED TO the clock ticking on the wall above her. She knew she was a prisoner of Belldorn, but her mind was having a hard time reconciling the comfort around her with prison.

She wore no chains, and there were no prison bars to speak of. And the woman, Eva, had checked on her more than once. She'd even returned Furi's backpack once it had been searched for weapons. There were others from Ballern around her, some bandaged, some recovering, but all provided for.

Furi dipped her fork into the strange mashed fruit and took another bite. At first, she'd assumed this was their ritual before executing their prisoners, but every time the woman Eva returned, she swore that Furi and her compatriots would not be harmed.

But why take prisoners if not to interrogate them? If not to make an example of them? Furi knew the stories of the savagery of Belldorn. She knew that to be captured was a death sentence.

Her eyes trailed back to the long rows of bookshelves, crowded with more tomes than she could read in a lifetime. And they were here, for their prisoners?

Beck sat at a table near the corner, a checkered gameboard between him and his opponent. Furi wasn't familiar with the game. Pieces started along the edge of all four sides and were only allowed to move in certain directions. It sounded something like chess, but her focus slipped when one of their guards was explaining it.

Furi pressed her palms into her eyes and squeezed. It didn't make sense. None of this made sense. They were treating prisoners better than Ballern treated their own soldiers. She took a deep breath and finished her lunch. A short time later, she picked up a small book she'd started the night before and made her way back to a private room that was little larger than a closet.

But it was hers and hers alone, with no cellmates to pester or threaten to kill.

So she returned to the story about a boy and his reptile companion, a tale that took them through the Dragonwing Mountains and across the world to the ruin of a city that had once been the heart of the Deadlands. It was a sad tale, rife with loss and longing and the barest thread of hope.

And it had been written by someone from Belldorn. *Belldorn.* At first, as Furi spoke to the guards and nurses in Belldorn's prison, she feared they were merely manipulating her, trying to scrape out as much information as they could before executing them all. Beck had felt the same in the beginning.

But day after day passed, and no threats came. No violence. The guards only defended themselves if attacked, and even then, they did not kill the Ballern soldiers. They restrained them and locked them in their private rooms until they agreed to be calm. And it was only that, a promise! Still, they were not bound, not shackled to some immovable object.

Furi took a sip of an odd drink that bubbled when it touched her lips. It had a sweetness to it that was not unwelcome. She paused at the end of the book and peered out through the small square window of her room. For she did think of it as a room by then, and no longer a cell. And that change in perspective led her to a truth she could not escape. The horrors she'd been raised to believe about Belldorn weren't true. They were lies of the most heinous kind.

Furi turned away from the vision of brilliant gray towers and glimmering seas. Hatred of Belldorn was such a key part of everything Ballern's children were taught. If those stories weren't true, then maybe the misgivings she'd had about her own leaders weren't so far off. Maybe that horrible, unsettled feeling she'd carried in her heart for the past year was because her heart knew the truth.

Tears threatened the corners of her eyes as she curled up on her bed and slept once more.

CHAPTER TWELVE

J ACOB HELD HIS hand outside the crawler, feeling the wind's resistance as they shot down the streets of Bollwerk. It was odd to be back in the city. It hadn't been long since they'd been there, but it felt like a lifetime ago.

The crawler slowed at the towering building that housed the Speaker and his people. But perhaps more importantly, the building housed Smith's workshop.

"You better go see Archibald first," Mary said. "You're on his good side. It's easier to stay there, even if you don't particularly like everything he has to say."

"Good advice!" their driver said as they all hopped out of the crawler.

Mary tossed him two coins as a tip and the driver nodded, pulling away once they had all their packs unloaded. The group made its way into the eight-story building through a polished copper archway that waited behind iron-braced doors.

The Council Hall didn't fail to impress. Open as the first four floors were, Jacob could see a handful of people wandering about above them. Mary led Jacob and the others to the lift, gated with the symbol of the Steamsworn, that would take them to Archibald.

Jacob remembered the first time he'd seen the risers in those halls, some ten rows deep, flanking the three tiers of the grand bench in the center. It made him feel small and inconsequential, which he supposed was exactly the point.

Only one man waited in those chambers today, seated behind one of the heavy benches as he scrawled something with a small pen. Archibald glanced up at the sound of the lift closing. He smiled and went back to writing for a moment before setting the pen down and coming to the floor to greet them.

Archibald never looked out of sorts. His hair was immaculate, as were his broad mustache and exquisitely tailored coat. The only thing that surprised Jacob now was the Steamsworn Fist pinned to his lapel as if he'd always worn it for all the world to see. The Steamsworn were shunned by many for their hand in the Deadlands War, and even their monuments were hidden from the public eye. For the Speaker to wear something as bold as that pin took Jacob by surprise.

"Jacob, Alice, it's good to see you all." Archibald opened his arms wide before rubbing his hands together.

"Thanks for sending Mary and Smith," Jacob said.

"Of course, of course." He offered a small smile and nodded to Mary. "I do appreciate you going out of your way."

"For the kids," Mary said, her voice somewhat flat.

Archibald grimaced, but let the comment pass. "Now, Jacob, tell me what it is you need our workshop for?"

So Jacob did, detailing his ideas for the glider designs, the bolt cannon, which he briefly demonstrated with his prototype, as well as his idea for using the designs of the Titan Mech for construction equipment.

Archibald nodded along with Jacob's explanations, only interrupting to clarify something here and there. When Jacob was done, Archibald spoke again.

"You are welcome to the workshops. And what tinkers are not already engaged can help with whatever you need." Archibald rubbed his chin. "Where did you find the schematics for a Titan Mech?"

"Charles's old workshop in the observatory." Jacob opened his backpack and pulled out a journal, handing it to Archibald.

"Oh my." Archibald gently turned a few pages. "I have not seen this in a very long time." He raised his eyes to Jacob and smiled before handing the journal back. "Take good care of that. It won more than one battle in its time."

"I will."

"Now, you are all welcome to stay here. There are dorms in the towers, or you're welcome to use a cot in the workshop."

"I'll be leaving with Smith and Alice in the morning," Mary said. "We have business in Belldorn."

Archibald inclined his head. "Please, take your things to the workshop and make yourself at home. I am happy to provide whatever food you may like."

"Thank you, Speaker," Alice said.

Archibald gave her a wide smile. "Call me Archibald. We have no need for such formalities now."

"Come with me, Jacob," Smith said. "I want to take a closer look at that bolt cannon. I think the tinkers in Belldorn would be happy to assist with the design."

They waved to Archibald as they returned to the lift.

"You think Theodosia will help?" Alice asked as the lift descended to the first floor.

"I do. She has a good heart, and I think she will appreciate what Jacob is trying to do, using Charles's designs for something good."

Jacob didn't think he had been so obvious with that strategy. But if Smith had realized it so quickly, it was likely others would too. He supposed that was okay, as the only people who might think he was weak because of it were those he would most like to avoid.

"I think it's a wonderful idea." Alice reached out and squeezed Jacob's arm.

Jacob smiled. He didn't put much stock in the opinions of many people, but he valued Alice's.

They exited the lift and turned right, heading toward Smith's workshop. Jacob had been there enough times he thought he might have grown accustomed to the rich décor, but he still found himself studying every copper etching as they passed it.

The door to Smith's workshop stood open when they reached it, and a small man with white hair was hunched over the workbench. He glanced up and smiled when he saw Smith and the others.

"Frederick?" Smith asked. "I would have thought you would be in Belldorn."

"No. After your story of Targrove and his work with biomechanics, I had to come see the city for myself."

"And Theo?"

"I doubt she will ever be too far from Lady Katherine. You can find her in Belldorn if you need her." Frederick paused and searched his pockets, handing over a small folded piece of paper. "One of Archibald's people delivered a transmitter to the tinkers. Should you have need."

Jacob looked at the small scrap of paper as Smith unfolded it. A series of letters and numbers was scrawled across it, the frequency for the transmitter.

Smith tucked the paper into his pocket and glanced at Jacob. "The workshop is yours. Whatever you need, Archibald will get it for you."

"That's awfully confident of you," Mary said.

Smith grinned. "Frederick, this is Jacob and Alice. Friends of mine, and people you can trust."

Frederick crossed his arms. "I like to make up my own mind about people I can trust."

"Me too," Jacob said.

"Jacob," Alice whispered.

But Frederick cast the pair a sly smile. "Well then, Master Tinker, if you need an assistant, I would be happy to help. You won't be working on anything biomechanical by chance, will you? I find myself rather curious."

Jacob knocked on his leg, the hollow metal thud filling the room.

Frederick raised an eyebrow. "I have known you for such a short time, and yet you have introduced me to some of the most fascinating people and ideas. I appreciate that."

Smith looked down at Jacob. "Don't let him take your leg off."

Jacob started to laugh, but Smith didn't smile.

Alice and Jacob sat their backpacks down on a bench adjacent to Frederick's. It was a relief to have the weight off, and Alice rubbed her shoulders.

"Do you have an idea of what we need to do?" Smith asked Jacob.

Jacob pulled out one of Charles's notebooks. "I bookmarked the design. I think if we scale it down by half, we'll be able to use it to rebuild the walls."

Smith spread the page out and studied it. He nodded to himself, going down the list of materials Charles documented. "Some of this would be unnecessarily durable. I think we can use lighter metals to decrease the load by half."

"Some of those stones it needs to pick up will be enormous."

"The braces will need to be reinforced, and we will need an extra set of cogs in the joints, but I doubt armored plating will be necessary."

"How long are you boys going to be?" Mary asked.

"An hour or two," Smith said. "Let us work up a prototype, and then we can get some food."

Mary blinked at Smith. "It's unnerving when you do that. Stay out of my head. It makes me feel like I've known you too long."

Smith's smile only widened with Mary's protests. Maybe they *had* known each other a little too long. It was a kind of sibling rivalry, and Jacob bit his tongue to avoid laughing at them.

"Then Belldorn tomorrow?" Alice asked.

"Returning to Belldorn?" Frederick asked, looking up at Smith from a tangle of wires.

"You're welcome to come if you'd like," Smith said.

Frederick shook his head. "As I said, I want to learn more about your biomechanics. There is precious little information to be found on that in Belldorn."

"Frederick," Alice said, waiting for the old tinker to focus on her. "If I wanted to find books on the beginning of the Deadlands War, where would those be?"

"The Crown Library, of course. Any book published in Belldorn has a copy made for the royal library. You'll have to do your research inside the building. They'll let anyone explore the old place, but you can't leave with any of the books."

"Thanks!"

Jacob recognized the look on Alice's face. There was an edge of excitement, much like the expression she'd worn when they found the abandoned bookstore beneath Ancora. He smiled and turned back to the schematics.

Smith was already reducing the measurements for every bolt, brace, gasket, and tube, wasting no time at all.

Alice settled into one of the few padded chairs in the corner and started reading while Mary explored the wall of spare parts and gadgets set up across the rear of the workshop.

One thing Jacob was sure of: when they were done, he was going to be ready for food.

✧   ✧   ✧

IT WASN'T UNTIL Jacob heard the snores from the cots in the workshop's corner that he realized how late it had gotten. They'd had a dinner of fish and rice that made him long for The Fish Head, even though he knew Gladys and George weren't there.

But when Jacob discovered the problems the arm would have when rotating with a heavy load, he hadn't been able to disconnect from the project. Instead, he spent hours swapping out parts, trying to get the prototype Smith had helped him build to pivot without falling.

Once he understood that would only be possible if the weight was centered, he took a new approach. Jacob removed the arm at the joint and replaced it with a ratchet that could spin in a complete circle.

The prototype was only a couple feet in length, while the final build would need to be almost the size of a crawler. Jacob's main concern was that he had never seen a ratcheting mechanism of that size. They'd have to fabricate it, and that would take time.

The door to the workshop squeaked open, and Jacob was surprised when Archibald appeared.

"You're still awake," Archibald whispered.

Jacob nodded. "We almost have the prototype working." He turned back to tightening the screws that would anchor the arm to the new ratchet. The ingot of lead they were using for testing should be an accurate stand-in for the stone blocks Ambrose was using, if Smith's calculations were correct.

He pushed two of the small hydraulic levers forward, and the ratchet spun, clicking as the miniature hand of the Titan Mech rotated. Another lever brought the hand down to the lead. A twist of a knob caused the fingers to wrap around the lead, and Jacob pulled a hydraulic lever back.

The arm pivoted until it was nearly upright. Jacob turned the ratchet and let the arm fold in the opposite direction. It didn't tip over this time; instead, the base held firm, and the ingot gently clicked against its target.

Jacob flopped back against his seat. "It worked."

Archibald crossed his arms. "You designed and built that in a day?"

"Sort of. We had Charles's notes to work off." He looked back at Archibald.

"Jacob, when the others have left for Belldorn, I would like for you to find me. I'd like to talk to you about the happenings in Dauschen and things we could do to help them."

"They're leaving tomorrow. Well, in a few hours, so it shouldn't be long."

Archibald inclined his head. "Frederick and some of Bollwerk's own tinkers can help build more of your design after you have refined it. Now, get some rest. I am afraid there are hard times yet ahead."

Archibald didn't say anything more before he left the workshop, and Jacob stared at the door long after he closed it.

"What was that about?"

Jacob almost shouted at the unexpected voice, juggling the wrench in his hand and barely catching it before it clattered to the ground. "Alice. A little warning next time."

"You mean other than my whispering?" She raised an eyebrow.

Jacob grinned at her. "I don't know exactly. He said he wants to talk about what's happening in Dauschen."

Alice tapped her chin. "Interesting. It can't hurt to talk to him. But be careful what you agree to."

Jacob nodded in agreement.

"He did say one smart thing. Let's get some rest."

Jacob didn't fight the yawn. He stretched his back and shuffled over to the leather couch, propping his feet up on a toolbox. Alice followed him over, dragging a blanket to where she curled up next to him. Jacob smiled and put his arm around her. He didn't think he'd be able to rest much, but sleep came easily.

A REPEATED CLICKING sound eventually woke Jacob up. He squinted against the light coming in from the windows. Smith and Frederick stood on opposite sides of the prototype, flicking the levers and knobs in a precise sequence that made the arm swivel, grasp, and return to its position in a matter of seconds.

Jacob looked around for Alice when he realized Mary was nowhere to be found, either.

"They took some supplies to the Skysworn," Smith said, noticing Jacob's searching gaze. "Do not worry. I am certain they will not leave me behind."

Frederick pointed to the ratcheted swivel. "This is brilliant, Jacob. It solves the tipping issue and the hydraulics provide enough force without any additional lines."

Jacob hopped up, shaking out hair that desperately needed trimming. "I got the idea from my leg." He slid the front panel open and pointed to the limited ratchet just below his knee.

Frederick slowly shook his head. "Smart. Very smart. We made a mistake last night, though."

"We did?" Jacob asked, his heart sinking. If they had to start the prototyping process over, it could be two or three days. He'd used all the spare braces he could find in the workshop.

"Oh, it's not a bad mistake," Frederick said, apparently catching on to Jacob's souring thoughts.

"Not at all," Smith said. "The problem is that ingot weighs four times more than the porous stones at Ancora."

"Four times?" The calculations flicked through Jacob's head. "But that means the original design would have worked. We didn't need the extra braces. I could have just used the bearings and been done with it."

"Don't you see?" Frederick asked. "This will pull four times the weight now, at a minimum. And unless I'm wrong, I think it will balance with nearly ten times the intended load." Frederick tapped on Charles's notebook with enthusiasm. "You didn't just fix the tipping problem; you fixed the issue that plagued Charles's original designs for a Titan Mech."

Jacob blinked at that. "I did what?"

Smith clapped him on the back. "You improved on one of the old man's designs. Not bad."

Frederick held up one finger and shook it as he talked. "But not only that. I've been thinking about your idea to use this along the rails between Ancora and Dauschen. If you built more of the Titan Mech's body, you could also use it to build airship docks. A machine that not only moved horizontally along a track, but could climb a track too."

"It would save us months of time," Smith said. He pulled out a length of square brass with a low-profile crank on the side. "I finished this while you were sleeping."

"Is that my bolt cannon?"

"Assembled and ready to go, based on your designs." Smith picked up a sheet of paper and passed it over. "You can see the few things I had to change to get the loading crank to work. The launching plate is thinner now, but it should still be durable with the additional brace bolted to it."

"And if anything breaks, the launching plate can be swapped out now. Brilliant! We just need the springs, and the observatory had a barrel full of them still."

"I'll get a couple dozen built with the help of the locals," Frederick said. "And they may have some of the springs we need here. Word is they're wanting to meet me because I knew Targrove."

"Just don't tell them I knew him," Smith muttered.

Frederick raised an eyebrow but didn't question it. Jacob had a feeling he knew why. There was still a bias, or perhaps fear was a better word, against Biomechs. It was still true in a few parts of Bollwerk, though they were far more accepting of Biomechs than Ancora.

Jacob took the bolt cannon from Smith when he offered it. The older tinker was more refined than Jacob in his joints and welds. Seeing that level of polish on what was little more than a prototype reminded Jacob how much more he had to learn.

CHAPTER THIRTEEN

A FEW HOURS later, Jacob, Mary, Alice, and Smith all stood along the swaying deck of the Skysworn.

"Come on, Smith," Mary said. "Give them some privacy, will you?"

"Privacy?" Smith said over the shouts of distant dock workers and occasional roars of engines firing. "We have all been living and fighting together for weeks. There is no such thing as privacy." But he followed her to the cabin nonetheless, waving to Jacob before vanishing inside.

"I don't like parting ways," Jacob said, taking Alice's hand.

"I don't either." She squeezed his fingers. "But you need to help Dauschen and Ancora, and I need to find out why this stupid war exists. It could be a chance to change things."

Jacob took a deep breath. On some level, he knew she was right. If they couldn't fix whatever history had broken, then only more wars could end the current ones. And that was a terrible thought.

"I'll be staying with Mary and Smith. You know I'll be fine. I can't imagine we'll be gone more than a week or two."

Jacob nodded. "And I'll check in. I have their transmitter numbers."

"Good. You be safe and help those cities rebuild. You know that bolt cannon alone will help Ambrose. And that portable crane could save lives."

Jacob liked that Alice had taken to calling the arm of the Titan Mech a portable crane. In many ways, she was quite right. He hesitated, and then leaned in, kissing her gently.

Alice threw her arms around him and squeezed hard enough to make his ribs ache. "I'll see you soon. Now go. Go rebuild our city."

With that, she pulled away and headed for the cabin without looking back.

Jacob waited until her bright hair vanished into the darkness, and then took his leave. He'd normally wait to watch the Skysworn disengage from the docks. But not today. Today there was a great deal to get done.

✧ ✧ ✧

"WE HAVE A surprise for you," Mary said, dropping two levers before spinning around in her captain's chair.

"For me?" Alice said, looking up from her book.

"I talked to Eva. She's going to meet us out at the wreck of one of the Ballern warships."

Alice frowned. "That doesn't sound like the good kind of surprise."

"It's the ship you and Jacob shot down. Only right you should get to loot and pillage it yourself."

Alice wanted to protest, but if she was being honest with herself, she wanted to see the ship up close. She wanted to see the debris from the people that had tried to kill them. But the idea of seeing bodies churned her stomach. She'd seen enough death in the past weeks to last a dozen lifetimes. She didn't have the heart to ask how many dead there were.

"It sounds like it should be safe," Mary continued, missing Alice's hesitation. "They've captured the survivors."

"What are they doing to them?"

"To them?" Mary asked. "Ah, right, Belldorn doesn't have the same penchant for prisons and labor camps as the eastern cities. They'll be held for a time, and then freed to either become a citizen of Belldorn, a spy for Belldorn, or to leave of their own accord."

"Just let them go?" Alice asked.

"I have often wondered about that policy myself," Smith said. "It would seem those who are freed and allowed to return to their homeland will simply return one day in another attack."

"I think you're wrong," Mary said. "It may happen some, but I think the stories of those who cared for them and freed them without harm would do more good than ill."

The desert passed by below them, patches of color in an ocean of sand until they reached the site of the airship battle. It would have been hard to miss with the scorched and ravaged sand flanked by the charred remnants of three titanic airships.

"There," Smith said, pointing toward a far-off destroyer that was mostly intact. A cluster of silver and gray ships sat in the sand around the warship. "One of those has to be Eva."

Mary swung wide and slowed the Skysworn. "Drop anchor."

Smith did, the rapid clicks of the unfurling cable drowning out every other sound for a moment until it thunked into the sand. Mary let the ship drift in a wide circle, making sure the anchor was holding fast before locking the control panel down.

"Here," Smith said, tossing Alice an empty backpack. "As much as you have crammed in yours, it'll be easier to use one of ours."

Alice agreed, but she still opened her own pack to retrieve the bolt glove from inside. Mary and Smith might have said it would be safe, but Alice had plenty of memories of when something safe nearly killed them all. Alice slid the glove and mesh over her fingers, flexing her hand and checking the cartridge.

Mary led the trio to the lines, opening a hinge in the railing and dropping two separate lines before handing both Alice and Smith a set of wheels. With that, Mary clipped her own wheels to the line and jumped.

Alice followed her down, smiling in the wind as the belayer slowed her descent, and she made a gentle landing on a small dune of sand. She froze at the sight of the destroyer. She and Jacob had done that. Blown out the gas chambers and sent the warship into a death spiral. It might have been finished off by Belldorn's Porcupines, but they'd done much to damage it.

She had little doubt the soldiers on that destroyer would have killed them if given the opportunity, but it was still gut-wrenching to see the destruction caused by her own hand.

The destroyer hadn't looked small when they attacked it, but standing next to it on the ground, it was enormous. The last surviving gas chamber loomed above them, broken away from its restraints and drifting lazily with the wind.

Mary hopped onto a large stretch of wood and slid down it to the bottom of a sand dune. Alice followed, but she didn't miss the splash of blood crusted in the sand and smeared across the boards.

If it had been from the initial conflict, it would've been long dry. But this was fresh, tacky, and Alice's hand flexed around the bolt glove.

Apparently, Smith had noticed the same thing as he drew a wrist cannon from his own pack and strapped it to his forearm.

Mary flagged down the nearest of Belldorn's soldiers, asking where they could find Eva.

"We had an issue with some scavengers. A Tail Sword and a couple Carrion Worms. They may have come for the corpses, but they got some of our soldiers as well. Eva and her crew have been clearing out the hold."

"Thank you." Mary gestured for the others to follow, heading for the steel ramp the soldier had indicated.

Alice relaxed a hair. Tail swords and Carrion Worms she could deal with. Their motivations were easy to understand, dangerous though they were. But the idea of fighting soldiers, humans, and their innate unpredictability, was far more unnerving.

The scent of charred wood and slag permeated the airship when they stepped inside. Alice tried to breathe through her mouth, but the scents still made their way in. She braced herself for the smells of burned flesh and hair and lives lost in the sand-covered hell, but they did not come.

"What is it?" Smith asked, apparently noticing her expression.

"I don't smell anything. I mean, I don't smell any rot."

Mary glanced back at them as they rounded a corner. "They would've moved all the corpses by now. Carrion Worms are a large problem in the desert. As you can imagine." She paused at a map hung in the hallway, a wide thing that held a shape Alice was not familiar with. Far to the east, shrunken to look small, waited the continent she knew. Belldorn and Ancora and Bollwerk, but the rest she only knew from rough sketches and rumors.

"I want to take that," Alice said.

Smith laughed and patted her on the shoulder. "I do not think we are going to fit that in your backpack."

"Then I want to find a smaller one," Alice said, as if it was the most obvious thing in the world.

Mary led them down the hallway past the worst of the fire damage. What had been dark and ashen brightened to polished bronze and thick copper pipes that ran the length of the hall.

The floor shifted below them, ever so slightly, but it was enough for Alice to notice. "We're moving."

Mary nodded. "They should have cut that last gas chamber free."

"Too much stress," a voice said as they rounded the corner. "We cut that gas chamber free, and those damaged lower decks are going to collapse."

Mary slowed and a wide smile cracked her stoic expression. "Eva."

"I didn't realize we were letting pirates on board," Eva whispered so none of the soldiers behind her could hear.

"I'm not one," Alice said.

Smith reached out and traded grips with Eva. "You would never know it from the company she keeps. And we did take down our flag today."

Eva grinned at Alice. "Now, you all hush. As far as my soldiers are concerned, I invited Smith here to analyze the armory we found."

Smith perked up at that. "Did you actually find an armory? Still intact after the crash?"

Eva nodded. "Follow me."

They turned left at another corner, and Alice peered into each room they passed. Some were clearly barracks for high-ranking officers, opulent and unnecessary on a military craft. Two wide cafeterias made up a mess hall. The only other soldiers in the corridor disappeared into the mess.

Eva paused and looked around, and when she confirmed no one else was with them, she leaned back and kissed Mary. It was as brief as could be, but Mary's face lit up with a grin.

"Collard," Eva said as she escorted them into a square room, every inch filled with dark gray racks. Several of the racks held swords and knives and conventional things. But others Alice didn't recognize.

The lone soldier in the room turned to Eva. "Yes, Captain?"

"This is Smith. He's one of Bollwerk's best tinkers. If anyone can help you figure out what these things are, it will be him."

Collard frowned. "I still think we could just pull all the triggers to find out."

Smith ran his finger across what looked like a simple gray box. A trigger sat on either side of it, guarded with a narrow band. It would make it hard to pull in the best of situations.

"Do you know what this is?" Smith asked.

Collard shook his head.

"Had you pulled these triggers," Smith said as he turned the gray box over. "You would have released the countdown on this timer. Judging by the dial, you would've had about thirty seconds to live before a bomb detonated."

Collard's eyes widened.

Eva grinned at the soldier. "Like I said, let Smith help you."

"Yes, Captain!"

"Alice, Mary, come with me."

They left Smith and Collard behind to comb through the armory. Alice wasn't sure if Smith was more excited to see the armory, or if Mary was more excited to see Eva.

While the thought amused her, she sobered as they passed another room. The wall was missing, and dark copper stains coated the floors and ceiling. That kind of carnage hadn't come from the crash. The way the walls had curled in and were scorched, Alice knew in her heart it was from one of their bombs. She shivered and turned away.

The next hallway stretched until it ended in a bank of sand where sunlight streamed in. Part of the ship had broken away here, but it was the last room that Eva led them into.

"Oh, wow," Alice said as she stepped inside. Maps were pinned to every wall, anchored by magnets where there was no wood available. A small table in the corner had been piled with books. Some of them looked brand-new, while others were worn from being read countless times. But on the floor in front of them was a small pile of scorched tomes.

"Did someone burn those?" Alice asked.

Eva shook her head. "We recovered those from the wreck. Figured I'd put them in here with the rest of the books. Feel free to take what you'd like. No inventory has been done of this place."

Alice's first instinct was to ask if Eva was sure. But Eva didn't strike her as the kind of person who would say something she didn't mean. Instead, Alice crouched down, most interested in the scorched books, as they would have been carried by the crew.

Some of them were nothing more than textbooks, airship maintenance and the physics of steam engines. Maybe Smith would've been interested, or even Jacob, but Alice wasn't. It was what waited beneath those textbooks that caught her eye.

The Great Lie. Alice turned the book over, intrigued by the title. There was no description on the back. Oddly, the description was only inside the front cover.

How the followers of the Great Machines became more than a cult and corrupted the third king of Ballern.

"Third king?" Alice said out loud.

"Two rulers ago, I think," Eva said. "Kings and queens have both ruled in Ballern."

Alice continued reading down the page. She was about to throw the book back on the pile when she absently flipped through to the middle. There, nestled close to the binding, was an illustrated plate that looked hauntingly similar to the illustration in the book she'd found in Charles's observatory.

Only this one was captioned "Great Machine Alpha, Valley of the Roots."

"Where is the Valley of the Roots?"

Eva pulled a map off the wall and folded it up. "Here, maybe not as detailed as the one in the hallway, but this should help."

Alice cringed at the rough folding of that gorgeous map before she took the paper from Eva, tucking it into the book and placing them both into her backpack. She grabbed a few other books. Two journals, and one simply titled *Burning Belldorn.* Apparently, it was a fictionalized account of Ballern's assumed victory. But Alice was well aware there were often truths about a people hidden inside their stories.

"If you want to learn about their history so much," Eva said, "why don't you come with me to Belldorn? I can introduce you to some of the more friendly soldiers from Ballern."

"Really?" Alice said, glancing between Mary and Eva.

"Sure. Maybe you can get more information out of them than our interrogators have been able to."

Mary scoffed. "Asking questions nicely is not an interrogation."

"What would you have us do? Take the path of the pirates and torture them to death? You'll only extract lies from a prisoner who knows they're going to die."

There was an odd tension between Mary and Eva, and Alice wasn't sure what had changed. She'd seen her parents like that on occasion, back when her dad was still alive. It was normally when he'd bring up an old argument that would have been better left buried.

"No," Eva said. "Anyway … meet me at the central docks in Belldorn."

✧   ✧   ✧

THE JOURNEY FROM the crash site to Belldorn was a bit shorter than the trip from Ancora to Bollwerk had been, once they managed to pry Smith away from the armory. He might have been done with his task, but he hadn't been quick to leave new gadgets behind. Alice was ready to get off the ship by the time the Dragonwing Mountains came into view. The brilliant jewel-like wings of the creatures for which the mountains were named made a nice distraction.

Dragonwings flitted by at nauseating speeds, sometimes landing on the edges of the Skysworn and preening before launching back into the air. Compared to the speed of those creatures, the Skysworn was practically sitting still.

Alice leaned forward, trying to follow a bulky shadow as it zipped by. "Did you see that?"

"See what?" Mary asked.

"I could have sworn someone was *riding* a Dragonwing back there."

Mary grimaced and opened the horn to the engine room. "Smith. Alice thinks she saw a Dragonrider. Get ready to jump."

Smith's lengthy burst of expletives came back over the speaker. "Countdown in ten."

"Get buckled in," Mary said to Alice.

Alice fumbled with the belt on her jump seat. "You mean that *was* someone riding a Dragonwing?"

"Yes, and they don't much like us. Dragonriders of the Shadowed Woods."

"Why?"

Mary glanced back at Alice and grinned. "We might have stolen something from them a long time ago. I'd say I'm not proud of it, but it was a lot of fun."

"Fun!" Smith barked. "Thrusters primed."

Two Dragonriders flitted by the sides of the ship, and Alice could make out long lances poised to strike.

"Mary?" Alice said.

"I see them." Mary slammed the throttle forward the instant the thrusters had fully extended. Dragonwings might have been fast, but the sudden sharp acceleration of the Skysworn left them reeling in the chaotic air currents.

"What about Eva?" Alice asked.

"They won't attack a Belldorn ship unless it's in their airspace over the Shadowed Woods. Now, let's get to the docks."

✧　✧　✧

THE REST OF the flight was uneventful, other than the exceptional view of Belldorn gleaming against the Crystal Sea as they cleared the Dragonwing Mountains. The city stretched into the foothills and followed the natural lines of the blue rivers and sandy streams.

The docks themselves towered above the city, not unlike the dark gray and rust of the monstrous Bollwerk docks. But Belldorn kept their docks polished and serviced to a level Alice could scarcely believe. It wasn't the first time she wondered who had been conned into polishing the metalwork so high in the air.

Mary had the Skysworn docked in no time with the help of the men and women who worked all across the structure. They served as both helpers and guards.

"To keep pirates out?" Alice asked as they traveled down the lift.

Mary blinked at her and Smith snorted a laugh.

"Come on." Mary led the way into a low, round building that looked as if it was built from roughly hewn stone.

As they approached it, Alice realized it wasn't low at all. It was at least ten stories tall, but it was dwarfed by the surrounding towers and buildings that tried to scrape the clouds.

Mary held the door open for Smith and Alice. While the outside had a stonelike appearance, the inside of the tower was as sparse and modern as it could be. Exposed framework, as clean and refined as the docks themselves, punched through the ceiling some ten feet above their heads. Every surface looked like polished metal except for a few blocky desks piled with papers.

Alice caught sight of a burst of red hair and pale skin seated at one of those desks when Eva stepped to the side and turned to face them.

"Come with me. I have all the paperwork in order."

They weren't escorted by guards or forced to declare anything beyond Eva's words. It either meant her rank as captain had a lot of weight, or the prisons in Belldorn truly were more relaxed than Ancora's.

A gated lift easily fit the four of them, and Eva threw the lever for the ninth floor.

The gate opened, and Alice marveled at the common room that waited on the other side. Soft furniture clustered by simple tables. Only a handful of uniformed soldiers were posted around the room, and some of them were engaged in tabletop games with the so-called prisoners. A counter served fresh food and drinks to those who asked.

The prisoners themselves had lighter skin than most Ancorans, but it was a range of complexions, much like any city Alice had visited. Visions of the downed destroyer flickered through her mind, and nausea swept over her as she remembered she'd killed friends of the people in that room.

Eva guided them over to a hallway. Plush carpet greeted their steps as they made their way past small rooms that Alice realized must have been prison cells. But there were no locks she could see from the outside, and each had only a high barred window in the door that allowed for a good deal of privacy. And beyond, the windows gave a beautiful view of the city.

It was nicer than many of the homes Alice had lived in during her time in the Lowlands. And that was a jarring thought.

Eva knocked on the last door in the hall before opening it.

"Eva?" a voice asked.

"I have some people for you to meet, if you're open to it."

Alice heard shuffling, and then the door opened wider. A girl not much older than her, with black hair and small eyes, met Alice's gaze with steel.

"Alice, I'd like you to meet Furi."

CHAPTER FOURTEEN

"YOU RAISE SUSPICIONS carrying saddlebags into the city," Drakkar said, moving to block another cluster of young men Samuel thought looked a bit unscrupulous.

Samuel glanced down at his leather tunic and the bronze plating of his generic greaves. "I should have kept my uniform on. That would have kept them away."

Drakkar gave him a look of disbelief. "*That* would have made you stand out worse than the saddlebags."

"I like the padding," Samuel said, lowering his voice. "If I'd put the coin in a backpack, it would have broken my neck."

"I offered to help you carry it, Spider Knight."

Samuel grunted.

"The fact I dragged you out of the Stone Dogs' lair does not mean you cannot accept my assistance."

Samuel hesitated at that. Was that why he didn't want to burden Drakkar? Maybe it was, and the fact the Cave Guardian realized that before he had himself rather annoyed Samuel.

Drakkar led the way up the steps to the temple. "Do not unburden yourself to any of the lower Guardians. While I trust them not to steal our lives, I do not trust a great many people with what you carry. The temptation is great."

Samuel nodded and followed Drakkar through the cots and temporary walls to the rear lift. This time, they rode it all the way to the roof, and Samuel froze when he stepped outside and looked out across the dim orange glow that was Cave's perpetual lighting.

"It really is a beautiful city."

Drakkar leaned closer to the railing that surrounded the roof. "A good place to call home, though it is odd to see it so busy. Cave has nowhere left to expand inside the mountains. It would be an odd thing to see the city sprawl into the open."

"At least more than the cavern by the fisherfolk?"

Drakkar laughed at that. "Yes. Indeed."

They climbed the tight stairs that led to the home mounted atop the temple. There was no door here, only a shadowed walkway through a rounded corridor.

At the end of the hall, cross-legged on a cushion that immediately reminded Samuel how tired he was, sat a woman with intricate tattoos across either side of her shaved head.

"Nameless," Drakkar said, taking a knee on the stair below her.

The woman slowly opened amber eyes and the hint of a smile crossed her lips. "Drakkar. It is not common for those who abandon the order to return. You need not call me Nameless here. Alana is suitable."

Alana turned that piercing gaze on Samuel, and he thought he might freeze to the spot.

"Umm, hi?"

"Drakkar? Why have you brought a stable hand to the highest room of the temple?"

Drakkar let out a low, slow laugh. "He is not a stable hand. He is my friend."

Alana's brows drew down. "Why does he carry saddlebags?"

"Can I talk?" Samuel asked, his voice between a hiss and a whisper.

Drakkar rubbed his face, briefly hiding a broad smile.

Alana gave him a dismissive gesture. "Of course, stable hand. You may speak."

"Drakkar thought this would be a good idea too. So if you don't think this is a good idea, I just want you to know you can blame him."

Alana turned to Drakkar. "Who is this man?"

"This is Samuel. He is a Spider Knight from Ancora."

Alana focused on Samuel, holding her hand up to stop Drakkar when he started to explain further.

Samuel took the pause in conversation as an opportunity to explain his presence. "I'd like to hire some of Cave's masons and artisans to help rebuild the city wall around Ancora."

Alana leaned back slightly. "It is my understanding that the walls of Ancora still stand."

"In the Highlands," Samuel said with a nod. "But it's the Lowlands I'm worried about. Their wall is gone, along with most of their homes. The Highlands will protect them for a time, but there are refugees flowing in from Dauschen."

"Hmm, and as the city becomes more crowded..." Alana pondered.

"Exactly. Things will escalate, and not in a good way. I'm sure you've seen some of that with the generosity you've shown to those who fled here."

Alana smiled. "We were long a city of pirates and thieves, young Spider Knight. The small inconveniences from harboring your people matter little. It is far more important to myself, and those who live in Cave, to assist all people who have suffered as we once did."

They were kind words. And it kindled a small hope in Samuel that Alana would be eager to help them. A hope she crushed immediately.

"But you must understand, while we have masons and artisans who may be able to assist you, they're helping to provide for the Ancorans who have fled here. I welcome them, and am willing to shelter and feed them, but the cost becomes significant."

Samuel exchanged a look with Drakkar and barely kept the smile from his face.

"I think I can help with that. My uncle gave his life to help defeat the Butcher. He was a wealthy man who lived in the Highlands."

"I am sorry for your loss."

"There are few in my city without loss." Samuel opened one flap of the saddlebag and tossed it toward Alana. The rattle and chime of a thousand golden coins silenced the room. "We are happy to pay."

Alana reached down and picked up one of the small coins that had spilled from the saddlebag. "This is a king's ransom."

"If Drakkar's estimates are correct, it should fund the city for at least a month."

"A month?" Alana said. She glanced between Samuel and Drakkar. "This is enough to replenish the food stores for three months at a minimum."

"And perhaps enough to restore the wages of your masons," Drakkar said.

Alana shook her head. "Our negotiations are not done yet."

That's good, Samuel thought. She was considering this a negotiation now. He had a chance. "We need ten masons for a month. I think that will be enough."

Alana scoffed at that. "I have heard of the unbridled optimism that dwells in Ancora. But a month to build a wall around an entire city? Of stone?"

"We have a very good tinker. He studied under Charles von Atlier."

Alana closed her hand around a single coin and leaned forward. "You will pay my masons as though they were your own. You have given us a generous gift here, but they will not be able to benefit from that while they are in your city."

"They will be fed and given shelter," Drakkar said.

Samuel dismissed Drakkar's words with a wave. "No, it's fine. The city will pay them. And if they fail to, I will pay them."

"Then we have an accord," Alana said. "They will need an escort to the city. Only a handful of them have been to Ancora. And I suspect much has changed since those times."

Samuel gave a quick nod. "Half the city is gone. If they weren't there during the Fall, things have greatly changed."

Alana turned to Drakkar. "Is this tinker truly an heir to the legacy of Atlier?"

"I like to think he is far better than Atlier."

Alana studied the coin in her hand and looked back to Drakkar. "I worry we may need another Atlier before the war is over. Perhaps his apprentice will not betray us."

Her words churned Samuel's stomach. The war should have ended with the death of the Butcher. *He* was their enemy. *He* handed down the death sentence on Jacob's head. Samuel remembered the curious kid who grew up a few streets away. It gutted him to watch what Jacob had had to endure.

But he didn't speak up against Alana. One thing he'd learned was to protect the longer strategies that would benefit the most people. And getting the walls rebuilt was his biggest priority.

"May all wars end," Drakkar whispered.

"And may the dead find their rest." Alana closed her eyes, and when she opened them again, she stood, her back rigid and her words absolute. "Take Samuel to the lost city. He needs to know what has come before. It is the only way to know what is to come."

Drakkar placed a fist over his chest and bowed.

"We don't have time for side trips," Samuel hissed. "We need to get the masons to Ancora."

Drakkar smiled. "I am of the opinion that Jacob and Alice's families could do a better job guiding than us."

Samuel started to protest and then paused. He'd never met anyone from Cave who couldn't defend themselves. If they took Walkers or crawlers through the mountain roads, they'd likely be safer than Samuel alone could manage.

Drakkar turned to leave, obviously taking this as a dismissal from Alana. Samuel hesitated, nodded to her, and followed Drakkar back outside the temple.

Samuel rubbed at his shoulders, glad to be rid of the saddlebags. "They can stay at Bat's; I mean at my house. Without me and the kids, there should be enough room."

Drakkar closed the door to the lift when they reached it. "It will not be long before they take issue at being called kids."

"I'll still call them kids when I'm fifty years old, so they'd better get used to it."

✧   ✧   ✧

SAMUEL WASN'T SURPRISED when Jacob's parents practically jumped at the opportunity to escort the masons from Cave to Ancora. They'd always been kind and willing to help people. And while their home might have been destroyed, there were still friends to think of who had stayed behind in Ancora.

"So where is this place you're taking me?" Samuel asked as Drakkar handed a small leather pouch filled with coins to a vendor.

Drakkar took a sack of dried meat and added it to a pack that was already bulging. He gestured for Samuel to follow and didn't respond until they were alone. "There are more relics from the Deadlands War hidden throughout the world than you know. Charles once worked with Cave, though perhaps *manipulated* would be a better word for it."

"What do you mean?"

"The old tinker was not always the benevolent person you knew. He was ruthless in war. And crossed more than one line to see a plan to fruition. One of his workshops is in the ruins of an old city beneath the Sea of Salt. Alana likely wants you to know the history so you will not betray us as Charles once did."

"Betrayed how?"

Drakkar frowned. "A broken word. And a sister city left to perish."

"I can't believe Charles would abandon an entire city."

"Before I knew him, I believed he was the epitome of all we despised about Ancora. The focus on oneself, the isolation from community that breeds in the Highlands. Never had I seen such a stark divide, a literal wall, between those who lived and those who ruled."

"There's some good there too," Samuel said. "Like Baddawick. Like Bat was."

"But they are the few who stand against the shadows who rule."

Samuel blinked at Drakkar's words. "Why did you come with us? If you thought Charles was such a menace?"

"To kill him if his path proved too great a threat."

Samuel cursed under his breath. "What the hell, Drakkar?"

"You have earned my honesty, as you have earned my trust. Your deeds have led Alana to open a dark chapter of our history to you. And I must warn you. Once you learn the truth of what happened beyond the Deadlands Spires, you will not look so kindly on some of those you call allies."

Samuel stopped when he realized where they were. A small ship bobbed at the edge of the southernmost stone pier.

Drakkar glanced back when the Spider Knight's footsteps fell silent. "I do hope your stomach can survive the seas."

"We really need to get Cave an airship dock."

Drakkar laughed and led the way onto the loading ramp.

CHAPTER FIFTEEN

JACOB SCRIBBLED THROUGH another line of measurements for the new glider design. The more he dug into it, the more he understood why Charles had to make the backpack so bulky. He could use different materials for the brackets themselves, but that wouldn't cut down on the bulk of the wing.

He crumpled up the page and tossed it onto the floor before laying his head on the workbench.

"Problems?" Frederick asked, bending down to retrieve the paper.

Jacob knotted his fingers in his hair before glancing at Frederick. "If I can get the arm to work, why can't I get the glider to be lighter?"

Frederick tapped the crumpled paper and stretched it out on the workbench. "What seems to be the issue?"

"It's going to be too heavy for little kids."

Frederick nodded. "True, true. And why is that?"

"The leather wings. But if I use a lighter material, the rough brass will cut it."

"So you stick with leather, and then the frame is too light for the wings?"

"Exactly."

"Then that is a problem you cannot fix until you learn more. More than I know, for I see no solution to that particular issue. And if one cannot fix the issue at hand, perhaps one has not looked at all angles of the problem."

"What do you mean?" Jacob asked, sitting back up.

"You're concerned about the weight. Change its distribution."

And those words brought Jacob's mind to a screeching halt. He'd been trying to lighten the entire mechanism, the springs, the bolts, the wings. But what if, instead, he changed the pack itself?

"It would have to be distributed like the shoulder harness Smith built for the chaingun. A loop over each shoulder. At least one chest strap."

Jacob's pencil moved across the page with a purpose. Piece by piece, he outlined the curve that could reach over the wearer's shoulder, spreading the burden over a much wider area.

Frederick smiled and started the calculations for a new build. Jacob watched in fascination as the tinker changed ratios and fractions to adjust to his new design. Charles had been fast to prototype things, and that was how Jacob had learned a great many skills, but Frederick outlined everything on paper, flipping through the math of it as though it all came naturally.

He leaned back and looked at Jacob. "We only need to build the shoulder harness to test this."

Jacob rubbed his cheek. "I'll need the chest strap too. And those bolts have to be solid when I jump off the roof."

Frederick froze. "When you what?"

Jacob grinned at the old tinker.

JACOB YAWNED AS Frederick stitched rigid leather pads to the shoulder harness. It fit perfectly onto the old frame of the glider. They had to replace some of the bent hinges with new metal, but that proved simpler than Jacob expected with the plethora of pre-manufactured plates and struts in Smith's workshop.

While the old tinker worked on the final changes to the glider, Jacob set his sights on improving the climbing mechanism for the arm. Some of the city smiths were already scaling up the prototype at the airship docks. When it was done, it would be delivered for testing in the field. Jacob hoped it would be enough to help Ambrose finish the walls faster than most thought possible.

Jacob bolted square hooks to a large wheel. He knew it would have to be removable, or at least retractable, or the arm wouldn't be able to be moved. Once he finished a second wheel, he slid them onto the base of the prototype.

One of the city tinkers had delivered a scale model of the airship docks they planned to use. Jacob's prototype was larger in scale than it would be in reality, but that was good enough for a test. He hefted the arm and the wheels and hung them on the side of the model.

"Well, it didn't fall over," Frederick said, watching Jacob work.

"Not yet." Jacob grinned. He clicked the igniter on a Burner and dropped it in beside the small boiler mounted on the arm and waited.

Archibald arrived a few minutes later as the assembly started to steam and sent a small fog of white clouds spiraling into the air.

"Is it supposed to do that?" Archibald asked.

In answer, Jacob threw the switch near the base, wincing away from the heat that had transferred into the prototype. He'd have to fix that or risk causing a fire. There was no hesitation as the wheels turned, and the arm of a Titan Mech slowly crawled upward.

With a now-gloved hand, Jacob flipped the switch to stop it at what amounted to a few stories up. From there, he fiddled with the hydraulic levers, making sure the heat hadn't caused any leaks and that rotating the arm outward wouldn't topple the tower.

A few corrections later, the arm picked up a bundle of metal rods, moving them precisely into position with help from the ratcheting joints. Alternating steam and hydraulics, the arm moved up and down the tower with ease. Satisfied, Jacob let the Burner drop from the steam engine into his glove before quenching it.

He turned to Archibald, confused by the blank look on both the Speaker's face and Frederick's. "Is something wrong?"

"Jacob," Archibald started. "Jacob, this could revolutionize our ability to construct towers and docks."

"Could?" Frederick said with a *harrumph*. "That boy just changed your entire industry, Archibald."

Archibald rubbed his chin. "How soon can we have one built?"

"Your tinkers are already working on one at the docks."

Archibald nodded. "Good, good. We need this in Dauschen."

"Dauschen?" Jacob asked. "This is for Ancora, to help rebuild the wall."

"And it will, Jacob." Archibald reached out with open palms. "It will, but with a dock in Dauschen, we'll be protecting Midstream, Dauschen, *and* Ancora."

Jacob was skeptical, and he did not try to hide the expression from his face.

"Frederick, a moment, please."

The old tinker stood and left without question. It made Jacob wonder how strict Theodosia was in Belldorn. Frederick didn't seem to hesitate at any order given to him, no matter how annoying it might be.

"Jacob," Archibald said when the door closed. "Fel soldiers are still in Dauschen. We have done all we can do to root them out, but we need more soldiers and more supplies. The train to Ancora is gone, which means the only way in is on foot, or by dropping in from an airship."

"What's wrong with an airship drop?" Jacob asked.

"It's not ..." Archibald fished for the right words. "It is not as imposing. Not the deterrent we need."

It felt wrong to Jacob. Ambrose needed the arm, but how was he supposed to say no to the Speaker of Bollwerk? Perhaps no wasn't the right answer. Perhaps there was another way.

"If I help you with this, I'll need your word on something."

Archibald straightened, looked like he was about to speak, and then held his tongue.

"Get Ambrose twenty bolt cannons in the next week, and I'll help build your dock in Dauschen. I'll train your people to operate the arm."

Archibald's eyes narrowed a fraction. "We have Charles's drawings. We do not need you to train anyone."

Jacob shook his head. "That's not enough. Smith and I changed too much, and that was before Frederick helped improve the ratios."

Archibald glanced at the bench where Frederick's schematics were scattered around, drowning in calculations and measurements. Apparently, the chaos left behind was all the convincing Archibald needed. "Twenty bolt cannons. Consider it done."

"And I'll need help building new gliders if I don't die today."

"Why would you die today?" Archibald's brow wrinkled.

Jacob smiled and hoisted the glider pack onto his back. "Can you unlock the roof for me?"

✧   ✧   ✧

"Theodosia would string me from the docks if she knew I was helping you with this madness," Frederick muttered. "I'm glad the pack is more comfortable, but that won't much matter if you're dead." He checked the springs and latches on the glider pack for the fifth time before stepping back.

Jacob hadn't much noticed. He stood at the edge of the roof, some eight stories in the air. It was higher than the city walls there on the roof. Of that, he was sure. But the view of Bollwerk, with its gray and bronze and stone patchwork, danced in the sunlight.

In the distance, the docks loomed, swarming like a nest of Sky Needles. The idea of helping build a monstrosity akin to the legendary docks of Bollwerk sent a surge of excitement through Jacob's bones.

"Jacob, are you sure you wouldn't prefer Frederick test this glider?" Archibald asked.

Jacob glanced back at the pair and smiled at the rather offended look on the old tinker's face.

"No," Jacob said. "I don't think you'd want to deal with Theodosia after that, from what I've heard."

"The boy's right about that."

Archibald cursed when Jacob hopped to the roof's edge and leaped.

He heard a scream below, cutting through the wind howling in his ears. A young woman, pointing up, drawing a dozen eyes to his careening fall from the tower. A few seconds passed, and Jacob stretched his arms wide, waited for his body to stabilize in the wind, and threw the lever to open the glider.

Jacob remembered the thrill of leaping from the city walls, soaring over rooftops and steering between chimneys as Charles cheered him on from below. This felt different. This felt like he had more of a purpose, and people were depending on him. And if he failed …

The wings snapped taut, jerking his body hard enough he suspected he should have pulled the lever earlier. An impromptu load test at best, and risking a catastrophic failure at worst. But the rattle and squeak of the new bolts and joiners subsided in an instant, pressure spreading from his thighs to his chest as the glider held him aloft.

His brief analysis and realization that he wasn't going to splatter on the cobblestones or go careening into one of the large glass windows on the busy street gave way to a burst of joy. He locked his hands into the braces on the steering levers, and dove.

Three floors vanished before he pulled back, and the updraft along the towers in Bollwerk lifted him almost as far as he'd fallen. It wasn't that the new ratios for the steering levers were necessarily better than what Charles had built, but they felt smoother, natural, and there was less force required when Jacob alternated them, swooping left into an alleyway.

This was a test he wasn't sure he was ready for. Small balconies and bay windows lined the narrow corridor. Jacob wove through them and around them, diving beneath a line of flags hung midway in the alley. He laughed with a furious joy he'd not felt since the times he'd spent in the workshop with Charles. The wingtip of the glider clipped a balcony, and Jacob's flight stuttered, the wing compressing for a moment before the springs forced it tight once more.

Only ten feet above the ground at the end, Jacob caught another updraft, locking the levers forward so the wings billowed into something more akin to the parachutes they used for airship drops. He half ran and half slid to a stop.

Jacob grinned, his heart swelling with the mad joy of the glider. Nothing made him feel that way except Alice … oh, and how mad would she be if he'd crashed into the ground? If he'd died, she probably would have killed him again.

A faint shout came from above. "You're mad, boy! Absolutely mad!"

Jacob waved to Frederick and started back into the tower. He figured Archibald and Frederick would meet him in the workshop and not wait for him to return to the roof. Jacob undid the locking mechanism and let the wings fold down.

Frederick had been right about redistributing the weight. Someone smaller and not as strong could easily carry the pack now. With enough of the gliders built, they could save countless lives. All Jacob had to do was leverage what Archibald needed into getting help building them.

Not unlike distracting someone while you picked their pocket, he thought with a wry smile.

CHAPTER SIXTEEN

ALICE MADE HER way back to the prison the next afternoon. She'd slept far later than she'd intended, but the bed at Mary's parents' house had been far too comfortable. If Samuel's home had beds like that, she might have never left.

Eva was kind enough to introduce her to the guards and get her a guest pass. Apparently, anyone could visit the prisoners unsupervised, which was a difficult concept for Alice to understand. In Ancora, they would have been worried about people escaping or attacking visitors or any of a dozen scenarios they were warned about in school.

But walking into the prison in Belldorn was jarring. And it challenged everything Alice thought she knew about those who had done something wrong, versus people who were truly evil. In the two days she'd been there, not one fight had broken out, she'd not heard a single threat. The worst that had happened was some of the quieter prisoners ignored her entirely.

Alice glanced down at the small parcel of strawberries in her hands, suddenly feeling like it was a silly idea. She took a deep breath and knocked on the door to Furi's room anyway. She wanted to talk to the girl and get more than the one-syllable answers she'd gotten yesterday. The silence that greeted her made her wonder if Furi had gone elsewhere, but a moment later, the door opened.

"You again," Furi said flatly.

"Hi, yes, me again. I brought you some strawberries."

"Some … what?"

That wasn't the answer Alice had been expecting. "Umm, well, they're a fruit here in the east. A delicacy in Ancora, but they're everywhere in Belldorn." Alice held up one of the ruby-colored pieces of fruit. She offered one to Furi.

Furi took it with hesitation. "It's not poison?"

"Poison!" Alice said with a laugh. "Why would it be …" She trailed off, a horrible idea coming to her. "Does Ballern poison prisoners?"

Furi didn't answer.

Alice took a strawberry and bit into it. Furi waited for her to chew and swallow before finally trying it herself.

"Wait!" Alice said. "Don't eat the green part."

"Poison?"

This time Alice laughed in earnest. "No, no poison, I promise. It just doesn't taste good."

Furi bit into the tip and chewed. She frowned a bit before her eyes lit up. "That's really good."

Alice offered the small basket. "Here. These are for you."

"All of them?" Furi asked, accepting the wicker vessel.

"I can get more if you like. But I'd like to talk to you about some things, if that's okay?"

Furi shrugged, and Alice thought that might be as close to a yes as she was going to get.

"Can I sit?"

Furi nodded and shuffled back to her bed.

Alice took the wooden chair, which turned out to be surprisingly comfortable. "You can dip those in sugar and they're fantastic."

"I'll get some at dinner." A brief smile crossed Furi's lips before she tucked the basket into a drawer. The end table looked nicer than anything Alice's family had back in Ancora. Alice gathered herself and dug in her backpack.

"I wanted to ask you about this." Alice held up the copy of *The Great Lie.*

"Where did you get *that*?" Furi asked, reaching out for it. "They banned it a decade ago in Ballern."

Alice frowned, confused. "Banned the book?"

Furi nodded. "They ban a lot of books in Ballern. But this one we learned about in school. It sparked a revolution against the Children of the Dark Fire and their Great Machines."

"Do you know what the Great Machines are? And what about the Children of the Dark Fire?"

Furi shrugged. "The machines are a legend mostly, I think. The Children of the Dark Fire are disciples who live in Ballern and worship them like gods."

Alice nodded. That was the impression she'd gotten from the book. She pulled another book out of her pack. *Climate Theories and the Lost World* was twice as thick as the book Furi now held. Alice flipped to the center and turned it toward Furi.

Furi cocked her head to the side when she saw the photograph inlaid in the binding. "That's not a drawing."

"No, it's a photograph. It's captioned 'Great Machine Alpha, Valley of the Roots.' I couldn't find the Valley of the Roots on a map, though."

"You wouldn't," Furi said. "It's a nickname the locals use. It's in the middle of a forest. And a dangerous forest, at that. Things live in the trees there. Things that don't like visitors."

Alice remembered the Tree Killers in the Skeleton. If anything like that lived in the Valley of the Roots, she wasn't sure she wanted to know about it. She still had visions of one of those creatures scything through Jacob's leg, and the blood in the sand she thought she might never wash away.

"Do you …" Alice started, trying to phrase the question properly. "Do you know what happened before the Deadlands War? Why Ballern and Belldorn have fought for so long?"

Furi frowned at Alice. "Of course. Do you not? The godless people of Belldorn came to cleanse the lands of the righteous followers of … of …" Furi's face fell.

"What's wrong?"

"I'm spewing their own words." She looked down at the book in her hands, her face crumbling. "Oh gods, oh *gods*. You don't understand. I don't follow their teachings. I don't even *like* the disciples of the Dark Fire. They're awful, spiteful people. But when you asked me that, my answer was automatic, like they'd trained me as they would a circus beetle."

Furi covered her mouth with her hand before yawning. "What do the people of Belldorn think happened? I never even … I never even wondered what they might have thought about it, Alice. I never believed everyone here could be evil like we were taught. But I never wondered what people here thought of Ballern."

Someone cleared their throat behind Alice. Furi wiped at her eyes and composed herself in an instant.

"Mary?" Alice asked when she turned around.

"I can help answer that. If you don't mind. My family has lived in Belldorn for generations. And then I need to talk to you, Alice. Smith and I need to make a run to Dauschen. For Jacob."

Alice nodded and turned back to Furi. "Furi, this is Mary. She's a friend. She helped us defeat the Butcher when he tore my home to the ground." Alice hesitated. "She's Eva's girlfriend. You can trust her, though I know it will take time."

"Girlfriend," Mary muttered. "Like we're twelve years old."

Furi eyed the pair before nodding. "Can you tell me what your history says about Ballern?"

Mary laughed. "How many days you have to listen, kid?"

Furi offered a small smile at that.

✦   ✦   ✦

JACOB STOOD IN the cargo hold of Bollwerk's largest transport ship. Beside him sat a crate filled with twenty bolt cannons, as requested. He sifted through the first two layers, inspecting the work of Bollwerk's tinkers. The only word he had for it was impeccable.

They'd taken the time to round the metal, cutting off every sharp edge before wrapping each in leather to create a solid grip for any gloved hand. As impressed as Jacob was with that, the eight barrels of anchoring bolts they'd provided surprised him. It was several times more than what was left in Charles's workshop, and quite possibly enough to wrap the entire city in stone.

He closed the last barrel before turning to face the construct behind him. It was one thing to see it on paper. Another to build a prototype. But to stand beside that mechanical beast mounted on a crawler base was something entirely different.

The only change Archibald's tinkers had made was that the teeth of the climbing wheels had to be removeable. If they'd been permanent, they would have suffered stress and likely breakage every time the arm was placed on the ground.

Jacob rather liked working with Frederick, and judging by the results of the city's tinkers, they hadn't minded working with an outsider from Belldorn either. Or Archibald had persuaded them not to mind. That was always a possibility with the Speaker.

The transport ship was nothing like the Skysworn, and Jacob knew he was in for a long trip from Bollwerk to Dauschen. It would be nearly a day before he put his feet on the ground again. Tomorrow he'd try to operate the Titan Mech arm. That should prove interesting under the best of circumstances.

A small cluster of soldiers walked by, one offering a nod to Jacob, who waved briefly in greeting. Bollwerk was sending more troops into Dauschen, and it reminded Jacob that his excitement about testing the arm might have more difficulties from outside sources than he'd prefer.

Jacob settled into a padded chair at the edge of the cargo hold before opening Charles's journal once again.

✧ ✧ ✧

SAMUEL BRACED HIMSELF on the railing of the speeder. The constant up and down and swells of the water, so hypnotic at a distance, had him curled up and ready to vomit at a moment's notice.

"Couldn't you have hired someone who knows how to steer around the waves?" Samuel shouted back to Drakkar at the ship's wheel.

The Cave Guardian grinned, the breeze snapping his cloak like a dark flag. "I see you are standing again! The tea helps, does it not?"

Samuel cringed. "If by helps you mean tastes like a rotted pile of spider dung."

"A few more hours, my friend. Look at the majesty of the Silver Gulf! It is a rare thing to be on the open waters."

"Rare for a reason," Samuel muttered, longing for a ride on an airship. Even if it was with Skysworn Mary and her death trap of a ship. Not that he'd ever say that to Smith.

But when Samuel looked up, the horizon had changed. It was no longer the endless expanse of unknown depths. Shadows lurked, rising and falling with the motion of the boat. Only it wasn't that the shadows themselves were moving like the spine of some great beast. It was the rocking of the speeder that lent itself to the illusion.

"The Spires!" Drakkar said, answering a question Samuel had not asked.

And Samuel had some small hope he'd survive the rest of the ride to the Sea of Salt.

CHAPTER SEVENTEEN

IT WAS NEARLY dawn when they reached Dauschen. Jacob hadn't slept well. The excitement of helping Dauschen and Ancora had grown as the hours grew late. Working the kinks out of the Titan Mech arm in Dauschen meant Ambrose might end up with a more refined tool.

Jacob walked outside the cargo hold when one of the soldiers mentioned they would arrive soon. He didn't know what to expect when he stepped onto the deck and started toward the bow of the airship. It was easy enough to make out the mountains that flanked Dauschen, but everything looked wrong.

He realized why as they grew closer. The slab of mountain he'd dropped on an unknowable number of soldiers had changed the face of the city entirely. The base was gone, hints of it littering the rubble at the base of the mountains. And where there had once been a fortified wall, there was now only open space, and the half-collapsed buildings that flanked it.

Memories came screaming back to Jacob. Of the shadows beneath the city, and the brutal demise of his friend and mentor. Images of Charles's last moments gutted him, and he braced himself on the railing, not looking away from the ruin he'd left of that city.

But it had changed more than that since he'd last set foot there. Scaffolding soared into the sky near the edge of the city, close to the area that had collapsed into the gaping pit in the mountainside. The start of Archibald's new docks. This was where he'd test the Titan Mech's arm.

This was where he'd repurpose Charles's work.

Somewhere below them, in that twisted pile of metal and ruin, Jacob knew Charles was with him. And perhaps, if the old man were still around, he would have been proud of his apprentice.

✧   ✧   ✧

Jacob thought the soldiers that had joined him on deck were about to have a heart attack when they screamed for him to stop. He grinned on the way over the side, throwing a sloppy salute as he fell. The city wall had been high. The tower in Bollwerk had been higher. Leaping from the supply ship was a thrill like no other.

The moment his fall stabilized, Jacob threw open the wings to the glider, clutching his backpack to his chest. He knew he needed a better way to carry the pack. Steering and trying to hold on to the pack at the same time was unwieldy at best.

He soared over the old graveyard where the cargo ship was deploying its soldiers. They stood in a lift in groups of ten, slowly lowered by cables. Jacob thought the whole process looked terribly inefficient. They could use landing lines and wheels and save half the time, if not more.

Then he remembered the main lift was currently occupied by the enormous Titan Mech arm. He nodded to himself and pulled the left lever, swinging around to sail over the northwestern wall of Dauschen. Not a wall so much as it was simply built into a sheer cliff face.

Jacob followed the line back toward the construction on the docks, remembering the underground train station and the Scythe Beetles that were hidden away there.

Another ship crossed the rising disc of the sun, and Jacob grinned when he saw the squat gas chambers and sleek forward cabin of the Skysworn. He felt bad dragging them across the continent again, but Mary seemed to like nothing better than flying.

A cool breeze cut through the mountains, lifting him as he rounded the construction site. A good deal of work had already been completed. Jacob suspected that meant Archibald had been planning it for some time. But if they intended to raise the dock as high as Bollwerk's, it would need to triple in height. A feat both dangerous and time-consuming.

Jacob studied the struts and braces along each side. Evenly spaced, and to his eye nearly identical to the scale Frederick had built. If the Titan Mech crane had enough power, Jacob suspected it could climb the structure.

If Frederick's calculations were wrong when it came to the struts' load-bearing capacity, the abyss that sat in front of the city might have more rubble joining it.

Someone waved to Jacob from a small group of workers. He couldn't make out a face, still in shadows from the rising sun, so he changed course to land nearby. Pulling up at the last second, Jacob made a somewhat clumsy landing that left him sprinting and cursing to catch himself.

Not the most graceful entrance he could have imagined. He collapsed the wings and turned back to face the group. More practice was needed.

"Jacob!" a man shouted, his face finally out of shadows. An unremarkable face with wide eyes. Someone who looked so average you might never notice they were there.

"Cage?"

The man laughed and nodded. "It's good to see you, kid."

"Last time I saw you, your helmet was cracked and I thought you might bleed out."

"Head wounds bleed a lot," Cage said, pulling his hair back so Jacob could see the line of stitches arching over his ear.

Jacob cringed at that. "Ouch."

"Hurt less than losing your leg, I imagine."

A nearby guard glanced down at Jacob's legs, his Mech components hidden behind leather boots and pale denim.

"Are you still with the resistance?"

Cage raised an eyebrow. "Not much left to resist these days, other than a few Fel soldiers sheltering in the ruins."

"But Archibald told you his plans for the city? The new airship docks?"

"Only that they're building them here. It will be easier to ship supplies and people."

Jacob squeezed his hands together. "You know, Bat told us to trust you before he died."

"Bat was a good friend. I was saddened to hear of his passing."

Passing, Jacob thought. As if a brutal murder could simply be called a *passing*.

Something clanked and squealed in the distance. Jacob looked up, his gaze finding the supply ship's cargo hold as the enormous lift began its slow descent again.

"Are they *mad?*" Cage asked, watching one edge of the cargo lift sag lower. Two tinkers stood beside the looming shadow of the Titan Mech's arm, but no one else was on the platform.

Jacob eyed the positioning between the airship and the supports of the dock. It was going to be a tight fit, but it could save them monumental effort, if it worked.

Jacob glanced at Cage. "You might want to clear the site. We tested this out with a scale model, but ..."

Cage nodded and started shouting orders to get all personnel clear.

He circled back to Jacob once everyone else was gone. "Now, tell me kid, why is Archibald actually building these docks?"

That was more the Cage he knew. Suspicious, keen, and not one to trust a gift from a politician. Even one who had helped them as much as Archibald.

"He wants Dauschen to be a deterrent to Fel and Ballern."

"Ballern?" Cage asked.

Jacob nodded. "They're deeply allied with Fel. I think he wants one of the warships, or maybe some of the smaller destroyers, stationed at Dauschen. Archibald didn't say that exactly, but they can easily reach Midstream, Bollwerk, or Ancora from there."

Cage shook his head. "It is farther to Midstream from here than Bollwerk. By a good distance too."

Jacob frowned. "Midstream will need more protection, then."

"That is a likely scenario, yes. But look at it from Archibald's perspective. Comparatively, there are more citizens in Dauschen, Ancora, and Cave."

Jacob blew out a breath. "So if he hopes to one day unite the land under a single government rule …"

"Exactly. To a ruler, a king, a government, a life is not a life. We are all only numbers." Cage did a double take as he looked up at the supply ship again. "What is that? It looks like … like an arm."

"It is, sort of. I changed the plans for a Titan Mech Charles designed for the Deadlands War. So we can use it for something more benevolent, I guess."

Cage smiled as the supply ship drifted backward, the tinkers letting the arm come to rest so they could begin attaching the hooked anchors that would propel the monstrosity up and down the airship docks. And when that was completed, they could remove them and exchange the climbing wheels for something fit for a railroad.

And a small part of Charles's legacy would not be soaked in blood.

"Assassin!" someone screamed from across the airship dock.

It was an odd thing, being in a place that had seen so much war and violence, whose people had been so downtrodden that a scream of assassin did not bring panic. It brought the area around the docks into a tense attention. A focus that rivaled anything Jacob had ever seen.

A lithe form clad in mottled blacks and browns slipped through the shadows of the dock construction, leaving a crumpled shadow behind them. They'd only struck down one worker before being spotted. Jacob's heart hammered in his chest, both impressed at how fast the assassin had been called out, and suspicious that they'd been seen at all.

Each shadow they slipped into wrapped them in near-absolute darkness. The more he watched the careful engagements, the deliberate evasion of line of sight with every raised crossbow and bolt launcher, those suspicions grew.

But the airship above them didn't know what was happening. They couldn't hear the shouts over the roar of the boilers and engines and the heavy clangs that echoed out from the descending arm.

Two times the assassin passed close enough to a leather-clad guard that they could have easily struck them down. Instead, the assassin danced away, drawing the soldiers into the framework of the docks, pulling the focus toward the airship lowering its load.

Every eye around him was focused on the assassin, Jacob realized with a start. Which meant … He spun, and his heart nearly stopped when he saw a dozen shadowy forms climbing out of the abyss that had once been the base at Dauschen.

"Behind us!" Jacob shouted as the soldiers closer to the scaffolding sprinted toward the rear guards. The warning came fast enough, but the assassins moved with a deadly grace.

One of the shadowy figures fell into a heap when a bolt caught him in the neck. But the damage was done. The guard who had struck the assassin down fell to a knee, clutching the throwing knife embedded in his chest.

Metal crashed against metal above them, the anchors for the arm latching into place as cables grew slack, finally falling away from the mechanism as the hooks slid from their loops. It was only then the tinkers noticed the chaos unfolding below them.

Jacob sprinted to the nearest ladder. It was a blend of rope and metal and swayed as he started up it.

"We could use a hand, kid!" Cage shouted after him.

Jacob glanced back, seeing the next line of assassins climbing from the cliffside. "Get the guards away from the cliff!" He turned back to the tinkers above him as he closed on the Titan Mech arm.

"Start the engine!"

"Are you mad?" the older tinker called down to him. "There's a battle on the ground!"

But the younger tinker with him didn't hesitate. Flames exploded from the side the of arm and the rollers pulled against the arm's braking system as Jacob climbed.

Charles had designed that. A thin, flat boiler, longer than anything he'd seen. It could be heated in an instant. For the Deadlands War, he'd had to abandon the design. It had been a weakness. But for a simple construction tool, Jacob had adopted it, and the tinkers of Bollwerk had executed it masterfully.

Jacob placed one foot on the towering spike of the airship dock and leaped off the ladder, catching the edge of the pilot's seat on the base of the arm. He slid inside, ignoring the seatbelt and instead wedging the now-extended plates of his Biomech leg into the grooves in the base.

"Off!" Jacob shouted to those who remained above him.

"You need more hands," the younger tinker said, dropping in beside Jacob. He buckled himself in like he'd done it a hundred times before.

Jacob didn't argue. Shouts and cries echoed up from below as another wave rose from the cliff. Jacob threw the two main levers, and the arm extended. He shifted the levers in opposite directions, wrapping the elbow joint around the tower of the dock.

His copilot already understood what was happening. He twisted the wheel to control the ratcheting mechanism in the forearm as Jacob increased the angle.

Jacob shifted another lever forward, spreading the fingers of the hand before dropping both main levers at once. He released the brake on the secondary ratchet that held the arm aloft, feeling the teeth retract with a clank. "Hold on!"

The arm gave way. Half a ton of steel and gears and bronze threatened to throw them into the air as the hand sped to the earth without resistance. The assassins had only a moment to wonder what the shadow above them was before the hand of a Titan Mech crushed six of them at once.

A retching sound rose from the seat beside him as blood and viscera oozed from the impact. Jacob engaged the ratchet and closed the fist, pulling up earth and stone. To the tinker's credit, he worked the hydraulics in sync with Jacob, even as he vomited over the side again.

Jacob extended the fistful of stone to the cliffside and released an avalanche on anything waiting below.

There was no more fight after that. Two of the assassins fell on their own blades, while the remaining either ran, or were taken down by Cage and his men.

Jacob looked at the ruin on the ground beneath the arm of the Titan Mech, blood staining the earth and the machine alike. He'd wanted to use Charles's creation for good. But again, again it had come to death.

He wiped at his eyes, trying to rid himself of the fury and pain that welled up inside his chest.

One day it would end. One day …

CHAPTER EIGHTEEN

ARCHIBALD STOOD ON the outskirts of Midstream, waiting for Gladys and George. He wanted to be sure the fortifications at Midstream were coming along. At the northern edge of the city, flanked by the ruined clay and stone homes that had fallen to countless wars, he could scarcely believe so many of its residents had returned.

Gladys had a great deal of influence over her people, and her return on the heels of Rana's death had brought a vibrance to the ancient city he had not fully expected.

"Confirmed, Speaker," the guard standing beside him said. "Anders and Cage survived. As did the city tinkers."

"What of the crew from the supply ship?"

"They never disembarked. The soldiers themselves unloaded on the far side of the city. Too distant to affect the ambush."

Archibald exhaled and rubbed the back of his hand. There were more wrinkles there now than he remembered. That always seemed to be how it went. He was one age, at one moment in his life, until he wasn't.

Jacob might be as brilliant as Charles, but Archibald wasn't sure how to get the tinker, so stalwart in his beliefs, to reconstruct some of Charles's old weapons. There were any of a dozen of the old machines that could protect Midstream, but the only builders who knew of them were long-dead now. Buried like the machines that had once ruled the deserts.

"Archibald!" a voice rang out, deep and kind, with every spoken syllable enunciated.

"Leave us," Archibald said to the guard.

There was no question, only a quick exit.

Archibald turned to find George, garbed in a long brown cloak that only gave hints and flashes of the armor the royal guard wore beneath it.

Gladys paced beside him, Princess of Midstream, and inheritor of a war she never should have had to see. But it was Alice, Jacob's friend, who had thrown down the burdensome tyrant named Rana. Archibald supposed he should be thankful for that. It might be his only hope of resurrecting the old war machines.

"Princess," Archibald said, offering a shallow bow. "George, it is always good to see you both."

"What do you need?" Gladys asked, her voice low, cutting.

Archibald blinked. He hadn't expected that kind of forcefulness from someone who amounted to little more than a child. "How are the fortifications coming along? I only wish to see if the city is in need of more hands."

"More hands are always welcome," Gladys said. "We can offer shelter and food but little else, despite your *generous* discounts."

Archibald bristled at her tone. "Princess, we offered you and your people shelter inside the walls of Bollwerk for years. We secured the funding for your restaurants and artisans to open their stores. They were provided real opportunities."

"And I appreciate that," Gladys said, some of her usual pep returning to her words. "But Midstream is our home, and we have longed to return here."

"The princess speaks too kindly," George said. "We are aware of the strategic advantage of Midstream. You wish us to be a distraction to Fel if they march, and a base of operations if *you* march."

Archibald glanced between the princess and the royal guard. He could deny it, spin a tale of the history of the city when it sat between two ancient rivers, but George would certainly see through it. And it seemed Gladys had inherited some of the cunning of her late mother.

"You are correct," Archibald said with a nod. "Midstream is strategic, as are my plans for Dauschen. Should either fall to Fel, we lose an advantage. Given Mordair and Newton's madness that led them to destroy Ancora, I have no wish to see that repeat."

"Madness?" George asked. "You see madness? I see cold calculation. A broken spirit is deadlier than any invasion. Moments of madness lived in the Butcher—Gareth Cave, the Bay of Sorrows, the burning of the North Woods. But a man who deceives an entire Parliament is not rife with madness."

The North Woods ... Archibald had almost forgotten about that. At the end of the Deadlands War, when the Butcher was hailed as hero or monster, he set fire to the dry timber of the North Woods, devastating the tree-dwelling villages who had dared support his enemies.

Charles had argued he be sentenced for war crimes. Archibald himself had defended the monster because the North Woods had been his enemy too. But George was too young to know about that incident. Slowly, Archibald realized George was not commenting on the history of the Butcher, but his knowledge of things Archibald thought long forgotten.

"What do you want?" Archibald asked, echoing Gladys's question in a much more reserved tone.

"Better defenses," Gladys said. "The old riverbeds keep the Tail Swords away. They don't like the pebbles and stones beneath the sands. But that isn't a barrier to an army. We need walls, like Bollwerk."

Archibald shook his head. "Walls will make you a bigger target."

"Then a wall you cannot see," George said. "Traps and defenses that lie hidden from an aggressor until it is too late."

Archibald blew out a breath. This was the moment. He could convince them, or lose the opportunity altogether. "Charles was the best tinker I ever knew. He could set a trap like no other. Build towering Mechs that stood as tall as the Knob." He gestured to the small mountain behind Midstream. It had a chunk taken out of the summit, almost as if it had long ago been a volcano.

"Charles is gone," George said.

"Jacob isn't," Gladys said.

Archibald tensed, forcing himself not to smile as the pieces shifted across his board. "Jacob is in Dauschen, building some of the old tinker's war machines as we speak."

Gladys shook her head. "He wouldn't do that."

Archibald nodded. "I admit, he is trying to repurpose them into construction equipment. But it does not change the fact they are machines of war. Only this morning he struck down a group of Fel's assassins with the arm of a Titan Mech."

Gladys and George exchanged a look. George shrugged. The princess turned her gaze back to Archibald.

"You could convince him. Go to Dauschen. Consider this my favor I once said you would owe me for shelter in Bollwerk."

"We give no favor after this," George said.

Archibald held his fist out to Gladys. She placed her open hand atop his, wrapping fingers around the fist. It was the greeting of the Steamsworn. An unbreakable oath. But this was his gamble. One he'd been setting in motion since he first met Jacob.

Charles von Atlier might have given up his warmongering, but his apprentice could be persuaded. Of that, Archibald was sure.

CHAPTER NINETEEN

MORDAIR SAT AT a corner table in an ancient pub near the outskirts of Fel. It was a place he'd been many times over the decades and was rumored to be where the plot was formed to overthrow the tyrant king a century prior.

His knife scraped on the pewter plate as he cut through a crunchy potato. While the history of the pub appealed to him, the food left something to be desired. The ale, at least, was passable.

Mordair let the guard stand in front of his table, nervously dancing from one foot to the other while he finished his meal. Only when the remnants were cleaned from his plate did he look up.

"You bring news?"

"Yes, Lord. Our scouts have returned from the desert. Midstream shows signs of fortification. Nothing of note, but there have been spikes laid in the riverbeds and a handful of metal plates raised before the homes near the border."

"Archibald?"

"Yes, Lord. The Speaker of Bollwerk was seen inside the city."

Mordair took a deep drink of ale, letting the strange spices burn his throat. He knew better than to ask what was in it. It had taken months for him to eat his own chef's fried noodles again when he discovered the meat was made from the hearts of Carrion Worms.

But in time, one could grow accustomed to most anything.

"I would have preferred to leave the desert people uninvolved."

"Perhaps a targeted strike to clear the city would be in order?"

Mordair shook his head. "I doubt the princess and her guards would be persuaded by less than an outright invasion." He paused, swirling the ale in his stein. "Though a targeted attack could draw Archibald away from Dauschen. Hmm …"

The guard waited in silence as Mordair pondered that idea. It was a risk, and those who attacked Midstream would likely be lost. If Ballern would commit their destroyers to the maneuver, it would have a better chance, but after losing three of them to Bollwerk, the queen was far more hesitant.

"One squadron. No more. Fire on their builders, whoever is raising the fortifications. Let us see who comes to their aid."

"At once, My Lord."

Midstream would be the key to defending Fel against Bollwerk, but Mordair could not abandon his plans for Belldorn either. Leaving his flank unguarded could be more disastrous than allowing Bollwerk to take Midstream in earnest.

Mordair finished his ale and smiled into the empty vessel. Interesting times awaited.

✧　　✧　　✧

ALICE'S EYES FLICKERED open. Confusion set in when half her vision was filled with cream and black blurs. She sat up, the pages of a book briefly sticking to her cheek. Alice rubbed her face and looked around the room. She was at Maxine and Mallory's, Mary's parents' home.

But what was that glorious smell?

Alice shuffled out of the small bedroom, leaving *The Dead Scourge* open to the page where she'd fallen asleep. She'd found some more excerpts about Ballern and wanted to ask Furi about them. It wasn't every day she had a chance to talk to someone from across the seas.

Laughter rose from the kitchen. Eva stood at the stove, a high flame licking the sides of a black skillet. Mary sat at the wide oval table, gesturing for Alice to take a seat.

"You're in for a treat!" Mary said. "It isn't often I can get Eva to cook."

Eva scoffed at that. "It isn't often you're home."

"Where are Maxine and Mallory?" Alice asked.

"Work," Mary said. "You slept in. It's already time for lunch."

Alice started and her eyes darted in search of a clock. She groaned. "I was supposed to be back at the prison an hour ago."

"Don't worry," Eva said. "You have unlimited access now. Decreed by Lady Katherine herself."

Alice blinked at that. "What? How?"

Eva glanced at Mary. "I suppose some old friendships are still honored."

Mary smiled, but it was small and reserved and Alice wasn't sure why.

"Well?" Eva said. "Tell her the other good news."

Mary sighed. "You can go to the Crown Library."

Alice raised an eyebrow. "I thought anyone could go to the Crown Library?"

"Anyone who isn't a criminal," Eva said. "Unless they have special permission from the Lady of Belldorn."

"I still don't like it," Mary said.

"Hush." Eva pointed at her with a steel turner. "Alice can take care of herself."

"What are you two talking about?" Alice said, still trying to wake up.

"You can take Furi to the library," Mary muttered.

Alice lit up. "That's wonderful! I think she'll love that. I mean, I'll love that too. But it will be good for her to get out."

"You need to be careful," Mary said. "We don't know anything about that girl. She could be just as dangerous as the worst of the warlords."

Eva crossed her arms. "I think we know Alice can handle herself around warlords."

"That's not what I meant, and you know it," Mary said under her breath.

Alice pulled out a heavy wooden chair by Mary and flopped onto the cushioned seat. "Thank you for that."

Mary grunted. "Just be careful, okay?"

Eva flipped the contents of the skillet. "All done!" She slid what looked like scrambled Pill-Bugs out onto a plate, but the dish had the appearance of a bright yellow pillow. Small ovals of sausage were set into the plate of food.

"What is this?" Alice asked, taking a deep breath.

"Chicken eggs," Eva said. "And the sausage is made from lizards they farm south of here."

"This must have cost a fortune!" Chicken eggs were a delicacy in Ancora, something usually only enjoyed around Festival. There was so much on the plate, Alice had thought they couldn't possibly be chicken eggs.

Eva glanced between Alice and Mary, her brow furrowing.

"They're hard to come by in Ancora," Mary said. "Their farms are limited due to the mountains."

"Ah," Eva said. "Well then, enjoy. They can get expensive here on occasion, when the pens are raided by young Fire Lizards, but for the most part, they're priced the same as a good cheese."

As much as Alice enjoyed the light texture and salt of the eggs, the sausage might have been the best burst of flavor she'd ever tried. Whatever spices were in it had dyed the meat a brilliant red and given it a subtle heat.

"I think she's hooked," Mary said, stuffing her own face with a towering forkful of egg.

Alice leaned back in her chair. "You have to make this next time Jacob is here. He'd love it!"

"I'll keep that in mind. Assuming Maxine and Mallory aren't opposed."

Mary shrugged. "Why don't we have everyone over to our place next time? Avoid the issue altogether?"

"Our place?" Eva asked, leaning a little closer to Mary. "You mean, you're going to move in?"

"Of course I am. It just always seemed silly with me being in the sky most of the year."

Eva grinned at her. "Don't be ridiculous. It's better than saying you still live with your parents! How old are you now?"

"On second thought …"

Eva laughed and leaned in to kiss Mary's cheek.

Alice finished her plate, scraping up every last bit of egg and sausage. She felt like one of the old men at the Wildhorse back in Ancora. Full and ready to loosen her belt. But she didn't have time to sit around. She needed to get back to Furi. She had questions no one from Belldorn, or this side of the sea, for that matter, could answer.

"We warmed the boiler this morning if you'd like to shower," Eva said.

Alice nodded. The bizarre multi-nozzled shower had been one of her favorite things in the house. She wondered if Jacob could build one for her mom, only to remember a moment later that her mom's home was gone. Alice shook off the dark thoughts at the edge of her mind. They'd rebuild Ancora and make it better than it had been before. Nothing would stop that.

CHAPTER TWENTY

THE GUARD AT the prison held up her ID and pointed to it as Alice approached. She hunted through her bag and pulled out the small rectangular card. The guard waved her through.

Alice still thought it was odd that they didn't search her bags or person. It seemed like it wouldn't be too difficult to smuggle something dangerous in. Or perhaps that was more of the leeway she enjoyed thanks to Lady Katherine. After all, they were going to let her take a prisoner outside.

She made her way through the common room, where one of the prisoners raised a hand in greeting. Alice waved back. He was a friend of Furi's and his name was Beck. She thought about asking to take Beck with them too, but she'd already established a connection with Furi, and worried if Beck was with them, he could be a deterrent.

Alice headed down the hall of narrow doors until she reached Furi's room. She knocked on the open doorway and waited for Furi to turn around.

"Hi, Alice."

"How would you like to get out and see the city today?"

Furi hesitated and stood up straighter. "What?"

"I have special permission from the Lady of Belldorn to, well, *escort* you to the library."

Furi's eyebrows rose. "A library in Belldorn?"

"*The* library in Belldorn. The Crown Library. It has a copy of every book ever published here, and some from other cities across the world."

Furi frowned. "Are you teasing me? This is real?"

Alice reached into her pack and pulled out a second badge tied to a long lanyard. "You have to stay close to me, but this is all you need."

Furi took the red and copper rectangle, sliding the lanyard over her head. "Okay. Why not?"

Alice grinned. "Then let's go! I've never seen the library here, and I can't wait."

✧   ✧   ✧

FURI FOLLOWED ALICE into the hall, trailing the flame-haired girl into the common room. She couldn't help the suspicions that bubbled in her mind. Most of the prisoners who were escorted out of their cells in Ballern were either released or executed. She didn't much believe she was going to be released.

But she also didn't think this young girl would lead her into an execution.

"Furi?"

She paused at the exit and turned toward her name, finding a concerned-looking Beck. "I'll be back shortly."

"Back?" Beck hesitated before leaning closer and whispering. "Where are they taking you?"

Alice had stopped too, walking over to stand with Furi. "Don't tell anyone, please, but I'm taking Furi to the library."

Beck's forehead wrinkled and he shook his head, his voice a hissed whisper. "What? A library?" He looked at Furi. "Are you sure about this?"

"I'll keep her safe," Alice said. "She has permission."

Furi glanced between the two before focusing on Beck. "I trust her."

Beck crossed his arms and sighed. "Furi … just, be careful. This is too strange. This hardly feels like a prison, and now they're letting you out into the city? You know the stories of these people."

Furi didn't answer.

"I want to hear those stories," Alice said in a hushed whisper. "I'm not from here, you know? Should we have brought Beck, too?" Before anyone could respond, Alice shook her head. "Too late for now."

"Is there a problem?" a deep voice asked from behind them.

Furi turned to find an armed guard standing there. She wasn't sure where he'd come from, much less why it looked like there could be an issue.

It was Alice who answered. "No problem at all. Thank you."

The guard nodded and walked away, slipping through a narrow doorway behind the reception desk.

Furi reached out and squeezed Beck's arm. "I'll be careful. You do the same."

He grunted and returned to a small game table in the corner.

"Let's go," Alice said, and Furi nodded as she followed.

Furi looked up at the towers of Belldorn all around them. Alice suspected it was as jarring to Furi as it was to her to see those clean lines and sharp edges in almost every building. Where Ballern was graceful arcs and arches in the drawings she'd seen, Belldorn was a broken shard of glass cutting into the skies.

"It's not far to the library," Alice said, "but we can take the long way around if you'd like."

Furi nodded, still looking up at the metal and stone and glass towers. She started counting the floors in the taller towers. "How can anyone build something so high and maintain stability?"

In the distance, a familiar shadow loomed.

"Is that their airship docks?" Furi asked, though Alice thought she already knew the answer. The outline of one of Belldorn's dreaded warships, a Porcupine, darkened the horizon.

"It is," Alice said. "I find the dock at Bollwerk a bit more charming, honestly, but Belldorn's is certainly imposing."

"What about Ancora?" Furi asked.

"We don't have a proper dock in Ancora. Archibald means to build one. He's the Speaker of Bollwerk. He's been helpful with the war against Fel, but he's greedy." Alice stopped talking and looked at Furi. "I probably shouldn't say that about the man helping us rebuild."

Furi shrugged. "Everyone has an agenda. You just need to find the people who won't ruin yours."

"Well, that's practical."

They made their way past a handful of storefronts, and Alice was taken again by the sight of an upper-class shopping district nestled in beside a prison. One storefront had a window display filled with chocolate and fruits.

"We may have to stop there on our way back," Alice said. "I'd rather like to see if they have Cocoa Crunch."

"You have Cocoa Crunch in the east?"

Alice nodded. "One of our favorite snacks. Me and Jacob, I mean."

"The tinker you mentioned?" Furi asked.

"The same."

"It's good to have friends in these times. I lost some when the Nightingale was shot down."

Alice's steps stuttered. She hadn't told Furi it was her and Jacob and the Skysworn that had shot down the destroyer. It didn't seem like a good way to earn trust. But eventually, she wanted to tell her the truth. She needed to know the truth. Because as much as Ballern thought everyone from the East with evil, the East had the same upbringing as the West.

"Are you okay?" Furi asked.

Alice nodded. "Let's get to the library." She led the way around the next corner. It was right where Mary had said it would be. Soaring columns reached up toward tarnished gargoyles. They looked like something out of the old stories, as if they belonged on a large stone castle.

The library wasn't the tallest building before them, but it might have been the widest. Two towering windows sat to either side of the grand columns. If they had been in Bollwerk, Alice would've expected the doors themselves to be just as ornate as those columns and gargoyles. But here, in Belldorn, they were heavy bronze with broad bolts and rivets sunk into the edge of the doors.

But all thought of those doors fell away as Furi and Alice pushed through and saw what waited beyond.

A short gate framed by latticework and manned by four guards blocked entry to the library, but it did not block the view. Four floors stretched out above them, and it was only as they approached the gate that Alice realized several more floors descended into the earth. Dozens of citizens of Belldorn walked through those halls, but the space in the library made it seem as though it was all practically empty.

Alice's steps slowed as she reached the gate, watching a lift traverse one of the supporting pillars near the center of the room. And even there, built into the grooves near the track of the lifts, were more bookshelves. Everywhere she looked, books upon books. More than she thought could have existed in the entire world.

"I've never seen anything like it," Furi said, the awe plain in her voice.

Alice shook herself and led the way a few steps over to the nearest guard. "Hello. My friend and I would like to visit the library."

"Your friend is a prisoner."

Alice blinked at the guard. "That does not change the fact she is my friend." She didn't miss the searching look on Furi's face.

"No offense was meant. You both bear the pass of the lady. You are, of course, welcome inside the library. Please take care, and do not hesitate to ask if you need help navigating the tower. As I am sure you are aware, no manuscripts may be removed from this place, but you are welcome to all of them. The most fragile tomes are in the basement, under closer guard. You're welcome to view them, but not alone."

With that, the guard opened the gate and allowed them through.

Alice exchanged a grin with Furi. Part of her thought the stories of the library had to be a myth. Another part of her wished Jacob was here to see it.

"Where do we even start?" Furi asked.

Alice already knew where. Eva had told her that the histories of the Deadlands War were on the second floor. Alice relayed the information to Furi and led the way to the nearest staircase.

"Okay, but what if the second floor is in the basement?"

Alice pointed to a large numbered sign hanging above them. Furi followed the sign up to its sister on the next level, where a large number two had been engraved.

Furi let out a quiet laugh. "You make a fair point."

"We don't have anything like this in Ancora. A handful of bookstores, but the only real library is inside the castle." Alice hesitated. "That's what we call the building where Parliament is. Not just anyone can go inside."

"That's sad," Furi said. "Even the slums of Ballern have a library. Although I must admit, they don't take as much care curating it. They allow too much propaganda to be filed away there."

The brass studs in the sides of Alice's boots clicked against the stairs, echoing in the cavernous space around them. Alice paused when they reached the second story. Mary had told her every row inside the library was meticulously labeled and cataloged. But as she looked at the numbers and letters along the edge of each row, she wasn't sure what they all meant.

They were four rows deep when she found the legend, a simple brass plaque, etched with an explanation of all the abbreviations. An eight-digit code identified every book inside the library by title, subject, author, and year.

With the identifier in hand for what she was looking for, Alice started down the next row. It didn't take long for her to realize they were in the right spot. Nestled on a shelf, just above eye level, sat a gilded spine she was quite familiar with. She reached up and slid the book out, running a finger over the embellished skull.

"This is only the third copy of *The Dead Scourge* I've ever seen."

"Three? Of the same book?" Furi raised an eyebrow. "That doesn't seem like a lot."

Alice shook her head. "It's not. Most of them were destroyed. I'm surprised to find one here."

Furi ran her finger across the spines on the row closest to her. "Alice. Some of these are in a language I don't know. Others … these are from Ballern!" She pointed to a spine with a strange eagle-headed lion on it. "The Griffin here, that's one of our oldest publishing houses. What in the world are these doing here?"

"They could have been seized in one of the battles?" Alice said. "But the books and documents I saw in the wreckage were all burned and damaged. These look like they have been taken care of for a very long time."

"It lends credence to a tale I heard on the docks a long time ago. That there was once open trade with Belldorn before the cities turned on one another. And after the wars began, a secret trade continued. A trade helmed by pirates."

Alice's head snapped back like she'd been slapped. "Pirates? I have a friend that … I'm going to have to talk to her."

"You know a pirate?"

Alice knew the curiosity in Furi's voice. It was a curiosity she shared about a great many things. And sometimes, it was a curiosity that could be dangerous. She liked Furi. There were things about the Ballern soldier that reminded her very much of herself. But she didn't know her well enough to trust her. She didn't know if she'd ever truly be able to trust someone from Ballern.

"I know someone who knows someone," Alice said.

"That's amazing," Furi whispered. "I've known crooks on the docks. Hustlers and thieves, but never a pirate. Most of the pirates in Ballern were executed before I was old enough to understand anything about them."

Alice couldn't stop the small smile that twitched across her lips. "Only the ones who got caught." She pulled two books down from the era she was looking for. *The Failed Treatise and the Third War* was a heavy tome with a faded blue cover.

Perhaps the book she was most interested in was not entirely written in her language. Strange symbols and jagged lines formed what she assumed was an entirely different alphabet, with few similar letters. But this book alternated paragraphs between her own language and whatever the other script was. A translation built into the pages themselves. She'd never seen the like.

"That's Mokuskrit," Furi said. "Can you read it?"

"No." Alice turned the page toward Furi. "Can you?"

"Yes, but look! It's translated. Brilliant!" Furi's gaze roved down the page. "The beginning of the war. That's what you're looking for?"

Alice nodded.

"Here," Furi said, pulling down a thin yellow volume Alice had barely glanced at. "We had to study this in school. Well, until they abolished school for the Skyborn, anyway."

"Abolished school?" Alice asked.

Furi frowned and gave a slow nod. "Only the ruling class is allowed a formal education in Ballern."

"That's awful," Alice said.

Furi stiffened. "Better than putting the lower class out as bait for the monsters."

Alice didn't miss the heat in Furi's words. Alice hadn't meant it as an insult, but she had little doubt Furi had taken it that way. "I didn't mean to say anything bad. Only that everyone should have school. How will your tinkers learn to build better things? How will you get more doctors? More architects?"

"Our doctors come from family lines," Furi said, rubbing the edge of the book in her hands. "You mean anyone in Ancora can become a doctor?"

Alice nodded. "That's simplifying it, but yes. If they study long enough. And that's a commitment many would not make."

"But you tore down your walls and let your lower class die."

Alice blinked at Furi. "What?"

"In the battle with Fel. It's all people talked about in Ballern before … before we were shot down by Bollwerk."

"Furi, we didn't tear down our own walls. The Butcher schemed with his brother to send an army of Red Death through our walls. That's what tore down the walls to the Lowlands. *I'm* from the Lowlands. I was there when it happened. When …" Alice trailed off, remembering that shadowy mass of legs and wings and chitinous death as it stormed across the Lowlands.

"Then it's true," Furi said, her voice barely a whisper. "I had a friend who always told me the queen was lying to us. That everything the criers shouted was propaganda to keep us in line. I just … I never thought it was that bad."

It was that moment, and the horror on Furi's face, that led Alice to question everything she'd ever known about Ballern.

✧ ✧ ✧

ALICE SAT ON the floor, leaning back against the large cushioned chair where Furi combed through the Mokuskrit book. Alice paged deeper into *The Failed Treatise and the Third War.* A few sections had caught her eye, outliers in a history she knew was wrong. Or at least thought was wrong. How was she supposed to know if what Archibald wrote in *The Dead Scourge* was the lie, or if this was the lie?

Or if they were both truths in their own way.

```
    Both the fifth king of Ballern and the Lady Esther
of Belldorn sought to forge a lasting trade. For years
their tariffs were stable, dictated by the terms of the
Treaty of the Woods, signed in the shadow of the Gray
Woods, and copies distributed wide across their territo-
ries.
    Late in life, near the flash point of the Third War,
the assassination of Lady Esther left blood in the
streets of Belldorn. And Belldorn's response was the
beginning of the Siege of Ballern. Taking the life of a
leader who wanted peace led to the most violent conflict
ever to visit the Crystal Sea.
```

Alice scribbled the passage down in her notebook. Maybe she'd have a chance to ask Archibald about it. But if nothing else, she could form her own vision of what had really happened between those two cities so long ago.

But if Furi was right, and pirates had anything to do with the history between Belldorn and Ballern, it was Mary she needed to talk to.

"Look," Alice said, laying out *The Failed Treatise and the Third War* next to *The Dead Scourge.* She put the conflicting passages side by side.

```
    We claimed a great victory in the bay north of Bell-
dorn. The aggressors from Ballern were turned back at
```

great cost to both fleets. Never had I seen such a sight
as an entire bay stained black by blood and oil. But
Lady Esther was a valued ally, and we could not afford
to abandon her in that time of need. Her support as the
war expanded and entered the desert would be critical.
    If not for Lady Esther, long would Bollwerk have
suffered.

"I don't see a conflict between them?" Furi said.

"Now look at the dates," Alice said.

Furi frowned and flipped back a page in *The Failed Treatise and the Third War*. She glanced at Archibald's book and her forehead crinkled. "What?"

"Exactly. Archibald's date is five years after this says Lady Esther was assassinated. But if Lady Esther was assassinated, why is he talking about her like she's still alive in *The Dead Scourge?* It doesn't make any sense. I want to ask him."

Furi glanced up at Alice and then back to the Mokuskrit book. She took a deep breath and slid it toward Alice. "You need to read this. I don't know if it's true, but if it is, I'm afraid there's a rot at the heart of Ballern I never knew."

Alice read, and with each line, her eyes widened.

    Forging the documents was difficult, but not impos-
sible for a gifted calligrapher. A simple theft of the
royal seal was the final deception. With everything in
order, and the placement of their forgery in the royal
vaults, the group who would become the Children of the
Dark Fire needed only to bide their time.
    When the last daughter of the second king passed,
the inheritors of Ballern became the Children of the
Dark Fire. With support at the highest levels of the
monarchy, their goals were realized. It took time to
replace the rulers of Ballern, but they have succeeded
more often than failed.
    Long have they waited, but many fear a new war comes
on the horizon. The dangers surrounding the Great Machines, divine Guardians according to the Children of

the Dark Fire, have grown too large for even the most
devout cultists. And make no mistake, a cult they are.
    As their homes are overrun by their own foolishness,
the Children of the Dark Fire will seek to expand east.
Suppressing the Skyborn, the largest threat to their
power, is their first priority. And in their wake, they
will leave the world a shattered ruin.

"Alice," Furi said, her voice shaky. "If this is true, then the queen of Ballern shouldn't be the queen. The whole line was wiped out and a false king crowned."

A shiver ran down Alice's spine. "They set the entire Deadlands War in motion. Gods, Furi. This changed the world."

CHAPTER TWENTY-ONE

S AMUEL HESITATED AT the stone staircase, the steps barely concealed in the rocky foothills of the Deadlands Spires. It was nice to be off the boat, but the hike inland had been exhausting. He glanced back through the small cluster of ironwood trees on the edge of the Silver Gulf. The washed-out green canopy was a burst of color in a barren land.

The Sea of Salt wasn't visible from their position on the opposite side of the foothills, but Samuel had an idea where it was.

"How long of a walk is this again?"

Drakkar turned toward Samuel, raising a freshly lit torch. "You would arrive sooner if you started now."

Samuel groaned, taking a longing look at the sun-drenched land before plunging into the shadows behind Drakkar. "You know, I don't live underground. The fondest memory I have of being underground involves almost dying. Repeatedly."

"Let us hope we do not add to that fondness today."

Samuel grumbled and blinked in the flickering torchlight, following the silhouette of Drakkar's cloak in front of him. Loose stone threatened to roll his ankles as something chittered in the darkness, the sound echoing all around them.

"There aren't Stone Dogs in the Spires, are there?"

"Not unheard of," Drakkar said, "but far fewer than what you saw beneath the Ridge Mountains."

"Didn't see much of anything beneath the Ridge Mountains," Samuel muttered, his hand moving to the hilt of his short sword. "Saw a lot of shadows and Fireworms and death."

"You lived. I would have been dragging a corpse out of those caves if it was not for those Fireworms."

"Good times."

Drakkar laughed quietly and led them deeper into the caves.

✧   ✧   ✧

IT HAD BEEN hours since they entered, of that Samuel was sure. He'd lost track of where they'd turned left and where they'd turned right. The tunnels were strange, branching and twisting in patterns that didn't appear to be carved by centuries of water passing through them. Instead, they were ribbed, as though something else had carved them out.

"What made these tunnels?" Samuel asked. "They're … odd."

"Caveworms," Drakkar said. "The stone eaters of legend."

"The what of who?"

"It is an old story of my people. One of the great worms that ate its way through the mountains."

Samuel ran his fingers along the stone. It was too smooth to have been carved by miners, and not smooth enough to have been a lava tube. Perhaps there was some truth in Drakkar's story, which gave Samuel pause.

"Caveworms don't still live here, do they?"

"No," Drakkar said with certainty. "No Caveworm has been seen in decades."

"Decades?" Samuel asked. "That … that doesn't seem like that long."

"You worry too much, my friend. It is a creature like any other. Do not anger it, or entice it, and it will leave you in peace."

"Okay, let's talk about something else. I'd rather not think about the fact we're walking through caves carved by some giant slimy worm."

Drakkar raised his torch to the wall, revealing a triangle. "Look, Samuel. These arrows were carved into the stone over a century ago, long before the Deadlands War, and even before Bollwerk rose to be the power it is today. They are untouched by man or creature. You have nothing to fear in this place."

Samuel's concern eased to a small degree, but he had a keen understanding of the creatures that liked to live in the dark underground. And very few of them were benevolent.

✧　✧　✧

SAMUEL HAD GROWN accustomed to the ribbed floor by the time Drakkar stopped. Sections had been smoothed away, but several maintained their form. Samuel wondered if that was because there was more than one way through the caves, and some had simply been worn down over the years.

"I thought some of the old folks might still be here. But I see no light."

"Be where?" Samuel asked.

Drakkar pulled on a handle sunk flat against a stone ledge, grunting as he freed it from rust and age with a squeal. He reached out with his torch, and something sparked in the darkness. A boiler started to hiss before a thin line of flame raced forward, cutting through the shadows like a knife of flickering light.

Samuel took a step backward when the flame arced over their head. Not a flame, he realized, but a series of tiny bulbs slowly brightening in the cavern above.

"Engines still work," Drakkar said. "You have to give it to the old tinkers. They did not always have the most elegant of solutions, but their creations often age well."

Samuel stepped closer, watching the rhythmic bursts of fire deep inside the stone. Warmth rose from the churning gears and pistons in the flames below. "What is that?"

"Combustion," Drakkar said. "An older type of engine. Charles thought them more efficient, but too dangerous when compared to steam. An irony when you consider he used steam engines to build weapons of war."

"What about the lights?"

"Gas and filaments of some sort. Horrendous to maintain, from the stories I have heard. They once had a team of citizens whose only tasks were to replace the expired lights. Come."

Drakkar led the way through a maze of stout stone homes. There was not a mixture of metal and wood here like Samuel had seen in Cave. This was the masterful work of gifted masons. Samuel hoped the masons Cave was sending to Ancora would have some of those skills.

The Cave Guardian wrapped his torch in cloth as they walked, extinguishing it so only the lights above remained in the cavern, like the spirits of some long-dead civilization. Samuel shivered at the thought.

Drakkar paused at the next intersection. "This is the last street, but I do not recall if … Ah! There is the bakery."

"The bakery?" Samuel asked.

"There is a particular workshop I would like you to see. Many horrors of the Deadlands War were created here, Samuel." He turned to meet Samuel's gaze. "It is sacred now, and cursed."

Drakkar stood before a simple wood door laid perfectly square into a slab of stone, a perfect arch chiseled away to frame the door, and above it, so small he almost missed the symbol, was a Steamsworn Fist. Green and tarnished and crusted with something white.

Water splashed down onto the fist and Samuel looked up. "Groundwater?"

"No, we are under the Sea of Salt here."

"Well, that's terrifying."

"It has stood guard over these caverns for millennia. You are quite safe, brave Spider Knight."

Samuel blew out a laugh as Drakkar pushed down on the latch to the old workshop and stepped inside. The Cave Guardian pulled a long black lever until it clicked against the stone, and a series of square lanterns overhead burst into life.

Only, they weren't lanterns at all. They were very much like the city lights in the Highlands of Ancora. Samuel's gaze traveled the room, taking in each station. Spools of wire and tensioners and strange wrenches he had no name for lined one station. Another held jars and gears and cogs and enough notebooks that it would take a lifetime to read, much less write.

Samuel moved closer to the bench, covered with a scattered array of schematics and letters. What he saw on the wall called to him immediately. A single photograph pinned to the wood. A man in a leather tunic. His hair wasn't so wild, and the beard not nearly so white in the monochrome frame. But the posture, and the smirk, and the penetrating eyes Samuel knew.

"Charles."

"Atlier," Drakkar said. "Yes, as our stories speak of him."

"I wish Jacob could see this place. We should bring him here."

"Samuel. *If* we ever bring Jacob here, it will be as a warning. These manuscripts hold some of the worst of Charles's inventions. Some of his weapons and experiments killed his friends. Allies inside these walls died at his hand. For a great many years, I believed it to have been intentional. That Atlier was the monster our history made him out to be."

Samuel eyed Drakkar. "And now?"

"He was doing what he believed to be right. As he did until the end." Drakkar crouched down to a brazier in the middle of the room, filled with ash. "This was his final act in this place before it was abandoned. He burned the manual that created the whitedamp."

"What's a whitedamp?"

"A poison that cannot be seen or smelled or tasted. A death sentence to all who lived in this block. Charles lost friends that day, and it is perhaps that moment more than any other that led him away from his focus on weapons of war."

Samuel cursed. He turned back to the workbench, reading through some of the papers. There was history there. Real history. Orders passed down from his superiors in the war. A letter from Archibald. Schematics for spring-loaded traps to be buried in sand. The stuff of nightmares.

But toward the bottom, Samuel found a strange page, written on the same letterhead as the orders he'd seen. "Look at this, Drakkar."

The Cave Guardian stepped closer, and they read the document together.

"When the dead no longer fall in battle, you'll know your job is completed."

Samuel tapped the date. His eyes flashed up to the row of salt-crusted journals, each with a date range scrawled along the spine. He found the one he wanted and slid it from its home.

```
    Damned fools, the lot of them. Asking me to modify a
soldier so they can't die. We've traded advancements for
madness in this war. Archibald is pushing to expand
research into biomechanics, but I fear what the addition
of more berserkers would do to the war effort.
    That's to say nothing of the psychological effect on
their friends and fellow soldiers. A machine, powered by
blood and a human heartbeat. There is little I consider
heresy in the goal of our mission, but not allowing a
dead man to die crosses a line.
```

Samuel flipped a few pages back. The entry was some weeks after the first, and his heart sank at the words.

```
    We had our first volunteer. It's not something that
can be attempted in our current location. I believe the
Cave Guardians and those who have welcomed us into their
homes would at best evict us, and at worst slaughter us.
```

"Outside the rule of law," Samuel repeated out loud. "What does that mean?"

Drakkar crossed his arms. "There are few who truly function outside the law of the land. But I know the stories of the dead who fight. Their last engagement was near the Skeleton when the Ballern forces pushed south to flank Bollwerk."

"There isn't anything left at the Skeleton like that."

"If there is, it is long buried. Legends say Charles succeeded. Dead men walking into war, fighting until there was nothing left of them. That is the Charles I knew from history, but knowing him in person perhaps taught me more about the duality of man than any history lesson ever could. Gather what you wish to take from this place. We make for Pirate's Cove."

CHAPTER TWENTY-TWO

THERE WAS A time Gladys had been nothing but grateful to the Speaker of Bollwerk. He'd taken her in after her family was lost to Rana and the warlords. But the older she got, and the more George spoke freely around her—she couldn't push down her growing suspicions.

For the time being, Gladys would accept Archibald's help. It was the best option for her people, and her people were by far her highest priority. Her family had let down Midstream and the surrounding villages far too many times for her to let that happen again.

They'd had warning that the warlords were forming a coalition, and that warning had come years before the raids started. Gladys twisted the ring on her thumb. George told her the plain band had been her mother's, but she didn't remember it. Regardless, it now served as a reminder, both of what she'd lost and what she hoped to surpass.

"Princess?" George asked, sitting down his hooked soup spoon. "What troubles you?"

Gladys shook her head, returning to the moment. The bar at the last inn at Midstream was no Fish Head, but the soup had remained a staple in her life as long as she could remember.

"I was just thinking about Archibald." She took a spoonful of soup. It had cooled somewhat, but the rough-cut vegetables and thick, salty broth were a balm to her worries.

"You need not concern yourself now," George said. "He needs Midstream to help defend against Fel. There is little threat while that remains true."

Gladys looked away for a moment, studying the reddish-tan plaster along the walls and thick ironwood beams overhead. "He's done a lot for us, George. I don't want to think of him as a threat." She paused. "Not that I don't *want* to, but I can't think of him as more than a helpful grandfather. It's like my brain won't get past that."

George smiled. "In a year, you will be fourteen, old enough to take the crown. Archibald will seek an alliance with us because *you* will have reunited the Deadlands. The villages are scattered, some still under threat from the surviving warlords. But that time will pass. Our allies grow with these battles. When I ask you to be suspicious of Archibald, I do not mean he is not an ally, Princess. I mean, you should be suspicious of all allies." He hesitated before a broad smile lit up his eyes with mischief. "Except for me, of course."

"Of course," Gladys said, dripping soup from her spoon as she laughed. Quieter, so not even the bartender could hear, she continued. "I trust Alice, and Jacob. Smith and Mary. They're our friends."

"Charles and Archibald were once friends," George said. "Do not forget that. Even friends can grow distant."

Gladys chewed on something crunchy. She was fairly certain the cook hadn't gotten all the chitin off whatever protein was in the soup, but it wasn't wholly unpleasant. "But in the end, Archibald helped Charles."

George took a deep breath and nodded. Gladys could tell he still disagreed to an extent. And it was a conversation they'd had more than once. George thought the only reason Archibald helped Charles was to again protect Bollwerk from the maneuvers of the Butcher.

Gladys thought it went much deeper than that. She felt a bond with the friends she'd fought beside against Fel. A bond she believed she'd carry to her grave. She lifted the bowl to her lips and sucked down the remaining broth.

"Let's join the patrols, George."

George opened his mouth, looking very much like he was about to protest, and then shrugged. "Very well. But only if you agree to wear your armor, regardless of the heat. At least you will be prepared for the flight to Dauschen."

Gladys sighed like it was the most difficult thing in the world to be armored and in the desert heat. But secretly she was happy George had given in so easily. It took some effort to hide the smile threatening her lips.

✦   ✦   ✦

GLADYS HAD FLED Midstream years before, and she hadn't remembered much about the city other than the food and the manor house they called home. It had been the largest building in Midstream, and one of the few with a more modern, inclined roof.

Though the home had been referred to as a manor house, Gladys scoffed at the name after seeing the manor homes near the outskirts of Bollwerk, each a giant compared to the home of Midstream's royal family. The idea a previous royal had built a manor house to emulate some wood and iron monstrosity from Bollwerk annoyed her.

"The new house is coming along," George said, calling her attention to the roof being hammered into place. "I appreciate the choices you made with the new manor."

"I think it fits Midstream better. It won't look like it's trying to fit in at Bollwerk." The oversized brick and exposed timber of the new adobe construction made her smile. It wouldn't stand out so much when it was done, other than the roof itself. A blend of tradition and things to come. Gladys liked that idea very much.

Along the ground, the sand was still mixed with ash from the great fire that had gutted the old manor house. It was a stark reminder of what the warlords had done, and how many of their people had not survived.

If she hadn't been looking so closely at the new construction, she might have missed the shadows sprinting down the alleyway. A glimpse made her think it was a small group of kids dashing through the pipes and wood and around frames of drying adobe.

But the glint of a blade's edge told her different.

"George!"

There was no hesitation in the guard's movements. George was on edge anytime there wasn't a locked door between Gladys and the rest of the world. Gladys might have had her eyes on the blades charging them from the left, but it was George who unfurled his armored cloak, catching a series of bolts before they could slam into Gladys's chest.

She didn't have time to let the shock wear off. She moved, dashing at the nearest squat building to cut off their assassins' line of sight. The steel of a throwing knife felt cold between her fingers as she slid it from one of the multiple sheaths across her breastplate. A quick snap of her wrist sent the first man grabbing at his throat as a fountain of blood sprayed the shadow beside him.

Luck, that was. The second sword stopped to wipe his eyes, and Gladys sank a knife into his leg. When his sword fell, and he moved to pull the knife out, a second hit him in the eye. No delay. No flailing. He simply fell into a heap as the narrow hilt slammed deep into his brain.

George had a spear in his hand when Gladys turned. He hadn't been carrying it a moment before, which meant it was a collapsible one from the tinkers. It soared through the air as George grunted, piercing the chest of the man armed with a crossbow that shot four bolts at once.

She didn't see the hand that took her from behind, catching her throat and squeezing tight. But memories of Rana flared in her chest, and what should have been a scream of terror became a scream of fury. Her left hand impaled the man's wrist on a blade, and as his grip weakened, Gladys clamped down, twisted, and leveraged his body weight over her back."

"Wait!" he cried, but the blade of George's sword found his throat a moment later.

One shadow stood frozen at the edge of the alleyway, turning to run as George pulled a small canister out of a pouch at his side. The guard squeezed the middle as he arched his arm back, a second spear expanding in his grip. He snapped it through the air.

George's aim had been uncanny, punctuated by a gristly crunch on impact. The man tried to crawl forward after he hit the ground, falling still soon after.

George looked to Gladys. He didn't ask if she was okay, and she knew he trusted her enough to say if she wasn't.

Gladys almost snarled. "I'd like to talk to Jacob now."

✧   ✧   ✧

They were silent most of the flight to Dauschen. But the attack in Midstream had eliminated Gladys's hesitation at asking Jacob for help. They needed better defenses, and Jacob was one of the best tinkers outside of Belldorn.

The airship was small, but far too opulent in Gladys's eyes. Practicality had been stripped and replaced with gilded furniture and long sofas to stretch out on. She did like the wide windows in the sides of the cabin. They gave a beautiful view of the Burning Forest and the North Woods' southernmost tip as they drifted into the mountain pass.

A crystalline lake shimmered in the distance, and Gladys watched as it slowly grew in her vision until they passed it, angling for the mountains where Dauschen waited.

George sat, his back rigid as he stared out the window. "What is that ..."

Gladys frowned, trying to see what he was looking at, and then she saw the arm. A monstrous thing, mounted to the framework of an airship dock. It bent and swiveled, hooked wheels climbing at will to deliver an impossible load of steel and two barrels to the topmost scaffolding where a crew of workers waited.

The closer the airship came, the more impossible the sight was. The arm was the size of a house, and not a small house. It could grab their ship from the air and crush it without effort. Steam belched from the sides of the monstrosity, mixed with fires and flame like some mad living forge.

Their pilot shouted back into the cabin, apparently unfazed by the vision before them. He said they'd be landing near a graveyard beyond the construction site.

Gladys looked down as they reached the city, her heart aching for the ruin in the collapsed cliff and the burned-out shells of so many homes. Dauschen had met with a tragedy not so unlike Midstream and Ancora. So many lives had been stolen away by the Butcher and Fel. It would be generations before this war would be forgotten. Part of her wondered what it would be called. A larger part of her just wanted it to be over.

✧   ✧   ✧

ON THE GROUND, standing below the Titan Mech arm, Gladys was at a loss for words. Someone near the top of the tower noticed them and waved a large red flag. The arm stopped moving, and Gladys smiled when she saw Jacob's face pop out the side of a small pilothouse.

Massive gears churned, reaching down as the arm reversed. It didn't quite reach the support below, dropping a fraction of an inch with the space, resulting in an enormous clang. The engine's fires roared as the gears shifted and the arm descended, finally stilling some ten feet above their heads.

Jacob hopped out onto a ladder and slid down the rungs. He wore a smile when he reached Gladys and George. And though it wasn't the most royal thing to do, Gladys almost tackled him to the ground with a hug.

Jacob ruffled her hair before exchanging grips with George. "It's good to see you two. What are you doing here?"

George looked up at the arm of the Titan Mech as it climbed again. "Is that bad?"

Jacob frowned and followed his gaze before laughing. "Oh, no. I trained Cage and some of his people on how to pilot it. I think they're getting used to it now." A second later, a large steel beam hit the earth with a crash. Jacob cringed. "They could use a bit more practice."

"The princess came to ask you a favor, in person," George said.

"We need help," Gladys blurted out, wringing her hands from a sudden bout of nerves. She'd felt determined after they were attacked in Midstream, but now, seeing the good Jacob was doing here, how could she pull him away from that?

"Well?" Jacob asked. "You came all this way. Ask me anything."

Gladys frowned and then hurried through what she had to say. "We need help building defenses in Midstream. I know you don't like building weapons, but we need help, Jacob. We can't defend the city on our own from Fel."

Jacob slowly crossed his arms, looking up at the contraption on the tower. "I want to help the cities rebuild. Ancora needs help too. I can talk Archibald into getting you some bolt guns to make the reconstruction faster."

"I do not believe bolt guns will help with adobe construction," George said with a small smile.

Jacob blinked. "Right. Hadn't thought about that."

Was he saying no? Of all the outcomes Gladys had thought might happen from their trip to Dauschen, Jacob saying no wasn't one of them. "Please," she said.

Jacob's face wrinkled at that plea. "I can't. I … I have to do some good in this world. There's been so much killing, Gladys."

"The princess herself was almost killed early today. Assassins from Fel attacked us inside the city proper."

Gladys felt that was a rather large exaggeration. They'd killed their would-be assassins quite readily. Except for the one … She remembered the iron grip on her throat and shivered. Maybe it wasn't such an exaggeration after all.

"What?" Jacob snapped. "Dressed in black with masks over their eyes?"

"Yes."

Jacob's hands turned white as they clenched into fists. He looked toward the edge of the cliff.

Gladys frowned at the brownish stains splattered across the stone. "What's that from?"

"Assassins," Jacob muttered. "They came here too. They've been regularly attacking the survivors. Cage and his soldiers have kept the worst of the attacks at bay, but Archibald doesn't think they'll stop until there's a regular presence of airships." He gestured back to the Titan Mech arm and the support structure.

George gave a slow nod. "If their focus is split between Midstream and Dauschen now, it will be entirely on Midstream should Archibald's plan succeed."

Jacob cursed. "I didn't … that's not what I wanted."

"Help us rebuild," Gladys said.

Jacob rubbed at his face. "Okay. Okay, I'll help. I'll help with the defenses. I can't say no to you."

Gladys thought that was an odd thing to say, since he'd been saying no to them since she first asked.

"I need to go to Bollwerk. The city tinkers can help, and Frederick. He's a tinker from Belldorn. One of Targrove's people. Helped me with the arm, in fact."

A small hope kindled in Gladys's chest. If they could build adequate defenses around Midstream, they'd be able to rebuild the city in earnest. In time, it could become the jewel of the desert, like it had been nearly a century before.

"Let's go," Gladys said. "We can take you now."

Jacob smiled. "Let me tell Cage and the others. I need to gather my things."

"Meet us at the airship when you're ready," George said. "It is one of Archibald's extravagant vessels. Fast, if somewhat small."

Jacob nodded, and they parted ways.

CHAPTER TWENTY-THREE

"I DON'T KNOW what I'm going to do," Jacob said, holding down the button on the airship's transmitter.

"Well, it would be helpful if—" Archibald started.

"Archibald. Gladys may not be asking you for soldiers, but they need them. Assassins attacked Midstream today, and I need time." Jacob angrily released the transmitter button.

Archibald remained silent for a time. "Very well. I have two skirmishers I can send that can land on sand. I do not expect the presence of smaller ships to draw much attention. But Jacob, if you form a perimeter around Midstream, it will draw Fel's eye."

Jacob shook his head and clicked the transmitter again. "They sent assassins today, Archibald. They're already focused on Midstream."

Another pause, and Archibald didn't protest again. "If you think it's for the best."

"Tell Frederick I'm going to need his help. And the city tinkers' help, for that matter. We have three cities to rebuild, so this needs to be done quickly."

"As you say. I would normally require a more formal request, but I do feel Midstream's preservation is in the best interest of all involved. Archibald out."

"Oh, he's mad," Gladys said.

Jacob smiled. "He'll be fine. He's getting some of what he wants, anyway. More weapons." He bit the last word off and ran his hand over the old leather journal. If Midstream needed protection, they had options.

✧   ✧   ✧

AFTER DOCKING IN Bollwerk came a rough ride on a crawler. Its treads cracked against worn cobblestones, delivering them to the factory where the first arm had been constructed. George insisted on seeing the facility, as he'd never been inside before.

Jacob hadn't seen much of it either, outside of the main hangar. But when they walked inside, he was greeted by something he didn't fully understand. "Two arms?"

"Jacob!" a familiar voice called.

He turned to find Frederick, the old tinker, making his way across an iron catwalk before taking a ride down to the floor on a smooth hydraulic lift.

"Frederick, what's going on?"

"Archibald gave the order as soon as you left for Dauschen. We're building another arm for Ancora."

"Then what's the third arm for?"

Frederick grinned. "We aren't waiting to finish the docks at Dauschen. We're sending a second arm to Dauschen to rebuild the tracks that lead to Ancora. Archibald didn't want to, I could tell, but I convinced him the increase in trade would benefit both. It will also be faster to move materials across the tracks while the airships have fewer drop points."

Jacob's smile widened the more Frederick spoke. These arms would do good. Ambrose would have one for the walls within the week, if his estimates were right.

"Who are your friends?" Frederick asked.

Jacob stiffened. "Oh, I'm so sorry. Frederick, this is George and Gladys. Gladys and George, Frederick."

Frederick stood a little straighter. "The Princess of Midstream? I apologize on behalf of Jacob, my lady. So familiar a tone with such a royal should never be tolerated."

George raised an eyebrow. "Perhaps I should execute him, My Princess?"

Gladys narrowed her eyes and tilted her head, studying Jacob as she tapped on her chin. "Not today. He may yet prove useful." She held her royal mask in place for all of ten seconds before erupting into laughter. "We are friends here, Frederick. Leave the formality of the courts behind. I appreciate your kindness."

Frederick inclined his head. "As you wish. It is lovely to meet you both. Smith told us stories of your trials and adventures. It would make a grand play for the stage."

Gladys grinned at Frederick.

Jacob flipped to the back of one of Charles's notebooks. Over half of it was blank, so he'd started some of his own sketches inside of it. "Frederick, I was thinking we could do something like this to the bolt cannons." He held it up so the other tinker could get a clear view.

Frederick eyed the sketch. It was essentially a wide box with twenty-five bolt cannons anchored to it. But instead of the regular triggers and individual crank, a series of lighter springs sat around each side, attached to a lever. A latticework of bronze was placed over the bolt cannons in two layers, serving two purposes. One, they would be held upright, their aim always true, and two, the uppermost layer doubled as a pressure plate, mounted just above the barrels of the cannons.

"This is fascinating, Jacob. Where do you hope to use it?"

"Buried in the sand around Midstream. Traps for anything coming from Fel on the ground. They've had trouble with assassins."

Frederick gently closed the journal in Jacob's hands. "You do not have to build weapons, Jacob. Your ideals are pure, and that is a rare thing."

But they weren't pure, Jacob knew. He'd felt the rush of battle more than once. The satisfaction of throwing down his enemy. He only hoped he could offset those darker times with better intentions.

"An ideal has to be worth the price. I can't lose my friends because I wasn't willing to help defend them."

Frederick paused and blew out a breath before nodding. "Work up a prototype. We'll do some tests. Reloading something buried in the sands will be difficult. You'll need an easier way to access the ratchets. And you'll want more than one pressure plate. You want to stop an attacker, not cut them into puzzle pieces."

Gladys and George exchanged a look. Jacob wasn't sure what passed between the two, but he hoped they'd feel like he was doing enough to help Midstream. The cities were pulling him in three different directions, and that said nothing for his concern about Alice off in Belldorn.

George placed a hand on Jacob's shoulder. "This means more to us than you know. Should you have need of our assistance, please ask. I will take Gladys to The Fish Head. I would like you and Frederick to join us later, if you are able."

When they turned to leave, Jacob was surprised to find Archibald waiting at the doors. He greeted them as they passed by.

"Jacob, I'd like to show you something."

Jacob nodded.

"Come, we must return to the workshop."

✧ ✧ ✧

BUT IT WASN'T the workshop Jacob found himself standing in a short time later. It was a hidden room, littered with artifacts from ages past, and one of the largest Steamsworn monuments he'd ever seen.

"What is all this?" Jacob asked.

"Much of it is the history of the Steamsworn," Archibald said, sifting through a trunk in the corner before frowning and standing up. "I could have sworn they were in there. Some of it was Charles's, you know. He was resistant to the cause, in the beginning, but almost became a symbol to the Steamsworn over the course of the war."

Jacob looked around the room. Some of it was scattered with worn gadgets he couldn't identify: long barrels that looked like cannons but had no opening at the end, only a spike, amulets with too many gears to be a simple amulet, and boots that had clearly been a weapon. Blades extended from the sole of one, and he didn't miss the stains on the rough leather.

Jacob made his way behind the Steamsworn monument, wondering if this one was the same as Gareth Cave. He reached down in the shadows and found the latch, pulling it to release the hidden drawer inside. Jacob froze when he met the gleaming eyes of a mask. A respirator was attached to it, with tubes flowing down to a pair of rusted air tanks.

He picked up the helmet. At first, he'd thought it was soft leather, but the weight told him otherwise. It was armor, and beneath it rested more pieces. He recognized the basic design. It was the same principles he'd used in the Titan Mech arm. But here everything was smaller, hollow.

"Ah, yes," Archibald said, his face appearing on the other side of the monument. "I'd nearly forgotten that was there. Not a successful project, to be sure."

"What was it?"

"A design Charles and Newton worked on. The idea was to make an exoskeleton, a Titan Mech that could be worn."

Jacob looked down into the eyes of the old helmet. Charles and the Butcher had worked together on it? That was hard to reconcile in Jacob's mind, but he'd only known them decades after the Deadlands War. After the Butcher had earned his name in full.

He recognized some of the design, having a sleekness that was un-mistakably Charles. Jacob turned it over, finding small tears in the hoses that he didn't think came from age. They looked blown out. Probably not heavy enough to survive whatever pressure had been flowing through them.

He set the helmet down and lifted one of the arms, almost dropping it when he saw the brace. It was the same design as the one Charles had once had in Ancora, but the slot for a Burner was a ball and socket instead of a simple joint. It was nearly identical to the brace he'd killed the Butcher with.

Jacob shivered and slid the drawer closed.

"Aha!" Archibald's excitement mercifully drew Jacob's attention away from the exoskeleton.

When Jacob stepped out from behind the monument, he blinked at the floor, now open to reveal a secondary vault. Whoever had crafted it had hidden it so well Jacob hadn't had a moment's thought there was anything beneath their feet.

Archibald held out a small notebook. "You already have some of Charles's notes on the Titan Mech. I thought you'd like to have the rest. Not that you need use them, of course."

"Of course," Jacob said, not hiding the skepticism in his voice. He took the leather-bound notebook from Archibald, the spine cracked but not broken. The first few pages told Jacob it was different from the schematics he had. One schematic showed the leg construction was entirely changed, and he hesitated on the fourth page.

The hip joint was intact, but below it was a locking ratchet, almost the same as what Jacob had done to get the arm working for construction purposes. He flipped forward, a musty scent rising from the pages. The first sketch of an arm looked exactly like the schematics he'd worked from, but part of the drawing had been scribbled out. On the following page, the arm had been changed, another ratchet installed below the elbow, the ratios nearly identical to those Jacob had used. Which meant

Frederick's math had been exactly right.

Charles had taught Jacob almost everything he knew. Jacob didn't think his mind worked that much in concert with the old man's. From the schematics, it was plain to see some part of him thought very much like Charles had.

"Great minds, eh?" Archibald said, as though echoing Jacob's thoughts. "There may be something useful in there for you in the defense of Midstream. Charles burned the schematics for some of his deadliest creations, but I think he would have liked you to have these."

Jacob closed the journal and ran a thumb over the rough leather. "I think he would have preferred I'd never need it."

Archibald inclined his head. "Charles had workshops all over the continent, did you know? As the war expanded, so did the reach of our allies. He had bolt holes and benches from Ancora to Pirate's Cove." A small smile flickered across Archibald's face. "Ancient history, I suppose, much like myself. Some of that can live on through you now."

Jacob slipped the notebooks into his backpack. He didn't tell Archibald about everything they'd discovered in Ancora. The more the Speaker asked him for favors, the more Jacob grew worried that the best interests of his friends and families didn't align with Archibald's ambitions.

✧   ✧   ✧

JACOB STOOD ON the smooth stone street and smiled up at the rusted iron fish skeleton hanging above the sidewalk. No matter how many times he saw the X's for eyes, it still made him chuckle. The crawler roared and churned out gray smoke as the pilot pulled away, leaving Jacob at The Fish Head.

He walked through the doorway and was immediately hit by a breeze filled with smoked fish and rich oil. The restaurant was crowded for being an off time of the day, and Jacob was surprised to see George behind the pale bar, deboning fish as though it was the easiest thing in the world.

Gladys sat on a stool, scowling at something George had said as she popped a handful of roasted seeds into her mouth. She swiveled back and forth, tapping her feet to some unheard tune as Jacob wove through the low tables between the door and the bar.

"Busy today," he said, throwing a leg over the barstool beside Gladys.

Gladys grinned at Jacob. "Finally, someone who won't call me princess."

"Anything you ask, Princess," Jacob said without hesitation, trying to intone George's formal use of her title.

George barked out a laugh, dropping his head to hide his hysterics as Gladys's smile hardened into a glare. Jacob smiled and took some seeds for himself. They were a bit chewy, quite salty, and just as addictive as almost everything on The Fish Head's menu.

"George," Gladys said, slowly turning to her guard. "When we get back to Midstream, I believe the gallows should be the first thing we rebuild."

"Of course, Princess." George winked at Jacob and slid two bowls across the bar. "Salmon from the southern tip of the Ridge Mountains. None finer, and I will miss it in Midstream."

"I'm sure Archibald would send you some," Jacob said.

George shook his head. "Not the same, I am afraid. But there is a fine Midstream dish fashioned from Tail Swords that is a reasonable substitute."

Gladys leaned closer to Jacob. "So? What did Archibald want?"

He told them of the monument and the hidden notebooks as he slid Charles's schematics across the bar to show them. "It's everything he did to build a Titan Mech."

A chef shouted orders from the window into the kitchen, sending a server scurrying over to grab piping hot bowls for some patrons at a table. George and Gladys didn't pay them any mind, so Jacob tuned out the organized chaos as well.

"Why don't we use one of these arms to help rebuild Midstream?" Gladys asked. "If it's working in Dauschen, won't it work for us?"

George raised an eyebrow and looked to Jacob.

"We'd need a solid base for it in the sand ... and something that could keep the worst of it out. But I don't think that would be too difficult to accomplish." Jacob flipped back through Charles's notebooks to the leg schematics. They were designed for a great variety of terrain, and making something similar to support the arm, rather than a rail car, might work in the sands. "Let me talk to Frederick. We might be able to make something work."

Gladys reached out and squeezed Jacob's hand, her sleeve sliding up enough to reveal a bracelet that held the fist of the Steamsworn, and the jagged crest of a Tail Sword that had once been the symbol of her house. A house that had been ground into the dirt by Rana and the warlords.

Midstream would never be caught off guard again. Jacob would make sure of that.

CHAPTER TWENTY-FOUR

"How do you feel about breaking the rules today?" Alice asked as she and Furi walked out under the gray skies of a looming storm.

"I feel like I don't want to be locked in prison for the rest of my life?" Furi's voice rose with the question. "Even a nice prison."

Alice scrunched up her face. "Well, I suppose it's more a bending of the rules than a breaking of them. A side trip. You can blame *me* if anything happens."

Furi slowly raised an eyebrow.

"It's a simple matter, really. I left my notebook at Mary's, so obviously we'll need it to finish our research."

Furi rubbed at her face. "I thought I was done with this kind of nonsense after Rin left."

Alice grinned at that. Furi had told her some of the tales of her childhood friend, Rin. He sounded like trouble. A trouble not so unlike Jacob, when it came down to it. Stealing to feed his family. But Rin had gone further, hiring out to other families as a thief for hire. Now that was something Alice thought she'd like to hear more about. What kind of stories would a thief for hire have?

It wasn't a long walk back to the house. Not really a house, Alice supposed, more like an excessively nice apartment with more rooms than most of the houses had in the Lowlands. Mary had planned to be home today, and if Alice timed it right, she hoped Furi might help get Mary to talk.

What Alice had not expected when she pushed in the front door with a wide smile on her face was to find Lady Katherine and Mary huddled over a map in the family room.

"Uh oh," Alice whispered.

"Uh oh?" Furi asked.

"That's Lady Katherine," Alice hissed.

Furi immediately leaped to the side and pointed at Alice. "It was her idea!"

"What are you two doing here?" Mary asked.

Furi's hand slowly lowered when no one started yelling, her gaze moving from Alice to the table and back.

Alice glanced between Furi and Lady Katherine. "Lady Katherine, this is Furi. We stopped by to pick up a notebook I forgot."

Furi wrung her hands together and gave what Alice thought might be the single most awkward smile she'd ever seen.

Lady Katherine tilted her head to the side. "A notebook? It must be of some value to risk escorting a prisoner off their approved schedule."

Alice gave her a nervous smile to rival Furi's.

Lady Katherine's decorum broke down a moment later when she chuckled and looked to Mary. "I suppose your request for a more lenient pass was apt."

"I told you they'd be trouble."

"Trouble?" Alice said, straightening. "I'd hardly say I'm trouble."

"Are you going to tell her?" Lady Katherine asked.

Mary shrugged. "I'm rather enjoying the moment, honestly."

The Lady of Belldorn smacked Mary's arm.

"Okay, okay." Mary grinned at Alice. "The pass Furi wears gives her freedom to roam the city so long as she's with an escort. After talking to Eva, she suggested we give you more space."

"More space for what?" Alice asked, exchanging a glance with a bewildered-looking Furi.

"More space to do your research," Mary said. "To see if you can find a weakness in Ballern. Something we could exploit."

Alice shook her head. "It's not Ballern you need to worry about. It's their alliance with Fel."

Lady Katherine grimaced. "Fel is a threat, to be sure. But how can you be certain of their alliance with Ballern?"

Alice looked at Furi and nodded.

Furi dug out one of her own notebooks and hurried over to the table. "Because it was Fel who assassinated Lady Esther. We found this in a book from Ballern that I'd never heard of. That means it was either rare, or they purged it."

Lady Katherine studied the passage beneath Furi's fingers, having no trouble reading the jagged-style Ballern writing. With every line her eyes took in, Lady Katherine's expression darkened until her hands curled into fists.

At the end, she leaned back in her chair, silent. No one spoke while Mary read the excerpt too.

Mary frowned and glanced at Lady Katherine. "I don't understand. What do the Children of the Dark Fire have to do with anything? They're just beggars on the docks around Ballern."

Lady Katherine's voice sounded like she was reciting a text, nearly forgotten. "Before the Third War, which preceded the Deadlands War by a quarter century, it was not Ballern who were allied with Fel. It was Belldorn. An arc of protection across the entire northwest border of the continent."

"What changed?" Alice asked.

"The assassination of Lady Olivia at the start of the Deadlands War," Lady Katherine said in a hushed tone. "Olivia courted the Lady of

Belldorn. She wanted to bring some of our customs across the sea. To widen the education of her people, and to stop the persecution of all who eschewed tradition."

"You mean Olivia wanted a queen?" Mary asked. "She pursued Esther? That's what you're saying, isn't it?"

"Yes, and while most of Ballern was open to our ways, in both marriage and economics, there were those who were not so welcoming."

"The Children of the Dark Fire," Alice said, not having to stretch to fit those pieces together.

"Yes. And do you know why?" Lady Katherine didn't give them time to answer. "To set in motion the rise of a cult. Worshipers of a machine who would see the world crushed beneath their heel. Fel has long meddled in the politics of foreign cities. You witnessed it in Ancora, but I had not dreamed their corruption had driven Ballern's descent into an authoritarian madness."

"You don't understand the extent of what's happened," Furi said. "Ballern is worse than you know." She told Lady Katherine of the divide in the city, the separation of the Skyborn from the proper citizens. The restriction of their education and the labor camps that were the only real jobs open to the Skyborn. "But at least we have the docks. The docks are a nice place to live."

Lady Katherine's eyes reddened, tears threatening to fall, but none did.

Furi turned to Alice and hissed, "What's wrong?"

Alice rubbed her hands together. "You just told her a pivotal moment in the history she's always believed is actually a lie. It takes some time to absorb that kind of thing. Believe me."

Lady Katherine slammed her palm onto the table. "The conflict with Ballern has *always* been a righteous one. Justified because they were the aggressors. *They* raided Belldorn and brought ruin onto our city. But all this time …" She shook her head and made a wordless growl. "Fel has been manipulating *everyone* like some mad puppeteer."

"Then we go to Ballern," Alice said. "We go to Ballern and explain what has happened. Set history right."

"I don't think that will go the way you want," Furi said quietly. "To speak against the doctrines of the state, our official histories, is punishable by death."

"Of course it is," Lady Katherine growled.

"There has to be someone who can help," Mary said.

"The only allies you might have in Ballern are the Skyborn. They've been cast aside by the monarchy for decades. But I was one of them. I *am* one of them. And until I met Eva and Alice, I didn't have a reason to believe Belldorn was anything but evil."

Lady Katherine listened to Furi's words, silent for a time when she finished speaking. "Furi, they would listen to *you*, would they not?"

Furi glanced down at the table. "A lot of my friends died in the desert. You have many more locked away, imprisoned here." She hesitated and took a deep breath. "Lady Katherine, the stories they used to start the conflict may have been a lie, but everything you've done since made them true."

"Furi," Alice hissed. "You can't say that to—"

Lady Katherine held up a hand before sagging into her chair. "No, Alice, it's okay. Furi's right. Things were set in motion too long ago. Fel's strategy has been playing out over decades. We've felt their influence without realizing it, and if it has penetrated Ballern's history so thoroughly as that, it is not something I myself can repair."

Mary crossed her arms. "Furi can."

"How?" Lady Katherine asked, incredulous.

"She can start a revolution from within. Free the Skyborn who still live there from a regime that wants no part of them to begin with. Drive another wedge between the factions."

A wordless exchange passed between Mary and Lady Katherine.

"You cannot," Lady Katherine said. "The Skysworn is marked by Ballern as a pirate vessel. They'll clip your wings without warning."

Mary smiled. "They're more accepting of pirates than you know. I can get Furi back to Ballern. We won't be shot down like a ship flying Belldorn's colors."

Furi hesitated. "I'll go if you let me take Beck."

"No," Lady Katherine said. "I cannot offer so much trust to a pair who can so easily betray my city and my friends." She gave Mary a meaningful stare.

"I'll go with her," Alice said. "From what she's told me of the Skyborn, they aren't so different from those of us who grew up in the Lowlands of Ancora."

Mary looked like she was about to protest, but she stopped and slowly nodded. "I like it. Alice is smarter than most of your spies, and I haven't made a good smuggler's run in years."

"And what will Smith think of that?" Lady Katherine asked. "You only just freed yourself of your debt to Archibald."

Mary's only response was a broad smile.

"I hate that smile. I *hate* that smile, Mary. I've had to endure that look since we were children. And it was consistently a precursor to us doing something incredibly stupid."

Mary held her smile.

Lady Katherine blew out a breath. "Fine. We'll try this your way. But understand, if you are held by Ballern, we can't come for you."

"I know you better than that," Mary said. "You always keep your promises."

"Eva's going to kill you."

Mary shrugged. "We have an understanding about me and stupid decisions." She placed a hand on the lady's shoulder. "We won't be caught. I'll make a trade, deliver some contraband, and leave the kids to meet with the Skyborn."

"And how will we get back?" Alice asked.

"Supply ships," Furi said. "It's easy to catch a ride. We can stowaway on a cargo ship to Fel or one of the trade vessels that go to the people of the Red Woods. It's … well, it's the only way most of us have been able to travel outside the military."

"Supply ships," Mary said, echoing Furi's words.

"Why do I have a bad feeling about this?" Alice muttered.

"We leave tomorrow," Mary said. "Get ready. Both of you."

CHAPTER TWENTY-FIVE

J ACOB LOOKED AT the box of sand, some three feet by three feet, that had been placed in the center of the workshop. "This isn't a good test."

"What do you mean?" Frederick asked.

"The grains of sand aren't in scale. They won't be nearly this large compared to the traps we'll be sending to Midstream."

"It's close enough. Just plan for more dust in the gears when they're in the field."

Dust. Jacob thought sand would be quite a bit more problematic in the desert than dust. He took a deep breath and slid the safety out from the small rectangle of loaded springs beneath the smooth sand.

"It's armed." He turned back to his bench, jotting a quick note when an idea came to him to enclose the gearbox completely. A gasket around the arming switch would keep the sand out well enough. Jacob glanced at Frederick, who was now making his way to the sandbox with a bucket.

"What is that?"

"Just a Pill-Bug to test the trap."

"Stop," Jacob said. "We don't have to kill anything to test the trap."

Frederick paused, raising an eyebrow. "It's only a bug. It is not as though we're testing it on a human."

"We can test it on a piece of jerky, or a sandbag." Jacob's tone darkened. "We don't have to kill anything."

Frederick raised a hand, not arguing further.

Jacob grabbed a small sandbag he sometimes used to test a model's load-bearing capacity. It was only five pounds, but depending on the scale, that could represent a weight many times greater. He frowned at the bucket, still in Frederick's hand.

"How much do you think that Pill-Bug weighs?"

"A pound, two at most."

Jacob tossed the sandbag to the side, instead grabbing a folded stack of webbing used to stitch harnesses and backpacks. It was durable and had enough heft it would be easy to weigh out two pounds. He laid the webbing on a scale and removed a few layers until he was happy.

A quick wrap in twine gave it more density, and with little effort, he had a perfect testing medium. It was strange working with experienced tinkers who weren't Charles. They were slower to come to solutions that Jacob saw almost immediately. But when he'd worked with Charles, *he* always felt like the slow one.

Jacob glanced up at Frederick. "Ready?"

The old tinker nodded and sat the bug down in a crate.

Jacob took a step back, lined up his aim, and tossed the bundle of webbing onto the sand. There was no warning. It was as fast as the strike of a Tail Sword. A small impact, followed by a click, and the webbing exploded into the air, chased by a narrow geyser of sand.

It spun and twisted with the gleaming polished bolts piercing its side, and Jacob's stomach soured at the thought of what that device would do to a person. But then he remembered the warlords of the Deadlands, and what they had been willing to do to Gladys, and Alice.

He almost snarled as he said, "We're ready to scale up."

✧   ✧   ✧

THE MORE THEY worked on the next model, the more Jacob grew concerned about sand interfering with the gears. The traps might work a handful of times, but eventually they were going to lock up, and

Midstream's defenses would be lessened for it.

But he had other options, he realized as he sketched design after design into Charles's old notebook. The same notebook with the original concepts for the air cannon. A closed system. A system he could repurpose to be the actuators for the sand traps.

While Frederick tinkered with the latticework to lay over the barrels themselves, Jacob redesigned the actuators from the ground up. The empty space around the barrels left plenty of room to build up the air pressure they needed, and if they divided the chambers, it would still be functional with multiple triggers. Meaning the trap itself would be good to fire up to ten times.

If they sank enough into the sands surrounding Midstream, the traps could chew through multiple companies before needing to be reloaded. Once that happened, Jacob knew the Midstream defenders would be exposed, but the psychological damage done to any aggressor might be enough for a reload to be unnecessary.

Just in case, he repurposed the original gearbox as an intake port and anchor to raise the entire unit through the sand for reloading, leaving the empty base below.

By the time Frederick finished the latticework and looked over Jacob's shoulder, the old tinker could only curse.

He flopped onto the stool beside Jacob and reviewed the calculations. "If the capacity is right, you're going to double the force of those projectiles."

Jacob frowned. They were already severe enough to penetrate steel based on the calculations. If they'd doubled that, or more if Jacob tweaked two of the valve casings ... "I think we could take down an airship with these."

Frederick blinked.

"A low-flying airship," Jacob corrected. "But considering that, I want to add bellows to the sides of the trap. We can be sure the sand will be kept out of them that way."

"It will be harder to bury with that design."

"It'll be harder to break too. And I think that's more important. Besides, if we ship an arm to Midstream, mounted on the same kind of protected base, they can use that to bury them."

Frederick sagged forward onto the workbench. "Jacob, Jacob that's brilliant. I never would have thought of using air pressure for all of this."

Jacob smiled. "I wouldn't have either if it wasn't for Charles's air cannon design. But it should work. It's the same concept on a larger scale."

Frederick nodded. "We best get started."

✧　✧　✧

IT WAS THE following day before they were ready to test the redesign. The gaskets had failed time and again until Jacob had the thought to reinforce the rubber with iron plates. With the extra structural support, they no longer ballooned into failure. He felt embarrassed for not realizing it sooner because it was almost the exact same technique Charles had used in the air cannons.

Jacob probed the sand with a long magnetic lever he'd assembled. It was the best idea he could come up with to avoid having to dig up the trap every time they needed to reload. He worried that when they were buried deeper, probing the sand would offer too much resistance, but it was still better than nothing.

The magnets were strong, which was both a problem and helpful. A bad angle left you stuck to the side of the trap. He'd solved that by anchoring the bellows with a non-magnetic alloy. With that done … the magnet mounted in the sand almost pulled the lever out of his hand, snapping it home with a thud.

Jacob pushed the lever forward, and the barrels rose through the latticework, iris valves keeping them clear of sand. Those had been Frederick's idea, and they worked perfectly. Jacob shifted the lever like it was a steering column on the Skysworn, and the valves opened, revealing a dozen barrels ready for bolts.

Another adjustment changed the angle of the battery until it was nearly at forty-five degrees. Jacob returned the lever to its original position, and the assembly returned to the sand. It would be little effort to cover it at that point.

"And how are you going to get the lever off the magnets now?" Frederick asked.

Jacob grinned and clicked the button on the end of the handle. It jerked when the plating slid around the end, shielding the magnet buried in the lever. He extracted it easily at that point, showing the shielded tip to Frederick.

"Charles would be proud."

Jacob started at that voice. He turned to find Archibald, though he hadn't heard the Speaker enter.

"Frederick tells me you're testing again today."

Jacob nodded, half annoyed that Frederick was pandering to Archibald, but also glad the Speaker could see what they'd accomplished. "We're almost ready to deliver the supplies to Midstream. The city smiths have made the adjustments to the bolts we asked for, and George will have thousands prepared."

Their final prototype, wrapped in rubber bellows and a latticework of half-inch-thick bronze, was two feet by one foot across. It took nearly an hour to bury it in the sandbox, but they had it done just before Archibald arrived to see their progress.

Jacob tossed his original webwork test bundle onto the sand, and nothing happened.

"Excellent," Frederick said.

"How so?" Archibald asked. "Nothing happened."

Jacob nodded. "He's right, we don't want it too sensitive, or a small bug or young Fire Lizard could set it off." Jacob picked up a long sheet of lead with Frederick's help. "On three. One. Two. Three."

They tossed it a fraction of an inch into the air and then skittered away from the sandbox. The lead weighed just over one hundred pounds, and it sent out a shower of sand as it landed. But the weight did far more than that. A series of muffled booms sprayed sand all across the room as the lead plate flipped once and landed back in the sand, six steel bolts stuck into it.

Jacob looked up at the ceiling and winced. "Sorry about that."

"About what?" Archibald asked, following his gaze. "Oh."

Above them, in the stone, were two more steel bolts, sunken halfway down their six-inch shafts. Jacob had little doubt those would remain in the ceiling until Bollwerk crumbled and the city returned to the dust from which it was built.

"I'll ready the supply ships," Archibald said. "How many have been completed?"

"In a couple hours, once we get the levers finished, we'll have a dozen," Jacob said. "But they'll need ten times that to defend Midstream."

"Frederick, stay here and assist the city smiths and any tinkers who wish to volunteer. Build as many as you can. If Jacob thinks they need a hundred of these traps, I want two hundred built." Archibald didn't wait for Frederick's response before he turned to Jacob. "Take one of the schooners to Midstream. George knows how to pilot them. Train the tinkers of Midstream on maintaining the traps, loading the traps, everything they need to know."

"I'll teach them to build them. That will help them fix any damage that happens."

Archibald nodded and turned to leave. At the door, he glanced back. "Good work. Both of you."

CHAPTER TWENTY-SIX

FURI SAT ON the edge of her bed, paging through the notebook Alice had given her. The notes the Ancoran had taken were more thorough than Furi expected. Several passages had been copied verbatim, but the more she read, the more conflicted she felt.

Half the history she'd learned about her city, about the entire empire she'd lived all her life in, was lies and when it wasn't an outright lie, it was embellished to be almost unrecognizable.

Furi and her friends had often talked about what the monarchy was keeping from them. They theorized about how the ruling class kept everyone else under control. But she'd never thought she'd get those answers with the help of an Ancoran.

Because whether she wanted to admit it or not, Furi knew hatred of the eastern lands had been bred into her. Belldorn and Ancora and Bollwerk were the *enemy*. But that was the monarchy's gift to them. A target. A finger pointed toward the outsiders, and a declaration that a nebulous enemy was responsible for the entirety of their hardships.

Furi ground her teeth. She felt like such a fool for buying into it. She'd been disenfranchised, to be sure, but never had she thought there could be such a thorough deception living in the minds of an entire population.

She took a deep breath and closed the notebook, leaving her room so she could get another snack from one of the exquisite cooks Belldorn staffed at their so-called prison. Furi made her way out to the common room, catching hints of an argument and a quiet sob.

Some of her allies inside the prison still thought they were going to be executed at any moment, no matter what Furi told them. She thought it more likely Ballern would kill them before they could return home and then raise them up as martyrs. The faith she'd had left in her city, however small, was crumbling to dust.

"Hello, Furi."

She glanced up at the man behind the counter. She was still surprised so many of the guards and staff had taken the time to learn everyone's names. "Hi, Jake. Could I get one of those grilled sandwiches again?"

"Of course." He adjusted a tall white hat on his head. "Did you like the butter we used last time? I've been experimenting with herbs."

"Yes!" Furi could still remember the sharp, earthy taste on her tongue, a mixture of yeast and salt that was not quite like anything she'd had before. She watched the cook from behind an iron trestle, enjoying the sizzle and smoke of the griddle. Belldorn may have been kind to their prisoners, but they were also cautious.

Furi thanked Jake as she turned away, not waiting to sink her teeth into that savory crunch with its creamy center. It struck her, in that moment, that it was easier to get food in a prison in Belldorn than it was to feed yourself as a Skyborn in Ballern.

She shook the darker thoughts off. She'd help raise the Skyborn. If they knew what she knew, they'd make a choice: fight, or flee to a better place. There were no other options.

Furi sat down on a sofa next to Beck. He was glaring at the checkered gameboard in front of him while one of the guards grinned from across the table.

"Getting your butt kicked?" Furi asked.

"Stop it, you." Beck's scowl lit up a moment later, and he slid one of the pyramid-shaped pieces one space to the left and one space forward.

The guard pursed his lips, studying the board. "Not a bad move, but I'm afraid you can't get out of this trap." He pushed a clear square piece two spaces closer to Beck.

Beck moved another pyramid in behind the guard's square, and as soon as the guard realized what was happening, he cursed at great length.

"I call crown," Beck said, a deep satisfaction in his voice Furi hadn't heard in a very long time.

The guard muttered and dropped two gold coins onto the board. "Not that you need coin in prison, but a bet is a bet." The irritation on his face slipped as he held a hand out to Beck. "Good game, kid."

Beck took the offered hand and gave it one firm pump, as was custom in Ballern. With that, the guard trailed back to the front, where the other guards were gathered. Furi recognized most of them, but one had a hat pulled low over his eyes.

Furi finished her sandwich, watching the guard approach. He turned from the rest of the room so only Furi and Beck could see him.

"Is there somewhere we can speak privately?"

Furi frowned. There was something familiar about that voice. She'd heard it before …

"I won that game square," Beck said, pocketing his winnings.

The guard's face broke into a grin. "Keep quiet." He raised the brim of his hat, revealing a narrow nose and deep-set eyes that made Furi's heart stop for a moment.

"Rin!" she hissed. "You're supposed to be dead!"

He held a finger up to his lips to silence their questions.

Furi shook her head in annoyance. Rin, alive, and *here* of all places. What in all hells was happening? "Come on." She grabbed Beck's sleeve and pulled him up before reaching out and briefly squeezing Rin's wrist.

It was him. Solid and real and in Belldorn with them. She led the pair back to her room, past a dozen empty doorways. She glanced back down the hall, and when she was sure no one was paying them any mind, slipped into her room.

"What the hell are you doing here?" Furi asked. But before Rin could answer, she crushed him in a hug. He was shorter than she remembered, which meant it had been so long that she'd grown. Years now.

"It's good to see you," Beck said, clapping Rin on the shoulder. "How did you get in here?"

"No guard I've ever met is immune to a little coin," Rin said. "I heard Belldorn had captured Ballern soldiers. I came to see if I could save them. You'd be amazed what you can get into with one of these passes." He flipped the badge hanging at his chest. "But you're all living in luxury here. What's happening?"

"What's happening?" Furi asked. "I think you've been dead for almost three years and all you can say is 'what's happening?' How about how are you alive? What are you doing in Belldorn? I thought you came here to fight in the war."

Rin sighed and sat down on the bed, looking down at his hands. "I did. But … Furi, I don't want to tell you what happened."

"Is it worse than getting shot down by a Porcupine and then rescued by the same people who shot you down? Worse than finding out the real villain in your life is the queen who was supposed to protect her people? The monarchy that stole our education and left us to rot on the docks?"

Rin blinked.

"What are you talking about?" Beck asked.

Furi launched into her story, not giving either of them a chance to interrupt or question. She told them about the library, the old Ballern books, and the story of what had really ground the Skyborn to the edge of survival.

Rin took his hat off when she was done. He glanced between them and cursed. "I was on one of the raids. We thought we were going to destroy a hidden factory." He shook his head. "That's what they told us. A factory where the worst of Belldorn's weapons were made. We destroyed it from above and then went in on foot to kill any survivors."

Rin's face twisted. "There were kids in there. No older than you were when I left. Captain tried to say it was because Belldorn was enslaving their children in factories. But it wasn't a factory at all. It was a school. I found the books. The teacher was still alive. Her last words were 'The children aren't your enemies' before she died. The captain congratulated us on a job well done. Me and Tatsu were there. You remember Tatsu?"

Furi nodded. How could she forget him? Even though he was older, he'd spent weeks with them in Kura's classroom. Always patient and kind, helping anyone who needed it on the Bones. Furi wondered how different he was now.

"We left the same day. Never got back on the airship. Just walked off into the woods, and that's where we've been for almost five years now."

"You could have come home," Furi said, thinking of the years that had passed without her friend.

"As much as I thought I deserved to die for what I'd done, I wasn't anxious to accelerate the process."

"You've just been in the woods alone?" Beck asked.

"No. We live with the Dragonriders of the Shadowed Woods."

Furi frowned. "The … what?"

"Outsiders who ride Dragonwings. They've defected from Belldorn. Or perhaps they were never part of Belldorn. I'm not sure, to be honest. It doesn't matter. They took us in, fed us. Let us earn our keep."

"Can they fight?" Furi asked.

"Like devils."

She exchanged a glance with Beck. "I'm going back to Ballern. To pass the truth to the Skyborn. They're in danger from the Children of the Dark Fire."

"I'll come with you." Rin stood immediately.

"You two have fun," Beck said. "I'll stay here and crown some more guards and live in luxury."

"You're still in prison," Rin said.

Beck blew out a breath. "Beats living on the docks."

Furi wanted to argue with him, but part of her agreed. There was a charm to the docks, to making your own way, but every day was a struggle. A fight. And sometimes it was nice not to have to fight to live.

"Then Furi and I will go."

"No," Furi said, squeezing Rin's arm. She was surprised to find muscle where he'd once been a lanky kid. She supposed they'd both grown up. "You need to stay here. See if the Dragonriders will fight with you. Will fight with us."

"Furi, they're not going to attack Belldorn. They don't hate them that much."

Furi's expression fractured. "I know, but Ballern is going to attack Belldorn. I should have told Alice. Oh, gods, I should have told Alice. They're going to be here in a week, Rin."

Rin grimaced and looked to the door. "I'll do what I can. Get to Ballern and spread the word. You know who you need to talk to."

Furi knew exactly who Rin meant, but the idea of pinning her hopes on Kura left a bitter taste in her mouth.

"I know you aren't always on the best of terms, but if we're lucky, enough Skyborn will listen to you. It could reduce their numbers in the fleet."

"I'll tell who I can here," Beck said. "I'm not telling the guards in case they want to skewer us, but the others … they've seen Belldorn's hospitality up front now. Maybe they'll believe us."

"I'll return in seven days with whoever will help," Rin said. He wrapped Furi up in a hug. "It really is good to see you, Furi."

She squeezed him back, slowly accepting the idea that she needed to talk to Kura. "You too."

With that, they broke apart. And Furi knew what she had to do.

✧　✧　✧

ALICE CAME FOR her the next day, just like they'd discussed. They'd make for the Skysworn, and then Ballern. Furi had notebooks carefully organized in her backpack, along with Alice's notes she'd given her. The more time she spent in Belldorn, the more she talked to people who lived such a vastly different life from her own, the more she realized Ballern was not well.

They were halfway through the city on their way to the docks before Furi took a deep breath and said what she should have said before.

"Alice, I have something to tell you."

"Did you find more in your research?"

Furi shook her head, looking down at the smooth stones of the side-walk. "Ballern is going to attack Belldorn."

"That's hardly news," Alice said. "It's to be expected at this point."

"No, I'm not being clear. They're going to attack Belldorn in force. If the attack on Bollwerk failed, which I think we can agree it did, the plan was to send half the fleet to Belldorn."

"I'm not surprised. Things are escalating across the continent. It feels like everything is hurtling toward a deadline we can never meet. Securing Ancora and Dauschen. Rebuilding Midstream. Turning away Fel's attacks. It's all too much."

"It will be in the next week. Two at most." Furi grabbed Alice's arm. "This will be the end of the war with Belldorn, one way or another. They'll send every destroyer they have, and it won't matter if Belldorn has Porcupines at that point. The city will fall."

"Well, that certainly sounds ominous."

Furi didn't understand why Alice wasn't screaming at her at that point. Maybe it just hadn't set in yet. Of course, there was more to tell. "Rin is alive."

"Your friend from Ballern?"

Furi nodded. "He's been living with the Dragonriders. Apparently, there is a group of Skyborn with them who defected from Ballern and Belldorn, both. He's going back to recruit anyone who will fight."

"I doubt Lady Katherine will say no to any help people will offer."

Furi rubbed her hands together. "We have to get to the docks in Ballern. There's a woman there, Kura. She's almost like a mother to all the Skyborn kids. She was a friend when I was growing up, but she despises those of us who volunteer for fleet."

"I thought you said most of the Skyborn joins the military?"

"Not because they want to, Alice." Furi wondered what Ancora had been like. If they weren't forced into service there, what did they do? Did they actually get to choose their careers? But she didn't think it was quite so simple. Alice's stories of the Lowlands echoed her own time on the docks too closely for that.

"Thank you for telling me about the attack," Alice said. "You may have saved a lot of lives."

Furi blinked. "I should have told you sooner. I'm sorry."

Alice rubbed the back of her neck and grimaced. "You told me now, and that means a great deal. You have nothing to apologize for."

Furi tried to understand Alice's reasoning. Furi had hidden Ballern's plot from her, from someone she was starting to think of as a friend. That wasn't the kind of thing that was easily forgiven in Ballern. The people she knew in Ballern held grudges like their lives depended on their bitterness. The thought reminded her of Kura, and a knot of dread coiled in her stomach.

"There's something I've wanted to tell you, too," Alice said as they reached the maze of booths and shops sprawled out beneath the docks.

"But I'm afraid you won't want to help us anymore."

Furi frowned. What could possibly make Alice think that? Furi had already told her about the incoming attacks planned by Ballern. And she didn't have any regrets over that. "What is it?"

Alice was quiet as she said, "I was on the ship that shot down the destroyers."

"I'm sure a lot of people were. Those Porcupines are massive."

"No, I mean the small ship. That bombed them from above."

Furi frowned as she remembered watching the strange vessel that moved like a schooner but was better armored. And, slowly, she remembered the faces that had appeared over the railing, and the shock of red hair. The bombs that had fallen, tearing out the turrets, killing Mei and the others. That had been … Alice? But that meant her own people had been trying to kill Alice and *her* friends, and Furi ground her teeth as she realized she felt closer to Alice than anyone in Ballern who wasn't Skyborn.

"Furi? I understand if you—"

Furi held a hand up to stop her, shaking her head. "You couldn't have known. My friends died on that ship."

Alice cringed at those words.

"But we were there to kill. It's not as though our ship wasn't firing on you. It's not as though we were a peaceful envoy." Furi wanted Alice to understand she didn't hate her for that. They didn't even know each other, and it was a conflict stoked by rulers detached from the people they'd sent to die. "It was war, it *is* war, and it's horrible, but is it so hard to imagine we were both wrong?"

Alice took a deep breath as they stepped into an enclosed lift, riding it into the skies as the only sound was the whir of the motors and pulleys. She met Furi's gaze. "No. No, it's not."

When the gates opened, they exited onto the docks, and Furi looked at the small ship anchored nearby. An odd ship she'd seen before. The Skysworn.

CHAPTER TWENTY-SEVEN

SAMUEL LET OUT a long sigh when they rounded the cape at the southeastern tip of the Deadlands. Drakkar kept the shore in sight at most times, but on occasion, they'd be so far out Samuel could see nothing but the clear blues of the Southern Sea.

So long as the waters stayed calm, he didn't much care about anything else. The nauseating journey from Cave to the Spires was one he wouldn't soon forget.

"I still think it would have been easier to take an airship," Samuel said.

Drakkar steered them around a shallow reef and grinned at the Spider Knight. "Even if Pirate's Cove is not so populated as it once was, you understand they are pirates, yes? They will take what they can from the skies, including an airship. But this old boat will not be of interest to them."

Samuel shook his head and went back to studying Charles's notebooks. While many of them were filled with schematics and designs the old tinker had given up on; others were more like journals. And those were what had kept Samuel's attention. Stories from the Deadlands War. Precise accountings of the engagements Charles fought in. It was both riveting and horrifying, knowing what Charles had been capable of.

The more he read, the more he understood why the people of Cave had feared the man they once simply called Atlier. Several of Charles's inventions at the height of the Deadlands War were absolutely barbaric.

To think the same mind that invented a device to fire a twenty-foot wall of flame at enemy lines was the same mind that had sacrificed so much for the good of Ancora was hard to swallow.

And it wasn't just the invention of those devices that made Samuel's skin crawl. It was the plain, matter-of-fact accounting for the fatalities after each field test. And the old man would tweak the assemblies to make it worse. Samuel made it to the last page, a summary of the deaths of twenty-three Fel soldiers, before he tossed it aside in disgust.

Samuel had long been a Spider Knight. Had fought, had *killed*, to protect the people of Ancora. But this was different, this glimpse into Charles's wartime battles. Samuel could have never seen those writings and been all the happier for it. Nonetheless, some of them would help Jacob. He had no doubt of that.

He held the notebook with the firebombs over the water, ready to drop it into oblivion.

"Not what you wished to read?" Drakkar asked.

Samuel hesitated. "I wouldn't want Jacob to see this."

Drakkar shrugged. "It may not be so terrible. For him to see what Charles once was, versus the good he did in the world."

"It'll break his heart."

"No," Drakkar said with a smile. "There is little that will deter our friend, Samuel. I do not think he would cower from the truth of things, and I do not think you should make that decision for him."

Samuel slowly pulled the notebook back over the boat. He took a deep breath and stuffed it into his pack. Perhaps Drakkar was right. Either way, he had time to decide before they saw Jacob again.

He picked up another of the journals and re-read a passage that reminded him of the man he knew. The story of an orphan and a widow who survived the destruction of a small village not far from the Skeleton. He'd sheltered them and abandoned his post to escort them to Bollwerk.

Charles's superior officer had wanted him tried for treason after deserting his post, but Archibald put a stop to it. Archibald, who had attained the rank of Magister, but was not yet the Speaker of Bollwerk, and wouldn't be until the end of the war and the assassination of his predecessor.

The boat tilted to the side as Drakkar spun the wheel, steam billowing away as water splashed onto the boilers. "Make ready!"

Samuel looked up at Drakkar's words, turning to see what the Cave Guardian was looking at. One thing he learned the deeper they traveled into Pirate's Cove: while many of the structures along the shore had long since rusted into ruin, it wasn't entirely abandoned.

In the scraps, more than one airship waited, concealed by tarps and netting.

"Are they trying to camouflage?" Samuel asked.

"Yes, and avoid the worst of the heat. It serves two purposes. It keeps the Dragonwings at bay and is much harder to spot if any pirates decide to break the covenant of the cove."

"The what?"

"An old agreement that the cove remains neutral. It is the only way to keep the pirates from killing each other. Or was, in older times. Pirates are a bit more civil now, what with those like Mary and Smith in the skies."

Samuel arched an eyebrow. He tried to get more information out of Drakkar, but the Cave Guardian would say no more about Mary and Smith.

"It is not my story to tell. Ask them the next time you see them." Drakkar pointed off to two short towers in the northeast. "If the old lab is still here, that is where we will find it."

Samuel grumbled and stuffed the last of Charles's notebooks into his pack.

"And Samuel," Drakkar said. "This area has long been outside the rule of law. Trust nothing."

✧ ✧ ✧

THE FARTHER INTO the cove they traveled, Samuel started to understand what had once been there. The wreckage of old fishing vessels littered the shore in places, flanked by collapsed piers. But beyond that, he could make out the ruins of waterfront villages, long since lost to time.

As the shoreline curved in, the ruins revealed more of themselves. And some, though they might have once been ruins, had been restored with care. The architecture reminded Samuel of the Skeleton—all sharp lines and harsh edges and too much glass—but here, modern stonework and brick mosaics swallowed the buildings' bones.

Drakkar slowed the boat, angling for a deep inlet beneath a cliff. It hadn't looked high at first, dwarfed by the Dragonwing Mountains in the distance, but the closer they got, the higher it loomed, finally hiding their view of anything beyond.

"Are we going to have to climb that?" Samuel asked.

"No, we are going underground. Last time I was here, the Stone Dogs were more of a threat than any man."

"Great," Samuel muttered. "Why did I agree to come here again?"

Drakkar smiled at the Spider Knight before stepping away from the wheel and picking up a length of rope. The Cave Guardian slowly steered the ship into the shadows, where it took Samuel's eyes a moment to adjust. Samuel couldn't follow the quick motion Drakkar used to tie their boat off to a wooden piling. Drakkar fastened another rope to a cleat and then shut the engine down.

Samuel followed Drakkar onto a stone platform that served as a dock. He glanced up and his steps slowed. Above them sat the remains of a great avalanche, as though a peak from the Dragonwing Mountains had collapsed onto the city.

The more he studied the random piles of rubble and decayed iron-wood trees, the more he was convinced that was exactly what had happened.

"Avalanche?" Samuel asked.

Drakkar shook his head. "The story long told here is that one of the bombs that destroyed the Skeleton buried this city too."

"A bomb brought down a mountain? How is that even possible?"

"Big bomb."

Samuel glanced at Drakkar, finding a broad grin on the Cave Guardian's face. "Still technically an avalanche, though. You have to give me that."

Drakkar inclined his head, leading the way to a set of narrow stairs. When they reached the top, Samuel froze. Pirate's Cove wasn't sunken deep underground like Cave and the outpost beneath the Sea of Salt. Instead, it was carved into the very rock of the fallen mountain; a jagged stone as large as the Lowlands themselves towered over them.

A handful of old buildings had survived, or been restored to some degree, and the effect was jarring. Stonework sat beside open-air towers protected by little more than canvas tarps and thick rope. But other sections were clad in iron, rusted by salt and water, but looking no less secure for it.

Closer to where they stood, a shadow moved. A person, Samuel thought, but as soon as he'd noticed the shadow, they were gone again.

"Be on your guard," Drakkar said.

They passed a small bar, bottles lining the shelves behind it as a bartender wiped down a series of glasses. It meant he'd either recently had more patrons than the one drunken sailor currently sitting in the corner, or he rarely washed the barware.

Either thought made Samuel shiver.

The bartender glanced up, frowning at Samuel before offering a nod to Drakkar.

Drakkar returned the gesture, and they continued on.

They started up a long ramp that wound back and forth before leaving the pair standing before a squat square building, an armored pod Samuel had seen from below. So close to it, he realized each pod was much larger than he'd thought. At least as broad as Bat's home. *His* home, he corrected himself. And some two stories tall.

Something skittered across the ground and vanished into a shadowy hole near the door.

"What was that?" Samuel hadn't gotten a good look at it.

"I believe it was a Stone Dog," Drakkar said, as casually as if a Pill-Bug had strolled across their path.

Samuel stifled a shiver.

Drakkar reached out to the door.

"What are you doing?" Samuel hissed.

"Going into the workshop, of course."

"That's where the Stone Dog went!"

"Yes, as I said. Look where you step."

"You never told me to look where I step," Samuel grumbled. But his irritation was soon forgotten as he crossed the threshold behind the Cave Guardian.

Samuel froze when he stepped inside. This was not a building left abandoned, rusting away beneath a layer of salt. The chime of a small hammer on metal, steady and deliberate, greeted them.

"Someone's here," Samuel whispered.

"Obviously," Drakkar said. "Now, announce yourself lest we find ourselves dead."

"Hello!" Samuel shouted.

The rhythmic hammering paused and then continued. "What is it?" someone called.

"We're, umm, we're looking for the old workshop of Charles von Atlier?"

"Is that a question or a statement?"

Samuel grew flustered at the question, but Drakkar appeared to be highly amused.

The Cave Guardian stepped deeper into the workshop. "I apologize for my friend's wavering resolve. We seek the history of the work done on Biomechs here."

The hammering stopped entirely. Something squeaked before a heavy thunk sounded on the stone floor. A small man who looked old enough to be Charles's father rounded the corner, switching out a lens over his eye to better study his visitors.

"Ah! Master Spider Knight. I wondered if you had survived the battle in Ancora."

"Do I know you?" Samuel asked.

The old tinker's smile wrinkled his face. "No." He turned to Drakkar and held out a fist. Drakkar placed his hand over it.

"For the Steamsworn."

"For the good of all."

"Now, what are you prattling on about? Looking for Charles's work?" He barked out a laugh. "Young sir, I *am* Charles's work."

Samuel stepped around the wall and gawked at what waited there. The old tinker was missing a hand. Well, that wasn't entirely accurate. His hand was mounted in a metal vise while the tinker replaced a series of bolts and joints.

"They get squeaky after a while. It's worse here by the sea, but I always said I'd die by the waters, and I intend to do just that."

"You're a Biomech," Samuel said.

The old tinker glanced at Drakkar. "Not the brightest Spider Knight I ever met. Rather think I'm more fond of Bessie."

"You know Bessie?" Samuel asked, confusion pulling at his thoughts.

"Aye. I know your friend Jacob too. Met him beneath the Highlands. He asked me to evacuate the people in the catacombs, he did."

Samuel slowly put the pieces together in his mind. This man must have been underground with him and Bessie when he was knocked unconscious. But as he tried to understand the timeline of what had happened underneath the streets of Ancora, a Stone Dog shot out from under a workbench.

"Look out!" Samuel screeched, trying to draw his sword, but cracking it against the wall instead.

He stared down at the spiny-backed creature, wide black eyes studying him as thick claws pinched at the air.

The old tinker clucked his tongue, and the Stone Dog retreated, climbing up the tinker's leg until it finally came to a rest on his shoulder.

Samuel stared in horror.

"They aren't so bad once they get used to you. Don't want to startle them, though, young sir. That's a good way to get dead."

"Oh, he is well aware of that," Drakkar said. "I once had to drag him out of a nest."

"Unconscious?"

Drakkar nodded.

"Seems you lose your mind quite a lot, young Spider Knight."

Samuel spluttered.

The old tinker scratched the Stone Dog between the eyes. The long quills on the creature's back shivered and lowered until it looked more like a disfigured crab than a monster. The old tinker held his arm out. The Stone Dog scurried down it, leaping onto the workbench before vanishing into another hole.

"Now, you find Stone Dogs in the wild, don't hesitate to put them down. Bad way to die, that. Bad way to die. But here, you're safe. Now, if you knew Charles, you must have stories about him. Come, tell me what you know of the man called Atlier. And if I like your stories, and you help me with this hand, perhaps I'll tell you some of what I know too."

Samuel and Drakkar exchanged a glance. Samuel wondered if this strange man was what they were looking for. Or if he would be a distraction to keep them from helping their friends.

Time would tell.

CHAPTER TWENTY-EIGHT

J ACOB STOOD ON the edge of the lift platform as it lowered from the supply ship. It was a beautiful view above Midstream, the small homes and taller groundwork for buildings of industry spread out before him. Worn mountains dotted the horizon, and a few rose close to the southern edge of Midstream.

"Not a view we often get," George said, smiling at Gladys.

The princess was quiet, watching the city rise from below.

Jacob's grip tightened on the cable in his hand when the airship rocked. He looked to the north. Far in the distance, he could make out more foothills and the wandering shadows of two Fire Lizards. He listened to the ship's captain shout back and forth with the crew, returning his gaze to the earth below.

Another minute and sand billowed out from beneath the lift. Jacob hopped into the pilot's seat for the Titan Mech arm. "Hold on!" he yelled when some of the Midstream crew started to board the lift.

He saw George ushering the men back, leading them away from crates filled with traps. Gladys trailed behind, sparing a glance and wave to give Jacob the all-clear.

Jacob pulled the firing knob below the levers that controlled the arm. Flames erupted from the sides, boiling the water in the closed system in moments. He waited for the pressure to rise high enough before swinging the arm around, careful to keep away from several onlookers. He couldn't help but smile at a few of the shocked faces.

Jacob and Frederick had replaced the rail car with the treads of a crawler for Midstream's arm. It allowed the entire system to rotate in place, and Jacob almost wished they'd included the same option on the other arms. He'd mentioned it to Frederick, but the other tinker had only shaken his head, rightly pointing out that treads would do no good on a train track.

The hand of the Titan Mech slid neatly beneath two pallets, each stacked high with traps. Jacob shook the arm slightly to make sure the load was properly secured and then took a deep breath. He pushed the lever for both tracks forward, and the arm lurched before settling into a steady forward motion.

Jacob had been worried about the sand, and whether he'd been right to choose crawler treads, considering the added weight. Relief washed over him when the sand churned up around the treads, and the entire assembly continued on.

He set the first two pallets near the dry riverbed. Tempted as he was to drive into the empty bed, he was in no rush to awaken any Tail Swords hidden in the sand. He shifted the steering levers again, spinning the arm around, and digging it into the sand.

Jacob looked over the side of his seat and cursed, afraid the treads had gotten too deep. But when he pushed both levers forward, the treads dug themselves out with little effort. He repeated the same trip until all the pallets were unloaded, leaving stacks of traps near the riverbed.

The last loads were bundles of steel and iron. Plates and rivets and enough material to raise a simple floating dock. Jacob overheard George talking to a member of the construction crew. She didn't look happy, but Jacob only heard her say something about not having nearly enough supplies.

"Another ship is coming," George said. "This is only to get started."

The annoyance on her face lessened as George explained the situation. Gladys signaled the captain of the supply ship when Jacob was clear, and the lift slowly rose back into the sky.

"Jacob!" George shouted. "I would be most appreciative if you could show Helena how to operate the arm."

"Why are you so kind to an Ancoran?" Helena asked.

"He's my friend," Gladys said, cutting off whatever response George had readied. "And his friends have saved my life more than once. You will treat him as well as you would treat me, if not better." She tacked on that last part in a flat voice.

Helena flinched as though she'd been struck. "Of course, My Princess. I did not realize."

Jacob looked away, his eyes landing on anything except the awkward exchange.

"Jacob," George called out again. "Show Helena how to dig pits first. I believe that should be our priority over the docks themselves."

He nodded and scooted into the copilot's seat. The arm could be operated from either position, but the copilot had easier access to reposition the arm, while the pilot's seat provided ready access to the levers controlling the treads.

Helena sighed as she made her way to the arm. Piercing brown eyes met Jacob's, and he gave the older woman a smile. A tight braid swung behind her head as she climbed into the pilot's seat. "Alright, show me how to run this contraption. George seems to think it will save us time, but that usually means I end up with extra work."

"It'll help you with the reconstruction," Jacob said. "I've seen it in Dauschen on the docks Archibald is building. They're sending another arm to Ancora too. The controls are just like a crawler."

"I've never piloted a crawler."

Jacob shrugged. "No problem. The left lever moves the left tread, and the right moves the right tread. Move them both in the direction you want to go, or opposite directions to spin."

"Spin?" Helena asked incredulously.

"Well, spin slowly," Jacob said with a laugh. "Maybe turn would be a better word. Let's take it to the edge of the riverbed."

Helena sighed and grabbed the steering levers, gently pushing them forward. The treads were smooth in the sand, and Helena was much kinder on the controls than Jacob. He explained how to turn while moving by adjusting the appropriate tread speed, and Helena deftly circled a large stone before coming to a stop beside a pallet.

"It is easier than I expected."

Jacob nodded. "The arm is a bit more complicated, but it's the same idea." He pointed to a dark bronze wheel. "This opens and closes the hand while the levers to either side raise or lower it. The slide across the top moves everything on a plane. The smaller levers here that are joined by another handle? These release the ratchet, which allows the wheel to rotate the arm instead of opening it. Watch."

The hand opened and closed with barely a sound, but the engine roared to life when Jacob moved the slide to swing the arm out over the riverbed. A few spins and pulls later, and the Titan Mech arm plunged into the sandy bed.

"Probably be easier if we stay on the edge of the bed. Those larger rocks could cause problems with the traps." Jacob twisted the arm, flexing the wrist until it raised a scoop of sand and pebbles into the air that would have taken hours for someone to dig by hand. Another round, and a pit large enough to hold a trap was ready.

Jacob used the Titan Mech hand to pluck a trap off the pallet and set it into the hole. He hopped off the arm and gestured for Helena to follow. In the pit, he showed her how to attach the lever and release the safety. The latticework rose as he pumped the chambers full of air. He'd been concerned about the intake pulling too much sand, but the filter

Frederick had added worked better than Jacob had hoped.

"And now we just have to bury it," Jacob said. "What did that take? Fifteen minutes? And you'll be faster than I am with some practice."

Back on the arm, he let Helena take over and settled into the copilot's seat. He was happy to see how fast she acclimated to the controls. A sign they were intuitive, and the arm could be controlled by those who weren't tinkers themselves. She buried the first trap and dug two more holes.

Jacob watched, offering little advice. Helena followed every step he'd shown her, a precision to everything she did. He could see why George wanted her to learn how to operate the arm. If she was as good at training people as she was at learning, Midstream would have a perimeter defense by the end of the day.

Jacob yawned and lost count of what hole Helena was on. He'd taken to watching the pressure gauges on the arm and making small adjustments to give the fingers more strength. If he hadn't been watching them so closely, he wouldn't have seen the sand shift. Wouldn't have noticed the glint of something dark in the pit a moment before something exploded from its depths.

"Tail Sword!" Jacob shouted.

Two Midstream workers sprinted away from the pallets as the curved arch of the Tail Sword's stinger lashed out.

"We have to run!" Helena hesitated. "I have no weapon!"

"Move," Jacob said, leaning across her as the Tail Sword stalked toward them. He slammed the lever down in an attempt to crush the Tail Sword, the same as he'd done to the assassins in Dauschen, but the Tail Sword was too quick. The beast might have been some ten feet in length, but it moved terrifyingly fast.

Jacob forced the steering levers in opposite directions, spinning the open Titan Mech hand to the side like an angry slap. This time it caught the Tail Sword, sending it reeling into the riverbed. But the angle was all wrong as it charged them again, and Jacob's heart sank.

Helena wasn't armed, and he'd left his air cannon back by the pallets. Maybe if he could …

The Tail Sword's leg came down, and Jacob recoiled when the entire body of the creature ruptured, spraying gore and viscera across the sands. It took him a second to realize what had happened, and Helena apparently realized it at the same time.

"It stepped on a trap."

One of the heavy bolts thunked down into the sand beside them a moment later. With that kind of delay, Jacob had little doubt the traps would be more than a match for an armored crawler. He grinned at Helena, a half-mad chuckle escaping his lips.

"The hell is wrong with you, boy?"

"A lot," Gladys said, startling Jacob when she appeared at his side, aiming his air cannon at the black carapace. She pulled the trigger, the boom echoing over the Titan Mech's engine, and pulping the Tail Sword further. "Just to be safe."

"That's enough for now," Helena said. "I want a guard out here in case anymore Tail Swords pop up. We may not be so lucky next time."

And Jacob knew she was right. There was luck involved in that Tail Sword stepping on a trap. If it hadn't, they might have been able to escape on the arm. But it's possible it could have run them down. It would have been a stupid way to die.

"Come on," Gladys said. "Let's get you two some food. And I'm sure George is going to want a word with you after that."

Jacob glanced up and found the royal guard standing at a distance, his arms crossed. It wasn't quite as intimidating as his mother's glare could be, but he suspected Gladys was quite right.

CHAPTER TWENTY-NINE

JACOB SAT DOWN at a low table beside Helena, crossing his legs beneath it in a far less graceful fashion than the Midstream folks. He wasn't used to sitting on the floor without chairs, and his instinct to slouch was met with a constant thwack across his back from Gladys.

"We don't slouch at a royal table."

"Sorry," Jacob whispered.

Gladys kept a straight face for all of ten seconds before bursting into laughter.

"This isn't a royal table, is it?" Jacob asked.

George gave a half shrug. "Technically, any table where royalty sits is considered royal. But no, my dining room is not a royal table."

"So this *is* your house."

"I told you it was," Gladys said.

"You also told me it was some kind of royal … royal … what did you call it?"

"It's my house," George said. "Or, it will be when the construction is done. Most of our belongings are still in the dwellings behind The Fish Head in Bollwerk. Now, enjoy your meal. I am afraid not all the news today is good."

With that ominous warning, Jacob took a rice ball from the offered platter. It was heavily seasoned, with dried fish in the center. Fish in the middle of the desert felt like a luxury in itself. A strange slaw, a bit too crunchy to be entirely vegetables, was served as a side dish. But the flavor was pleasant and complemented the saltiness of the rice balls well.

"I missed these," Gladys said, sinking her teeth into a rice ball. "You should put them on the menu at The Fish Head."

"Perhaps," George said. "I am not sure how well the people of Bollwerk would respond to such fiery spice."

"Take it to Ancora, then," Jacob said. "Because I love it."

"Now that's an idea!" Gladys said. "We could open a restaurant in every city."

George took a deep breath. "We can discuss that at length after Midstream has been rebuilt. I think it would be rather nice to open a restaurant in our own city."

Gladys nodded at that.

"That would be wonderful," Helena said. "It is too long a journey to Bollwerk for one of your meals. I have missed these."

They moved on to dessert, a crispy fritter in a sweet cream sauce. Jacob had tried something similar back at The Fish Head, but this one had more texture, more chunks.

"You like the Stone Dog?" Gladys asked.

Jacob recoiled. "It's poison?"

"Yes," Gladys said flatly. "I'm eating poison."

George gave a slow laugh. "They must be boiled to be prepared. The poison breaks down in heat. And you are left with a sweet flavor."

Getting over his initial revulsion, Jacob took another bite. "Well, whatever it is, it's delicious."

"To the matter I am concerned with." George wiped his hands down and took a sip of his drink. "We have been watching the passes on the edge of the desert. In the north, our scouts have made some disturbing discoveries. Fel has been deploying forces along the edge of their territory."

"How far south?" Helena asked.

"The border of the grasslands. They are amassing a concerning number in the pass to the north. Should they decide to march on Midstream, they need only cross the edge of the smallest foothills and dunes. Archibald sent a pair of clippers to take stock of what awaits farther to the west."

"What of the crawlers?" Gladys asked.

George nodded. "Several armored crawlers were spotted. They will make short work of the terrain between Fel and Midstream. I can only hope the traps will be enough to slow them."

George glanced at the clock, slowly ticking away the seconds. "Archibald should be contacting us shortly." He sat a small copper box on the table. Jacob had seen its like before, a transmitter and speaker built into one unit.

So not so much a lunch break, Jacob thought. George wanted everyone at his house, in a private setting, so they could talk to Archibald.

"Does Archibald plan to send us a warship?" Gladys asked. "We have a chance against a ground invasion, but that won't stop them from bombing us."

"The traps can take down a smaller airship," Jacob said. "If they're low enough."

"That is more of an uncertainty than I care to entertain," George said.

The speaker on the table hissed and clicked before Archibald's voice sounded around them. "George, this is Archibald."

George clicked the transmitter. "We are here, Speaker."

"Who is with you?"

"Gladys, Jacob, and Helena."

"Good. I don't have much positive to share. Fel has gathered a squadron of airships near the Red Woods. They can flank you easily enough. I'm sending two destroyers to flank them first, but Fel is also moving toward Dauschen via the North Woods."

"You do not intend to send one of the warships here?" George asked.

"Not at first. Warship One is moving past Dauschen now. If we can turn back Fel's squadron before they cross the river, I'll give the order to make for Midstream."

"And if not?"

"Dauschen will be lost," Archibald said in a simple statement of fact. "And you'll be left fighting with two destroyers and whatever you can muster."

George held a hand up when Gladys leaned toward the transmitter, looking like she was about to chew Archibald's arm off. She paused, took a deep breath, and nodded.

Gladys pressed the transmitter. "Tell your destroyers to drive the airships low. Jacob's traps may be of more use than just defending against the ground troops."

"It will be done." Archibald hesitated. "Should things go poorly, it would be wise to have a plan of escape."

"We've run long enough," Gladys said. "From Fel and warlords and every city who has come for us. Fel will remember this day."

"How long do we have?" George asked.

"From the time they start moving, only a couple hours. Gods only know when that will be."

"It'll be soon," Jacob said. "They're in the open now. They won't want to give us more time to prepare."

"He's likely right," Archibald said. "Prepare yourselves. I hope to speak to you again soon. And when the battle comes closer, use code names. It will at least delay comprehension of the message should it be intercepted."

The static over the connection went dead.

Gladys stared at the transmitter. "I thought we'd have more time."

Helena stood up. "I'll be setting traps. You best tell the guard what's coming."

George started to answer, but Gladys interrupted. "I will. We'll be ready."

✧   ✧   ✧

HOURS PASSED, AND Jacob thought he might collapse as they mounted the last trap from the second pallet to a crawler. It was George's idea. Make them mobile, like a ballista, only far more maneuverable. Whatever required less digging, Jacob was all for it.

The arm moved things along, but they quickly realized they'd have to bury some by hand if they wished to be done by sunset. He'd only helped dig two holes and wouldn't have been surprised if he fell over dead in the blistering sun. He made his way back to George's house later in the evening, surprised to find Gladys there.

"I thought you'd be rallying your troops."

"My troops are my friends and family, Jacob. There are only a few hundred of us in Midstream. I'm not sure what we can do against Fel."

"I'd rather fight Fel than a wall of Red Death. Maybe they'll run away when they hit the traps."

Gladys blew out a breath. "Have you talked to Alice?"

Jacob shook his head. "Not in a couple days now. Do you think George would mind if I used his transmitter?"

"Not at all. Well, honestly, he probably would, but if I'm telling you to use it, there's not much argument, right?"

Jacob grinned as Gladys pulled the small copper box off the table and sat down on the couch. She handed it over, lifting the lid to expose the dials inside. Jacob spun the two around until he was on the Skysworn's frequency. If anyone knew where to find Alice, it would be Mary.

He clicked the transmitter. "Skysworn, are you there?" Jacob waited and was about to click the button again when the speaker crackled to life.

"Is that you, Jacob?"

"Alice?" He asked. "What are you doing on the Skysworn?"

"What am *I* doing on the Skysworn? What are *you* doing on the transmitter?"

In the background, he heard Mary complaining that they weren't using code names.

"Right, sorry," Alice said.

"I'm with … the princess out in the desert. Helping build some defenses."

"Of course you are," Alice said. "Do you ever do anything that might *not* get you killed? That would be nice to hear sometime."

Gladys pushed the button. "Hello! He's assisting us. I think the rebuilding is going to go a lot faster now that we have one of those arms."

"Arms?" Alice asked.

"It's part of a Titan Mech, like we found in the notes."

"You got it working already?"

"Well, just an arm. But I had a lot of help."

Alice was silent for a time. "I can imagine who would want to help."

"So what have you been doing?" Jacob asked, feeling like the question was incredibly lame.

"Well, I made a new friend from Ballern. It's possible we shot her ship down in the desert …"

"What?" Jacob tried to wrap his head around that statement. "One of the destroyers we brought down?"

"Yes, she's here. Say hi."

Jacob exchanged a mortified glance with Gladys. "What do I even say to that?"

"I don't know," Gladys said. "I didn't shoot her out of the sky."

Jacob groaned and clicked the transmitter. "Hi?"

"Hello."

There was a bit of shuffling before Alice's voice came back on the line. "Okay, bad idea. That was awkward. Anyhow, did you know that in Ballern they refer to the kids who live on the docks as Skyborn? It's like how the Highlands call us Steamborn in Ancora. I thought that rather interesting.

"We've been in the library at Belldorn. Oh, Jacob, you simply *have* to see it. More books than I imagined existed. But, we discovered some inconsistencies in the history of the Ballern and Belldorn conflict. So we're going to Ballern to clear some things up."

"You're … what?" Jacob asked. "Mary is flying you to *Ballern?*"

"She'll be safe," Mary said. "Likely safer than you two have been in the past month."

Jacob grimaced at that. He didn't like it, even if it might be true. "But we don't know anything about Ballern."

A long sigh came across the line. Alice again. "Jacob. I'll be with Furi. She's lived on the docks for years. And if that's not enough to stop you from worrying, I did confirm our captain and her first mate were pirates."

Jacob heard Mary squawk something before the transmission cut out. He took a deep breath. Worried as he was, heaping that onto Alice right then wasn't going to do anyone any good. He clicked the transmitter.

"Sorry. I just worry sometimes."

Gladys twiddled her thumbs, avoiding the awkward exchange altogether. She was probably the smartest one in the room.

"We all do," Mary said. "But you know this has to be done."

Did it, though? He wondered. Was their time better spent learning more about the past, or helping their allies who were alive right then? Perhaps splitting up had been the best solution. Alice could dig, and Jacob could help Midstream fortify itself against Fel. And perhaps that, more than anything, was what had his nerves on edge.

He debated telling them at all, but he knew they'd find out soon enough.

"I have more to tell you. Fel is organizing outside of Midstream. Archibald suspects an attack. I can't say more over the transmitter."

"Bad timing," Mary said. "We can't turn back now. I already have contacts expecting us."

"I don't want you to turn back." He glanced at Gladys. "We're preparing, but it's going to be rough."

"Jacob?" Alice said. "Jacob, you get the princess and get the hell out of there."

"I can't. She's made her choice, and I won't leave her."

Only static answered for a time until Alice spoke again. "Be careful."

"You too."

"We'll get there when we can," Mary said. "But it'll be a day at least."

"Understood."

Jacob sighed and hung his head as they disconnected. He looked to Gladys. "We better get back to the traps."

CHAPTER THIRTY

Furi sank back into her notebook. She'd copied a great many passages from books published in both cities. But it was still the excerpts from *The Failed Treatise and the Third War* that sent shivers down her spine. Published in Ballern, but it had made its way to the great library at Belldorn.

Furi looked up from her book when the Skysworn lurched to the side.

Mary cursed and wiped at her pants. "Of all the things Jacob has invented, he should really invent a lid for these damn cups."

Smith's voice came over the horn, tinny and barely hiding his amusement. "If you need a lid, I am sure I can make one for you."

Mary glared at the horn while Alice and Furi exchanged a grin.

"You know what's odd?" Furi asked.

"If you tell me you have lids in Ballern, so help me," Mary muttered.

"No, no. Well, I mean, we do, but that's not what I was going to say. I've been reading *The Dead Scourge*, and it talks about the history leading up to the war, but there's no mention of the labor camps Belldorn used to hold prisoners."

"Labor camps?" Alice asked. "I've never heard of that."

"When I still had a teacher, her grandmother had been in one. And she wasn't a follower of the Children of the Dark Fire, so I can't see why she would have lied about it."

"I've heard of them," Mary said. "Mines mostly, so they only needed to guard the entrances. And they weren't humane. More than a few prisoners died in those camps."

Furi nodded. "Those who escaped back to Ballern told terrible accounts. If it wasn't the guards beating them, it was their own friends killing them for scraps of food. Some starved to death. Others died where they stood, pickaxes in hand."

"That's horrible," Alice said. "Why wouldn't that be in Archibald's book?"

"He may not have known," Mary said. "You'll find Belldorn enjoys remembering the best of itself. And the less savory things, well, those are often forgotten or polished away into a footnote."

"How did you know about it?"

Mary glanced back at Alice. "Well, that's a rather long story."

The horn beside Mary squawked to life. "Because she is a pirate at heart, Alice. And because you learn the worst parts of a place when you are smuggling."

"Do you have the chainguns primed?" Mary asked, redirecting the conversation. "We're heading for Midstream after we drop this cargo off."

Smith grunted, an odd sound over the horn. "I heard you, Mary. We'll get there in time. Have faith."

Mary rolled her eyes.

"Mary," Alice said. "What cargo are you smuggling exactly?"

"Pill-Bug eggs."

"You must be joking!" Furi said. "All four barrels?"

"Yes," Mary said.

"Pill-Bug eggs?" Alice asked. "That's … that seems somewhat disappointing on the scale of things pirates might transport."

Mary chuckled. "They've been outlawed in Ballern for decades. Classified as an agricultural parasite."

"That's ridiculous," Alice said. "I raised them with my mom for years, and we never had a problem."

"I heard they ate an entire crop of cabbages one year," Furi said.

Alice shook her head. "They eat dead things. The only way they're going to eat an entire crop of cabbages is if the cabbages were already rotting."

Furi shrugged.

"Well," Mary said. "Whatever happened, they're a delicacy now."

Alice pinched the bridge of her nose. "So you're a smuggler? Who transports *food*?"

Mary grinned. "Sometimes. Other times we transport fugitives like you and Jacob."

Alice shrank back into her chair a bit at that. "Right. Well, that's different. I think. What did you do that you ended up owing Archibald?"

"Archibald?" Furi asked.

Alice nodded. "They owed him a debt, and he owned the ship until they paid it or something."

Smith barked out a laugh over the horn. "You may as well tell them. Our debt is paid."

Mary's fingers strangled the lever in her hand. "Archibald. It was a long time ago. When we knew less about the world than we do now. We smuggled old textbooks into Ballern."

"Books?" Alice said. "I'm rather impressed, and somehow disappointed."

"Among other things," Smith said. "Remember that barrel of explosives?"

"Smith," Mary said with a warning edge to her voice.

"That airship crashed before we even left the docks. Should have timed the fuse better."

But Furi didn't care about what else Mary and Smith had done. She wanted other answers. "Where did you deliver the books? For who? I've never heard a story about illegal texts before."

Mary crossed her arms. "An ostracized teacher. She took care of some of the dock kids. We didn't know much more than that. It's easier to hide your trail the less you know."

Furi narrowed her eyes. "What was her name?"

"Kathy, I think?" Mary said. "Did you know her?"

Smith laughed over the horn. "*Kathy?* How many loads did we deliver to her, Mary? Her name was Kura."

An electric chill bolted down Furi's spine. Kura, the same woman who had sheltered her as a kid? Surely not. It couldn't be. Why would she have known smugglers? *Pirates!* But the more she pondered that question, the more she remembered the small gatherings in cargo holds and the floating warehouse they used to meet in for story time.

But that was the answer. The warehouse was the only place Furi ever saw Kura with a book in her hand. Hidden away in the clouds where no one but the maintenance crews would ever tread, and those crews were more loyal to the Skyborn than they were to the crown.

"Furi?" Alice asked. "Are you okay?"

Furi blinked rapidly, willing away tears as she gained a new perspective on the care Kura had given her and the others. The risks she must have taken. "Kura was like a mother to me growing up. She gave you money?"

Mary nodded. "Quite a bit of it."

"She could have used it for food, or a home. For herself. She used to feed me and Rin and some others. Most of the Skyborn ate at charity kitchens. You know the type, funded by some good Samaritans? I always thought the monarchy only allowed them to operate so they didn't have to clean up the corpses from the docks."

Furi didn't miss Alice's cringe. And she thought she knew why. They probably had the same kind of thing in Ancora, where it sounded like the divide between the rulers and the common folk was just as severe.

"Kura is why I can read Mokuskrit, Alice. She taught us everything we knew. Reading, writing, history, all of it."

Mary nodded along to Furi's story. "Kura told us you didn't have schools in Ballern."

"That was only half of it," Furi said. "The Skyborn didn't have schools. We weren't allowed to attend school. Who would be the cog if they knew they could be more?"

"The Butcher did much the same in Ancora," Smith said. "Although I would say he was more subtle about it."

"Smith's right," Alice said. "We still had schools, at least. But I was raised to believe if I worked hard enough, I could be one of those living behind the walls of the Highlands. But the divide is too great, and the gatekeepers too many. That was never meant to be my world."

Furi reached out and squeezed Alice's arm, but jerked back a moment later. It wasn't the kind of gesture you gave to someone who was your enemy, who had shot you out of the sky. But Alice was something more. Furi felt like Alice was a mirror of her time in Ballern, like she could have been Alice if she'd grown up in Ancora instead.

And now, now she'd seen the books in the library at Belldorn. The truth of her city's past could never be taken from her mind. But that meant the monarchy of Ballern was an enemy to the people of Ballern. It meant she didn't have a reason to run from Alice and the others when they reached the city. Because she knew, in her heart, the city she had known was only a waking dream.

✧ ✧ ✧

ALICE HUNKERED DOWN behind the hidden panel in the Skysworn's supply hold. A few cracks of light and Furi's breathing were all that told her the world still existed outside. They'd waited until the last minute to slip into the smuggling hold.

Furi argued that Alice didn't need to hide with her because no one in Ballern would know who she was. But Mary disagreed. She didn't want anyone knowing either of them had come from the Skysworn. She thought it would be safer for everyone that way, and Alice rather agreed.

A door slammed open nearby, the handle cracking against the wall twice. That was their signal. Mary's customer was here. Muffled voices sounded in the cargo hold, and Alice held her breath. One voice rose higher, anger plain to hear, but Alice couldn't make out the words behind the wood and steel of their bolt-hole.

Something scraped along the ground and thudded outside. Alice grabbed Furi's arm on instinct alone, squeezing it to choke back her own rising panic. Again the scraping came, louder this time until it faded. When it came the third time, Alice realized someone was moving the cargo.

She released Furi's arm and waited until a knock sounded on the wall. Only then did she undo a simple bolt on her right and push the door open. The dim light was blinding after an hour in the darkness, and her legs threatened to cramp as she straightened out.

"All clear," Smith said.

"What was that arguing about?"

Smith shrugged. "Apparently, they didn't want four barrels. Something about not being able to sell them before they went bad. Or hatched." A slow smile crept over Smith's face. "Mary changed their minds."

The door to the cargo hold opened, and Mary stepped inside. "They're gone. You two are in the clear. Smith and I will gather a few supplies, and then we're heading to Midstream." She flipped a small copper box to Alice.

Alice caught it and frowned at the warm metal. "A transmitter?"

"Best we have. It'll reach Bollwerk from Ballern without an antenna. You may have to wait until night to reach us if we're too far out. The signal travels farther then."

"We can catch a supply ship," Furi said.

"Hold on to it anyway," Mary said. "In case you can't. Better to be prepared than dead."

Furi didn't argue that point.

"Lead the way," Alice said, throwing a small pack over her shoulder.

Furi adjusted her own and took a deep breath.

"Be careful, you two," Mary said. "I expect to hear all about your escapades. And I'm sure Jacob will be anxious to hear from you."

Alice hesitated and then hugged Smith and Mary before opening the door for Furi. What waited beyond—the sprawl of soaring airship docks to dwarf those of Bollwerk against a cloudy blue sky—took her breath away. Far below them was a city that looked like another world.

Graceful arches and spires soared closest to the docks, but even those were left well below the lowest levels and ships. The more Alice looked around, the more out of place she felt. This was no airship dock. This was a city above the city.

Huge tanks sat at regular intervals, massive pipes flowing from them and into them, terminating in small shacks and open-air bars set up all along the dock. At the edges, protected by a mesh Alice suspected served multiple purposes, gas chambers large enough for a destroyer floated, stabilizing the docks on the few anchors and lifts that connected them to the earth.

When Alice thought of the docks at Bollwerk, she thought of the rust and dirt and oil that crusted everything around the airships. Like a floating tinker's workshop with traces of use at every corner. But here in Ballern, no rust showed on the sprawling docks. It looked more like they had been painted, even sanded and waxed in some areas.

"Come on," Furi said, taking a right as they left the Skysworn.

Alice followed, looking over the railings at two levels of schooners, clippers, and private ships docked below them. Their current walkway split every hundred feet, creating a U-shaped dock for a bevy of trading vessels. On the ends, larger supply ships waited, while above them, like a floating shield, sat the destroyers and warships of Ballern.

One thing Alice realized, despite their quick pace across the walkways, was that Ballern had far more destroyers than what they'd seen near Bollwerk. They outnumbered the fleet she'd seen in Belldorn, and she suspected the only reason Ballern hadn't conquered Belldorn ages ago was due to superior firepower. One destroyer against a Porcupine would never have a chance.

"This place is amazing," Alice said. "It's … honestly, it's nicer than the Lowlands."

"Really?" Furi asked, glancing back as they skirted one of many large gas chambers. She waved to a cook working a wide griddle who held up a spatula in greeting.

Furi lowered her voice. "We need to be careful. Anyone who knows I was stationed on the Nightingale could raise an alarm."

The thought pulled Alice back into the present. Thoughts of scraping by in the Lowlands fled when she remembered how much of a risk they were taking. What would happen if the authorities in Ballern realized they had a spy in their midst? Alice doubted she'd have to worry about *that* for long. It was a sobering thought.

A long walkway extended out over nothing behind the gas chamber. Alice wasn't afraid of heights so much, but as the steel trembled beneath her boots, her heart leaped a little faster. There were no lights on the narrow path, no bars or restaurants or dock workers gathered.

"No one comes to the edge," Furi said. "If you ever need to move through the docks undetected, you take the Bones."

"The Bones?"

Furi tapped on the walkway with her foot, drawing Alice's eye back to the grate under their feet. "The way they rattle like an old ghost story. We call them the Bones."

Alice shivered and looked away as the edge of a low fog bank drifted in beneath them. She wasn't sure if the opaque vision made it better or worse. She pulled her pack tighter against her shoulders and stayed close to Furi.

"Not far now." Furi grabbed a ladder that shifted with the levels of the docks until the angle was nearly past 100 degrees.

Alice grabbed the cold metal, slicked with condensation. She didn't look down after that. Just followed Furi's boots from rung to rung until they mercifully reached stable footing again.

"Kura lives here," Furi said.

"On the Bones?" Alice asked.

Furi nodded and tapped the side of a metal hut. "These are the nicer ones. For years, I lived in one made from the leather of an ancient gas chamber. Didn't like that much in the winter."

Alice shivered at the thought of being so high in frigid temperatures. How the condensation she saw now would likely be ice then. "Don't you have lifts or something nearby?"

"Not too far," Furi said, "but that's where everyone goes. Too likely to be seen." She knocked on a metal door with a porthole in it, the corners rounded and framed by rivets. It reminded Alice very much of the door to the cabin on the Skysworn.

Furi frowned and tried the handle when no one answered. "She's always here. And this is never locked. Unless …" Furi glanced over her shoulder and then up.

"Not up," Alice muttered.

"One more level. To the warehouses. The only time Kura locked her house was when she was hiding something. Or someone."

House, Alice thought. *To call that squat thing a house?* It couldn't have been more than twenty feet square. Unless there was more in the back she couldn't see, but she doubted it.

"It's so small," Alice said.

"If you hadn't noticed, anything that's not open air is a premium here. I guess your house in Ancora was bigger?"

Alice nodded, starting to feel like her family had been much better off than she'd realized.

Furi shrugged. "Home is home. Our homes are small here."

Alice cringed when Furi started past Kura's house. Beyond a fluttering tarp waited another ladder. As bad as she'd thought the first one was, this one had two broken rungs. "You can't be serious."

Instead of answering, Furi started up. She glanced down at Alice. "Kura replaced good rungs with broken ones. Keeps people away. Just don't put any weight on them."

Alice groaned and followed her up, slowly realizing that the ladder was quite a bit longer than the last. A steel cage encased the top where the last three rungs had been broken out. She reached back to take the last few steps on the cage itself, holding her breath as she took one long stride to reach the next level.

But what waited for them there stole her breath. It was a floating city in earnest, far more than the docks below had been. This held warehouses, some two stories tall, and a sparse scattering of restaurants hidden behind vibrant awnings.

Furi's pace increased, taking them off the grates on the edge and onto solid footing. If Alice didn't know what waited below them, she might have thought she was walking on the streets of Ancora itself.

There were homes in the distance, capped with graceful arches that set them apart from the plain blocky warehouses of the edge.

"This is where I went to school," Furi said. "If you can call it that." She twisted a doorknob and led Alice inside one of the sheet-metal buildings. It was dark except for a light in the far corner. Shadows loomed around them, crates and barrels piled high on shelving that looked far too narrow to handle the load.

The farther they walked, the more Alice understood how much larger the facility was than she'd thought. It must be hanging out past the edge of the docks. What had been a small light when they first entered grew into a doorway, and beyond a room with a few tables and a cracked chalkboard.

Beside the chalkboard sat a woman scribbling furiously in a stained notebook.

A smile split Furi's face. "Kura?"

The woman cursed, bobbling her pen before taking a steadying breath. "Furi? Furi!" Her eyes lit up beneath a wild halo of salt and pepper hair. She jumped to her feet, throwing her arms around Furi to crush her in a hug. Alice didn't think the woman looked more than twice her own age, far too young to be caring for the number of children Furi had spoken of.

"I thought you were dead," Kura whispered into Furi's hair. "How are you here?"

Furi glanced at Alice. "It's … it's a bit of a long story. Do you have time?"

"Of course, of course. Grab a seat. And bring your friend." Kura paused and stared at Alice. "Where in the world are you from, girl?"

Alice gave Kura an awkward smile. "That's rather a long story too."

CHAPTER THIRTY-ONE

Furi told her story first. The battle, which made Alice cringe, hearing it again and seeing the horror on Kura's face. And then the prison. Alice studied Kura's reaction, surprised at the woman's *lack* of surprise. From there, Alice came into the story, and their trips to the library.

It was the first time Kura looked skeptical. And Alice couldn't blame her.

"Banned Ballern texts in Belldorn?" Kura shook her head. "We've had plenty of books pass the other way, and some older Ballern texts were brought in by smugglers. But you're talking about treason." Kura's voice dropped to a whisper. "About high treason by a member of royalty."

"Kura," Furi said. "Do you trust me?"

"Of course I trust you. We looked out for each other for years on the docks."

"And you looked out for me before I was smart enough to look out for myself." Furi opened her notebook and passed it to Kura.

Kura's kind smile faded as she read, shaking her head as things she had thought were their true history were contradicted entirely. The last paragraph she read out loud, and Furi could hear the heartbreak in her voice.

"As their homes are overrun by their own foolishness, the Children of the Dark Fire will seek to expand east. Suppressing the Skyborn, the largest threat to their power, is their first priority. And in their wake, they will leave the world a shattered ruin."

Kura looked up and met Furi's gaze. "You saw this?" Her voice trembled, and she glanced at Alice. "With your own eyes you saw this?"

"It's in Belldorn's library," Furi said. "A gilded griffin on the spine."

Kura grimaced. "That house was one of our most reliable presses. Before the monarchy crushed them." She barked out a humorless laugh. "Crushed them for treason, of all things. I still managed to get a few of their titles for you kids, you know? Scraped the spines so no one would be the wiser. But nothing so incriminating as this."

"Who are you?" Kura asked, staring at Alice.

"I'm …" Alice started, then glanced at Furi, who nodded. "I'm from Ancora."

"*Ancora!*" Kura sat up straighter. "Surely not. That's the other side of the world."

"Almost," Alice said. "But there are more cities across the sea, farther east than us. I've never seen them, but I'm told my family came from there long before the old wars."

"And how do you know Furi?"

Alice sighed. "We were on opposite sides of a battle near Bollwerk. The same battle where her ship was struck down."

"She came to visit the prison," Furi said. "That's actually how we met. I'd like to think you wouldn't have bombed me if you knew me."

Alice gave a small, uncomfortable laugh. "Of course I wouldn't have."

"You two met in battle?" Kura asked.

"More or less," Furi said. "After the battle, obviously. But that's how I got to see the Crown Library."

"So you've really seen it?" Kura leaned back. "You've been in the Crown Library of Belldorn? How I wish I could see it one day."

"She met the Lady Katherine, too," Alice chimed in.

Kura's eyes widened, blinking rapidly. "What?"

"She seemed nice," Furi said.

"Oh, Furi," Kura said. "You have brought knowledge here that will spread like the wasting."

"What do you mean?" Furi's words were hurried, almost panicked.

"This is the heart of everything that has poisoned our city. And I fear it's too late to save it. It is like the story of Anabelle and the Apple Tree."

Furi's face darkened. "I am not so naïve as that. I didn't unknowingly bring poison to my home."

"No," Kura said. "You brought a light to show them the poison that has been killing them as long as their memories."

"What is Anabelle and the Apple Tree?" Alice asked.

"A children's tale," Kura said. "A tale of warning. One I teach to the youngest of my students. If the apple breeds ignorance, ignorance begets death."

"Then the ignorant will lead themselves into oblivion," Furi said quietly.

"And I have raised the Skyborn better than that, child. They will rise, and they will burn down the oppressors who call themselves kings."

There was passion in Kura's voice. So much that it made Alice shiver. She seemed a good Samaritan, a good soul, wanting to help people. It reminded her of Jacob. But where Jacob wanted to do good often for the sake of good, it seemed to her Kura wanted to burn down an empire for the outside *chance* of something good.

"What do you mean to do?" Furi asked.

Kura looked down at Furi's notebook. "If this is all true … or even a fraction of the truth … much of Ballern's power comes from Fel. Fel is as much a threat to the Skyborn as anything."

"There's more you don't know," Alice said. "They destroyed part of my city. Half of Ancora is in ruins because of Fel, and Dauschen may never be the same."

"Word travels here faster than you may think," Kura said. "I'm aware of the war in the east. And if it comes here?" she asked, raising an eyebrow as she turned to Furi. "That I cannot allow."

Alice glanced down at Kura's notebook. It took time to make out the words as they were upside from Alice's perspective, but they slowly came together.

Kura hastily closed the notebook when she saw Alice looking. Some of the text didn't make sense, but other parts did.

"You're going to Fel?" Alice asked, taking a step back. "Are you one of them?"

"No!" Kura said.

Furi glanced between the two. "What are you talking about?"

Kura sighed and opened her notebook. "It's a code. Furi, what you brought here is only the proof of a conspiracy some of the mercenaries have been speaking of. Things are already in motion."

"What kind of things?" Alice asked, suddenly concerned about what they might have just stepped into.

"They're going to Fel." Furi wasn't asking a question as she glanced up from the notebook.

Kura's voice lowered to little more than a whisper. "A small group of mercenaries mean to infiltrate the Fel forces staged near the Red Woods."

The quiet caution in Kura's whisper, so far on the edge of Ballern and the docks, made Alice's skin crawl. What kind of threat did they live under to worry about being overheard at the farthest edge of a city?

Alice shook her head. "Not a good idea. Midstream already knows about the soldiers stationed there. Your mercenaries could get themselves killed."

"Our friends will make sure the soldiers in the Red Woods are sabotaged. They are not fools." Kura glanced at the clock on the wall. "You already know some of them, Furi. They'll be here soon."

"We are already here," a voice boomed.

Alice spun as she stood, priming her wrist launcher when she saw the crossbow leveled at Furi's head. She raised her arm, cocking her wrist so the launcher started to spin.

"Drop it," Alice commanded.

Furi turned slowly, freezing when she locked eyes with the mercenary, much as the mercenary froze when he saw her.

"Furi?" He almost threw the crossbow away, but Alice kept her sight trained on the man, just above his outrageous mustache.

"Jakon?" A range of expressions stormed across Furi's face, but she finally stood and stepped forward and hugged the old man. "You're a mercenary?" She backed away and frowned at him. "But you work in the palaces."

"Mercenary is a strong word," Jakon said with a gentle smile. "Perhaps informant would be better?"

"A spy," Alice said, relaxing. "But for who?"

"Whoever has the coin to pay."

The man sent Alice's hackles up immediately. A spy inside the royal palaces of Ballern? Who was also a mercenary? Suspicions plagued her thoughts as she tried to pin down the extent of the threat he presented.

Kura handed Jakon her notebook. He didn't read it at that moment, simply tucked it away into his jerkin.

"Where have you been?" Jakon asked. "The Nightingale was shot down. How did you get home?"

"Alice saved me," Furi said.

Alice waited for her to expand on the story, but she didn't. So however Furi knew Jakon in Ballern, it wasn't enough to tell him the entire truth. But Furi did tell him about Rin and Beck and the raid where they'd been forced to fire on children. Jakon's face darkened, but Kura didn't seem surprised at all.

"Children," Jakon said. "It is bad enough they recruit their own children for war. But to target the children of an enemy ..." He shook his head.

"What do you know about the Children of the Dark Fire?" Furi asked.

Jakon gave her a weak smile. "You go to a dangerous place, Furi. It is not safe to speak of them. Eyes everywhere. Ears in every wall."

Furi bit her lip. "But you know they're bad, right?"

Jakon took a deep breath. "Furi ... yes. But you cannot stop madness that has grown such deep roots."

So Furi told him in detail about what she and Alice had found in the library at Belldorn, ignoring Jakon's questions when he asked how they could possibly have gotten inside. She showed him the excerpts from her notes and Alice's, the rise of a religion that brought down an empire from the inside.

At the end, Jakon looked up to Kura, who only nodded. He cursed and closed the notebook, handing it back to Furi. "There are many who will not believe this without the book itself as proof. I fear there are many more who will not care. The Dark Fire is all they know."

"Then the Skyborn will remove them as they once removed us," Kura said, her knuckles whitening on the table.

"You are as stubborn as those pirates," Jakon muttered.

"What pirates?" Kura asked.

"I needed a single barrel of Pill-Bug eggs, and they forced me to buy four."

"Mary?" Alice asked before she could stop the question.

Jakon raised an eyebrow. "Do you know the thief? I suppose I should not be surprised that a pirate would change the terms. But it is still an annoyance." He grinned. "Though it did give me the idea to journey with my mercenaries. I'll sell the extra barrels to the soldiers in the Red Woods before we sabotage them."

"Do you know of any ships they could take to Fel?" Kura asked.

Jakon shook his head. "The Red Woods are as close as you'll get right now. You're welcome to join my crew."

"Will you cook on the way?" Furi asked.

"Of course!" Jakon said. "It's a long flight, and we will all need to eat." His mustache rose with his smile.

Furi turned to Alice. "What do you think? We won't have to risk talking to anyone else on the docks."

From that perspective, Alice thought it was a great idea. But she worried about Jakon. If Furi hadn't known he was a mercenary, and he was a spy inside the palaces, what else didn't she and Furi know? But if it would get them closer to Midstream, she thought it might just be worth the risk.

Alice nodded.

"Excellent!" Jakon said. "You'll have an egg like nothing you've tasted before. And then you'll be sick of them because I have too many eggs."

Alice smiled despite herself. Seeing the fallout from Mary's rather skillful negotiations was an entertaining sight indeed.

"You know I lived in Belldorn for years as a spy," Jakon said.

Alice froze. To so freely admit he was a spy to someone he didn't know was insane. But the words that followed chilled her.

"I know the only way you could have gotten into the library was as a guest, or a prisoner." Jakon studied Alice. "I suppose you were a prisoner of this one."

"Her name is Alice," Furi said. "And, well, yes, you're right, but she's my friend."

Alice blinked at that.

"It is tiresome to lie to those you care for," Jakon said. "The older I get, the less taste I have for it. But the old library." He nodded slowly. "That was a place I rather enjoyed. It is also the place I learned more about Ballern and the western cities. The Children of the Dark Fire may be a threat to the empire today, but religions have come and gone before. Some ruling for a time, some forbidden to rule, and some scoured from the world by a rival.

"Not all the old wars were fought over land and food. Some were waged in the name of ideals and stories, principles of religion that their own followers ignore when it suits their goals." Jakon looked to Furi. "You tread in dangerous waters, but you do not tread alone. Our ship is crewed by defectors fleeing Ballern. Only a few of us will return to the city at the end of this journey."

"It sounds like you already know what we need to know," Alice said. "We need an insider who can tell us about the palaces and workings of Ballern."

"So you can invade it," Jakon said. It wasn't a question.

"Yes," Furi said quietly when Alice hesitated.

"You will need an army. A fleet of airships to breach the docks. It would take a battle the likes of which has not been seen since the Deadlands War." Jakon paused for a time. "Come to the ship at midnight. You'll find The Ray four docks over on the northeastern edge of the Bones. I can help you with some of what you need."

CHAPTER THIRTY-TWO

I F THE DOCKS had been unnerving in the daylight, at night, they were terrifying. Sparse lights along the walkways gave brief visibility in the cover of night as Alice and Furi looked for The Ray. Every step they took on the solid metal around the warehouses rang out.

Alice cringed, waiting for someone to stop them, to question what they were doing. "I can't believe no one has asked us what we're doing out here."

"Have you seen anyone?" Furi asked. "Of course not. Every sensible dock rat is asleep. They'll have to be awake in a couple hours as the supply ships finish refueling and start to leave."

The noise of their footsteps changed, and Alice glanced down. They were back on the horrible grating that let her see the city far below. She'd almost grown used to the constant swaying of the docks in the hours since they'd arrived. But she had most certainly not grown used to the vision of city lights beneath her feet, so distant they might have been glowworms in an endless chasm.

Alice shivered and kept her eyes on Furi's back, following her around the corner of another warehouse, and almost running into her when she stopped. Alice was about to ask her why when she saw it. A golden swirl of text glinted in the dim dock lights. *The Ray.*

She couldn't make out all of the ship, but she guessed it was at least twice the size of the Skysworn. It was an older beast, with great sails sweeping out from beneath the gas chamber. It would steer as much by wind as it would power, but Alice had little doubt the ship would be faster than it looked.

No self-respecting smuggler took more risks than were absolutely necessary.

"Don't worry," Furi said. "It's faster than it looks."

Alice grinned, amused that Furi had almost guessed exactly what she was thinking.

Furi paused and cocked her head, as if listening to something Alice couldn't hear. She looked both ways across the walkway and then turned onto the gangplank leading to the ship. A thin rope railing was all that stood between Alice and a very long drop to the earth below. At that moment, she was glad of the dark and the fact she couldn't tell just how high they were, even if she knew it in her mind.

A shadow lingered just inside the orange glow of the airship. Furi's steps slowed until the man turned, and Jakon's features were plain to see.

"Welcome to The Ray!" Jakon said, gesturing for them to come on board. "I'd introduce you to my crew, but most of them will be gone after we unload at the Red Woods. Defectors, you know. Looking for a better life on the other side of the sea."

"It's not the best time to visit," Alice muttered. "They're going to get themselves dropped into the middle of a war."

Jakon smiled. "Ah, but that's what's so easy to forget about Ballern. We all fight in the wars. All except the monarchy."

Alice blinked at that. It was so different from Ancora, where the guards and knights were volunteers. She glanced at Furi, remembering the stories of how the Skyborn were all forced to serve. How so many of the soldiers on those airships would rather be anywhere else.

Furi stepped into the hold of The Ray, and Alice followed.

Jakon handed Furi a book the moment she crossed the bulkhead. "Keep it safe. Do not let anyone see what is inside this until you are well and truly away from any of Ballern's influence."

Alice looked over Furi's shoulder, eyes widening as Furi flipped past a map, a schedule, and a legend that detailed what each symbol on the schedule meant. Some of the pages were the queen's daily itinerary, while another detailed the patrols in the gardens.

"I have other copies," Jakon said when Furi glanced up with a question on her lips.

"Thank you," she said. "What … what if you got caught with this?"

"Well, it's mostly nonsense without the legend. I've learned to talk myself out of a lot of problems. But if you are caught with the legend, and they understand what that actually is." He nodded to the book. "I doubt very much you will live to warn anyone else."

Wordlessly, Furi passed the legend to Alice. She studied it for a moment before folding and tucking it into her own journal. Hidden away, it felt like an extra weight had been added to her pack, though it was only a single sheet of paper.

"Another barrel is leaking, Captain." Alice turned toward the voice and found a broad-shouldered man who looked like he might be larger than Smith. From his lighter complexion, she thought he'd fit in better in Ancora or Bollwerk than Ballern.

Jakon cursed and followed the man into a narrow hall. "Come along, you two."

Furi and Alice trailed behind, pausing when the corridor ended and opened onto a second supply hold.

"I thought we were in the hold already?" Alice said, studying the cavernous space.

Jakon grinned. "You're in the secondary gas chamber here. As you may have noticed by the fact you aren't dying or sounding like a baby Fire Lizard, we've repurposed it."

He led them around a stack of crates that obscured the front of the hold, and as Alice rounded the corner, she saw two dozen seats in the front, filled with people. Most of them were at least her age, but several more were older, and a handful were small children.

"Alice, Furi, meet my crew. Crew, this is Alice and Furi." A few hands rose in greeting, but most offered them little more than a glance.

A crew, in a secondary hold, hidden behind a door in a maintenance corridor. "You're smuggling people," Alice said.

Jakon blinked. "Obviously, yes. Which barrel is it?"

"Here." The large man indicated a barrel that Alice recognized. It had a small brand burned into it, the same as one she'd seen on the Skysworn. But Mary hadn't been storing liquid in them. They were full of Pill-Bug eggs.

Jakon frowned at the puddle forming beneath the barrel. He waved off the crewman, who returned to the corridor. "Help me with this, would you, Alice?"

"How well do you know Mary?" Alice asked Jakon as they cracked the lid off the barrels.

"Well enough. She's the best smuggler of fine ingredients I've ever known."

Inside the barrel waited a soup of Pill-Bug eggs and some kind of fluid. Jakon muttered something Alice didn't catch as he grabbed a bucket and started pouring more liquid into the barrel.

"But you know if Mary finds out anything happened to us on your ship, you likely won't live out the week?"

"Alice," Furi hissed.

"Oh aye," Jakon said. "I'm well aware of the stories of Skysworn Mary. There are some pirates you do not cross. And a pirate who's earned their blood wings is at the top of that list."

Furi's warning glare softened with Jakon's words.

Blood wings. Alice had read the expression in a series of grand adventure stories she'd read in Ancora. Pirates who repaid a debt in blood were said to have earned their blood wings. It meant Mary had killed someone who wronged her, and Alice wanted to know that story.

"Do you know how she earned them?" Alice asked.

"No." Jakon pursed his lips. "And I don't need to know, so you can keep it to yourself. Some stories are best left in the past."

Alice gave him what she thought was a mischievous smile. He didn't need to know *she* didn't know. If the mere thought of the story was enough to keep him on their side, that was good enough for Alice. Of course, Furi seemed to trust Jakon, so maybe her paranoia wasn't entirely needed. On the other hand, they'd been betrayed in the past. Caution was rarely a bad plan.

"So what are you doing to the eggs?"

"Pickling them in a brine. Keeps them from hatching, and they make a nice snack. Well, these are pretty sizable, so each one is probably more like a meal."

"You can scramble them and mix them with cream too."

Jakon raised an eyebrow. "You *are* Ancoran, aren't you? Most folks in this city would be sickened at the idea of adding cream to an egg. I suppose you enjoy them with a hint of fire sauce?"

"Yes, I do," Alice said with a warm smile.

"Why's the barrel leaking?" Furi asked when Jakon started mopping up the brine.

"Too old and dried out, I suspect. It should stop once the wood absorbs enough moisture. In the meantime, we'll just have to mop it up." He passed the mop off to an irritated-looking passenger, but they agreed to keep an eye on the barrel in exchange for a discount on their fee.

"You two, come with me." Jakon led Furi and Alice out of the supply hold. When they had closed the door to the hold, it looked like no more than a maintenance hatch to a gas chamber, the porthole so dirty no one could see through it.

He took them down another corridor to their left, toward the front of the ship. A spiral staircase sunk into the interior wall led the way up to the second floor. From there, Jakon led them down a hallway lined with elegant wood floors and what looked like velvet on the walls.

The change from bare metal to an ostentatious décor was jarring, and Alice couldn't help but run her fingers along the soft wall and marvel at the fine paintings anchored along the way. Each was protected by a pane of glass that looked as thick as the windows in the Bollwerk towers.

She stopped near the end of the hall, studying a painting done with thick brush strokes and dark colors. A squat building stood near the center, shaped like a trapezoid, pipes and smokestacks rising from it as though it was trying to pierce the sky and cut down the trees around it.

"Ah," Jakon said. "One of the Great Machines. I like to keep it here in case I get any unwelcome visits from the Children of the Dark Fire. They don't approve of smugglers, but they have a soft spot for believers. The fools."

"It's more detailed than the illustrations we found in the books," Furi said.

Jakon pointed to the corner by one of the tree's roots. "See how small they are by the trees."

Alice squinted, looking away from the cluster of pipes she'd been studying in the painting, and almost gasped when she saw the pair of humans, like leaves fallen to the earth beneath towering giants. "Surely those trees aren't really that large."

Furi nodded. "They are. They aren't far from Ballern. Off to the west, past the Gray Woods."

"Gods, I'd like to see that one day." Silently, she hoped Jacob would be there to see it too. The longer they were apart, the more she missed him. Hopefully, Jakon and his ship would get them to the Red Woods, and from there, they could return to Midstream.

Another idea struck Alice. "Could you take us all the way to Midstream?"

Jakon shook his head. "They keep a schedule on these docks for departures and arrivals. If I'm not back in my allotted timeframe, I can lose permissions altogether. Helps prevent collisions in bad weather too."

Alice nodded.

"Now, you two can stay here." Jakon led them into the cockpit. It made the Skysworn's look raw and unrefined in comparison. The Ray had fine leather wrapped around every lever, and most of the buttons on the console were lit from behind, pulsing in various patterns as though each had a meaning. And Alice suspected they did, at that.

Jakon pulled a jump seat from the floor. It didn't rise like a flat folding chair; instead, two feet of flooring spun, revealing a cushioned beast of a chair that unfolded as the mechanism clicked into place. Jakon grinned at the shock on both Alice's and Furi's faces.

And then he pulled up another seat, digging his toe into a button to release it. "Belts are tucked under the cushion if you'd like one." He moved to one of the horns, sliding a large pad from the front of it, which Alice quickly realized was a mute. "Raise anchor and lock in. Countdown starts in sixty seconds."

"Aye, captain," a pair of voices boomed back simultaneously.

There was plenty of room for Alice to stuff her pack into the chair beside her as she dug out the belt. She had it fastened just as Jakon's countdown ended, and The Ray rose slightly as all its anchors and ties were released.

"Moving out. Cargo, please remain seated."

Furi grinned at that.

The whine of thrusters warming up grew louder as The Ray pulled away from the dock. Small lights sat at the end of the Bones, and they were the only real indicator Alice could see that they'd cleared the structure. Jakon pulled on an old-fashioned ship's wheel, and the craft drifted to the right, angling toward the Crystal Sea.

"I can't see anything," Alice said.

Jakon cast a smile over his shoulder. "That makes two of us."

"Oh, that's reassuring," Furi muttered. "I liked you better as a chef."

"I'll have you know I'm still an excellent chef. We'll be on the ground near sunrise. But, over the ocean, there isn't much to do. If one of you can pilot The Ray, I'll get some breakfast ready."

"I've never piloted an airship," Furi said.

"I've seen one piloted loads of times," Alice said.

"Good enough!" Jakon said. "Come, let me show you some of the intricacies of The Ray, and I'll let you watch the heading for a time."

✧ ✧ ✧

It wasn't long before Alice found herself strapped into the harness in the captain's chair, her hands gripping the wheel as if the airship might suddenly get a mind of its own and take them off course.

"How's our heading, *Captain*," Furi said with a laugh.

Alice pointed at the compass. "I'm keeping the needle between those two bearings. Just like he said."

"Jakon said we can go faster. Let's try it."

Alice took a steadying breath and nodded. "Okay. You push the thrust and I'll hold the bearing."

Furi clapped her hands together and made it over to Alice's left side. She flipped two switches above a pair of muddy green lights. "Ready?"

Alice tightened her grip on the wheel again. "Go."

Furi gradually pushed the lever forward, and the same whine Alice had heard when they left the docks filled the cabin around them.

"Steady," said Jakon's voice over the horn. "I have a vat of boiling oil down here." It wasn't as tinny-sounding as the horns on the Skysworn, and Alice wondered why that was.

"Is he really frying food?" Alice asked Furi.

"He is," Jakon answered.

Furi inched the thrusters forward, and the wheel shook in Alice's hand. "How's that?"

"The eggs aren't breaking, so I'm okay with this."

Furi rolled her eyes. "I was asking our current captain."

"Of course, whatever was I thinking?"

Alice grinned. "The compass is shaking a bit, but I can hold the heading."

"Excellent!" Jakon said. "Warn me if you reduce thrust. Otherwise, I'll be up shortly with food. As soon as I feed the cargo."

Furi slid the mute over the horn. "Is it just me, or is his referring to people as cargo really unnerving? I thought it was funny at first, but it's kind of weird."

Alice shrugged. "I've heard people called worse. And, I mean, he *is* technically delivering them across the Crystal Sea."

✧   ✧   ✧

JAKON RETURNED TO the cabin a short time later, three steaming bowls balanced on his hands. He pressed a pedal off to the right of the console, and a table slid out of the wall.

"Are you kidding?" Furi asked. "What *don't* you have on this thing?"

"It's my home away from home," Jakon said, setting the bowls down. "Now, you two eat. You have a long day ahead if you mean to make it all the way to Midstream."

Alice unbuckled the harness and slid it over her shoulders. Jakon took her seat, checking over the console and their heading.

"How'd we do?" Furi asked.

"Fantastic!" Jakon said. "Our bearing is good. Altitude is ideal for the thrusters. We'll be landing ahead of schedule at this rate."

Alice stood at the high table and took a deep breath over the steaming bowl. "What's in this?" It smelled remarkably similar to a bisque her mother used to make, and her mouth immediately longed for that old salty dish.

"A bit of cream from the Clickers they farm in Ballern. Best milk you'll find outside of a cow. And you know how rare and expensive a cow can be."

Alice did at that. The only livestock like cows and chickens in Ancora were closely guarded in the Highlands in an area nearly as secure as the castle itself. It was a rare thing for anyone in the Lowlands to get their meat or dairy from a cow. Most of the larger mammals of the world had been overrun by the bugs decades before. Or at least, that was the common belief.

She took a sip of the broth and was stunned at the complexity of salt and cream and the hints of richness from the pickled Pill-Bug eggs. Alice knew their flavor would only improve the more time they spent in the brine, but they were already fantastic.

"This is wonderful. Thank you!"

Jakon smiled.

"Even better than the last soup you made down by the city," Furi said. "All it needs is some bread."

"Sacrilege," Jakon said with a laugh. He picked up his own bowl and sipped at it before taking it back to the captain's chair. "Best guess, we'll be passing over the Red Woods in an hour. I can see the beginning of the sunrise."

Alice looked out at the faint light. Barely a glow in the darkness, but soon it would warm the world below. She wished she could have slept more. It was going to be a long day indeed.

✧　✧　✧

JAKON'S ESTIMATES WERE spot on. They tied off against a rickety dock not ten feet off the ground at the edge of the Red Woods, where sparse grasslands created a narrow barrier between the gnarled trees and the desert beyond.

Alice had worried there would be an ambush waiting for them. That Kura, or even Jakon himself, should not have been trusted. But Furi trusted them, and Alice was growing to trust Furi. She hoped the same could be said for her.

"A quarantine zone, you say?" Jakon asked as he made his way back up the ramp with two burly dockhands.

"Yeah, some nonsense about the warlords threatening Fel. Nothing to worry yourself about here. You should see the perimeter around the base. Never seen the like."

Alice frowned at the exchange.

"Why would the warlords threaten Fel?" Furi asked.

Alice leaned closer. "They wouldn't. You read the same thing I did. They're allied with Fel."

"So he's wrong?"

Alice wrung her hands together and lowered her voice. "He's wrong, or Fel is claiming the warlords are threatening them. Building a case against them, so their soldiers won't hesitate in the war."

Furi glanced to the side and then focused on Alice. "They're going to move on Midstream. That's what it is. That has to be it."

"What do you mean?" Alice asked.

Furi grabbed another dockhand as he walked by. "Do you know where the warlords are holed up?"

The man looked surprised. He looked at Furi's hand on his arm and then back to her face. "Midstream, of course. Same place they always are."

Alice felt sick. Mordair had his people convinced the warlords were rising against them and were sheltering in Midstream. They'd roll through the city and burn it down as their king commanded, and feel great about doing it.

Furi frowned as the man walked away. "Warlords? They're going to kill the warlords too." She ran a hand through her hair, her lips almost curling into a snarl. "And Ballern is helping them?"

"I have to tell Jacob and the others. They need to know what's coming."

"Alice, *we* don't even know what's coming."

"We know why they're coming, though. They think Midstream is a dire threat. They're doing to burn it to the ground and leave nothing behind."

"You don't know that."

Alice turned on Furi, anger rising. "You didn't see what they did to Ancora. You didn't see the bodies. You didn't see an entire city crushed into the earth."

Furi blinked rapidly, and Alice didn't miss the tears at the corners of her eyes.

"I'm sorry," Alice said, squeezing Furi's arm. "It's going to be bad. Please, I've trusted you about Jakon and Kura. Trust me in this."

"I don't want it to be true."

Alice gave her a weak smile. "Neither do I."

They were almost to the small line of vendor tents and shacks beneath the gnarled and twisted trees of the Red Woods when they heard it. A handful of phrases that all meant the same thing. Chatter spread through the landing area and the stalls. A battle was starting. The lines were moving out. Fel was finally going to put down their desert rivals once and for all.

But the battle cries curdled her blood.

"All glory to the king!"

"His righteous fury will cleanse the world of the unworthy!"

"Glory to Fel before all!"

Alice's heart pounded in her chest.

Midstream.

Jacob.

CHAPTER THIRTY-THREE

MORDAIR STOOD UPON the great wall of Fel. The edges of the ramparts had been broken away into jagged stones over countless years and battles. And an arsenal tower had collapsed during the Deadlands War. But it had never been repaired. Instead, it remained as a symbol of Fel's persistence. A reminder that they would always persevere.

A handful of barges drifted down the river in the distance, carrying the resupplies he knew his armored crawlers and soldiers would need. His people might have been convinced Midstream would be an easy target, weakened as it was by the warlords, but Mordair knew better. They'd meet resistance there. Archibald was no fool. He'd know Mordair would have to come for Bollwerk, and the easiest path without Dauschen and Ancora under Fel's rule would be through Midstream.

He had a moment of regret for the failed gambit in Ancora. It would have been easy to reinforce the mountain passes of that city and force Bollwerk to divide their attention. But his brother's failures would not be the end of his own ambitions.

"The battalion is moving, My King, split between the north front and the west, as you requested. Have you reconsidered the plan of attack?"

Mordair turned to face one of his most trusted generals, a woman who had come to be known as the Red Hand. "No. Sacrifice the west so we can drive Midstream into ruin from the north. One company of crawlers will be adequate. Lessons must be learned."

"Of course, my king." The Red Hand bowed and took her leave, the gold epaulets of her gray wartime uniform catching the morning sun.

The question burning at the back of Mordair's mind was a simple one. Would the apprentice of Charles von Atlier prove the equal of his mentor? The idea sent a thrill down his spine. It might be too late to recruit the boy to their own ranks, but that didn't mean he wouldn't have his uses.

The battle for Midstream would determine much. Should the desert princess manage to turn his forces away, he had little doubt Midstream's allies would come to Fel. But the armaments of Fel were not insignificant. He could protect his city. Or he could leverage an invasion to the favor of his allies in the west.

There were many options to explore. But one thing Gregory Mordair was sure of, blood would be spilled. And there was never a bad time for blood.

✦   ✦   ✦

GLADYS STUDIED THE maps of the desert around Midstream. Their scouts had found a large group of Fel's soldiers closing from the north. Excitement had almost won out over worry because she knew they were as ready as they could be. The traps were buried, and a handful of airships drifted near the outskirts of town.

If George's calculations were right, they only had an hour before the first wave of soldiers reached them. It wasn't the troops that concerned her. It was the companies of crawlers, armored against most anything Midstream could throw at them.

But the traps were something new. And she'd seen them penetrate steel with her own eyes. Still, she worried they would be no match for a battalion of crawlers.

Gladys looked up from the map spread across her table when the rhythmic bursts of static filled the room. She made her way over to the bookshelf and the hidden panel that concealed their transmitter.

"Fireworm," she said, finally using a code name, like George and Archibald had insisted on.

"This is Dragonwing," Alice said. "Near the Red Woods, crawlers are headed your way."

"The Red Woods? No. Scouts found them in the north, not the west."

"They may not have been scouting far enough west. I can see the dust clouds two miles ahead of us. They're moving fast. A full company, I'd say. At least twelve."

Gladys cursed and clicked the transmitter. "Thank you. We'll be ready." But would they? Gladys wondered. The thrill of one force walking into their traps from the north vanished entirely as she realized the threat had evolved.

"We'll be there as soon as we can."

"Be safe."

"Dragonwing out."

Gladys slid the transmitter back into its concealed compartment and returned to the maps. They only had a few hundred soldiers in Midstream. With the clippers circling above, they had some air cover, but if Jacob was wrong about those traps, Midstream was going to fall.

Gladys slammed her palm onto the table and hurried out to the front lines. She needed to find Jacob. She needed George. And Midstream needed them all.

✧　✧　✧

"Jacob," Gladys called when she reached one of the A-frame steel plates Jacob had raised with the Titan Mech. She frowned at the trap still in the Titan Mech's hand. "I thought we'd buried all of those?"

Jacob smiled down at her. "Except this one. Helena thought we could leave it in the hand for a larger range of targeting. I think it's actually a great idea. I was also thinking we could miniaturize it to be installed on airships."

Gladys first question was how in the world was he going to fire it, but she shook her head to focus on the problem at hand. "We have crawlers coming in from the west."

"The west is fortified. Both sides of the river have traps buried, and the wind has been high enough today you can't tell where the sand was disturbed."

Gladys blinked. "Then, how will *we* be able to tell where the traps are?"

Jacob opened his mouth like he was going to answer and then frowned. His eyes lit up a moment later. "The reloading levers! The magnets are strong enough to pull them through the sand, so you can use them like a dowsing rod."

"A dowsing rod?" Gladys muttered. "Dowsing rods don't work!"

Jacob shrugged. "Okay, bad example, but you get the idea."

Gladys jumped when a hand touched her shoulder. She spun, relieved to find George and Helena.

"Do you know how many, Princess?" George asked.

"Alice said it's a full company."

"Alice?" Jacob asked, shutting down the arm and hopping from the treads to the sand. "How does she know about a company of crawlers?"

"She already left Ballern," Gladys said. "They were in the Red Woods when I talked to her."

Helena frowned. "Fel has forces stationed there. Is she behind their lines?"

"She has to be," Gladys said. "She said she could see the dust cloud from the crawlers."

"Then they are moving quickly," George said. "A crawler would need speed to generate a cloud, and if it was large enough for her to mention it, time is not on our side. Helena, position our troops behind the A-frames and the temporary walls you and Jacob helped design. Signal the clippers to all draw closer to the city except for two. Keep them forward as scouts."

Helena nodded and ran back into the city proper.

George's switch in demeanor, from his casual tone to a commanding one, sent a frisson of fear down Gladys's spine. He only sounded like that when things were bad. And now she worried just how bad off they really were.

George turned to Jacob. "Alice is safe. Safer than we are right now. Rest easy knowing that. You are welcome to join us on the front or shelter in the city."

Jacob shook his head. "I'm staying with you. And if anything gets close enough, I'm going to test out Helena's idea with the arm."

Gladys looked to George, and then past him. On the horizon was the first sign of a dust storm, only Gladys didn't think it was a storm at all.

George followed her gaze and handed her a telescope.

She raised it to her eye, finding a line of shadows, bulkier and taller than they had any right to be. When she thought of crawlers, she thought of the open-air transports of Bollwerk. But this was something different. It was hard to guess their size, but they were taller, armored, and moving faster than she could have imagined.

"I see ten of them. They're huge." She handed the scope back to George.

He cursed and let Jacob take a look.

Gladys shivered when the tinker frowned and glanced at the trap in the Titan Mech's hand.

Jacob scratched the back of his head. "I have no idea how thick their armor is, but I'm confident in the traps."

"We are better protected to the north," George said. "They may only need to sacrifice a few crawlers to break our lines." He took a slow breath. "Remain confident around our soldiers. They have enough worry, and we don't need to show doubt. Come."

✧   ✧   ✧

JACOB HAD MORE plans to execute than the traps alone. In the shadow of the easternmost A-frame bunker, he cracked open a crate, revealing a series of Bangers. He removed the top tray, passing it to George. Below that waited compound bombs from Bollwerk. Accelerant lined the large shells, and an explosive ring within.

He'd changed his original design some, and Frederick had executed the changes with precision. These had been etched with lines like a grid, the metal thinning between the plates. It would encourage the bombs to create more shrapnel and hopefully cause more damage than the originals.

Jacob sighed and tested the hinges of a few. There was no use for these other than killing, and he knew it. He could tell himself the Titan Mech arms would work to help rebuild, would save lives over time. But he had no illusions about what the modified bombs would do.

Gladys dropped a bundle of long, gray metal launchers beside him. Each looked something like a mixture of a crossbow and a harpoon gun, not unlike what he and Alice used to launch bombs from the Skysworn's deck.

She wiped a line of sweat from her forehead. "They're almost here."

"Are you sure you want to be on the front?" Jacob whispered.

Gladys offered a smile. "If I ask my people to fight for me, then I must fight for them." She passed a launcher to Helena. "You heard Jacob. Don't throw these by hand and get behind a barrier if you do have to fire them."

The A-frames gave them a reasonable barrier, and Helena had the idea to place them in such a way that the crawlers would be funneled toward the thickest clusters of traps. Jacob had thought it was brilliant, and George said as much.

Then all they had to do was wait. It had started slowly, a distant roar and the clatter of treads that were a bit too loose. The sound had grown as the crawlers approached, until a peek around the barriers showed Jacob just what had come for Midstream.

Each was at least eight feet tall and broad as a street in the Lowlands. That he hadn't planned for. With enough distance between the treads, they could drive past a trap without triggering it. But that's why they'd staggered them, he reminded himself.

The first crawler reached the dry riverbed, too far to the north to trigger a trap, but not too far from the Tail Sword that had been sleeping just below the surface. It erupted from the sands, claws spread wide as it screeched. The crawler tried to veer away; even armored, the driver understood the danger of a threatened Tail Sword. And Jacob had never seen one as large as what waited in the sands.

Sparks sprayed the landscape as a claw cut the tread like it had been fabric and not metal. The dark chitin gleamed in the rising sun, a blinding torch as the Tail Sword's stinger slammed through the roof of the crawler. Jacob didn't take his eyes off the unfolding scene as two other crawlers changed course to close on the creature.

It was a pointless effort. The first crawler was nothing but blood and torn metal by the time they reached the Tail Sword. Turrets fired, bursts of flame sending cannonballs to slam into the Tail Sword. The beast screeched at them, scuttled forward, and then retreated to the east. Down the center of the riverbed.

Jacob thought it was pure luck the Tail Sword had kept to the middle of the dry river, but then he remembered the creatures preferred the low ground.

A soldier leaped from the smoking ruin of the first crawler. He froze where he landed, watching the second crawler bounce into the air as it triggered a trap, firing massive bolts into its undercarriage while a plume of sand exploded from beneath the crawler. The vehicle rolled forward in a lazy arc before falling still.

The third crawler clipped the edge of a trap, and Jacob didn't stop the savage smile spreading across his face as bolts shattered the tread of one side, stranding the crawler. But this crawler wasn't out of commission entirely. Its turret swiveled, taking aim to Jacob's right, and fired.

Cannonballs clanged against one of the A-frame barriers, causing it to rise from the sands slightly before slamming back into its original position.

"Good thing we sank those supports deeper," Helena said.

Jacob nodded. "Look."

He pointed to the north. A cloud similar to what they'd seen in the west was now bearing down from the north. But the crawlers weren't alone. A line of airships coasted along above them.

The transmitter hidden in the leather collar of George's armor burst to life. "Clippers, four destroyers north. In range estimate … ten minutes."

George clicked the transmitter. "Message received."

Jacob frowned. Destroyers? Against clippers? That wasn't likely to end well. He listened as George gave orders for them to come in from above, and he worried those orders would be intercepted. If the Butcher had known about the transmitters, then Mordair surely would too. He took a steadying breath. But for that to be the case, they'd have to find the frequency. That would take time, and George kept the frequency rotating on a schedule.

Another cannonball crashed into their A-frame, bringing Jacob back to the moment. He picked up a launcher and spun the crank, the quiet clicks drawing the thick rubber back and adding tension to the crossbar. He turned the crank until the guidelines on the draw mechanism matched the notches on the stock.

The fourth crawler crossed into the riverbed, passing over the initial traps before crashing into the other side of the bank as it tried to climb the steeper incline. A trap fired into the undercarriage as it hit the sand, puncturing the crawler so thoroughly that the highest armor plate peeled back with a screech.

Jacob clicked the button on a Banger and slid it into a compound bomb, locking the shell together before dropping it onto his launcher. He'd fired the launcher enough that he had a good sense of range, but the crawler still looked too far out when he leaned outside of their shelter.

But the bomb was primed. He couldn't stop now.

He raised the nose of the launcher a bit higher and pulled the trigger. The sudden release of tension threatened to pull the launcher out of his hands, and the snap of rubber briefly drowned out most of the noises around him.

The gray orb rose in a graceful arc, and Jacob was worried the shot would be short regardless of his higher aim. But he heard the distant clink when it cracked into the front of the crawler and bounced into the gaping hole the trap had left.

It was the fireball that came first, bowing out the sides of the armored crawler like someone inflating the gas chamber of an airship. But as the light faded, Jacob could see the extra divots all around the plating where shrapnel from the bomb had torn into the armor, and anyone inside it.

A moment later, a second explosion rocked the remains of the crawler, triggering some of the traps in the sand as Jacob suspected whatever incendiaries had been onboard had been triggered. With all four crawlers disabled, George gave the order.

"Attack!"

The soldiers of Midstream flowed out from behind the A-frames, charging down the slopes that would take them to the riverbed. They wouldn't have long before the next wave arrived. But the Midstream soldiers, under the command of the royal guard, didn't need much time at all.

Jacob frowned at a small form sprinting through the sand beside George, realizing it was Gladys when she threw open her cloak, revealing knives set into her armor. One of the crawler turrets rotated toward her and George as she flicked two knives through the slit below the barrel.

The machine stilled as George bounded up the broken tread and pulled open the side door. He led with his sword, leaving no chance for surrender or escape. Jacob didn't miss the blood that stained the steel when the royal guard moved on.

Crawler by crawler, they moved through the sands, dispatching enemy soldiers even as the final crawlers realized what was coming. In the end, the first wave managed to take down two of Midstream's soldiers with crossbow fire. But George and the others adapted after that, letting their cloaks billow around them, obscuring their bodies.

And as the front line cut down the soldiers from the crawlers, those behind them worked on the traps, sinking levers into the sands and raising them to reload. The process was fast, faster than Jacob had hoped, and by the time more of the northern crawlers would reach them, and the western flank moved in force, the Midstreamers would have already returned to their shelters.

"Clippers are engaging," Jacob said, pointing up to the battle unfolding above them.

George cursed as he leaned in beside Jacob and raised his telescope. "Landing ship ... those are not destroyers." He clicked the button on his collar. "Clippers disengage! *Disengage!*"

"What is it?" Helena asked.

"Heavily armed landing ships," George said. "Who called them destroyers? No scout of mine would have declared those destroyers."

"It came over the transmitters," Gladys said, standing up straighter.

"They have our frequency!"

And as the words left her mouth, the landing ships opened fire on the clippers. Jacob could see the smokey trails of cannon shot and the small arms fire that followed. The first clipper ruptured, its small gas chamber parting like falling leaves before a fireball blew it into a rain of debris.

The second swung around, diving past the bow of the landing ship, only to be caught by a gun pod that swiveled to track it, cutting it down in moments. It didn't explode, instead drifting aimlessly to the desert below.

George clicked his transmitter. "Switch to backup frequency." He pulled a small box from his pocket, adjusting the dial of his own transmitter.

Jacob looked at the Titan Mech arm holding a trap. It had seemed like a good idea at the time, but now it seemed wholly inadequate after seeing those clippers shot down in rapid succession.

What happened next sent a chill into his bones.

The front-most landing ship fired on the riverbed, triggering a line of traps several feet wide. In moments, another burst of shells exploded around the river, revealing the mangled metal of half a dozen traps.

They'd cut a path into the city, which meant nothing would stop the crawlers.

Jacob and Gladys exchanged a glance.

But it was George who spoke. "This is not good."

CHAPTER THIRTY-FOUR

Alice and Furi returned to The Ray before Jakon left. They'd planned on making a slow journey to Midstream, but that was out of the question now. They needed to get there. And fast.

The captain crossed his arms and shook his head where he stood at the entrance to the cargo hold. It stood empty, his people smuggled to their intended destination.

"I can't get involved, Furi."

Alice clenched her hands into fists. "Then just take us to Midstream and leave us!"

"No. And you need to stay far away from what's coming to that town."

"My friends are there," Alice said. "I can't leave them to die!"

Furi nodded. "We're behind enemy lines. You could turn the tide of the battle! Those Fel crawlers are slow and clumsy, and you already know that."

"Slow and clumsy?" Jakon scoffed. "Did you see their speed?"

"Compared to The Ray?" Furi snapped back. "Yes, *slow.*"

Jakon looked toward the rear of the hold. "It doesn't matter. They've been gone for half an hour. They'll be at Midstream long before we could get there."

"I need your transmitter," Alice said.

Jakon gestured to the cockpit. "At your disposal. Then you need to leave my ship if you're determined to kill yourself today."

Furi watched Alice go before turning back to Jakon. "What is it? Why won't you help us?"

"I won't help you get yourself killed," Jakon snapped. "I've done enough of that. You stand up to Fel, and that's all that's going to happen, Furi. I don't want to see my friends dying on the sands of some backwater ruin."

"Neither does Alice," Furi said. "Neither do I." With that, she turned and made her way down the corridor, following Alice.

Alice was already talking. "… don't know, but not long. We're at a base at the edge of the Red Woods."

"I know it," Mary said. "How long to get us there, Smith?" She paused. "Are you sure?"

Alice looked like she was about to scream, her hands turning white she'd clenched her fists so hard. "What did he say?"

"Under an hour." Mary lowered her voice. "He made some adjustments to the thrusters, so we'll either be there or we'll explode over the Crystal Sea."

Furi raised her eyebrows. "How can they possibly get here that fast?"

"We aren't docked," Mary said. "Been sightseeing in the Gray Mountains. Smith's priming the thrusters now. Get to the south side of the base. We'll drop landing lines to you at the tree line."

Jakon stood in the doorway when they disconnected. "I wish you well, but this is not my fight."

Furi frowned at him. "Then what is your fight? You want to protect Ballern? The city that betrayed us all? If you don't choose, someone will choose for you."

Jakon stepped to the side and let them go. Once they were outside, Furi and Alice watched the loading ramp retract and seal. Jakon might have been thinking about staying longer, but seeing the beginnings of the battle headed for Midstream had certainly changed his mind.

"Jerk," Furi muttered.

"I'm mad too, but I understand why he wouldn't do it." Alice turned to Furi. "You've seen what war is. And who knows what Jakon has seen over his life. How long has he been a mercenary?"

"I don't know, but he knows what Ballern has done to the Skyborn. That should be enough, Alice. How could you *not* fight for those kids!" Furi pressed her palms into her eyes, determined not to show any more emotion than she already had. "It has to change."

"Come on," Alice said, gently squeezing her shoulder. "Let's get to the southern edge of the base and wait for Mary. Knowing Smith, they probably won't blow up, but they might get here faster than Mary planned."

Furi smiled at that. Jakon may have abandoned her, but she had other friends too. Of course, Jakon had never tried to shoot down an airship she was on. But these were strange days indeed.

✧　✧　✧

ALICE CHEWED ON the jerky Furi had given her. It was some of the best she'd ever had—apparently, one of the secret recipes Jakon protected like his life depended on it. She was still angry with the captain of The Ray, but she understood why he'd made the decisions he had.

If it weren't her friends out there, would she be so anxious to plunge headlong into another battle? She liked to think she would, to always fight for what was right, what was needed. But the war had already taken such a toll on her city and family and friends. How did people in the old wars do it? They fought for years.

And will this war last for years? She shuddered at the thought.

Furi sipped at a Sweetwing Tea and leaned against a tree. "It's peaceful here, isn't it?"

Alice nodded, still chewing on her jerky. "I just wish I could relax. I can't stand just sitting here while I know what's out there."

Furi took a drink and sighed. "I can't explain how strange the last few weeks have been, Alice."

She knew exactly what Furi meant. "I've been dragged from one end of the continent to the other, not sure if I'll ever see home again, or another sunrise for that matter. And is Ancora really even home anymore? My mom's house was destroyed with the Lowlands. It'll be different now, even if they rebuild the city."

"I'm sorry, Alice. I can't even imagine."

Alice shook her head. "You've been through just as much. Just different."

"I suppose." Furi squinted at the sky. "What is that?"

By the time Alice turned, the first wave of bombs had shattered the base to the north. Fireballs towered over the trees and her ears rang with the thunder of the blasts. Heat seared her eyes in a fiery wind. Furi's glass fell to the ground and splintered on a root as she hefted her pack onto her shoulders. Alice didn't think, didn't stop to consider a plan, only grabbed Furi's arm and ran.

They sprinted into the woods, putting distance between them and the camp before cutting left, heading south where they could watch for the Skysworn *if* they reached the far side of the woods. A startled mantis reared back to threaten them, but the giant bug was just frightened, Alice knew, and it let them pass without striking.

"What was that?" Furi screamed, panic ringing in her words. "Who's attacking!"

"I don't know," Alice said, "but we aren't staying around here to find out."

But she realized that wasn't entirely accurate as they broke through the south side of the forest, stumbling over the arched root system of the Red Woods. In the distance, on the other side of the trees, was a small grassland that gave way to a wide beach. Beyond, waited the Bay of

Sorrow.

Alice turned back, horror crawling through her as she took in the visage of the gray warship hovering in the clouds.

"That's a Fel ship!" Furi said. "But I thought this was a Fel base?"

"It might have been," Alice said, "but they cleared out, didn't they? The crawlers already left. If they learned the base was being used to smuggle people and trade with pirates …"

"Oh gods, the *people*. Everyone who was on The Ray …" Furi put her hand over her mouth. "Do you think Jakon got away?"

The ground shook as the Fel warship released another round of bombs onto the base.

If one of those monsters attacked Midstream, and Archibald didn't have a warship stationed there, Jacob wouldn't have a chance. Gladys's people would truly be lost. Erased. A small cry escaped Alice's lips as the heat from the latest blasts reached them.

"Come on," Furi said, dragging Alice forward until they'd crossed half the grasslands.

A shadow passed over them and Alice looked up, seeing a ship eclipsing the sun as it circled once and drifted back toward them. She slipped her hand into the bolt glove and tightened the straps. If this was going to be the end, it would be met with fury.

The ship sank lower, crossing the sun, and Alice could make out the squat, armored gas chamber that formed the center of the Skysworn.

"Oh, thank the gods," she whispered. "It's Mary."

A rope smacked into the earth some twenty feet away, two sets of wheels clipped to the end.

"You first," Alice said, hurrying Furi onto the rope. "Hold on tight. These will carry you up to the ship after you click the button." She hooked Furi's pack to the belayer as a precaution.

Furi nodded and took a deep breath before clicking the Burner set into the wheels. It jerked twice and then soared into the air, carrying her to Smith, waiting at the railing.

Alice clipped the brace for the bolt glove into the belayer before wrapping her hand around the grip mounted to the wheels. She clicked the Burner and waited for the pressure to equalize. A moment later, she was racing through the air.

And then the Skysworn lurched to the side. Alice screamed when the fireballs exploded beneath her, the wheels breaking free of the rope as she started to fall.

"Alice!" Smith shouted.

The belayer caught, and Alice dangled from the rope. Cannon fire from the warship buzzed by her, clanging against the Skysworn as Smith started hauling the rope in by hand. This was it. She knew it. If they tried to save her, Mary couldn't evade the warship. If they avoided the warship, the inertia alone would be enough to kill her.

Another shadow tore through the sky above them, a glint of gold on the bow of a bloated airship that had no right to move so quickly. The sides of the beast opened wide, unfurling like a flag to reveal four long cannons to either side.

The skies roared with fire as The Ray unleashed hell across the bow of Fel's warship. Glass and steel exploded as Jakon pulled away from that gray monstrosity, only to spiral up above it, stalling the airship until it turned in a graceful arc, plunging down once more as another round transformed one of the warship's gas chambers into a torrent of fire.

Before she realized what had happened, a hand clamped down on Alice's wrist hard enough that it could have broken bone.

"I have her!" Smith cried. "Go!"

Smith tore the belayer off the rope, bending the steel so much it wouldn't be holding anything for some time. Alice caught a glimpse of the flags dripping from The Ray, the skull and crossbones against a field of black as Mary raised the same colors on the Skysworn.

Smith slammed the door to the cockpit closed and Mary hit the thrusters.

Alice tucked her face against the hard biomechanics of Smith's chest and wept.

CHAPTER THIRTY-FIVE

THE ONLY GOOD thing Jacob could say about the landing ships was they'd made the pilots of the crawlers overconfident. Not every trap had been destroyed, and not every damaged trap was non-functional.

"Three of them," Gladys said into a portable transmitter. "Archibald. If you don't send support now, Midstream is going to be a base for Fel. We can't stop this."

Helena took aim at a stalled crawler and launched a bomb. It bounced off the roof and fell to the side. The detonation rocked the crawler, but Jacob was fairly certain those bombs weren't enough to stop a crawler unless they had a lucky shot like he'd had.

The boom of the second landing ship's cannons opened up, bombing out the other side of the riverbed and continuing on until it reached one of the A-frames. Jacob watched, helpless to do anything as the barrier took the brunt of the blast, but more than one soldier fell still behind it.

"Helena," Jacob said. "We need to get to the arm."

"Jacob, no," she said. "We don't even know if that will work."

"It *will* work. It has to." He didn't wait for any more word. His feet dug into the sand and he sprinted toward the arm. The front of it was shielded by another A-frame. That would give them some cover while they tightened their aim.

He reached the seat on the Titan Mech arm as the ships continued to fire on the traps. Helena slid into the seat next to him a moment later.

"I'm going to be annoyed if you get me killed, Jacob."

"You and me both."

Jacob turned the base so the arm was aligned with the nearest ship. Helena adjusted the angle to aim above the airship. They'd only get six shots out of the battery. The fingers of the Titan Mech were too wide to get more precise than that.

He took a deep breath and slid a narrow lever down, curling just the index finger against the latticework of the trap. The metal creaked and then slammed against the base of the mechanism. Four bolts triggered, and Jacob cringed when one of them shattered the casing on the fingertip.

But the other three cleared the hand, silent slivers of light arcing through the air. For a moment, it looked like it would be short, the arc too low, only the bolts didn't lose their velocity as fast as he'd expected. Instead, they crashed into the hull of the landing ship.

Helena leaned back as the loading bay doors bent beneath the impact. The second bolt caught a cannon. Sparks flew as the barrels swung free. Whatever mechanism had held it in place broke, and the barrel slid forward, finally falling to the sands below.

The third bolt cleared the bow of the landing ship and pierced the gas chamber above. It was a small hole, and Jacob doubted it would do any real damage.

"That got their attention," Helena said.

With some dread, Jacob watched the landing ship turn to the west so its remaining cannon could fire on them. Helena adjusted the angle of the arm, and Jacob threw the next lever, firing a second volley. Two of the bolts caught the bay doors and tore them from their hinges, sending the twisted metal careening into whatever waited behind them.

Jacob blinked when the third bolt shot through the deck of the airship and continued on into the gas chamber. But the fourth, which had again clipped the finger of the hand, spiraled forward like a throwing knife. The angle was wrong, but it shattered part of the bow and skittered along the gas chamber, tearing the chamber's shell so deeply that a tightly woven panel collapsed entirely.

From one moment to the next, the landing ship's graceful turn changed into a death spiral, the gas chamber losing its air as a catastrophic failure rippled through it, the volume exploding out the sides and sending some of the crew flailing through the sky as the chamber evacuated in a tremendous blast of wind.

The pilots of the remaining landing ships were smart. They wheeled away from the wreckage of the first landing ship, well out of range of a precise attack from the arm, and opened fire.

"Run!" Helena shouted as the first rounds sent fountains of sand into the air beside them. She leaped to the earth, hurrying back to the A-frame where Gladys and George were still sheltered. But Jacob stayed with the arm.

The third airship landed behind a line of crawlers, and the bay doors opened, revealing a company of heavily armored troops inside. Jacob refined his aim after another shell hit the A-frame in front of him, the concussion rattling his teeth.

He fired, four bolts arcing through the air, and missing completely. The second airship adjusted its cannon again, and this time Jacob didn't wait. He leaped down, sand invading his boots as he stumbled forward, barely clearing the arm before a rain of bolts slammed into the seat where he'd been.

"Our only chance is to take them while they're on the ground," Gladys said as Jacob slid back into their shelter.

"No!" George snapped, making Jacob think they'd been having this argument for some time now. "We may be fast enough to take their soldiers, but those crawlers are too much."

Gladys primed a launcher and slid three of the compound bombs and their Bangers into her cloak. It weighed the fabric down so it didn't billow in the breeze. "Then we put them down as best we can."

"Those bombs will work best against the soldiers on the ground," Jacob said. "You won't have to get close to them. And it … it'll be bad when they go off around people."

Gladys grimaced. "Good. If we can't destroy their crawlers, then we have to buy time for Archibald to get here."

"Gladys," George said. "We have two small carriers in the south of the city. We need to evacuate to those. You cannot fight."

Bolts and shells pinged off the A-frames as the second wave of crawlers reached the riverbed. The soldiers behind them were organized into ranks and already marching into the center of the dry river.

"Go," Gladys said to George. "Take Helena. Get our people out of here. I won't stand by while Fel destroys us again."

"Gladys …"

"Go!"

George grimaced and gestured to Helena. He hesitated and turned back to Gladys. "If the battle grows too intense, retreat into the city itself. Hide if you must. I will return."

Jacob picked up another launcher and clipped a sack of bombs to his belt, priming the launcher as he glanced around the edge of their shelter. One cluster of crawlers was already reaching the top of the opposite bank.

The first ran into a surviving trap, but the second made it through. Time was something they didn't have much of.

"We fire and we run," Gladys said. "They're across the river."

Jacob nodded and passed the word down. "Fire and fall back."

"Keep moving until we're in the city," Gladys said. "Then set up what ambushes you can, and stay hidden if possible."

The word whispered down the ranks, a soldier from each A-frame hurrying to the next, spreading Gladys's orders. Another crawler breached the river and ran into an A-frame as if it meant to knock it over on anyone sheltered behind it.

Instead, the crawler ramped up it, tilted, and rolled back into the riverbed. Jacob raised an eyebrow. "Didn't expect that."

"I don't think they did either." Gladys clicked the fuse on a Banger and snapped it into a shell. She stepped out from the shelter of the barrier as the foot soldiers rushed to help right the crawler. The launcher jerked in her hands, sending the bomb arcing through the air only to clang off the crawler's undercarriage.

One soldier frowned at the orb a moment before a fireball enveloped everyone standing near the crawler. Blood and viscera sprayed across the sand as Gladys reloaded and fired again.

The second round bounced off a dying soldier, and the blast tore the face off another man rushing in to help. Jacob vomited into the sands. He'd done that. He'd made that bomb. Gladys grabbed his arm and hauled him backward.

"Run!"

They abandoned the A-frame as a volley of bolts came down around them. A soldier beside Gladys went down without a sound, a bolt glistening in his neck. Gladys grunted as something caught her arm, and Jacob didn't miss the splash of blood on her cloak.

He turned as he locked his own bomb in place and fired back at the corner of the A-frame where the first foot soldiers had now progressed. He didn't watch the fireball, or the shrapnel, do its work. The screams were enough.

The thunder of metal on metal crashed behind them, followed by a series of explosions. Gladys threw Jacob to the ground as the small home in front of them vanished into a fine cloud of sand and rubble. Jacob scrambled to look at what else might be coming for them. One of the crawlers had its cannon aimed right at them, and judging by the damage done to the buildings, they'd opted for explosive rounds.

Charles had always warned Jacob about explosives. The wrong mixture, or the loss of focus at the wrong time, and you might not have a hand left, or your life. And to carry those inside a crawler? Something that would surely take fire from an enemy force? Jacob shuddered at the thought.

The turret rotated, and Jacob pulled Gladys to her feet. He didn't miss the princess's wince as she flexed her arm and led the survivors down a narrow alley.

Another explosion ripped through the city above them, echoing in their ears and sending bricks and wood to rain down as part of an unrelenting tide. One thing Jacob was sure of as the buildings collapsed behind them: if Archibald's reinforcements didn't get there soon, there wouldn't be a Midstream left to salvage.

CHAPTER THIRTY-SIX

DEEPER INTO THE city, the shelling slowed. Jacob jumped at every sound, tracking the movement of every bug and lizard that crossed their path.

"They'll have the city surrounded by now," Gladys said. "Did you see how those crawlers were starting to circle as we left."

Jacob nodded. He *had* seen it, and they didn't have traps to the south of Midstream. "Once they have a perimeter, they'll move into the city."

"We need to get higher and see what's happening."

"Lead the way." The buildings of Midstream weren't tall, but being tucked away in the tight alleys didn't give Jacob a view of what waited on the outskirts of the city.

Gladys ducked into one of the few three-story structures that remained from the last time Midstream had been burned to the ground, and Jacob stayed close to her. Ancient area rugs, woven with intricate designs and symbols of the old desert, silenced their footsteps.

Jacob followed Gladys up a wooden staircase, parts of the banister still scarred from sword strikes and pocked with shrapnel from whatever had happened there when the warlords came. A simple ladder led from the second floor to a squat square room on the top. A single window graced each wall, and a few pieces of musty furniture sat covered by aged sheets.

Gladys crept to the eastern window while Jacob peered out the corner to the north.

He cursed when he saw the shadows on the horizon. More airships, and these were no landers. The long narrow hulls, crossed at regular intervals with what looked like perpendicular pontoons, could only mean one thing.

"Bombers," Jacob hissed. "We need to get into the basements if we can."

"We don't have basements," Gladys said, joining Jacob at the window. She stared out at the looming shadows closing on them. "The water table is too high here, even in the desert."

"Can we get south?"

"No, the crawlers have already surrounded us, but they aren't moving into the city."

Jacob shook his head. "They wouldn't be. They're going to destroy Midstream and us with it. We have to get to George on the docks."

"The docks are outside the perimeter, Jacob," Gladys said.

He clenched his teeth. "Then tell him to go. We need to split up everyone who followed us. Scatter through the perimeter. They can't catch us all."

"Catch us?" Gladys said. "They're going to kill us. Come on. There's another transmitter downstairs. The lower floor used to be a school, and George always kept one here."

"Don't you have a portable one?"

Gladys ran shaky fingers through her hair before she opened her cloak by the streak of blood. Jacob's eyes widened when he saw the shattered transmitter box. It had cut into her, yes, but it had likely saved her arm in the process.

"Okay, let's find it."

Jacob hurried down to the first floor, and Gladys followed close behind. She made her way over to a bookcase, not unlike the one in George's place, and opened a panel hidden in the bottom of a shelf.

Gladys pulled out another copper box.

She turned the dial and clicked the transmitter. "George, it's Gladys. We're surrounded. A bomber is heading into Midstream. Take the ships and escape to Bollwerk. This is an order from your princess."

A burst of static came back a moment later. "No! I will do no such thing. Where are you stationed? We can …"

"George," Gladys said. "George, it's too late. Fel has a perimeter set up around the city. Save who you can."

The line was silent, but Jacob could only imagine how much cursing George was doing at that minute.

"I'll be back for you, Princess. Take the corridor to the mountains. It won't get you to the docks, but it will provide shelter for a time."

Gladys exchanged a glance with Jacob. "I'm a fool. I forgot we dug out the old passageways. It's how we maintain our wells."

"You're not a fool, Gladys. Now show us how to get there."

Gladys turned the knob on her transmitter. "This is your princess. Get underground. Get to the old wells and shelter there as long as you can. May the gods watch over us all."

They were back in the street when the earth shook beneath their feet as if the desert itself meant to swallow them.

"Are they bombing the riverbed?" Jacob asked.

"I guess your traps bothered them," Gladys said with a brief, savage grin. She sprinted down an alley, following another cloak, while several more trailed them. But even as they moved farther into the city, the explosions didn't stop.

Bomb after bomb blew gusts of sand and debris into the air, and the sky itself vibrated with every clap of thunder.

"Not far now," Gladys said, hurrying into what looked like a small square near the center of the city. But as the shadows drifted in above them, Jacob feared that not far was going to be too far. Another explosion deafened them, and bits of wood and brick pelted down in smoking hail.

Jacob glanced back. The bomber had reached the city limits, and they were out of time. He dove at Gladys as a timber spiraled through the air above them, crashing into a decorative gazebo in the center of the square.

Gladys dragged him back to his feet without pausing. "Everyone run!"

It was the last thing Jacob heard before something slammed into him from behind, and everything went black.

✧　✧　✧

MARY LOWERED THE scope from her eye and slowly collapsed it.

"What is it?" Alice asked.

Mary shook her head. "They're bombing the city."

"What?" Alice undid her harness and hopped out of her seat, snatching the scope out of Mary's hand.

"Get back in your harness," Mary said, but there was no fire in her words.

Alice raised the scope to her eye so she could better see the shadows around Midstream. Crawlers had surrounded the city, large gray things that looked invulnerable to almost any kind of attack. But Alice could see the broken ruin of more than one of those tanks.

She swept the scope closer to the city and gasped. Fel's bomber had cut a swath through the center of the entire city. Buildings lay in smoking rubble while fires had taken hold near the outskirts. Relief flooded her chest when she saw two small airships fleeing from the mountains.

"Two ships past the mountains, headed south."

"Let me see," Mary said.

Alice handed her the scope, and even without it, she could see the smoke and fire rising from the city.

"Why would they do this?" Furi asked, leaning close to Alice.

"Those are the airships Archibald gave to Midstream," Mary said.

"Hopefully Gladys and Jacob are on there. It won't matter if those schooners catch them."

Mary shouted into the horn. "Smith! We're going to engage four schooners."

"Four!" Smith's annoyed shout came back. "Why don't you just fly us into a mountain instead?"

"They're chasing Midstream's only airships."

Smith didn't respond for a time. "Send Alice and Furi down here. We'll need them on the guns."

"No," Mary said. "I want to use the guns you installed in the hull. I don't want to slow down."

"You want to engage with the thrusters on?" Smith cursed. "Mary, that's insane!"

"We have about two minutes until we're in range. Be ready. Alice, Furi, buckle in."

Alice could hear Smith banging around over the horn. The sounds faded and something like steel dragging over steel screeched through the ship.

Mary flashed a bitter grin. "Smith's loading a belt in the new chainguns."

"Look," Furi said, pointing to the windscreen. "The bomber is circling back around."

Mary shook her head. "They're going to destroy Midstream entirely. Just like Ancora. Just like the Bay of Sorrow." Her fingers whitened as they choked the life out of a lever. She took a deep breath and opened a copper panel to expose their transmitter.

"Airships fleeing Midstream, this is the Skysworn. You have four schooners closing from behind."

The transmitter crackled and George's voice burst to life. "Skysworn! We are not equipped for combat."

"We are. One minute out from engaging their rear. It doesn't look good for Midstream. Fel's bomber is circling back."

George's voice choked up. "Gladys and Jacob are still in there!"

"What!" Alice squeaked as her heart dropped into her stomach. "No. No!"

Furi reached out and grabbed her hand.

"She ordered us to leave," George said. "It was the right thing to do. We have hundreds of souls on these ships."

"It won't matter if you're all dead," Mary growled. "Split your formation. At least give them a hard target."

"You have to stop the bomber," George said. "There could still be survivors down there."

"First, I need to make sure there are survivors up here," Mary said. "Keep a line open. Smith, did you catch all that?"

"I caught it. Now take down the schooners so we can figure out a way to bring down a bomber. Belts are locked in."

"Then you better lock yourself in." Mary slid a panel out from underneath the console. It looked shiny and new compared to the aged patina of the rest of the buttons and levers. She hit the pale yellow one on the left first, and the ship shook.

"What is that?" Alice asked.

"Drag from the chainguns."

Alice leaned as far to the right as she could, releasing Furi's hand. At the edge of the porthole, she could just make out the railing flipping and locking into place. And on the far side, now starting to spin, sat a chaingun like the one Smith had used in Gareth Cave. Memories of Rana flashed through her mind before she came back to the moment.

Mary hit the green button, and the barrels started to spin. And as the speed accelerated, Alice realized these were far different from what she'd seen in Gareth Cave.

"You know this will either be brilliant, or we'll explode, right?" Smith said with an odd calm to his voice.

In answer, Mary flipped the brass locking mechanism off the red button and slammed her palm down onto it. It was as though they'd stepped into a swarm of Sky Needles, the chaingun buzzing like a saw powered by compressed air. Only instead of a single needle to cut down their prey, the chainguns sent bolts of fire screaming across the skies.

The first schooner never had a chance. Mary's volley cut through the cabin and gas chamber alike, sending a spray of metal and wood into the air before the gas chamber collapsed entirely, and the ruined ship plummeted to the earth.

At the speed they were moving, Alice didn't even see it crash into the mountains. By the time it hit, they were well past it. Mary targeted the next, the chainguns again thundering outside the Skysworn. This volley took the stern of a schooner, but it managed to evade being shot down.

"Brace yourselves!" Mary said. "Thrusters down in three, two, one."

The inertia slammed Alice against her harness, and she didn't miss Furi's boots scraping against the floor as if she could slow them down on her own. But their ambush had done its job.

"Schooners are retreating," George's voice crackled over the transmitter. "Thank you, Skysworn."

"I wish they were retreating," Mary said. "Smith, we're taking to the mountains."

Smith groaned, and Alice heard the ringing of metal on metal. "Ready when you are. Secondary boilers are primed, but I would still prefer you not run into anything."

"I can go below deck." Alice started to unbuckle her harness.

"Not now," Mary said. "I don't want anyone in those gun pods while we're in the valleys."

Alice hesitated and then refastened her harness.

The Skysworn dove, skimming a mountain ridge as it slipped into a valley.

"We should take the high ground!" Furi said. "We're an easy target for cannon fire here!"

Mary released a bitter laugh at that. "Or so they'll think."

Two schooners appeared along the valley above them, cannons swinging toward the Skysworn.

"Let's see you match this. Hold on!" Mary slammed two levers down and the bow of the Skysworn lurched into clouds. She increased the thrust, and a cannonball screeched past them, detonating in the valley below. By the time the second schooner could have even thought about firing, the Skysworn had reached the top of its arc.

"Who has the high ground now?" Mary whispered. She primed the chainguns and fired again, cutting through the gas chamber of the second schooner. "Two down."

Before she finished getting the words out, small arms fire ripped through the cabin of the Skysworn. Furi screamed as splinters exploded into the air and metal clanged against the cabin door. Something boomed below them and Smith's hurried cursing echoed over the horn.

"Switching to secondary boilers. Don't take another hit like that!"

"Steering's slow," Mary shouted back.

"We lost one of the chainguns too. Damn! I should have shielded that. Stupid."

"You can yell at yourself later; just fix the steering! Rudders are down. I'm taking to the valley again."

"Why would you do that when we can't steer!" Smith squawked.

Alice thought that was a perfectly reasonable question as the Skysworn dove into the valley again. But it was also a perfectly reasonable question as to why she was unfastening her harness, opening the door to the cabin to Mary's protests, and scampering down the access hatch in the middle of the deck. She heard Mary's voice come across the horn.

"Alice is heading your way, Smith."

"What? Why?"

Alice paused when she reached the hatch above the gun pod, spinning the lock to open it and then slipping inside. She opened the horn. "Because we already lost one gun, and I don't want to die today."

"Gods be damned! Shoot straight, and if it looks like the mountains are getting too close, get out of the pod."

Alice locked her harness in and grabbed the controls. She'd seen them work before, and she knew the wheel would rotate the entire pod. She spun it clockwise, tracing the sights of the chaingun until it was aimed behind them.

One of the schooners had followed them into the valley, and it was a mistake they'd regret. Alice flipped the trigger guards off the top of the levers as she put the ship in the crosshairs and squeezed the buttons down with her thumbs.

The chaingun burst into life, scouring the side of the valley as she strafed across the bow of the ship behind her. Small bursts of wood and sparks lit up behind them, but the schooner still had time to fire back. Cannon fire ripped into the mountain beside Alice, peppering the glass gun pod with rock and debris.

They didn't have time for this. They had to stop the bomber, and at this rate, there'd be nothing left of Midstream by the time they got back to it. Alice tracked to the right, following the curve of the canyon, and unleashed another volley as the schooner made the turn. This time the shots sparked against the armored struts of the gas chamber before cutting into the cannon mounted above the cabin.

Alice flinched when something caught fire and detonated a moment later, sending the schooner to the floor of the valley in a tumbling, flaming wreck. There was an odd sense of satisfaction, followed by the gut-wrenching realization that anyone on that ship was dead.

"It was them or us," she whispered.

"It still might be us, kid!" Mary shouted over the horn. "Smith, I can't adjust altitude."

"I had to disconnect the drive rod. Hold on!"

"Their cannon is locked on, Smith! We're in a straightaway! Fix the damn rod!"

Alice unbuckled her harness and leaped out of the gun pod. If Mary couldn't adjust their elevation, then the gun pod would be the first thing to get smashed on the rocks. She made her way up to the deck and back to the cabin, where she saw the first cannonball miss their bow by inches.

"Sorry, girls," Mary said. "I didn't think we'd get trapped like this."

Alice fastened her harness and reached out to squeeze Furi's hand. But the moment she did, Furi pointed out the windscreen.

"Look!"

"Another ship incoming!" Mary shouted into the horn. "Starboard!"

But before Alice could so much as worry about Mary's warning, the sides of the ship unfurled, and the flags shifted beneath the gleaming gold of the bow. The Ray dove, opening fire on the schooner with such a fury that the ship was rent in two. Alice watched in horror as the schooner spilled its guts and its burning crewmen into the sky, only to be smashed into the mountainside that waited below.

"Skysworn, this is The Ray. You can thank Furi for my short bout of conscience."

Mary clicked the transmitter. "Ray, thanks for the assist. Can you help us take down that bomber?"

"Bomber?"

"You didn't see the bomber over Midstream?"

"Negative. I came from the north. Had to harass some Fel clippers in the desert before I made my way here. Your crew may have left your frequency on my transmitter. I've been listening for a while now."

"Drive rod ready!" Smith said.

Mary pulled back, and the Skysworn arced out of the valley. She guided it up alongside The Ray, signaling Jakon in the cabin.

Furi leaped out of her seat and hit the transmitter by Mary. "Jakon, it's Furi. Thank you."

"No names. You never know who's listening."

"Apparently, you are. You didn't answer Mary. Can you help?"

There was a brief moment of dead air when Alice dreaded Jakon's answer. Then he spoke. "I didn't come all this way not to help. Let's take care of your bomber, and then I can get back to cooking for a living."

"And smuggling," Furi said, but she'd already released the transmitter.

"The bombs are carried in the cargo pontoons, away from the hull," Jakon said. "They're armored, but they can be penetrated by a good shot to the seams."

"You only need one good shot out of a hundred," Mary said.

"Well, I suppose that's true, but it would take rather a long time to load a cannon one hundred times."

Smoke filled the horizon before Alice saw the shadow. She couldn't judge the distance between the bomber and Midstream very well, but from where they were, it didn't look like the city had much time left at all.

Apparently, Mary noticed it at the same time. "How fast can that old rust bucket run?"

"Old rust bucket!" Jakon said. "I doubt you can keep up."

"Smith, making the jump."

Furi fumbled with her harness and locked it in a second before Mary hit the thrusters. They shot ahead, leading The Ray, though Alice was fairly certain she heard a rather large piece of metal tear away from the Skysworn.

"Damn," Jakon said, a moment before twin flames burst from the rear of The Ray, and though the Skysworn might have stayed ahead of Jakon as they closed on the bomber, it wasn't by nearly as much as Alice had expected.

"Get in the pod, Smith. We're going to dive under the gas chambers and you're going to put as many rounds as you can into those pontoons. Jakon, take the port side. We'll hammer the starboard."

"No, I'll follow you in."

"Be ready to run."

The Ray slowed, pulling into the Skysworn's slipstream and out of Alice's line of sight. She clenched her teeth as the bomber loomed ever larger. The closer they got, the more she realized how massive it was. If they shot it down over the city, and it exploded, she doubted they'd save much of anyone.

She said as much to Mary.

"I know. We're only two miles out. It's going to be close. Cutting thrusters." It was all the warning she gave before slowing the Skysworn and dipping down beneath the wide, flat gas chambers of the bomber. They'd arrived so fast, Alice wondered if Smith would react in time.

But the moment she'd had that thought, the chaingun below the Skysworn roared to life. She could feel the vibration through her seat, but nothing like when she'd been seated in the gun pod herself.

"What the hell are you firing!" Jakon shouted over the transmitter.

"We survive this, I'll have Smith make you one as thanks."

"Well, then you better survive because I need a pair! Bomber deploying cannons. Get out of there!"

Smith's hail of shells punched dozens of holes into the pontoons, but still, the bomber continued on. Mary swerved hard to starboard, veering out from beneath the bomber as a line of small cannons opened fire on their former trajectory.

But while the barrels were pointed down, The Ray swung wide, angling in from the aft as its cannons unfurled and the skull and crossbones snapped in the wind. Jakon passed close to the Skysworn, so close it made Alice's skin crawl as the ship shook. But a moment later, the ship shook for an entirely different reason.

She watched in awe and horror as the pontoon ruptured. The Ray dove beneath it, and a fireball nearly as large as Midstream itself flashed upward into the gas chambers of the bomber.

Alice had once heard stories of ships that could only fly on gas that was as flammable as the air in the Burning Forest. She'd never really believed it until the explosion threatened to deafen her, and the Fel bomber was consumed by waves of fire.

"Jakon!" Furi shouted. "Did he clear it?"

"Skysworn to Ray. Skysworn to Ray!"

For a moment, there was only static. "Ray here. A little burnt, but I'll survive. Bomber is falling, but it's going to hit the southern outskirts of the city. I hope they got everyone out."

Even as Jakon spoke, the bomber crumpled into the sands below, sending up a cloud of fire and steam and death that spread like a furious sandstorm. More than one of the smaller homes on the edge of Midstream collapsed in that gale, and two functional crawlers vanished in the blast.

Alice silently hoped Jacob and Gladys were still alive.

"Ray, we're setting down to look for our friends."

"You're mad. There's still two dozen crawlers down there."

"Why don't you make yourself useful and take care of a few?"

Jakon laughed. "Aye, that I can do."

Fire streaked from The Ray, sending up plumes of sand and shrapnel as the first crawler met its quick demise. By the time Jakon reached the third, soldiers were scattering outside the city, returning to their crawlers, and retreating to the north.

"Smith, we're landing."

"No," Smith said. "We'll take the lines down. Stay airborne. Be ready to leave if you need to."

Mary hesitated and then nodded. "Will do. Be careful."

CHAPTER THIRTY-SEVEN

J ACOB BLINKED IN the flickering light and shadows, trying to understand where he was and why the walls were moving. Slowly he realized he was being dragged on a stretcher. He checked himself over for injury, finding a crude bandage on his head.

"What happened?" he asked, wincing at the pain that shot through his skull.

He grunted when the stretcher dropped, and Gladys suddenly appeared above him.

"Sorry!" She reached out and hugged him. "I thought we lost you. A brick hit you in the back of the head. Helena patched you up."

Jacob frowned as Gladys pulled away. "Helena? I thought she went with George."

"His memory is still good," Helena said. "Positive sign. I was helping evacuate the city and came back to gather who I could when the bombing started."

Jacob looked around at the smooth stone walls. A quiet rush of water sounded in the distance. The only light came from torches that were slowly filling the top of the corridor with a thin veil of smoke.

Something like distant thunder echoed around them, and a small trickle of dust and sand fell from the ceiling. More memories came rushing back to Jacob, and he jumped up from the stretcher, much to Helena's protests.

Midstream, the bomber, the crawlers …

"You shouldn't be walking," Helena said.

Jacob felt a little slow, but he'd been hit harder before. Or so he thought. "I can walk, and I won't slow you down. Lead on, Princess."

Gladys grinned at him while Helena rolled her eyes. But they didn't argue, leaving the stretcher behind as he picked up his air cannon and pack from the stretched canvas.

"There's an opening to the wells ahead," Gladys said. "We have three options. Take the underground river to the oasis, continue on to the other side of the mountain where the docks are, or shelter here and fight anyone who followed us."

"We have too many injured to take the river, Princess," Helena said. "It's nearly a minute underwater at the end of the stream."

Just the thought of trying to hold his breath made Jacob's head spin. And if anyone else was injured, like Helena had said, it was a losing prospect.

Gladys nodded as she led the way into a circular cistern. The walls had been lined with stone, but above them were natural rock formations clinging to the arched ceiling. Jacob wondered how old it was for the water to have deposited such large stalactites. Had the river once been above them, or was it just groundwater?

More thunder chased away his thoughts.

"I don't think the docks are safe," Gladys said. "If they saw George and the others leave, they could bomb those next."

Helena nodded. "It is possible."

Gladys took a deep breath. "Then we fight. Here. We form a barrier to both sides of the path. They can only come in two at a time, three at a time at most. Anyone who has bolts or arrows can line up to target the doorway. Swords and spears in front."

Helena went to work without question, directing the injured to the back of the pathway that arched above the underground river. They shifted several heavy stones and aged crates closer to the entryway, creating a funnel for anyone entering the cavern, and offering shelter to those at the front of the lines.

Jacob didn't count the number of Midstreamers who came into the chamber behind him, but it was obvious a great deal of the citizenry hadn't escaped with George. He pulled the air cannon off his back and racked the slide. He might be injured, but if he didn't help fight, he might be dead.

✧　✧　✧

IT WASN'T LONG after the last of the Midstreamers had entered the cistern that they could see the light of torches at the far end of the hall. Helena signaled everyone to draw back from the entrance. No incoming soldier would be able to see what waited for them.

But the waiting was agony. Jacob's heart pounded and his fingers flexed around the barrel of the air cannon. Memories of the battle of Ancora screamed in his memory, and he tried to focus on the moment, tried to block out the thought that he already knew what was coming down that corridor.

Jacob sprawled out on the floor at the edge of one of the crates, taking a deep breath of the musty air. His new position gave him a line of sight to the corridor while keeping him almost completely hidden in the shadows. He'd expected to hear footsteps synchronized like a march, but when the sound reached his ears, it was anything but.

The torches grew brighter, and the first two soldiers crossed into the light. Jacob had never seen armor so heavy before. Metal plates covered their bodies from head to toe, and their helmets, which should have had weaknesses at the eyes at least, were shielded themselves with a curved transparency.

"Fire!" Helena shouted.

Bolts and arrows slammed into the armored figures. A few found passage in the joints of the armor, but the vast majority pinged off them harmlessly. Jacob clicked the button on a Banger and slid it into the air cannon's barrel. He steadied himself and fired. The boom caused almost everyone in that room to freeze as the metal orb cracked through the first soldier's faceplate and caved the armor in beneath it.

Jacob didn't wait for the screams to stop before he reloaded. Didn't wait for the Banger to fail in a spray of teeth and gore as he aimed at the second soldier. This one was still stunned, staring at his fallen comrade. Jacob's shot took him in the chest, and the armor failed in earnest, cutting a deep bloody wound before the man collapsed. The Banger detonated, and blood streamed across the floor, pooling around the dead.

Shouts rose in the corridor, and Jacob had little doubt they were about to find themselves battling far more of the armored troops. But while the screams and thunder echoed through the tunnel, no one came. It continued for some minutes before a bloody form hobbled into the chamber, two bolts hammered into its arm.

"Hold fire!" Gladys shouted. And when she did, the remaining soldier spun to face the tunnel.

Jacob didn't understand why Gladys had called to hold fire until a flash of red hair gleamed in the torchlight. Alice. She looked savage with the stream of blood matting down one side of her hair. Smith's heavy footfalls followed her down the corridor.

But beside Alice was someone he didn't recognize. She was small, but Jacob thought she might be older than them both. And when she flourished a bloody blade in her right hand, she showed a terrible skill that made Jacob never want to find himself on the wrong end of its edge.

It had to be Furi, the Ballern girl Alice had told him about.

She sprang on the last soldier, weaving under the sweep of a sword before pulling his helmet back as her blade slid into his neck. He gasped and gurgled and then fell onto the pair of soldiers they'd recently fought.

Alice's fiery gaze roamed the cavern until she found Jacob and Gladys. Something in her expression softened, even as she reloaded the wrist launcher she'd taken from Charles's lab. She held a hand out to Jacob and pulled him to his feet, offering a quick embrace before doing the same to Gladys.

"How bad is the city?" Gladys asked.

"Bad," Smith said, straightening a bent rod near his shoulder with some annoyance.

"Could have been worse," Alice said. "One of Furi's friends from Ballern helped destroy the bomber."

"Ballern?" Helena said. "You're from Ballern?" She turned to Furi, and something warred across her face. Jacob suspected he knew the feeling. A mixture of curiosity and long-instilled fear.

Furi nodded. "I fought in the airship battle not far from here. That's where Belldorn captured me, and how I met Alice."

Helena frowned. "Then why would you help Midstream? Help *us?* Ballern has never been a friend to the desert cities."

"It still isn't," Furi said quietly. "But their alliance with Fel is a threat to more than just Midstream. It's a threat to all of us, in every city on this continent, and others."

Helena held up her hand. "Midstream is my only concern right now. You can talk to George and Gladys about the rest."

Smith rubbed the back of his neck as Gladys pounced on him, giving the mountain of a man a crushing hug. "It's good to see you too. Feels like it's been too long."

"You and Mary need to come visit. I know it's only been a week, but it feels like forever."

Smith smiled. "Well, a lot has happened. And it sounds like a lot more is going to happen." He gave Furi a meaningful look before turning back to Gladys. "Do you wish to retreat to Bollwerk? We can fit your people on the Skysworn and The Ray. I am quite certain of that."

"We'll make do here," Gladys said. "After all, if that bomber crashed nearby, that will give us a lot of steel to work with. Let's get above ground. I need to see what's happened to the city."

"It's not good," Alice said. "At least a block was destroyed across the entire city. Right through the middle."

Gladys looked to Jacob. "Do you think Archibald would send more Titan Mech parts here? So we could work on more buildings at once?"

Alice blew out a breath. "If it keeps Fel from attacking Bollwerk? I'm sure he'll be happy to send you as many parts as you want."

Jacob didn't doubt Alice was right about that.

Smith clicked the transmitter in his collar. Nothing came back but static. He frowned. "Too far underground. Let us get these people back to the surface. I have not heard an explosion in some time. I suspect The Ray has done its work."

✧   ✧   ✧

THEY STOOD AT the edge of the city where the bomber had crashed. Nothing had survived the impact, and the sands themselves had been scorched into glass, trapping the burnt remains of buildings and soldiers alike beneath the debris.

"Ash upon ash," Gladys said, the wind catching her cloak and revealing a torn sleeve. "We will rebuild again and again until Mordair has been thrown down and we can live in peace."

"Sometimes, I think it would be easier to move elsewhere," Helena said, looking toward the wound cut through Midstream.

"It would be," Gladys said. "But I wouldn't want to be the leader who abandoned our home. Our history is here, and no man, no *king*, will take that from us."

Smith's transmitter crackled, hard to hear in the gust of wind.

"Understood." Smith turned to Gladys as he released his transmitter.

"Mary talked to George. The passengers voted unanimously to return to the city."

Gladys's shoulders slumped a hair. "Oh, good. Almost all of our builders were with George. I was afraid I'd have to rely on Jacob and Helena to rebuild everything."

Jacob blinked at that.

Gladys started to speak and then paused, raising her hand to shield her eyes. "A little late, I'd say."

Jacob followed her gaze. Looming behind the two small ships floated one of Bollwerk's warships. It was a terrifying vision. As large as Fel's bomber had been, the warship dwarfed it by magnitudes. More than once, he'd heard the warships referred to as floating cities, and that was the best description Jacob could think of.

"Come on," Gladys muttered, stalking toward the ship as it fired anchoring harpoons into the foothills. "It's time to have a talk with Archibald."

✧   ✧   ✧

JACOB COULD TELL Gladys was disappointed that Archibald himself wasn't on Warship One. But that didn't slow her down. She cut the captain off mid-sentence as he tried to explain why they hadn't arrived earlier, and made her way back into the city. Mary had docked in the mountains, and Jacob was somewhat surprised to hear The Ray had anchored there too.

Smith and Helena left to help George at the docks, but Jacob, Alice, and Furi stayed behind with Gladys. They crossed a section of street that the bomber hadn't entirely demolished, and Gladys led them back to George's home.

Inside, she pulled the transmitter from the shelf and switched the dial.

"Archibald. This is Gladys. *Archibald.*"

The transmitter crackled, and Archibald sounded like he might be out of breath. "Gladys, thank the gods. George said you hadn't gotten out."

"I didn't. Your warship just arrived. Nearly an hour late, I might add."

Archibald remained silent for a time, and Jacob had heard his placating tone before. "I apologize for that, but as you know, the warships are not built to be quick vessels. For the time being, it will remain anchored at Midstream. Should Fel strike at you again, they will be driven back."

Gladys nodded. "Good. I need more of those Titan Mech arms Jacob built. How fast can you get them to me?"

"Our smiths are currently building several. I will have two of them mounted on crawlers and brought to Midstream within the week."

"The last one only took a couple days," Jacob said.

Gladys hesitated. "Make it two days, Archibald. We lost a block across the entire city. We'll need to clear the debris and rebuild."

"It will be done. You'll have more materials on the next supply ship as well. I would recommend rebuilding the outskirts with metal. I know it is not traditional, but it will give you better shelter."

"Send the framework for a bunker too. The tunnels that lead to our wells will need reinforcement. If we lose access to water, rebuilding won't matter anyway. And Archibald, this is no favor to me. Midstream will pay you for your goods, even if we cannot repay you for the warship's presence."

"You owe no favor, Princess. Watch for us in two days' time. Speaker out."

Gladys sighed and released the transmitter.

"He's leaving the warship here for now," Alice said. "That's more than I expected."

"It's more than I hoped," Gladys said with a brief smile. "But don't tell him that. He may not think I see his broader plans for using us as a shield, but I do. And I'll take what I can from it to help my city."

CHAPTER THIRTY-EIGHT

T HEY SAT AROUND a bonfire that evening, near the northern edge of the city, where the remains of six armored crawlers had fallen still. Many homes had been lost to the bombing, but the hospital in the west had been spared and had plenty of beds for those who wanted to stay in the city.

Others left for the warship. Several of the children from Midstream were excited to see one of the massive vessels up close. Jacob remembered that sense of wonder. It didn't feel like that long ago when he'd marvel at almost any kind of technology he didn't understand.

But now things had changed. Now, when he didn't understand something, he'd want to take it apart and learn its secrets for himself. Charles had taught him some of that, he knew. A useful curiosity, the old man would call it, because curiosity without action didn't bring understanding.

His bandage had been removed by a local doctor. The process of prying the dried blood out of his hair, sterilizing the wound, and stitching it closed had been less pleasant than being knocked out in the first place. He gently prodded at the edge of the bandage, only to get his hand slapped by Alice.

"Stop touching it. You're going to get it infected."

Jacob grinned at her.

"Tell me about Ballern," Gladys said to Furi.

Furi sipped at her soup and pursed her lips. "Well, from what I've learned here, it sounds a lot like Fel. I mean, I guess Fel is more open about ruling with an iron fist, but Ballern isn't so different."

"I thought Ballern was divided into districts like Belldorn?" Gladys said. "Where they had representatives of the various districts meet in the courts."

Furi shook her head. "Technically, they do, but the monarchy has overridden them so many times they might as well not exist. I think they just keep doing it because it looks better to the outside world. But, honestly, they're just as bad as Fel. One ruler sets the laws and breaks them as they please."

"Like what the Butcher did to Ancora," Alice said quietly. "We always had Parliament to keep things fair. Until we didn't."

"Parliament!" Gladys said with a laugh. "Please, they kept the Lowlands as poor as they could. How else could the Highlands control them? And that wasn't new with the Butcher's manipulation. George told me that's how your city has been for a century."

"It still sounds nicer than Ballern," Furi said. "We've been overrun from the inside by a religion that worships old machines in the west."

Alice nodded. "Well, that *is* somewhat insane. And they really think their machines are guarded by mutants and horrors?"

"Holy mutants," Furi muttered. "The Children of the Dark Fire are a disease in themselves, and most of Ballern doesn't know what they've done. I'm afraid Ballern will have to be broken to ever get rid of them."

"What do you mean?" Jacob asked.

"I think Ballern will have to go to war with itself. And I don't know if those of us who are sane can win that fight. Some of their symbols are etched into our coins now. If you've ever seen a king's crown, that trapezoid on the back represents the Great Machines. I never even realized that until Alice and I went snooping through the library."

"It wasn't snooping." Alice passed a block of salted meat to Furi that one of Gladys's people had brought them for food. "We were there with permission from the lady herself."

Furi laughed. "*That* was an accident. You didn't expect her to be at Mary's any more than I did."

"Well, no, but still, she gave her blessing."

"You met the Lady Katherine?" Gladys asked, arching an eyebrow.

Furi grinned at that. The bonfire crackled and sparked, casting shadows among the gathered groups.

"I'd like to see the library one day," Jacob said.

Alice scooted closer and put her arm around his waist. "You'd love it. It's as tall as the Highland walls and filled with books from top to bottom."

"I can't even imagine that."

"Neither could I."

"What's Midstream like?" Furi asked, turning to Gladys. "How do you rule here?"

Gladys looked off into the distance for a moment. "For a long time, I didn't. We hid in Bollwerk while the warlords ran the desert. That all changed when one of them abducted me, and Alice killed him."

"It was a bit more complicated than that," Alice said.

Furi blinked. "And, how *will* you rule?"

"Like my parents did," Gladys said. "I have four advisors, those closest to me, who are both guards and consults. It is a monarchy of sorts, but I listen to my people. And should I ever choose to stop listening, my family will be removed from the throne and a more benevolent ruler installed. It's a rare thing, but it's happened twice in our history. Those who report to the council must be unanimous in their request."

"But still, it can be done," Furi said. "I like that. It compels you to do the right thing and gives your people a sense that they have some say in their city."

Gladys nodded. "As they should. It's home to all of us."

Furi sighed and peeled a strip of meat from the block she'd been whittling. "I like some things about Ballern, but maybe I'll just move here instead."

"You should come for the Fire Lizard migration, at least," Gladys said. "It's one of the only times they gather in groups, and you can see their flames all across the horizon as they migrate between the Burning Forest and the Bay of Sorrow."

"I'd like that," Furi said. "I'd like that a lot."

✧　✧　✧

AFTER SOME REST and food, Jacob and Alice made their way to the dry riverbed. It was jarring to see the sand and stone displaced by explosions from the bomber. Just twelve hours before it had been undisturbed but for the traps they'd laid.

"Wow," Alice said, climbing into the driver's seat of the Mech arm. "You really built this."

"Well, I had some help. A lot of help, actually. Frederick is pretty amazing. I still can't believe he came all the way from Belldorn to help build the arms.

"How many are there now?"

Jacob shrugged. "Four, I guess?" He studied the panels and joints that had broken off the one they were in. "Three and a half?"

Alice looked at the ground and laughed. "Yes, well, I suppose this one has seen better days."

"Can you pull that lever on the right to lower the arm? I want to take a closer look at the damage."

Jacob winced at the grinding sound the arm made as Alice lowered it. If he was lucky, some debris was just working its way past the gears. If he wasn't lucky, they might have to remove the arm from the treads to work on it.

He hopped up into the palm of the Titan Mech's hand. Of the four fingers, the smallest had taken the most damage. Its armor had been ripped away by the trap he'd fired, and a cannonball had blown apart the interior.

"We'll need to replace two joints, and I'm not sure if there's a workshop in Midstream that can handle it."

Alice pointed to the sky.

"What?"

Alice stretched her arm up until Jacob's gaze followed it to the massive airship floating above Midstream.

"Oh. That's a good point."

Alice grinned. "I'm pretty sure they'll have anything you need to pull the arm apart."

"And if they don't, I can have Frederick send a lift with the next arm!"

"That sounds … *Jacob*," Alice hissed. "Jacob, don't move."

He froze, slowly turning to see what Alice was looking at. To his credit, he didn't scream when he found the titanic Tail Sword standing just behind him, its stinger raised to the sky. He had nothing to fend it off with, nowhere to run except perhaps to dive off the other side of the hand.

But this was the largest Tail Sword he'd ever seen. And he remembered what it had done to a crawler. It had to be nearly fifteen feet from tail to claw, and as he stared with a mixture of shock and horror, the Tail Sword started rubbing against the hand. The tail flattened out, and the creature shook itself.

It took Jacob a moment to realize what was happening. The Tail Sword wasn't coming to attack them. It probably didn't even realize they were there.

"It's molting," Jacob whispered back to Alice.

"Oh, that's great. Now we can be its snacks when it's done."

"It won't attack," Jacob said, standing and slowly making his way to the seat beside Alice. "They're vulnerable after they molt."

"Pretty sure *we're* more vulnerable."

Jacob grinned at Alice. "We're safe."

Alice wrapped her hands around his arm and leaned closer. "You know, some of the desert clans used to make their armor out of Tail Sword shells."

"Some of them still do," Jacob said. "When we were underground, more than one guard had armor carved out of chitin."

They watched the Tail Sword as it slowly backed out of its exoskeleton. It looked oddly pale, but Jacob knew it would darken as the days passed. The Tail Sword sat motionless for a time, its body rising and falling with its breath before it scurried off toward the larger sand dunes.

Alice leaned over to look down at the long stretch of exoskeleton the Tail Sword had left. "Well, I think they'll have enough to make some new armor now."

Jacob squeezed her closer and looked up at the stars. Midstream didn't have city lights like Ancora and Bollwerk, and the view was spectacular. Distant nebulae and galaxies drifted behind the stars above them. And for a moment, Jacob felt peace.

CHAPTER THIRTY-NINE

MORDAIR WAITED IMPATIENTLY for his general to finish the report. The loss was more substantial than he'd expected. Over a dozen armored crawlers, four schooners, and a bomber. The bomber surprised him more than anything. For a ship of that size to be taken down, something must have penetrated the holds and triggered the bombs before they were utilized.

Someone would need to have been very lucky, or have a working knowledge of Fel's warships. Mordair could deal with luck. But the idea that someone from Fel might have betrayed their city darkened his thoughts.

"And what of the casualties?" Mordair asked, tapping his finger on the arm of the throne as he interrupted the general's report.

"Severe. Close to eighty percent of those deployed did not return."

Mordair's tapping stopped. "Schedule a rally for tomorrow. Those soldiers died heroes, martyrs for our great cause, and the people of Fel will know it. Donate five thousand bars to each family."

"Five … five *thousand*, my king?"

"Yes. This is not the time to have our people question the validity of this war simply because their friends and family have died. Pay them for their loss, and we will remember them with the greatest honors a king can bestow."

"And for those who do not … see in the proper way?"

"Eliminate them."

"Exile, my king?"

"Execution. Blame them for the plague the mountainfolk are battling and burn them."

The general gestured to one of the guards standing by the sharp gray stone closest to the king. The general handed the guard a note scribbled on a thin pad of parchment. "Get this to the lieutenants. Have them secure the gold from the vaults."

Mordair held up a finger. "Leave the gold in the vaults. Take it from the common bank."

"My king, those taxes are for the restoration and maintenance of—"

"Of course. Be sure to increase our takings for the next quarter. We'll need to recover the gold we used to purchase the allegiance of the families."

The general took a deep breath and passed the note to the guard. "Go now."

After a short bow, the guard left, his armored boots rattling across the stone floor.

"Archibald means to protect Midstream," Mordair said. "I know his mind well enough. He seeks a return to the brutality of the Deadlands War. And he shall have it."

CHAPTER FORTY

The next morning, Jacob found himself back on the arm of the Titan Mech with a set of tools from a Midstream tinker. He'd managed to get the first joint of the broken finger off by himself, and one of Gladys's tinkers was working on rebuilding the exterior for him. If all went well, he thought they'd be able to start building with the arm again by midday.

Jacob wiped a line of sweat from his brow and leaned into the ratchet. It finally budged when he slid an extension over the handle and put all of his body weight into it, digging into the flesh of his hands. It shouldn't have been that tight, and he suspected the bolt had been bent in the battle. He grumbled to himself and hopped down to the toolbox. The repair would have been a thousand times easier if he'd had the bay at Bollwerk, or even the workshop.

But transporting the arm back to Bollwerk, or to the warship, would take more time than it would save. He found what he was looking for in the bottom of the toolbox: a strange cylinder with abrasive metal inside.

Jacob climbed back up onto the hand and slid the sander over the end of the bolt before tightening it against the threads. It was a hand crank, so it would take some time, but time he had.

It wasn't long before he felt like he'd been spinning the handle for an hour, a small pile of filings forming at his feet when the bolt had finally been stripped. Not only was the thread gone, but the end protruding from the joint was a bit thinner too.

He took a hammer to it, the metal impact ringing through the air as he worked the bolt out of the joint. It might have cost them an oversized bolt, but at least the socket was saved. Far easier to replace a bolt.

"Jacob!"

He glanced over the side of the arm to find Gladys and Alice and a face he hadn't expected to see in Midstream.

"Archibald?"

"Hello, Jacob."

"What are you doing here?" Jacob hopped down from the arm, sinking into the sands when he landed.

"Gladys can be quite … motivating when she applies herself." Archibald cast a smile to the princess.

Gladys stood a little straighter. "I told him we needed the docks expanded here so we can move the construction equipment in from Dauschen."

Jacob's eyebrows rose a hair. "Dauschen still needs the arm, though, don't they?"

Archibald nodded. "We'll move some of the construction from the docks at Dauschen to Midstream. We do not need towering docks in that part of the Deadlands. Fel will not risk sailing over the Burning Forest. Some of those fireballs rise too high. The chainguns and the bolt cannons will be enough to buy a Porcupine the time it needs to reach altitude."

"A Porcupine?" Jacob asked.

"Yes!" Gladys said, her words coming out in a rush. "Because Archibald moved Warship One here, Belldorn agreed to post a Porcupine at Dauschen and with batteries installed in the Ridge Mountains, Fel's going to have a hard time reaching the city."

"And breathe," Alice whispered.

Gladys grinned.

Archibald held a notebook out to Jacob. "You left this behind in

Bollwerk."

"Thanks," Jacob said, taking the yellowed parchment from Archibald. He flipped through it, briefly studying Charles's Titan Mech designs.

Alice leaned over his shoulder. "You left that behind? On purpose?"

"You don't always have to read my thoughts like that," Jacob muttered. "I don't know. I just … I want Charles's designs to do some good in the world. This was just made for war."

Gladys tugged on his sleeve until he was facing Midstream and the scorched ash that had been a city block barely a day before. In the distance, the wreckage of the bomber still smoldered, sending a trail of smoke to curl into the air.

"It won't do us any good to rebuild our city, only to have that happen again and again."

Jacob looked away from Gladys. "Even if we built a Titan Mech, it can't stop something like that bomber. Not unless …" He stopped and sighed.

"Think it over," Archibald said. "For the good of Midstream, and to help protect your friends."

"He will," Alice said when Jacob didn't answer. "Give him some time."

"Of course." Archibald looked out across the dry riverbed as if he could see into the city of Fel itself. "Alice, you have made an interesting ally in Furi. My spies inside Ballern failed to understand the depth of the unrest there. Part of that blame falls to me as well. I should have realized that a city with a thriving pirate trade had deeper issues than what I was aware of."

Alice frowned for a moment before her expression evened out. "What are you asking?"

"Only that if you learn something of significance, you report it to me."

"She's my friend," Alice said. "I won't betray her and prove the people of the east are just as bad as she'd been led to believe."

"I am asking no such thing." Archibald turned back to face the group.

"I hope you aren't." Alice sorted through her pack and pulled out a stack of parchment. "I've been making copies of some of the more interesting things we found out. The Children of the Dark Fire have infiltrated their monarchy, like the Butcher did in Ancora. They're allied with Fel, but I don't know if Mordair even realizes how unstable that city actually is."

Archibald took the papers and flipped through them, briefly pausing to read a paragraph. "Thank you."

"You should send a copy to Lady Katherine. We told her some of what's in there, but she should know more about it. Some of it has to do with the refugees who moved to the Shadowed Woods. Furi has friends there."

A smile crossed Archibald's face as he patted the parchment. "An interesting ally indeed." He turned to Jacob. "As for your supplies, I have two ships on their way from Bollwerk. Frederick gave us the designs for a portable workshop to help keep the sands out of the grease, as he says."

"My supplies?" Jacob asked.

Gladys dragged her foot through the sand. "I might have mentioned to him what you needed. I probably missed some things, but figured this would be a good start."

Jacob shook his head. "Thank you. Both of you. Some of the people here don't have homes to get back to, and I want to get them rebuilt as soon as we can."

Archibald nodded. "For now, they're welcome in the barracks on Warship One. And Jacob, please think on those plans. There is much to be said for an unexpected asset." With that, the Speaker of Bollwerk took his leave, walking back toward the lift descending from Warship One.

To the untrained eye, it might have looked like Archibald was alone, but Jacob hadn't missed the cloaked shadows that were following him, only to reveal themselves as his guard when he was away from the others.

Gladys squeezed Jacob's arm. "You're a good man, Jacob."

He smiled at the desert princess. He hoped she was right. Because if she wasn't, he could leave a legacy worse than Charles had in the Deadlands War.

A Fire Lizard roared in the distance, and a plume of flame stretched into the sky.

CHAPTER FORTY-ONE

ALICE SAT AT the writing table nestled in the corner of George's house. Furi sank into a nearby couch, cracking open her second book of the day. Once Furi realized George had books dating back to some of Midstream's earliest history, and they were in a language she could read, Alice wasn't sure if she'd ever see Furi again.

"So you don't mind staying here for a while?" Alice asked.

Furi peered over the top of her book. "I know I said I didn't want to stay here, but look at these books, Alice! It's like the restricted section of the Crown Library, but we can read them whenever we want."

"I know. But you realize we'll see more soldiers from Bollwerk as the days go on. If Archibald already set foot in Midstream himself, he's confident in the loyalty of his people here."

"Eh," Furi said, closing her book. "Archibald is confident that his people want money from him. There's a big gap between that and actual loyalty. I'm not saying he's as bad as the monarchy in Ballern, but I don't trust him."

Alice hesitated. "I've known worse people."

"*That's* a resounding endorsement," Furi said with a laugh. "Can you honestly say he hasn't asked you to spy on me? Or use me to get some kind of *inside* information about Ballern."

Alice didn't answer, remembering how recently he'd asked for almost those same things.

"Exactly. You've known worse people, and I'm sure I have too, but politicians are politicians."

"I know. But Gladys is my friend too. If nothing else, I want to see Midstream safe for her. And yes, I know that if it weren't for Archibald, they wouldn't have to worry about it being safe."

Furi shrugged. "Maybe. From what I've read about the warlords, I think Archibald is the better option. I think it's low of him to use Midstream as a staging ground to keep the battle away from Bollwerk, though. And you can't tell me you think he's doing anything but that."

Alice shook her head. "No, I know you're right. It's why I want to stay here. If I can help Jacob or Gladys, I'm going to do it."

"So what's the story with you and Jacob, anyway? Are you planning a wedding yet?"

"What!" Alice croaked out, juggling her pen and splashing ink across her notes.

"I'll take that as a no," Furi said. "It's just, you both seem old enough. I don't know what your customs are in Ancora. I thought … I didn't mean to pry. Well, maybe I meant to pry a little bit."

"I don't know, Furi." Alice blotted at the splashes of ink. "There's no one else I want to be with, but look at the world. There's so much to see. So much to explore! I'd rather see the world with him than tie ourselves down to one city. You know … that's nothing I'd want anytime soon. I'd barely left Ancora at all until last month. And now …" She gestured widely.

Furi rubbed at the back of her hand. "I always thought I'd spend my life with Rin. And then he was gone. Dead as far as I knew until he showed up at a prison in Belldorn. Sometimes it seems like fate only exists to rub our faces in what could have been. And I don't appreciate that very much. Maybe Mary and Eva have the right idea. Just settle down with a wife."

"Settle down!" Alice scoffed. "Mary and Eva are two of the least settled people I've ever known. A soldier and a pirate who happen to be friends with the Lady of Belldorn? Sure, settled. Let's go with that."

Furi flopped back into the couch cushions. "Whatever."

"Well, I cannot comment on Jacob's worthiness as a spouse," George said with a wide grin as he stepped into the room, "but I suspect Furi is right about Archibald."

Alice felt her face flush at the royal guard's sudden appearance. "How much of that did you hear?"

"Your secrets are safe with me. Although perhaps secrets are the wrong word when your adoration is on such vibrant display."

Alice groaned and laid her head down on the desk.

George settled onto the couch, leaning against the opposite armrest from Furi. "Gladys is well aware of Archibald's motivations, you see. But those motivations have protected us over the years. Without them, we would not have been sheltered by Bollwerk, and I certainly wouldn't have had the finest restaurant in all of that rusted city."

"You have a restaurant?" Furi asked.

"The Fish Head!" George said. "Surely even Ballern has heard tales of my fine cooking."

"Umm …"

George grinned at Furi.

"I have a friend who's a chef. Well, Jakon, actually. You've met him?"

George nodded. "On the docks, yes. I find myself drawn to his ship. It has a flair you do not often find among the pirate vessels."

Alice was thankful the conversation had veered away from her and Jacob. "You should see the smuggler's hold on The Ray. It puts the Skysworn to shame."

George raised an eyebrow. "Don't let Mary hear you claim something so bold as that."

"I think Smith would be more offended than Mary," Alice said with a laugh before lowering her voice. "You trust Archibald, right?"

George nodded. "I trust in what he is. There is a predictability in politicians. If they do not protect their own, then their people will flee. Or their people will throw them down and replace them with a new ruler."

"You make it sound easy," Furi said.

"Oh, no. It is not easy, my friend. It is a rare thing for a ruler to be thrown down without bloodshed. And I have seen my share of it. So long as sacrificing Midstream does not forward Archibald's goals, we can rely on his assistance."

Furi ran a hand through her hair. "I hadn't thought of it like that."

"It is best when there is a mutual benefit. Trust without reason can get you killed."

They chatted with George for a bit. And the royal guard eventually promised to fix Furi the best fish stew she'd ever had.

The skeptical look on Furi's face contrasted with the absolute confidence on George's, making Alice laugh. She went back to copying her notes, hoping to have them completed before George's feast later that day.

CHAPTER FORTY-TWO

The old tinker flexed his wrist and frowned at the clicking sound it made. "It's getting close now." He threw a clasp to the side, which let him turn the mechanism farther before it popped off his forearm. "Still needs a bit more work."

Samuel groaned and tried to sink into the stiff-backed chair.

"You aren't a bad tinker, young Spider Knight, but you could use some finesse with the smaller gears."

"I told you Drakkar could do a better job," Samuel muttered.

"Ah, yes, but that is why *you* must do the job. How are you to get better without practice?"

Drakkar patted Samuel on the shoulder. "Forgive him, tinker. He is used to riding on the back of a Jumper where all the finesse is handled by his mount."

The old tinker chuckled. "Now, that is a sight I would like to see. No giant Jumpers down here near the Dragonwing Mountains since the war. Reckon if there ever were, the Dragonwings themselves ate them all."

"Well, that's terrifying," Samuel said, taking the mechanical hand from the tinker when it was offered. He mounted it back in the vice, fingers down, and then slid a large magnifying lens in front of it. Everything the old tinker had said to look for was in place. The springs, the plate, the locks to make sure it wouldn't spin freely in its mount. "If Jacob was here, he'd fix this in a minute."

Samuel flexed the joint, and it clicked. Drakkar and the old tinker were talking, but Samuel stared into the opening of the wrist, flexing the joint again. It was a consistent click, which meant it had to be tied to one of the two pivots. He raised the lens and fished around the end of the bolt with a probe, cursing when it hit something that shouldn't have been there.

Changing the angle, Samuel found the problem, and he felt a bit like a fool for not finding it earlier. "The bolt's too long." He started removing it, so focused he only caught a snippet of the conversation behind him, but it was enough to draw his attention.

"And it was Charles's apprentice who killed the Butcher. That's something, I tell you. It's a shame Charles didn't kill that monster in the Deadlands War. Told him he should have, you know. He might still be alive if he'd listened."

"When a man has had enough of war, he has had enough."

The old tinker nodded. "You don't have to tell me. I've been in this cave long enough now to know."

Samuel clipped the now-extracted bolt into a spiral cutter. It closed like the lens on a camera, one that was formed of blades. It took a dozen strokes to sever the bolt, but it left a clean cut. Samuel reassembled the hand and sighed when it didn't click in the vise.

"Okay, I think it's done."

The old tinker slid it out of the vise and twisted it onto the socket on his wrist before throwing the latch down again. He grinned when he flexed his metal hand, and only silence greeted them.

"Thank the gods," Samuel muttered. "How long have we been here?"

"Two days, at most," the tinker said. "And I do appreciate you helping me organize the workshop. Some of those barrels are awfully heavy at my age."

Samuel groaned. "We have things to do! I'm glad we could help you, but we have to go."

"Does the Cave Guardian feel the same?"

Drakkar smiled. "The Cave Guardian is more patient than the Spider Knight."

"I do appreciate your time here. It's good to talk with allies on occasion." The old tinker ran his finger along the spines of several books before pausing and pulling one down. "This is some of the earliest work done on biomechanics. You'll find Charles's work toward the end. I warn you, some of the earlier experiments were ghastly, and you'll find more detail about the berserkers than you ever wished to know."

Samuel took the volume and flipped through a few pages. Some were filled with diagrams and formulas that looked more complex than anything he'd seen in all the years he'd known Charles. Other pages were just blocks of text.

He flipped back to the front of the volume. The first date was before the journal he'd found beneath the Sea of Salt. But the date at the end was well after. This was what they'd been looking for.

"These are the dates we were missing," Samuel said. "Maybe we can piece together the entire story now."

The old tinker tapped his finger on the workbench. "If you have need, you may ask me what that book does not tell you. Take it and go. I must return to my work here now that my hand doesn't make that infernal clicking."

He scribbled a note on a scrap of parchment and held it out to Samuel. "I assume you're aware of Archibald's transmitters."

"Yes," Samuel said, frowning at the frequency with the name Targrove written next to it. "Is Targrove a codeword? That was Smith's mentor's name."

The old tinker smiled. "Perhaps, before you go, it is best you know. I was once the Master Tinker of Belldorn. My name, you see, is Targrove."

Targrove. Mentor to Smith. Ally of Charles. Legendary tinker of the

Deadlands War. A man who had supposedly died decades before. A thousand questions ran through Samuel's mind. But all he managed to say was, "But you're dead."

Targrove's laughter echoed around them in the workshop, and Samuel realized they might not be leaving Pirate's Cove quite yet.

Note from Eric R. Asher

Thank you for spending time with Jacob and Alice! I've been blown away by the reader response to this series, and am so grateful to you all. The next book of Jacob and Alice's adventures is called Skyforged.

If you'd like an email when I release a new book, sign up for my mailing list (www.ericrasher.com). Emails only go out about once per month and your information is closely guarded by a ravenous Pilly.

Also, follow me on BookBub (bookbub.com/authors/eric-r-asher), and you'll always get an email for special sales.

If you enjoyed Skyborn, please consider leaving a review on a platform of your choice. Reviews can make a huge difference and help make sure we get more Steamborn books.

Thanks for reading!
Eric

Please enjoy the following excerpt from

Skyforged

The Steamborn Series, Book #5

By Eric R. Asher

S AMUEL SCRATCHED AT a knot in the wooden bar top. Once, it had been stained nearly as dark as the shadows in the corners of that place, but time and customers had worn the color thin. When the Spider Knight turned away from the bar, it wasn't a worn counter that filled his vision. It was a sparkling cove, flanked by the ruined buildings of a forgotten history and the pirate city that had been built on its corpse.

Drakkar's explosive laugh brought Samuel's attention back to the Cave Guardian and the old tinker. Targrove wore a welcoming smile as he sipped at his drink. The barkeep clearly knew who the old tinker was because Targrove didn't whisper quietly. If Samuel or Drakkar asked a question, no matter how sensitive it might be, Targrove's answer would confidently boom through the cramped bar.

"No, no, it's true!" Targrove shook his head. "You have to understand. I'd only heard about Cave through tall tales told in Belldorn. And … hell, are you even old enough to remember the old ceremonies?" He waved the thought off with a flourish of his hand. "But Charles had me convinced entry to Cave required a tithing. So yes, I showed up with a Stone Dog in a crate as a gift for the king."

"There has never been a King of Cave," Drakkar said with a chuckle.

"Well, I found that out rather quickly. Not before they locked me in shackles for an assassination attempt, mind you. Damned fool, Atlier was."

"Was that the old prison that became The Rock Inn?" Drakkar asked.

Targrove nodded and threw back the rest of his drink. "Aye. A right eyesore that was. And the smell. That sour blend of sick and meat gone bad. Cave's come a long way since they chased out the worst of the pirates."

"They got rid of you, didn't they?" The barkeep wiped down tap handles and grinned at Targrove.

"That they did. That they did." Targrove held up a hand to stop the barkeep when he offered to refill his glass. "Three days I spent in that hole. Long enough I think Charles *almost* felt bad about it."

"Do you remember much about the beginning of the war?" Samuel asked. "We've found some of Charles's journals, but that shows what he was doing, not really why he was doing it."

"Not always a reason why for a tinker, Samuel. Sometimes we do a thing to see if we can. Other times we do it out of desperation, though I suppose that would be a reason in itself. You read enough of those journals and you'll start to see how Charles thought. See why he did what he did." Targrove glanced at Drakkar. "You weren't wrong about him. Not entirely. But I think when Cave feared Atlier, they overlooked his history."

"How so?" Drakkar asked.

"You look at those journals and see nothing but engines of war. But every time Charles designed something to kill, he did it with the hope the wars would end. A village would be spared. A child might live who would have been destined to die in battle. I always thought he was a fool for that. Kill to prevent killing? Nonsense. But I think you need to understand that about him—about who he was—to fully appreciate those journals."

"I understand," Drakkar said. "It fits perfectly with the man I knew."

Targrove nodded.

Samuel didn't say anything. The man he remembered was different than the man Targrove and Drakkar knew. Samuel had known Charles during a long peace. A time where open war had been relegated to history books and short bouts of conflict in the Deadlands. He remembered the tinker who amazed kids at Festival and took Jacob under his wing. A kind man who skirted violence at every turn, until he didn't. Until the choice had been taken from him. And maybe that's what the Deadlands War had been to him. The taking away of any other option.

"Now, is you want to know more of the good he did, you should visit Fire Island," Targrove said. "The distillery he helped build is one of the best in all the cities."

"Drink is not what we seek," Drakkar said.

The barkeep scoffed at that. "Then you're in the wrong place."

Targrove nodded. "No fresh water on Fire Island, you know? At least, not more than a few small lakes, and that's not nearly enough for a city."

"A city?" Samuel asked, frowning. "Fire Island has been abandoned for decades. The last great eruption killed everything living there."

"It's a good story to keep people away," Targrove said. He drummed his fingernails on the bar and waited until the barkeep had vanished around the corner. "More there than you know. Charles built a plant to convert salt water to fresh. There's long been a society of tinkers there. If anyone has records from the early days of the war, it will be them."

Drakkar turned to Samuel. "I am afraid we will be journeying on the seas once more."

Samuel groaned and looked up at the smooth wood of the ceiling. "Fantastic."

"It's a fascinating place," Targrove said. "Parts of it remind me of the Highlands in Ancora, but it's not so polished as that."

"Many of Cave's founding residents immigrated from the island,"

Drakkar said. "But the settlements there are rarely spoken of. I did not realize such a large number had remained behind."

"I've never even heard of it," Samuel said.

Targrove shrugged. "Why would you? History buried it, much like the small villages lost to the Deadlands War. Once-great cities can fall to ruin and memory, given enough time. It is not so strange."

Samuel thought of the skeleton and the soaring towers that must have once held so many people. The city had been reclaimed by the desert and left to decay over the decades and centuries. But even that cursed place had once been home to countless souls. It was a hard thing to imagine, having only seen it after it had fallen.

"I will need to restock our supplies," Drakkar said. "Our speeder does not hold much, and the journey will take more time than our current stockpile will last."

"Get food for three," Targrove said. "It's been some time since I visited the island. I think I'll travel with you."

Samuel blinked at the old tinker. Having a guide along in a new city could save them days of researching trying to find the right tinkers. Maybe their luck was turning around. And then he remembered the impending boat ride and groaned.

✧   ✧   ✧

TARGROVE FINISHED RATCHETING an outrigger onto the side of their boat. It rose in a low, graceful arc only to end with a lengthy pontoon in the water.

"That should help keep us stable. I suspect Samuel won't mind a smoother journey."

"That obvious?" Samuel asked.

"Boy, you turned green at the mere mention of sailing."

Drakkar laughed and patted Samuel on the back before sliding a wicker basket into the hold.

Targrove wrestled the cover off the main boiler set near the rear of the speeder. "Now, let me make sure this old boat is seaworthy and we can be on our way."

"It got us here," Samuel said.

"Aye, that it did. But I didn't live to be older than dirt by sailing across the Southern Sea on a ship deemed seaworthy by a Spider Knight, of all things."

Samuel blinked at that.

"I don't mean that as an insult, just that I have sixty years of experience elbow-deep in boilers."

Samuel waved the thought off. "None taken." He went back to helping Drakkar load the last couple of crates. It was likely more food than they'd need, but Drakkar wanted to be sure they'd be supplied even if Fire Island turned out to be a wasteland. The thought hadn't crossed Samuel's mind, and it was a stark reminder he wasn't fully cut out for the wilds away from city life.

Another hour passed, and Targrove was satisfied with some small changes he'd made to the boilers. The largest had been reinforcement at the seams.

"And you believe we can push the engine harder with that?" Drakkar asked.

Targrove nodded. "As hard as you like. That boiler won't breach with the furnace as high as it will go." He glanced at Samuel. "Might not be the smoothest ride, though. You best drink that down before we raise anchor."

Samuel looked down at the purple concoction Targrove swore would stave off any kind of motion sickness. It smelled like the Lowlands after the Fall. A mixture of rot and decay and wood. He grimaced and slammed the drink before gagging.

"Tastes just like it smells," Targrove said to Drakkar as Samuel fought to keep the drink down.

"That is … unfortunate."

"Indeed."

Once Samuel was sure he wasn't going to vomit all over the deck, he turned back from the waters of Pirate's Cove and took a deep breath. "You better be right. That was disgusting."

Targrove grinned at the Spider Knight, crinkling the deeply tanned wrinkles on his face. "Weigh anchor! We make for Fire Island!"

Samuel threw the lever to pull the anchor in as Drakkar untied the boat from the dock. The furnace sputtered as Targrove adjusted the flames, and in short order, they'd wheeled away from the city, headed south through Pirate's Cove.

Samuel wasn't sure how well Targrove's adjustments would perform once they reached the open sea. In the small waves of Pirate's Cove, the pontoon minimized the swaying and that awful feeling they were one bad wave from capsizing.

He spent the time on the smoother waters reading through the latest journal they'd acquired from Targrove. The experiments detailed in that book, the accidental creation of berserkers, were hard to read. He understood Charles had never set out to cause that kind of deranged behavior, but he would never have thought the leaders in the Deadlands War would have pushed him to make it worse.

They came to lean on the berserkers like a tool instead of the sick soldiers they actually were: warriors without conscience, pointed at the enemy and left to do as they would. Samuel shivered at the description Charles wrote of the fate of a village not far from Midstream.

The opposition might have had soldiers stationed there, but Samuel had little doubt innocents had been killed in those raids—raids that sounded more like the warlords of the Deadlands than the organized forces he thought of in Bollwerk and Belldorn.

He looked out at the Southern Sea when they approached it sometime later, closing the journal and wondering if their friends were faring better than they were.

Skyforged
The Steamborn Series, Book #5
By Eric R. Asher

Books by Eric R. Asher

Shop ebooks, audiobooks, and paperbacks at ericrasherstore.com

The Theme Park at the End of the World

The Steamborn Series

Steamborn

Steamforged

Steamsworn

Skyborn

Skyforged

Skysworn

Stormborn

Stormforged

Stormsworn

The Vesik Series
(Recommended for Ages 17+)

Days Gone Bad

Wolves and the River of Stone

Winter's Demon

This Broken World

Destroyer Rising

Rattle the Bones

Witch Queen's War

Forgotten Ghosts

The Book of the Ghost

The Book of the Claw
The Book of the Sea
The Book of the Staff
The Book of the Rune
The Book of the Sails
The Book of the Wing
The Book of the Blade
The Book of the Fang
The Book of the Reaper
Dreams of the Forgotten Dead
Garden Gnome Graves

The Vesik Series Box Sets

Box Set One (Books 1-3)
Box Set Two (Books 4-6)
Box Set Three (Books 7-8)
Box Set Four: The Books of the Dead Part 1
Box Set Five: The Books of the Dead Part 2

Mason Dixon: Monster Hunter

Episode One
Episode Two
Episode Three
Episode Four

Want to receive an email when one of Eric's books releases?
Visit ericrasher.com to get started.

About the Author

Eric is a former bookseller, cellist, and comic seller currently living in Saint Louis, Missouri. A lifelong enthusiast of books, music, toys, and games, he discovered a love for the written word after being dragged to the library by his parents at a young age. When he is not writing, you can usually find him reading, gaming, or buried beneath a small avalanche of Transformers. For more about Eric, see: www.ericrasher.com

Enjoy this book? You can make a big difference.

If you've enjoyed this book, I would be very grateful if you could take a minute to leave a review on the platform of your choice. It can be as short as you like. Thank you for spending time with Jacob and Alice.